More praise for
SEARCHING FOR CALEB

"The Pecks are marvelous—literally marvelous, by turns heartbreaking and hilarious. . . . It is not possible for me to convey adequately the magic of this book. There is not a wrong word or a false emotion. . . . These people seem part of our own lives and the search for Caleb becomes as important to us as it does to them."

The Washington Post

"It is about growing up, mating and breaking away. It is about living by prescription and living by instinct. It is about loving the past and yet defying it, and taking responsibility for terrible things while holding onto joyfulness. It is about rebellion and adjustment, the simultaneous lust to wander and to take root, to move and to stay. It's about trying, up till the moment of death, to discover what it was we rebelled against, what it was we adjusted to, what we loved and what we lost. Anne Tyler has made something magical out of common life, fulfilling our belief that it can be magical. She is the best of magicians, a born artist. She has created an epic. . . . Wonderful . . . Perfect."

The Philadelphia Inquirer

Also by Anne Tyler:

THE ACCIDENTAL TOURIST
BREATHING LESSONS
CELESTIAL NAVIGATION*
THE CLOCK WINDER*
DINNER AT THE HOMESICK RESTAURANT*
EARTHLY POSSESSIONS
IF MORNING EVER COMES*
MORGAN'S PASSING*
A SLIPPING-DOWN LIFE*
THE TIN CAN TREE*
SAINT MAYBE*

*Published by Ivy Books

SEARCHING FOR CALEB

Anne Tyler

IVY BOOKS • NEW YORK

Ivy Books
Published by Ballantine Books
Copyright © 1975 by Anne Tyler Modarressi

ISBN 0-8041-0883-8

This edition published by arrangement with Alfred A. Knopf, Inc.

Manufactured in the United States of America

First Ballantine Books Edition: February 1993

1

The fortune teller and her grandfather went to New York City on an Amtrak train, racketing along with their identical, peaky white faces set due north. The grandfather had left his hearing aid at home on the bureau. He wore a black suit, pearl-gray suspenders, and a very old-fashioned, expensive-looking pinstriped collarless shirt. No matter what happened he kept his deep-socketed eyes fixed upon the seat in front of him, he continued sliding a thumb over the news clipping he held in his hand. Either the train had turned his deafness absolute or else he had something very serious on his mind, it was hard to tell which. In any case, he would not answer the few things the fortune teller said to him.

Past his downy white head, outside the scummy window, factories and warehouses streamed along. Occasionally a left-over forest would coast into view and then out again—twisted bare trees, trunks ripped by lightning, logs covered with vines, tangled raspy bushes and beer cans, whisky bottles, rusted carburetors, sewing machines, and armchairs. Then some town or other would take over. Men wearing several layers of jackets struggled with crates and barrels on loading docks, their breaths trailing out of their mouths in white tatters. It was January, and cold enough to make the brick buildings appear to darken and condense.

The fortune teller, who was not a gypsy or even Spanish but a lanky, weedy blond woman in a Breton hat and a faded shift, took a *National Geographic* from a straw bag on the floor and started reading it from back to front. She flicked the pages after barely a glance, rapidly swinging one crossed foot. Half-way through the magazine she bent to rummage through the bag again. She felt her grandfather slide his eyes over to see what she was keeping there. Tarot cards? A crystal ball? Some other tool of her mysterious, disreputable profession? But all she showed was a spill of multicolored kerchief and then a box of Luden's cough drops, which she took out and offered him. He refused. She put one in her mouth, giving him a sudden smile that completely upturned every one of her pale, straight features. Her grandfather absorbed it but forgot to smile back. He returned to his view of the seat ahead, a button-on antimacassar with an old lady's netted hat just beyond.

In his hand, stroked by his puckered thumb, the newspaper clipping first rustled and then wilted and dropped, but the fortune teller knew it by heart anyway.

TABOR

Suddenly on December 18, 1972, Paul Jeffrey, Sr., of New York City, formerly of Baltimore. Beloved husband of Deborah Palmer Tabor. Father of Paul J. Tabor, Jr., of Chicago and Theresa T. Hanes of Springline, Massachusetts. Also survived by five grandchildren and seven great-grandchildren.

Services will be held Thursday at the . . .

"My throat is dry, Justine," her grandfather said.

"I'll get you a soda."

"What?"

"A *soda.*"

He drew back, offended. No telling what he thought she had said. Justine patted his hand and told him, "Never mind, Grandfather. I'll just be gone a minute."

She left, sidling between shopping bags and weekend cases along the narrow aisle, holding tight to her saucerlike hat. Three cars up, she paid for two root beers and a sack of Cheez Doodles. She returned walking carefully, opening doors with her elbows and frowning at the plastic cups, which were filled to the brim. Just inside her own car, the Cheez Doodles fell and a man in a business suit had to pick them up for her. "Oh! Thank you!" she said, and smiled at him, her cheeks grown suddenly pink. At first glance she could be taken for a young girl, but then people saw the fine lines beginning to show in her skin, and the faded blue of her eyes and the veined, parched, forty-year-old hands with the scratched wedding band looking three sizes too large below one knobby knuckle. She had a ramshackle way of walking and a sharp, merry voice. "*Root* beer, Grandfather!" she sang out. If he didn't hear her, all the rest of the car did.

She put a cup in his hand, and he took a sip. "Ah yes," he said. He liked herby things, root beer and horehound drops and sassafras tea. But when she tore open the cellophane bag and presented him with a Cheez Doodle—a fat orange worm that left crystals on his fingertips—he frowned at it from beneath a tangle of white eyebrows. He had once been a judge. He still gave the impression of judging everything that came his way. "What *is* this," he said, but that was a verdict, not a question.

"It's a Cheez Doodle, Grandfather, try it and see."

"What's that you say?"

She held out the bag, showing him the lettering on the side. First he replaced the Cheez Doodle and then he wiped his fingers on a handkerchief he took from his pocket. Then he went back to drinking root beer and studying the clipping, which he had laid flat on one narrow, triangular knee. "Theresa," he said. "I never cared for that name."

Justine nodded, chewing.

"I don't like *difficult* names. I don't like foreignness."

"Perhaps they're Catholic," Justine said.

"How's that?"

"Perhaps they're Catholic."

"I didn't quite hear."

"*Catholic!*"

Faces spun around.

"Don't be ridiculous," her grandfather said. "Paul Tabor went to the same church I did, he was in my brother's Sunday school class. The two of them graduated from the Salter Academy together. Then this—dissatisfaction set in. This, this *newness*. I can't tell you how many times I've seen it come to pass. A young man goes to a distant city instead of staying close to home, he gets a job, switches friends, widens his circle of acquaintances. Marries a girl from a family no one knows, lives in a house of unusual architecture, names his children foreign names that never were in his family in any preceding generation. He takes to traveling, buys winter homes and summer homes and vacation cottages in godforsaken states like Florida where none of us has ever been. Meanwhile his parents die and all his people just seem to vanish, there's no one you can ask any more, 'Now, what is Paul up to these days?' Then he dies himself, most likely in a very large city where there's nobody to notice, only his wife and his barber and his tailor and maybe not even the last two, and what's it for? What's it all about? Now in Paul's case I just couldn't say for certain, of course. He was my brother's friend, not mine. However I will hazard a guess: he had no *stamina*. He couldn't endure, he wouldn't stay around to fight it out or live it down or sit it through, whatever was required. He hadn't the patience. He wanted something new, something different, he couldn't quite name it. He thought things would be better somewhere else. Anywhere else. And what did it get him? Watch, next time I'm in Baltimore I'll tell the family, 'Paul Tabor died.' 'Paul *who?*' they'll say. 'Paul Tabor, it was in the Baltimore *Sun*. Don't you read it any more? Don't you know?' Well, of course they do read it and would catch any familiar name in a flash but not Paul Tabor's. Forgotten, all forgotten. He discarded us, now he's dead and forgotten. Hear what I say, Justine. Do you hear?"

Justine smiled at him. "I hear," she said.

She had moved away from Baltimore herself. She and her husband and daughter now lived in Semple, Virginia; in another place last year and another the year before that. (Her husband was a restless man.) Next week they were moving to Caro Mill, Maryland. Was it Caro Mill? Caro Mills? Sometimes all these places would run together in her mind. She would mentally locate friends in towns those friends had never set foot in, she would await a visit from a client whom she had left two years ago without a forwarding address. She would ransack the telephone book for a doctor or a dentist or a plumber who was actually three hundred miles away and three or four or fourteen years in the past. Her grandfather didn't guess that, probably. Or care. He had scarcely bothered to learn the towns' names in the first place. Although he lived with Justine and made all those moves with her he called it visiting; he considered himself a citizen still of Baltimore, his birthplace. All other towns were ephemeral, no-account; he shuffled through them absent-mindedly like a man passing a string of shanties on the way to his own sturdy house. When he arrived in Baltimore (for Thanksgiving or Christmas or the Fourth of July) he would heave a sigh and lower the sharp narrow shoulders that he held, at all other times, so tightly hunched. The brackets around his mouth would relax somewhat. He would set his old leather suitcase down with finality, as if it held all his earthly goods and not just a shirt and a change of underwear and a scruffy toothbrush. "There's no place in the world like Baltimore, Maryland," he would say.

He said it now.

This morning they had passed through the Baltimore railroad station, even stopping a moment to let other, luckier passengers alight. The thought of having come so near must have made him melancholy. He looked down at his clipping now and shook his head, maybe even regretting this trip, which had been entirely his own idea. But when Justine said, "Are you tired, Grandfather?"—thinning her voice to that special, carrying tone he would be certain to hear—he only looked at her blankly. It seemed that his mind was on Paul Tabor again.

"They don't say a word about where they buried him," he said.

"Oh well, I imagine—"

"If you died in New York City, where would you be buried?"

"I'm sure they have—"

"No doubt they ship you someplace else," he said. He turned his face to the window. Without his hearing aid he gave an impression of rudeness. He interrupted people and changed the subject willfully and spoke in a particularly loud, flat voice, although normally he was so well-mannered that he caused others to feel awkward. "I never made the acquaintance of Paul's wife," he said, while Justine was still considering cemeteries. "I don't recollect even hearing when he got married. But then he was younger than I of course and moved in different circles. Or perhaps he married late in life. Now if I had known the wife I would have gone up for the funeral, then asked my questions afterwards. But as it is, I hesitated to barge in upon a family affair and immediately put my case. It would look so—it would seem so self-serving. Do you think I did right to wait?"

He had asked her this before. He didn't listen for the answer.

"By now she will be calmer," he said. "Not so likely to break down at any mention of his name."

He folded the clipping suddenly, as if he had decided something. He creased it with one broad yellow thumbnail.

"Justine," he said.

"Hmm?"

"Am I going to be successful?"

She stopped swirling the ice in her cup and looked at him. "Oh," she said. "Why—I'm certain you are. Certainly, Grandfather. Maybe not *this* time, maybe not right away, but—"

"Truly. Tell me."

"Certainly you will."

He was looking too closely into her face. Possibly he hadn't heard her. She set her voice to the proper tone and said, ''I'm sure that—''

''Justine, how much do you know?''

''What?''

, ''This telling fortunes. This bunk. This—*piffle*,'' said her grandfather, and he brushed something violently off his sleeve. ''I hate the very thought of it.''

''You've told me all that, Grandfather.''

''It's not respectable. Your aunts go into a state whenever we speak of it. You know what people call you? 'The fortune teller.' Like 'the cleaner,' 'the greengrocer.' 'How's that granddaughter of yours, Judge Peck, the fortune teller. How's she doing?' Ah, it turns my stomach.''

Justine picked up her magazine and opened to a page, any page.

''But, Justine,'' her grandfather said, ''I ask you this. Is there anything to it at all?''

Her eyes snagged on a line of print.

''Do you really have some inkling of the future?''

She shut the magazine. He locked her in a fierce, steady frown; his intensity made everything around him seem pale.

''I want to know if I will find my brother,'' he said.

Yet immediately afterward he turned away, watching the train's descent into the blackness beneath Manhattan. And Justine repacked her straw bag and brushed cheese crumbs off her lap and put her coat on, her expression calm and cheerful. Neither one of them appeared to be waiting for anything more to be said.

Because they were trying to save money, they took the subway from Penn Station. Justine loved subways. She enjoyed standing on them, gripping a warm, oily metal pole, feet planted slightly apart and knees dipping with the roll of the train as they careened through the darkness. But her grandfather distrusted them, and once they were off the shuttle and onto the IRT, he made her sit down. He continually rotated his face, scanning the car for enemies. Silent young people returned his stare. "I don't know, Justine, I don't know what's happening. I don't like this city at all any more," her grandfather said. But Justine was enjoying herself too much to answer. She watched each station as they drew into it, the murky light and bathroom-tile walls and those mysterious, grimy men who sat on benches, one or two at every stop, watching trains come and go without ever boarding one. Then when they were moving again she drank in the sensation of speed. *Getting* somewhere. She loved going fast in any kind of vehicle. She particularly liked the rickety sound of these tracks, on which something unexpected might happen at any moment. She hoped the wheels would howl in that eerie way they had while heading through the deepest stretch of darkness. Once the lights went out and when they came on again her face was surprised and joyous, open-mouthed; everybody noticed. Her grandfather touched her wrist.

"Are you watching for the proper station?" he asked.

"Oh yes."

Although she hadn't been.

Clutched in her hand was Mrs. Tabor's address, which she had copied from a telephone book. She had suggested calling ahead from Penn Station, but her grandfather refused. He was too impatient, or he wanted to hold onto his hopes just a little bit longer, or he was afraid of being turned away. Also he might have been anxious to reach Mrs. Tabor's bathroom. He preferred not to use any public facilities.

When they were above ground again—Justine taking gulps of the ashy, foreign air, the old man limp with relief—they walked a block and a half west and entered a gray building with a revolving door. "Look," her grandfather said. "Wood for the door and polished handles. Marble floor. I like old buildings. I like places like this." And he nodded to a lady just stepping out of the elevator—the first person in all New York whose existence he had recognized. He was disappointed, however, that the elevator was self-service. "*Once* upon a time they would have had a boy to do this," he said, watching Justine jab a button. The elevator toiled upward, creaking and sighing. Its walls were fine oak but on one panel there was a concentration of four-letter words that the old man covered immediately, stepping square in front of them without appearing to notice and then staring upward. Justine smiled at him. He pursed his lips and studied an inspection certificate.

On the eighth floor, at the end of a long dark hall, they pressed another button. Bolts slithered and locks rattled, as if connected somehow to the button. The door opened three inches and a roughed, seamed face peered out from behind a police chain. "Yes?" she asked.

"Mrs. Tabor?" said Justine.

Puffy eyes took her in from top to toe, her streaky ribbons of hair and her brown coat with the uneven hemline. "What is this," Mrs. Tabor said, "are you selling something? I don't need a thing and I already have religion."

So the grandfather had to step up and take over. There was no mistaking the elegance of his bow, or the way he raised one hand to his head even though he wore no hat. He presented her with his card. Not his business card, oh no, but his calling card, cream-colored, aged yellow around the edges. He slipped it beneath the police chain into her jeweled hand. "Daniel Peck," he said, as if she could not read, and she looked up into his face while one finger tested the engraving. "Peck," she said.

"I knew your husband. Paul? Back in Baltimore."

"Why didn't you *say* so?" she asked, and she unhooked the chain and stood back to let them in. They entered a room that Justine might have grown up in, all wine-colored and velvety, giving off a scent of dust although every piece of furniture gleamed. Mrs. Tabor's white hair was precisely finger-waved, webby with beauty parlor hairspray. She wore black wool and ropes and ropes of pearls. Her focus was on the old man and she barely looked at Justine even when he remembered to introduce her. "Of course you do know about his passing, Mr. Peck," she said.

"I beg your pardon?"

"You'll have to speak up," said Justine. "He left his hearing aid at home."

"You know he *passed*, Mr. Peck."

"Oh. Passed. Oh yes. Yes, naturally, I read it in the paper. You see we hadn't heard of Paul for many many years, we—" He followed, absently, to the couch where she led him. He sat down beside Justine, pinching the creases in his trousers. "We had no idea where he might be until that death notice, Mrs. Tabor. Why, I've made several trips to New York in my life and never even knew he was here! Never guessed! We could have talked over old times together."

"Oh, it's sad how people lose track," said Mrs. Tabor.

"Well, I wanted to offer my condolences. Our family thought highly of Paul and my brother Caleb in particular was very close to him."

"Why, thank you, Mr. Peck. It was painless, I'm happy to say, sudden and painless, just the way he would have wished it. All the more shock to *me*, therefore, but—"

"What was that?"

"*Thank* you."

"My brother's name was Caleb Peck."

"What a fine old-fashioned name," said Mrs. Tabor.

The old man looked at her for a minute, perhaps wondering whether it was worthwhile asking her to repeat herself. Then he sighed and shook his head. "I don't suppose you knew him, did you?" he said.

"Why, not that I remember, no. I don't believe so. Because of Paul's work we moved about so, you see. It was difficult to—"

"What? What?"

"*No*, Grandfather," Justine said, and laid one hand on top of his. He looked at her dimly for a moment, as if he didn't recognize her.

"I assumed he might have kept in touch with Paul," he told Mrs. Tabor. "Written, or sent Christmas cards. Or visited, even. You know they were very close. Perhaps he stopped to see you on his way to someplace else.''

''We never had many visitors, Mr. Peck.''

''Pardon?''

He looked at Justine. Justine shook her head.

''Or possibly Paul just mentioned his *name* on some occasion,'' he said.

''Possibly, yes, but—''

''Yes?''

He snatched his hand from Justine's and sat forward. ''When would that have been?'' he asked.

''But—no, Mr. Peck, I can't say I remember it. I'm sorry.''

''Look here,'' he said. He searched a pocket and came up with something—a small brown photograph framed in gold. He leaned over to jab it in her face. ''Don't you know him? Doesn't he look familiar in any way? Take your time. Don't be in a hurry to say no.''

Mrs. Tabor seemed a little startled by the picture, but it took her only a second to make up her mind. ''I'm sorry,'' she said. Then she looked at Justine. ''I don't understand. Is this important in some way?''

''Well—'' said Justine.

''We've lost track of Caleb too, you see,'' her grandfather said. He shoved the photograph back in his pocket. He turned down the corners of his mouth in a bitter smile. ''You must think we're very careless people.''

Mrs. Tabor did not smile back.

''However it was no more our fault in this case than in Paul's; he left us.''

''Oh, what a pity,'' Mrs. Tabor said.

''Our family is very close knit, a *fine* family, we have always stuck together, but I don't know, periodically some . . . *explorer* sets out on his own.'' He scowled suddenly at Justine. ''The last time I saw Caleb was in nineteen twelve. I have never heard of him since.''

''Nineteen twelve!'' Mrs. Tabor said. She sank back in her chair. Wheels seemed to be clicking in her head. When she spoke next her voice had become softer and sadder. "Mr. Peck, I'm so very sorry that I can't help you. I *wish* I could. Might I offer you some tea?"

"How's that?" he said.

"*Tea*, Grandfather."

"Tea. Oh. Well . . ."

This time when he looked at Justine he was handing the rest of the visit to her, and she straightened and clutched her carry-all. "Thank you, but I don't think so," she said. Phrases her mother had taught her thirty years ago came wisping back to her. "It's kind of you to . . . but we really must be . . . however, I wonder if my grandfather might freshen up first? He just got off the train and he . . ."

"Surely," said Mrs. Tabor. "Mr. Peck, may I show you the way?"

She beckoned to him and he rose without question, either guessing at where she was leading him or no longer caring. He followed her through a polished door that swept open with a hushing sound across the carpet. He went down a short hall with his hands by his sides, like a child being sent to his room. When she pointed him toward another door he stepped through it and vanished, not looking around. Mrs. Tabor returned to the living room with careful, outward-turned steps.

"That poor, poor man," she said.

Justine would not answer.

"And will you be in New York long?"

"Just till we find a train home again."

Mrs. Tabor stopped patting her pearls. "You mean you only came for this?"

"Oh, we're used to it, we do it often," Justine said.

"Often! You go looking for his *brother* often?"

"Whenever we have some kind of lead," said Justine. "Some name or letter or something. We've been at this several years now. Grandfather takes it very seriously."

"He'll never find him, of course," said Mrs. Tabor.

Justine was silent.

"Will he?"

"Maybe he will."

"But—nineteen *twelve!* I mean—"

"Our family tends to live a long time," Justine said.

"But even so! And of course, dear," she said, leaning forward suddenly, "it must be hard on *you*."

"Oh no."

"All that wandering around? I'd lose my mind. And he can't be so easy to travel with, his handicap and all. It must be a terrible burden for you."

"I love him very much," said Justine.

"Oh, well yes. Naturally!"

But the mention of love had turned Mrs. Tabor breathless, and she seemed delighted to hear the bathroom door clicking open. "Well, now!" she said, turning to Justine's grandfather.

He came into the room searching all his pockets, a sign he was preparing to leave a place. Justine rose and hoisted her straw bag. "Thank you, Mrs. Tabor," she said. "I'm sorry about your husband. I hope we haven't put you to any trouble."

"No, no."

The grandfather ducked his head in the doorway. "If you should recollect at some later date . . ." he said.

"I'll let you know."

"I wrote my Baltimore number on my calling card. Justine has no phone. If you should chance to think of something, anything at all . . ."

"Will do, Mr. Peck," she said, suddenly jaunty.

"You do?"

"What?"

"She *will* do. Grandfather," Justine said, and led him into the hall. But he did not hear and was still turned to Mrs. Tabor, puzzled and unhappy, when the door swung shut and the locks began tumbling into place again.

* * *

In the railroad station they sat on a wooden bench, waiting for the next train home. Justine ate a sack of Fritos, a Baby Ruth, and two hot dogs; her grandfather would not take anything. Neither of them liked Cokes and they could not find any root beer so they drank warm, bleachy New York water begged from a concession stand. Justine finished the last of her cough drops. She had to go buy more, paying too much for them at a vending machine. When she came back she found that her grandfather had fallen asleep with his head tipped back and his mouth open, his empty hands curled at his sides. She moved some sailor's unattended seabag over next to him and adjusted his head to rest upon it. Then she opened her carry-all and took out magazines, scarves, a coin purse, road maps and unmailed letters and a snaggle-toothed comb and a clutch of candy wrappers, until at the very bottom she came upon a deck of playing cards wrapped in a square of old, old silk. She unwrapped them and laid them out on the bench one by one, choosing places for them as surely and delicately as a cat chooses where to set its paws. When she had formed a cross she sat still for a moment, holding the remaining cards in her left hand. Then her grandfather stirred and she gathered the cards quickly and without a sound. They were back in their silk before he was fully awake again, and Justine was sitting motionless on the bench with her hands folded neatly over her straw bag.

2

On moving day they were up at five, not because there was any rush but because the house was so uncomfortable now with everything packed, the walls bare and the furniture gone, no place to sleep but mattresses laid upon newspapers. All night long one person or another had been coughing or rearranging blankets or padding across the moonlit floor to the bathroom. People fell out of dreams and into them again, jerking awake and then spiraling back to sleep. The hollow walls creaked almost as steadily as the ticking of a clock.

Then Justine rose and stalked around the mattress, working a cramp out of one long, narrow foot. And Duncan opened his eyes to watch her fling on her bathrobe, all flurry and rustling and sleight-of-hand. Darkness swirled around her, but that was only chenille. "What time is it?" he asked. "Is it morning yet?"

"I don't know," she said.

Neither of them wore watches. On them, watches broke or lost themselves or speeded up to keep some lawless schedule of their own so you could almost see the minute hand racing around the dial.

Duncan sat up and felt for his clothing, while Justine sailed through the living room. Her gritty bare feet whispered on the floor and her bathrobe sash galloped behind. "Coming through! Excuse me! Coming through!" Her daughter's bedclothes stirred and rumpled. In the kitchen, Justine switched on the light and went to the sink to make tap-water coffee. The room gave off an icy chill. Everything was bare, scraped and smudged by the past—four bald spots on the linoleum where the table had once stood, and dimples where Duncan had tipped back in his chair, scorches and chips on the countertop, the uncurtained window filmed with cooking grease, the rickety wooden shelves empty but still bearing rings of molasses and catsup. Justine made the coffee in paper cups and stirred it with a screwdriver. When she had set the cups on the counter she turned to find her grandfather teetering in the doorway. Noise could not wake him, but light could. He wore withered silk pajamas and held his snaptop pocket watch open in his hand. "It's five ten a.m.," he said.

"Good morning, Grandfather."

"Yesterday you slept till noon. *Regularity* is what we want to aim for here."

"Would you like some coffee?"

But he hadn't heard. He pursed his lips and snapped the watch shut and went back to his bedroom for his clothes.

Now throughout the house came the sounds of people dressing, doors opening and closing, teeth being brushed. Nobody spoke. They were struggling free of their dreams still—all but Justine, who hummed a polka as she darted around the kitchen. In her flimsy robe, flushed with heat when anyone else would be shivering, she gave an impression of energy burning and wasting. She moved very fast and accomplished very little. She opened drawers for no reason and slammed them shut, pulled down the yellowed windowshade and let it snap up again. Then she called, "Duncan? Meg? Am I the only one *doing* anything?"

Duncan came in with his oldest clothes on: a white shirt worn soft and translucent and a shrunken pair of dungarees. His arms and legs gawked out like a growing boy's. He had a boy's face still, the expression trustful and the corners of his mouth pulled upward. With his hair and skin a single color and his long-boned, awkward body he might have been Justine's brother, except that he seemed to be continually turning over some mysterious private thought that set him apart. Also he moved differently; he was slower and more deliberate. Justine ran circles around him with his cup of coffee until he stopped her and took it from her hands.

"I could be dressed and gone by now, the rest of you would still be lolling in bed," she told him.

He swallowed a mouthful of coffee, looked down into the cup and raised his eyebrows.

Justine went back through the living room, where Meg's mattress lay empty with her blanket already folded in a neat, flat square. She knocked on the bathroom door. "Meg? Meggie? Is that you? We're not going to *wait* all day for you."

Water ran on and on.

"If you set up housekeeping there the way you did yesterday we'll leave you, we'll walk right out and leave you, hear?"

She tapped the door once more and returned to the kitchen. "Meg is crying again," she told Duncan.

"How can you tell?"

"She's shut up in the bathroom running the faucet. If today's like yesterday, what are we going to do?" she asked, but she was already trailing off, heading toward her bedroom with her mind switched to something else, and Duncan didn't bother answering.

In the bedroom, Justine dressed and then gathered up heaps of cast-off clothing, a coffee cup and a half-empty bottle of bourbon and a *Scientific American*. She tried to fold her blanket as neatly as Meg's. Then she straightened and looked around her. The room swooped with shadows from the swinging lightbulb. Without furniture it showed itself for what it was: a paper box with sagging walls. In every corner were empty matchbooks, safety pins, dustballs, Kleenexes, but she was not a careful housekeeper and she left them for whoever came after.

When she returned to the kitchen her grandfather and Duncan were standing side by side drinking their coffee like medicine. Her grandfather wore his deerskin slippers; otherwise, he was ready to leave. No one was going to accuse him of holding things up. "One of the trials I expect to see in hell," he said, "is paper cups, where your thumbnail is forever tempted to scrape off a strip of wax. And plastic spoons, and pulpy paper plates."

"That's for sure," Duncan told him.

"What say?"

"Where's your *hearing* aid?" Justine asked.

"Not so very well," said her grandfather. He held one hand out level, palm down. "I'm experiencing some discomfort in my fingers and both knees, I believe because of the cold. I was cold all night. I haven't been so cold since the blizzard of eighty-eight. Why are there not enough blankets, all of a sudden?"

Duncan flashed Justine a wide, quick smile, which she returned with the corners tucked in. There were not enough blankets because she had used most of them yesterday to pad the furniture, shielding claw feet and bureau tops and peeling veneer from the splintery walls of the U-Haul truck, although Duncan had told her, several times, that it might be best to save the blankets out. This was still January, the nights were cold. What was her hurry? But Justine was *always* in a hurry. "I want to get things done, I want to get going," she had said. Duncan gave up. There had been no system to their previous moves either; it seemed pointless to start now.

Meg came into the kitchen and claimed her coffee without looking to left or right—a neat, pretty girl in a shirtwaist dress, with short hair held in place by a sterling silver barrette. She was scrubbed and shining, buttoned, combed, smelling of toothpaste, but her eyes were pink. "Oh, honey!" Justine cried, but Meg ducked out from between her hands. She was seventeen years old. This move was the worst thing that had ever happened to her. Justine said, "Would you like some bread? It's all we've got out."

"No, thank you, Mama."

"I thought we'd have breakfast when we get to what's-its-name, if it's not too long to wait."

"I'm not hungry anyway."

She said nothing to her father. It was plain what she thought: If it weren't for Duncan they would never have to move at all. He had gone and grown tired of another business and chosen yet another town to drag them off to, seemingly picked it out of a hat, or might as well have.

"Your father will be driving the truck all alone," Justine said, "since last time it made Grandfather sick. Would you like to ride with him?" She never would let a quarrel wind on its natural way. She knew it herself, she had no tact or subtlety. She always had to be interfering. "*Why* not go, he could use the company."

But Meg's tears were back and she wouldn't speak, even to say no. She bent her head. The two short wings of her hair swung forward to hide her cheeks. And Duncan, of course, was off on some tangent of his own. His mind had started up again; he was finally awake. His mind was an intricate, multigeared machine, or perhaps some little animal with skittery paws. "I am fascinated by randomness," he said. "Do you realize that there is no possible permutation of four fingers that could be called absolutely random?"

"Duncan, it's time to roll the mattresses," Justine said.

"Mattresses. Yes."

"Would you?"

"Hold up your hand," Duncan told the grandfather, leading him through the living room. "Then take away two fingers. The first and third elements, say, of a four-element . . ."

"Last night," said Meg, "Mrs. Benning asked me again if I would like to stay with her."

"Oh, Meg."

"She said, '*Why* won't your mother allow it? Just till the school year is over,' she said. She said, 'You know we'd love to have you. Does she think you'd be imposing? Would it help if I talked to her one more time?' "

"You'll be leaving us soon enough as it is," said Justine, stacking empty paper cups.

"At least we should consider my schooling," Meg said. "This is my senior year. I won't learn a thing, moving around the way we do."

"Teaching you to adapt is the best education we could give you," Justine told her.

"Adapt! What about logarithms?"

"Now I can't keep on and on about this. I want you to find the cat. I think she knows it's moving day. She's hiding."

"So would I," said Meg, "if I could think of a place." And she slid off the counter and left, calling the cat in her soft, sensible voice that was never raised even when she argued. Justine stood motionless beside the sink. When she heard footsteps she spun around but it was only her grandfather.

"Justine? There are neighbors here to see you off," he told her. He sniffed through his long, pinched nose. People who were not related to him ought to keep to themselves, he always said. He watched narrowly while Justine rushed through the house, hunting her keys and struggling into her coat and jamming her hat on her head. "Check your room, Grandfather," she called. "Turn off the lights. Will you help Meg find the cat? Tell her we're just about to leave."

"Knees?"

"And don't forget your hearing aid."

"They don't get better *that* fast, the cold has sunk into the sockets," her grandfather said. "Ask me again tomorrow. Thank you very much."

Justine kissed his cheekbone, a polished white blade. She flew through the living room and out the front door, into the chalky dawn. Cold air yanked at her breath. Frozen grass crunched under her feet. Over by the U-Haul truck, Mr. Ambrose was helping Duncan load the last of the mattresses. Mrs. Ambrose stood to one side, along with the Printzes and Mrs. Benning and Della Carpenter and her retarded daughter. And a few feet away was a newsboy Justine had never seen before, a canvas sack slung from one shoulder. Except for the newsboy they all wore bathrobes, or coats thrown over pajamas. She had known them for nearly a year and there were still these new things to be learned: Alice Printz favored fluffy slippers the size of small sheep and Mrs. Benning, so practical in the daytime, wore a nightgown made of layers and layers of see-through pink or blue or gray—it was hard to tell which in this light. They stood hugging themselves against the cold, and the Carpenter girl's teeth were chattering. "Justine, I never!" Alice Printz was saying. "You thought you could slip out from under us. But we won't let you go that easy, here we are at crack of dawn waiting to see you off."

"Oh, I *hate* goodbyes!" said Justine. She went down the row hugging each one, even the newsboy, whom she might after all know without realizing it. Then a light came on over the Franks' front door, three houses down, and Justine went to tell June Frank goodbye. All but the newsboy came along with her. June appeared on her cinderblock steps carrying a begonia in a plastic pot. "I had this growing for you ever since I knew you would be moving," she said, "and if you had run off in the night the way you're doing and not give me a chance to say goodbye it would have broke my heart in two." June rolled her hair up on orange juice cans. Justine had never known that before either. And she said not to thank her for the plant or its growth would be stunted. "Is that right?" said Justine, her attention sidetracked. She held up the pot and thought a minute. "Now why, I wonder?"

"*I* don't know why, I only know what my mother used to say to me," June said. "Justine, honey, I won't come any further, but you tell the others goodbye for me too. Tell that pretty little Meg and your sweet old grandfather, tell that handsome husband, hear? And I'm going to write you a letter. If my sister decides to get married again I have to write you first and ask you what the cards say. I wouldn't think of letting her go ahead without it. Can you manage such a thing long distance?"

"I'll surely try," said Justine. "Well, I won't say thank

you for the plant then but I promise to take good care of it. Goodbye then, June.''

''Goodbye, old honey,'' June said, and she grew sad all at once and came down the steps to lay her cheek softly against Justine's while the others looked on, suddenly still, tilting their heads and smiling.

Meanwhile Meg had settled in the rear of the battered Ford with an enormous gray tweed cat in her lap. The cat crouched and glared and Meg cried, causing a mist of tears to glaze the squat little house with its yellowed foundations, its tattered shrubs, the porch pillars rotting from the bottom up. In the front seat, her great-grandfather placed his hearing aid in his ear, adjusted a button, and winced. Duncan slammed the tailgate on the last of the mattresses and climbed into the truck cab. He turned on the headlights, coloring the gray and white scene in front of him—Justine being passed from hand to hand down a row of neighbors in their nightclothes. ''Ho, Justine,'' he called softly. Of course she couldn't hear. He had to beep the horn. Then everybody jumped and screeched and a window lit up half a block down, but Justine only gave him a wave and headed for the car, unsurprised, because wasn't he always having to honk for her? She was late for everything, though she started out the earliest and the fastest and the most impatient. She was always leaving places the same way, calling scraps of goodbyes and then running, flying, bearing some shaking plant or parcel or covered dish, out of breath and laughing at herself, clutching her hat to her head as she sped along.

At nine o'clock in the morning, Red Emma Borden was wiping the counter in the Caro Mill Diner when these four unfamiliar people walked in—a man and wife, a teenaged daughter and a very ancient gentleman. Red Emma was about to have a cigarette (she'd been on her feet since four) and she wasn't eager to wait on anyone else. Still, it was nice to see some new faces. She had been born and raised and married and widowed in this town and she was sick of everybody in it. So she puffed up her orange curls, tugged her uniform down, and reached for the order pad. Meanwhile the strangers were trying to find acceptable seats, which was not all that easy to do. Two of the counter stools were broken, just topless aluminum pedestals, and another would tip you off as soon as you tried to perch upon it. They had to cluster at one end down near the exhaust fan. Even then, the old gentleman had a long tail of cotton batting dangling out from under him. But none of them made any complaint; they just folded their arms and waited for her behind four pairs of blue, blue eyes.

"Well, now," said Red Emma, slapping down cracked plastic menu cards. "What you going to have?"

She addressed the woman first—a skin-and-bones lady wearing a hat. But it was the husband who answered. "Speedy here will have everything in the kitchen," he said.

"Speedy! I barely *inched* along," the woman said.

"I thought you had entered the Indy five hundred. And your seat belt flopping out the door, after I took all that time installing it for you—"

"I will take coffee and three fried eggs," the woman told Red Emma. "Sunny side up. And hotcakes, link sausages, and orange juice. And something salty, a sack of potato chips. Grandfather? Meg?"

Red Emma feared she would be cooking all morning, but it turned out the others just wanted coffee. They had the dazed, rumpled look of people who had been traveling. Only the woman seemed to care to talk. "My name is Justine," she said, "and this is my husband, Duncan. Our Grandfather Peck and our daughter Meg. Do you have the keys?"

"How's that?"

"We were told to stop here and pick up the keys for Mr. Parkinson's house."

"Oh, yes," said Red Emma. She would never have supposed that these were the people for Ned Parkinson's house—a tacky little place next to the electric shop. Particularly not the old gentleman. "Well, he did say somebody might be by," she said. "Have you took a good look at it yet?"

"Duncan has. He chose it," said Justine. "You haven't told us *your* name."

"Why, I'm Red Emma Borden."

"Do you work here all the time?"

"Mornings I do."

"Because I like to eat in diners. I expect we'll run into you often."

"Maybe so," said Red Emma, breaking eggs onto the grill. "But if you come after noon it'll be my late husband's cousin, *Black* Emma Borden. They call her that because she's the one with black hair, only she's been dyeing it for years now." She poured coffee into thick white cups. "You say your husband chose the house?" she asked Justine.

"He always does."

Red Emma flung him a glance. A fine-looking, straw-colored man. His conscience did not appear to be bothering him. "Look, honey," she told Justine. She set the coffeepot down and leaned over the counter. "How come you would let your husband choose where you live? Does he understand kitchens? Does he check for closet space and woodwork that doesn't crumble to bits the first time you try to scrub it down?"

Justine laughed. "I doubt it," she said.

Red Emma had once sent her husband to a used car lot to buy a family automobile and he had come home with a little teeny red creature meant for racing, set low to the ground, slit eyes for windows. It ate up every cent they had saved. She had never forgiven him. So now she felt personally involved, and she glared at this Duncan. He sat there as calm as you please building a pyramid out of sugar cubes. The grandfather was reading someone's discarded newspaper, holding it three feet away from him as old people tend to do and scowling and working his mouth around. Only the daughter seemed to understand. A *nice* girl, so trim and quiet. She wore a coat that was shabby but good quality, and she kept her eyes fixed on a catsup bottle as if something had shamed her. *She* knew what Red Emma was getting at.

"There's other places," Red Emma said. "The Butters are letting, oh, a *big* place go, over by the schoolhouse."

"Now on the average," Duncan said, and Red Emma turned, thinking he was speaking to her, "on the average a single one of the blocks in Cheop's pyramid weighed two and a half tons." No, it was the grandfather he meant that for, but the grandfather only looked up, irritated, maybe not even hearing, and turned a page of his paper. Duncan spun toward Meg, on his left. "It is accepted that wheels as such were not used in the construction," he told her. "Nor any but the most primitive surveying tools, so far as we know. Nevertheless, the greatest error to be found is only a little over five degrees on the east wall, and the others are almost perfect. And have you thought about the angle of the slant?"

Meg looked back at him, expressionless.

"It's my belief they built it from the top down," he said. He laughed.

Red Emma thought he must be crazy.

She flipped the hotcakes, loaded Justine's plate, and set it in front of her. "The Butters' house is a *two*-story affair," she said. "They also have a sleeping porch."

"Oh, I believe Mr. Parkinson's place is going to be just fine," said Justine. "Besides, it's near where Duncan's going to work. This way he can come home for lunch."

"Now where's he going to work?" Red Emma asked.

"At the Blue Bottle Antique Shop."

Oh, Lord. She should have known. That gilt-lettered place, run by a fat man nobody knew. Who needed antiques in Caro Mill? Only tourists, passing through on their way to the Eastern Shore, and most of them were in too much of a hurry to stop. But Red Emma still clung to a shred of hope (she liked to see people *manage*, somehow) and she said, "Well now, I suppose he could improve on what that Mr.—I don't recall his name. I suppose if he knows about antiques, and so on—"

"Oh, Duncan knows about everything," said Justine.

It didn't sound good, not at all.

"He hasn't worked with antiques before but he did build some furniture once, a few jobs back—"

Yes.

"The man who owns the Blue Bottle is Duncan's mother's sister's brother-in-law. He wants to ease off a little, get somebody else to manage the store for him now that he's getting older."

"We've used up all my mother's *blood* relations," Duncan said cheerfully. He was correcting the pitch of one pyramid wall. The truth that was coming out did not appear to embarrass him. "The last job was with my uncle, he owns a health food store. But no one in the family has a fix-it shop, and fixing is what I really do. I can fix anything. Do you need some repair work here?"

"No indeed," Red Emma told him firmly.

And she turned back to Justine, ready to offer her sympathy, but Justine was munching potato chips with a merry look in her eye. Her hat was a little crooked. Could she possibly be a drinker? Red Emma sighed and went to clean the grill. "Of course," she said, "I don't mean to say anything against Ned Parkinson's house. Why, in lots of ways it's just fine. I'm sure you'll all be happy there."

"I'm sure we will be," Justine said.

"And certainly your husband can handle any plumbing and electrical problems that might arise," Red Emma said, wickedly sweet, because she did not for a moment think he could.

But Duncan said, "Certainly," and started plunking his sugar cubes one by one back into the bowl.

Red Emma wiped the grill with a sour dish rag. She felt tired and wished they would go. But then Justine said, "You want to hear something? This coming year will be the best our family's ever had. It's going to be exceptional."

"Now, how do you know that?"

"It's nineteen seventy-three, isn't it? And three is our number! Look: both Duncan and I were born in nineteen thirty-three. We were married in nineteen fifty-three and Meg was born on the third day of the third month in nineteen fifty-five. Isn't that something?''

"Oh, Mama," Meg said, and ducked her head over her coffee.

"Meg's afraid that people will think I'm eccentric," said Justine. "But after all, it's not as if I believed in *numerology* or anything. Just lucky numbers. What's your lucky number, Red Emma?''

"Eight," said Red Emma.

"Ah. See there? Eight is forceful and good at organizing. You would succeed at any business or career, just anything.''

"I would?"

Red Emma looked down at her billowing white nylon front, the flowered handkerchief prinked to her bosom with a cameo brooch.

"Now, Meg doesn't have a lucky number. I'm worried that nothing will ever happen to her.''

"Mama."

"Meg was due to be born in May and I wondered how that could happen. Unless she arrived on the third, of course. But see? She was premature, she came in March after all.''

"I always ask for eight at the Basket of Cheer lottery," said Red Emma. "And I've won it twice, too. Forty dollars' worth of fine-quality liquor.''

"Of course. Now, who's the fortune teller in this town?''

"Fortune teller?"

The grandfather rattled and crackled his paper.

"Don't tell me you don't have one," said Justine.

"Not to my knowledge we don't.''

"Well, you know where I'll be living. Come when I'm settled and I'll tell your fortune free.''

"You tell fortunes.''

"I do church fairs, bazaars, club meetings, teas—anybody's, any time. People can knock on my door in the dead of night if they have some urgent problem and I will get up in my bathrobe to give them a reading. I don't mind at all. I like it, in fact. I have insomnia.''

"But—you mean you tell fortunes *seriously?*" Red Emma asked.

"How else would I tell them?"

Red Emma looked at Duncan. He looked back, unsmiling.

"Well, if we could have the keys, then," said Justine.

Red Emma fetched them, sleepwalking—two flat, tinny keys on a shower curtain ring. "I really do need to have my fortune told," she said. "I wouldn't want this spread around but I'm considering a change in employment."

"Oh, *I* could help out with that."

"Don't laugh, will you? I'd like to be a mailman. I even passed the tests. Could you really tell me whether that would be a lucky move or not?"

"Of course," said Justine.

Red Emma rang up their bill, which Duncan paid with a BankAmericard so worn it would not emboss properly. Then they filed out, and she stood by the door to watch them go. When Justine passed, Red Emma touched her shoulder. "I'm just so anxious, you see," she said. "I don't sleep good at all. My mind swings back and forth between decisions. Oh, I know it's nothing big. I mean, a mailman, what is that to the world? What's it going to matter a hundred years from now? I don't fool myself it's anything important. Only day after day in this place, the grease causing my hair to flop halfway through the morning and the men all making smart remarks and me just feeding them and feeding them . . . though the pay is good and I really don't know what Uncle Harry would say if I was to quit after all these years."

"Change," said Justine.

"Beg pardon?"

"Change. I don't need cards for that. Take the change. Always change."

"Well—is that my fortune?"

"Yes it is," said Justine. "Goodbye, Red Emma! See you soon!"

And she was gone, leaving Red Emma to pleat her lower lip with her fingers and ponder beside the plate glass door.

Justine drove the Ford down Main Street with the cat racing back and forth across the rear window ledge, yowling like an old, angry baby while people on the sidewalks stopped and stared. Meg sat with her hands folded; by now she was used to the racket. The grandfather simply shut his hearing aid off and gazed from his bubble of silence at the little wooden Woolworth's, the Texaco, the Amoco, the Arco, a moldering A&P, a neat brick post office with a flag in front. This time Duncan's truck was ahead, and Justine followed him in a right-hand turn down a side street lined with one-story buildings. They passed a drugstore and an electric shop, and then they came to a row of small houses. Duncan parked in front of the first one. Justine pulled in behind him. "Here we are!" she said.

The house was white, worn down to gray. On the porch, square shingled columns rose waist-high and then stopped, giving the overhang a precarious, unreliable look. Although there was no second floor the dormer window of some attic or storage room bulged out of the roof like an eyelid. A snarl of wiry bushes guarded the crawlspace beneath the porch. "Oh, roses!" Justine cried. "Are those roses?" Her grandfather shifted in his seat.

"This house is even worse than the last," said Meg.

"Never mind, here you'll have a room of your own. You won't have to sleep in the living room. Isn't that going to be nice?"

"Yes, Mama," Meg said.

Duncan was already pacing the yard when the others reached him. "I'm going to put a row or two of corn here," he told them. "Out back is too shady but see how much sun we get in front? I'm going to plow up the grass and plant corn and cucumbers. I have this plan for fertilizer, I'm going to buy a blender and grind up all our garbage with a little water. Pay attention, Justine. I want you to save everything, eggshells and orange peels and even bones. The bones we'll pressure-cook first. Have we got a pressure-cooker? We'll make a sort of jelly and spread that around here too.''

Meanwhile the cat had streaked under the crawlspace, where she would stay till the moving was over, and the grandfather was climbing the front steps all hunkered and disapproving, muttering to himself, making an inventory of every splinter and knothole and paint blister, every nail worked loose, windowscreen split, floorboard warped. Meg sat down on the very top step. ''I'm cold,'' she said.

Justine said, ''Your father's going to take up farming. Maybe we'll have tomatoes.''

''Will we be here to harvest them?'' Meg asked nobody.

Justine found the keys in one of her pockets and opened the door. They stepped into a hall smelling of mildew, littered with newspapers and broken cardboard boxes. The kitchen leading off it contained a refrigerator with a motor on top, a dirty gas stove, and a sink on stilts. There was a living room with a boarded-up fireplace. In the back were the bathroom and three bedrooms, all tiny and dark, but Justine swept through flinging up windowshades and stirring the thick, musty air. ''Look! Someone left a pair of pliers,'' she said. ''And here's a chair we can use for the porch.'' She was a pack rat; all of them were. It was a family trait. You could tell that in a flash when they started carrying things in from the truck—the bales of ancient, curly-edged magazines, zipper bags bursting with unfashionable clothes, cardboard boxes marked *Clippings, Used Wrapping Paper, Photos, Empty Bottles*. Duncan and Justine staggered into the grandfather's room carrying a steel filing cabinet from his old office, stuffed with carbon copies of all his personal correspondence for the twenty-three years since his retirement. In one corner of their own room Duncan stacked crates of machine parts and nameless metal objects picked up on walks, which he might someday want to use for some invention. He had cartons of books, most of them second-hand, dealing with things like the development of the quantum theory and the philosophy of Lao-tzu and the tribal life of Ila-speaking Northern Rhodesians. But when all of this clutter had been brought in (and it took the four of them two hours) there was next to nothing left in the truck. Their furniture was barely enough to make the house seem inhabited: three rust-stained mattresses, four kitchen chairs from Goodwill, Great-Grandma's hand-carved rosewood dining table, a sagging sofa and easy chair donated by a neighbor two moves back, and three bureaus of Justine's mother's, their ornate feet and bow fronts self-conscious next to the bedsteads Duncan had constructed out of raw pine boards that gave off a yellow smell. For dishes they had a collection of dimestore plates, some light green, some flowered, some dark brown with white glaze dripped around the edges, and thermal mugs given away free when Esso changed to Exxon. The cutlery with its yellow plastic handles had been salvaged from Aunt Sarah's English picnic basket. There were two saucepans and a skillet. (Justine did not like cooking.) They owned a broom and a sponge mop, but no dustpan, no vacuum cleaner, no squeegee, scrub bucket, or chamois cloth. (Justine did not like cleaning either.) No washing machine or dryer. When all the clothes in the house were dirty the family would lug them to the laundromat. Of course that was not much fun—the four of them struggling with their bulging pillow slips, the grandfather's head ducked way, way low in case of passers-by, all of them a little bedraggled in their very last clean clothes unearthed from the bottom of the drawer or the back of the closet—but wasn't it better than moving those shiny, heavy appliances from place to place? Why, by late afternoon they were completely settled in. There was nothing more to do. It was true that most of the boxes remained to be opened but that was nothing, some were still packed from the *last* move. There was no hurry. Justine was free to stretch out on her mattress, which had the piney-wood smell of home, and work her feet from her shoes and smile at the ceiling while the cat lay on her stomach like a twenty-pound, purring hot water bottle. Duncan could sit on the edge of the bed fooling with a stroboscope he had forgotten he owned. Meg could shut her door and unwrap, from its own special box, from seven layers of tissue paper, her framed photograph of a young man in a clerical robe at least a size too large, which she rewrapped almost immediately and slid to the back of her closet shelf. And in his room across the hall the grandfather could take a photo of his own from his pocket: Caleb Peck in tones of brown, framed in gold, wearing a hat and tie, his face stark and dignified, playing a violoncello while seated in an open stable door twenty feet off the ground.

3

Duncan took a tour of the Blue Bottle Antique Shop with Silas Amsel, the owner. Since he had already seen it when he applied for the job, he was not very interested. He ambled along behind fat, bearded Silas, yawning and drumming his fingers on passing tabletops. Spider-legged spinet desks, clocks with cherubs and shepherdesses and Father Time, dusty goblets, mirrors framed in knobby gold plaster, occasional tables too weak to bear the weight of a lamp—what was the sense in all this? To tell the truth, he had never thought about antiques before. He had been reared in a world where they were taken for granted. No one ever *bought* them, no one bought anything; the rooms were crowded with mellowed, well-kept furniture that appeared to have grown there, and whenever children departed they took several pieces with them but left the rooms as crowded as ever, somehow, as if more had sprouted in the night. No, what interested Duncan was the bin of contrivances he had found behind Silas's counter: rusty cherry pitters, potato quillers, apple corers, fish scalers, an ingenious spiral cone for separating the white of an egg from the yolk. Beside the bin was a wicker valise that opened to make a chair for sitting by the seashore. Where had all that inventiveness got to, now? How had it faded away? The bin was marked with a felt-tip pen: *Your choice, $1*. The valise, which was broken, could be bought for $2.50, if anyone could find it among the boots and paper bags. When Duncan took over, he would put the valise in the front window. (He leered suddenly at Silas's broad, ponderous back.) He would polish the utensils and lay them out in rows. He would sell everything humdrum and buy ancient tools at barn auctions and flea markets, until the shop resembled a nineteenth-century inventor's workroom and he could sit inhaling a combination of machine oil and wood and oxidizing iron, his favorite smells.

"Oh, I'm getting old, getting old," said Silas, creaking up the steps at the back of the store to show him where the telephone was. "Be sorry to let loose of the reins but glad of the rest, believe me."

In fact Silas was a good thirty years younger than Grandfather Peck, who could have run the shop with one hand tied behind him, but Duncan was used to this premature aging among people outside the family. Besides, if Silas weren't retiring Duncan would still be looking for a job. He had thought, this time, that he might finally have used up all his mother's relatives. He had wondered if he would ever escape from the health food store, which he had turned into a paying proposition and then, out of boredom, allowed to run down again. Weevils took over the stone-ground wheat and mold got the soy grits and the unsulphured raisins turned to pebbles. He lost his natural gaiety and his recklessness, he fell back on bourbon, solitaire, and a flat-faced silence that not even Justine could penetrate. Was there anything worse than feeling you were *sealed* in a place, to grow old and stale and finally die? His careless bookkeeping and erratic hours, already a matter of principle, became so obvious no employer could overlook them. That was the pattern of Duncan's life— ventures begun light-heartedly, with enthusiasm but only half his attention, the other half devoted to plans for a perpetual motion machine made entirely of screen door springs or a method of breeding stingless honeybees or the entering of a contest, sponsored by an Englishman, for a one-man flying machine no bigger than an armchair. In the last twenty years he had been, among other things, a goat farmer, a photographer, and a cabinetmaker; he had worked in a pet store, a tobacconist's, a record bar, and a gourmet shop; he had taken census, shorn sheep, and fertilized the lawns of a suburban development on a toy tractor. Almost all these jobs had been enjoyable, but only briefly. He began to grow restless. He noticed that he was treading an endless round of days just as his pinched, unimaginative family had done before him. He would start going to work at ten and then eleven, four days a week and then three; and next came the bourbon, the solitaire, the silence in which to reflect upon the bars of his cage. Next another venture. He was his own perpetual motion machine.

Sometimes he worried about Justine. He didn't *want* to be the way he was, uprooting her yearly or even more often, switching Meg to still another school. He knew how the neighbors shook their heads over him. Yet it seemed he suffered from some sort of chronic dissatisfaction which came and went like malaria, and the only way to hold it back was to learn more and more new facts, as if continually surprising his mind. Now peculiar scraps of knowledge were stuck to him like lint from all his jobs. He knew a Toggenburg goat from a Saanen, he could measure a dachshund, by sight alone, for a plaid mackintosh with matching Sherlock Holmes-style hat. He was an authority on the making of yogurt and the application of poisons to broad-leafed weeds during dandelion season. He had also discovered that every shop, even the most unlikely, has a circle of daily customers who become its experts—the elderly gentlemen capping each other's list of imported cheeses, the ladies debating on the use of slippery elm bark, the teenagers intoning the life history of every member of every rock band. At the tobacconist's, college boys could spend hours recalling the time a legendary freshman had found a fully aged and yellowed, hand-carved meerschaum pipe sitting on the top of someone's garbage can. Perched on his stool behind the counter, gloating over the drawings for his pedal-driven flying machine, Duncan absorbed this stray knowledge like sunlight. Never mind that it was useless. And now he was about to find something else to learn, here among these ancient navigating devices and cracked foggy lanterns and ropes of amber beads like half-sucked butter rum balls.

"This is potassium lactate," said Silas, tapping a brown bottle on the telephone table. "We use it to replace the acids in the covers of old leather books."

And he looked surprised at the sudden light that flashed across Duncan's face.

"Now this pad I always keep handy, and the pencil chained. People will call with items to sell, you want to get their addresses. Here, by the way, is a message for you."

He ripped it off the pad. *Habit-Forming Entertainments called, come to lunch first Sun. in Feb.*

"What?" said Duncan.

"He said you would know him. He phoned four times in the last two days. He said if you couldn't make it call back, he's still listed as Exotico."

"Ah," said Duncan, and pocketed the slip. Silas waited but Duncan didn't explain.

"Well, then," Silas said finally, "if you can't think of any questions—but I'll be by, I'll drop by often, of course."

"Of course," said Duncan, and he sighed, but Silas was groaning back down the steps by now and didn't hear him.

Habit-Forming Entertainments, which had been Exotico, Inc., last year and Alonzo's Amazing Amusements the year before that, was located in a cow pasture on the outskirts of Parvis, Maryland. It was a carnival company, of sorts—the kind that is called a forty-miler, although in this case the circuit was considerably wider. It traveled from one tiny town to another, supplying the entertainment for firehouse fairs, church and school bazaars, homecoming celebrations, and the gala openings of new shopping malls. In between trips the entire company lived in trailers in the cow pasture, with a pumpkin-colored tent flying pennants in the middle. They worked year round. Even in the dead of winter, Habit-Forming Entertainments would come trundling across the frost-bitten Maryland countryside to whoever asked for them.

They brought mechanical rides, two ponies, a concession stand, a few simple games of chance whenever local law allowed, and five girls to run the games in satin bathing suits with dirty seams. There was also a merry-go-round. It was hard to transport and something was always going wrong with it, the mechanism sticking or the animals toppling over, but Justine preferred it to any other merry-go-round she had ever known. It played only one piece: "The St. James Infirmary Blues." Whenever Justine heard that tune sawing through the air she had to climb on, she didn't care if she *was* too old. She sat astride a laughing white horse, hugging the mane and laughing herself or occasionally crying, because the music was so tinny and sweet and sad and made her nostalgic for times before she was born. And whenever she saw Alonzo Divich, who owned that merry-go-round and all the other equipment, he was whistling "The St. James Infirmary Blues" like a theme song. He said it was the only tune *he* knew, too. He and the merry-go-round: two clumsy, hopeful, cheerful creatures, lumbering along where you would least expect to find them.

He was whistling when Justine and Duncan arrived; they tracked him down by his song. They left the car at the edge of the field and made their way across the frozen stubble toward the trailers, which sat around the tent in a cold, huddled circle like covered wagons braced for Indian attack. In the spring, when the countryside was blooming, this sort of life could seem pleasant, but not today. Today everything was lit with a sickly white winter sun, the inhabitants were shut inside their trailers, the ponies hung their heads. "Oh, the poor things!" Justine cried, and she felt the same when she passed an orange ride all folded on its truckbed like a crumpled baby dinosaur. But the whistling continued, happy as ever, sailing out from behind a plowshed, and when they had rounded the shed there was Alonzo Divich looking untouched by cold or loneliness or time. He was sitting on a boulder braiding rawhide—a large, dark man with a drooping black mustache and drooping eyes. He wore too many colors of clothing, all a little soiled, greasy, strained across the stomach and crotch and under the arms: a rose shirt, a woven Mexican vest, suede dungarees and crumpled boots. When he stood to hug them, he gave off a smell of leather and honey. "Aha!" he said to Justine. "But you haven't changed at all! Even the hat is still the same! Is it rooted there?"

He had no accent—only a curious certainty to his speech. But where did he get his hybrid name, and his coloring, and his flashing gold molars and his habit of hugging other men so unself-consciously? Justine had asked him outright, once, what nationality he was. "You're the fortune teller, you tell me," he said.

"I read the future, not the past," she told him.

"Well, the past should be easier!"

"It's not. It's far more complicated."

But he had never told her, even so.

He led them to the tent, where folding chairs were grouped around long wheeled conference tables. This was the company's communal hall, although in cold weather it was nearly empty. In one corner a blonde wearing slacks, gilt sandals, and several sweaters was combing out a miniature poodle. Two men in overalls were seated at a table drinking coffee from green mugs, but they left when Alonzo entered. "Aah, don't go," he said, flopping an arm toward their backs. He pulled out chairs at the center table, and seated himself at the head. Almost immediately a dark old lady appeared and spread a tablecloth. Then she brought a bottle and three small glasses, which she set before Alonzo. He filled the glasses exactly to the brim. The old lady reappeared with paper plates, plastic forks, and then trays of rice, hunks of meat in tomato sauce, eggplant, chicken dusted with some peculiar red powder, wrinkled black olives, bowls of beet soup and chopped cucumber in yogurt, great flat disks of bread and pitchers of green Kool-Aid. Steam rose from the platters, and from Alonzo's mouth as he talked in the cold, rubbery-smelling air. "Take some, don't be shy. First Duncan, he's thinner than ever. He's stretching out tall and thin like a dandelion. How tall are you, Duncan?''

"Six two."

"Double rice for Duncan, Nana!"

The old lady shoveled a mountain onto Duncan's plate.

"Rice prevents heart attacks, stroke, and impotence," said Alonzo.

"It's the thiamine," said Duncan.

"More slivovitz?"

"Oh, I might as well."

Justine ate everything she was given and accepted seconds and thirds, egged on by the approving eye of the old lady who stood behind Alonzo's chair with her hands folded under her apron. Alonzo and Duncan mainly drank, though Alonzo outdistanced Duncan very early and even managed to work in a few slabs of bread stuffed with meat and rice, meanwhile talking steadily. "When I heard you were moving back to Maryland I thought, well then, I can wait. I was contemplating a certain action. But we'll go into that later. I had been thinking, now how will I reach Justine? Then I got your card. It came as a great relief to me."

He leaned back and laced his hands across his stomach, his face a buttery color in the light of the tent. Alonzo was a happy man but forever complaining, as if hoping to fool any jealous gods. Although he loved his carnival business he said that only a fool would stick with it. "Imagine," he always said, "some people suppose this life to be romantic, dancing around the wagons at night. If they were only in my boots! You need to be a mechanic, a lawyer, an accountant. It's all the assembling and disassembling of machinery, and repairs and insurance payments. I'm being robbed by my insurance agency. Disability and liability and major medical and fire and theft and acts of God. Then there is the social security, a headache in itself when you consider all these employees coming and going and the pregnancies and the girls deciding to finish school. And you have to negotiate in every town, some don't allow so much as a ring-the-bottle game, and there's the safety inspectors and the police and the church that wants to put a tray of cupcakes in your hot dog stand . . ."

It was Duncan he talked to; men were best for discussing business. But it was Justine he took away with him at the end of the meal, one large warm thumb and forefinger gripping her upper arm. "May I?" he asked Duncan. "Only long enough to say when I'll become a millionaire."

Duncan said, "Do you still have your mechanic?"

"Lem? Would I be here if I didn't? He's in the purple trailer. He knew you were coming; go right in."

Alonzo walked with his head down, still holding Justine's arm. "You must excuse the state of my place," he said. "I have too many people in it now. My wife has left me but one of her children stayed behind to keep me company. And also Bobby. You've met Bobby, my stepson. Actually my fourth wife's stepson, her ex-husband's boy by a woman from Tampa, Florida. Would you care for Turkish coffee?"

"No, thank you," said Justine, and she stepped inside the little green trailer. Although it was crowded it was neater than her own house, with pots and pans arranged in rows in the tiny kitchen and account books stacked at one end of the corduroy daybed. There was a coffee table that had a stripped look, as if he had just recently cleared it. He smoothed it now with both hands. "For the cards," he said.

"Thank you," said Justine.

She sat down on the daybed. She removed her crumb-littered coat, although even here it was cold. From her carry-all she took the cards in their square of silk.

"Where did you get the silk?" Alonzo asked. (He always did.)

"They came with the cards," she said, unwrapping them. She shuffled them several times, looking off at the blue air outside the trailer window.

"And where did you get the cards?"

"Cut the deck, please."

He cut it. He sat down across from her and looked at her

soberly from under curled black brows, as if his future might be read in her face.

Justine first met Alonzo Divich at a church bazaar in 1956, when she was telling fortunes in the Sunday school basement. She was with the white elephants and the potted plants; his carnival was outside. He came in to have his cards read. He was one of those people, she saw, who are addicted to outguessing their futures. Whenever he had an hour to kill, a layover in some town or a lull in his work, he would search out the local seeress. If there were five local seeresses, fine. He would go to all five. He would listen without even breathing. He had heard his fortune, he told Justine, from well over a thousand women, and it had not once been done right. He had not only had his cards read but also his palms, his skull, his moles, his fingernails, his dreams, his handwriting, his tea leaves and coffee grounds. He had been to astrologers and physiognomists, not to mention specialists in bibliomancy, clidomancy, crystal-gazing, and ouija boards. A lady in Montgomery County had set a gamecock to pick corn from a circle of letters; a Georgia woman studied smoke rising from a fire and another dropped melted wax into cold water, forming small nubbly objects that she claimed to be able to interpret. In York County, Pennsylvania, he had had to bake his own barley cakes, which were then broken open and examined under a magnifying glass. And in a marsh near St. Elmo, Alabama, a very old woman had offered to kill a rice rat and study its entrails, but he had felt that such an act might bring bad luck.

He had told Justine all this at once, leaning toward her across the table in her curtained booth while a line of church ladies waited their turns outside. Justine, although she did not know it, wore the tolerant, disillusioned expression of a doctor hearing that his new patient has been to forty other doctors before him, none of them satisfactory. It gave her a look of wisdom. Alonzo decided she was going to turn out to be special. "Lady," he had said, setting his palms on her table, "tell me the answer to my problem. I feel you can."

"What is your problem?"

"Don't you know?"

"How should I?"

"*You're* the fortune teller."

So Justine had to give the speech she had made more often than she could count, and would make many times again, sometimes even to him. "Now I am not a mind reader," she said, "and I have no way at all of guessing what you want to ask, or where you come from or anything else about your past. I read the future. I have a talent for predicting change. If you help me we can search for an answer together; but I'm not going to *outwit* you."

"My problem is this," Alonzo said instantly.

And he sat on a Sunday school chair and took his hat off—a sudden, changeable man, all black and bright and multicolored like a fire that could leap in any direction at any second. "My name is Alonzo Divich," he told her. "I own a carnival business." He jabbed a thumb at the merry-go-round music above them, "The St. James Infirmary Blues" spinning itself out among the cries of children and hot dog vendors, and teenagers clinging to the Tilt-A-Whirl. "I'm divorced, I have this kid. Now I've met a rich widow woman who wants to marry me. She likes the kid, too. She would even live in the trailer. I don't have to change one thing in my life for her. And I'm a marrying fool. I love being married, I tried it twice before. So what's the trouble? The same day we start the talk about a wedding, exact same day, a man I used to know calls and asks me to come and prospect for gold with him beside a lake in Michigan. He says he's onto something. He's going to be a wealthy man, and so am I. But of course there's the kid, and the mortgaged machines, and the woman who doesn't like Michigan. So which do I do?"

Justine was listening with her mouth open. When he finished she said, immediately, "Go look for gold."

"Huh? What about the cards?"

"Oh, the cards," she said.

So she let him cut them and she laid them down, her beautiful cards as limp and greasy as her baby's oilcloth picture books. She chose the simplest formation she knew. She pointed out the meaning while he hung over the table, not breathing: a happy journey, reunion with a friend, a pleasant surprise, and no possibility of money.

"Aha," he said and she raised her face. "So it's lucky I ran into you. No money!"

"Mr.—"

"Divich. Just call me Alonzo."

"Alonzo, is the money all you're going for?"

"Well, but—"

"Go anyway! Go on! *Don't* just sit around hemming and hawing!"

Then she slapped his money back on his palm, for lack of any better way to show how she felt. And she gathered up her cards without looking at him even though he sat there a minute longer, waiting.

It was four years before she saw Alonzo again. On Independence Day, 1960, she set up a booth at a picnic in Wamburton, Maryland. Nobody there seemed much interested in the future. Finally she repacked her cards and took a walk toward the courthouse, where rides were spinning and balloons were sailing and the merry-go-round was playing "The St. James Infirmary Blues," sending out little shimmering catgut strings that drew her in. She started toward the wooden horses. And there beside the tallest horse was—why, Alonzo Divich!—wiping his face on a red bandanna and quarreling with a mechanic. Only when she came up he turned and stopped in mid-sentence and stared. "You!" he said. He ringed her wrist with his hand and pulled her away, toward a bench where the music was not so loud. She came, holding onto her hat. "Do you know how long I worked to find you?" he shouted.

"Who, me?"

"How often do you move? Are you some sort of forty-miler all your own? First I asked at the church, who was the fortune teller? 'Oh, *Justine*,' they said. Everyone knew you, but they didn't know where you lived. And by the time I found *that* out you had moved but left no forwarding address. Why? Did you owe money? Never mind. I haunted all your ladyfriends, I hoped you were a letter writer. But you are not. Then at the tobacconist's where your husband used to work they said—''

"But what did you want me for?'' Justine asked.

"To tell my fortune, of course.''

"I *told* your fortune.''

"Yes, back in nineteen fifty-six. Do you think my life is so steady? *Now* that reading has no bearing at all.''

"Oh. Well, no,'' said Justine, who saw that with him, that would certainly be true. She reached into her bag—at that time a leather pouch gouged by her neighbor's puppy—and pulled out the cards. "And you didn't go look for gold,'' she said.

"You *do* read the past!''

"Don't be silly. Here you are in Maryland; it's obvious to anyone.''

"I didn't, no. I thought about it. Instinct said to follow your advice, but I held back. You know the rest.''

"No.''

"Yes, you do. I married the widow,'' he said, "who turned out to be a disappointment. She had no money after all, the kid got on her nerves, what she had wanted all along was to start us a troupe of belly dancers with her as the star. Belly dancers, when half the towns make our game girls wear sweatshirts! I said absolutely not. She left me. I haven't heard from my friend in Michigan but I expect he has a whole sack of gold nuggets by now and meanwhile here I sit, where I was to begin with, only I happen to be married again—oh, you were right! If I had listened to you, think where I might be today!''

"Cut the cards,'' Justine told him.

"My new wife is pregnant and I have too many kids already,'' said Alonzo. "She is morning-sick, afternoon-sick, and evening-sick. When I walk into the trailer she throws fruits and vegetables at me. I don't think we are getting along at all. However, that's not my problem, no . . .''

But what his problem *had* been Justine couldn't even remember now. There were so many years in between, so many different formations laid out for him on park benches, tent floors, and trailer furniture. Once he found her he never again lost track of her. He supplied her with change-of-address cards already stamped and filled out, with blanks left for the old address and the new. He adopted her entire family, unfolding for Duncan the mysteries of his diesel engines and his cotton candy machines and the odds on his games of chance, bringing Meg gaudy circus prizes for as long as she was a child, treating the baffled grandfather with elaborate old-world respect and sending Justine a great moldy Smithfield ham every Christmas. He would drive halfway across the state just to ask her a single question, and then overpay her ridiculously when she answered. He mourned her moves to Virginia and Pennsylvania and rejoiced when she was safely back in Maryland. He beat on her front door at unexpected times and when she was not home he threatened to fall apart. ''I have to know!'' he would cry to Duncan or Meg. ''I can't make a move, I am utterly dependent on her!''

Yet the peculiar thing (which Justine had seen too often before to wonder at) was that he very seldom took her advice. Look at all his marriages: seven, at last count. Maybe more. And how many of those had Justine approved? None. He had gone ahead anyway. Later he would come back: ''Oh, you were right. I never should have done it. When will I learn?'' His wives tended to leave him, taking the children along. Then sooner or later the children drifted back, and there were always a few living in his trailer—sons and stepsons and others whose relationship was not quite clear, even to him. ''My wives are gone and I sleep alone but still I have three kids at me night and day, all ages. Next time I will listen to every word you say, I'll follow it to the letter,'' he said.

He said it now, nearly seventeen years from the day he

had first ignored her advice, while Justine laid out the cards on the coffee table in the trailer. "I'm going to do everything you tell me to this time," he said.

"Ha," she said.

She bent closer and peered at the cards. "Money and a jealous woman. You're not getting *married* again."

"No, no." He sighed and stroked his mustache. "Who would marry me? I'm growing old, Justine."

For a second she thought she had heard wrong.

"I'm fifty-two," he said. "Do your cards tell you that?"

It was the only fact he had ever handed her. For some reason it diminished him. Alonzo, possessing an *age?* When she first met him, then, he would have been thirty-five—a young, unsteady number of years for a man, but Alonzo had never been young or unsteady. She raised her eyes and found a sprinkling of white in his hair, and deep grooves extending the droop of his mustache. When he smiled at her, creases rayed out from the corners of his eyes. "Why, Alonzo," she said.

"Yes?"

"Why—"

But she couldn't think what she was trying to say. And Alonzo shot his cuffs impatiently and sat forward on his stool. "Well, never mind *that*," he said. "Get on with my problem."

"Tell me what it is."

"Shall I sell the business to Mrs. Harry Mosely?"

"Who's Mrs. Harry Mosely?"

"What does it matter? A rich lady in Parvis, divorced, wants some kind of business different from all her friends."

"The jealous woman."

"Not of me."

"*Envious* jealous."

"She wears jodhpurs," Alonzo said, and shook his head. Justine waited.

"Well?" he said.

"Well, what?"

"Do I sell or do I not? I'm asking."

"But you haven't said what the choice is," Justine told him. "What are you selling it *for*? Are you joining another gold rush?"

"No, I thought just something quiet. I have a friend who's in merchandising, he would find me something or other."

"Merchandising?"

"What's wrong with that?"

"I'm going to have to study these cards a bit," Justine said, and she bent over them again and rested her forehead on her hand.

"This life is hard, Justine," Alonzo told her. "That tent out there cost five thousand dollars and has a life span of only six years. I pay very high taxes on this pasture but Maryland has gypsy laws so we *have* to live here, it's too expensive to camp around. And occasionally people fail to pay me or the weather keeps the customers away, and a ride rusts to bits at exactly the time I clear the mortgage on it. I have so many people to be responsible for. Also these kids all the time. Can't you understand?"

"Yes, yes,"

"Then why are you studying the cards for so long?"

"Because I don't know what to say," she said, and she laid an index finger on the six of hearts and thought a moment. "I see the woman and the money, but everything else is indecisive. No sudden fortune and no disasters. A few petty reverses, a friendship breaking off, but otherwise just— weak."

"Weak?" said Alonzo.

She looked directly at him. "Alonzo," she said. "Don't sell your business."

She left it up to him to decide whether it was she or the cards who spoke.

In the late afternoon, when the sun grew warmer, they sat outside on a collapsed sofa and watched two of Alonzo's teenaged boys pitching a baseball back and forth in the long grass behind the trailers. A girl was hanging out diapers, and a man was rotating the tires on his Studebaker. In the field beyond the baseball players, Duncan and Lem were fiddling with a hunk of machinery. Really it was time they started back, but Duncan said this machine was something special. He wanted to invent a ride for it to run. And the sun was warming the top of Justine's head right through her hat, and the dexterous twist of the baseball glove as it rose to meet the ball and the slap of leather on leather lulled her into a trance.

"If I were president, I would not have a personal physician in the White House with me but you, Justine," said Alonzo. "You could read the cards for me every morning before the Cabinet meeting."

She smiled and let her head tip against the back of the sofa.

"Till then, you can join my carnival. *Why* do you always say no? Coralette, who works the concession stand, she just takes her husband and kids along. They stay in the trailer and read comic books."

"Duncan doesn't like comic books," Justine said.

Out in the field, Duncan raised a sprocket wheel in one gaunt, blackened hand and waved it at her.

"And Meg, she's all grown up? She doesn't come on visits with you now?"

"She doesn't come *anywhere* with us," Justine said sadly. "She studies a lot. She works very hard. She's very conscientious. Other girls wear blue jeans but Meg sews herself these shirtwaist dresses and polishes her shoes every Sunday night and washes her hair every Monday and Thursday. I don't think she approves of us. To tell the truth, Alonzo, I don't believe she thinks much of carnivals either or fortune telling or moving around the way we do. Not that she says so. She's very good about it, really, she's so quiet and she does whatever we tell her to. It kills me to see her bend her head the way she sometimes does."

"Girls are difficult," Alonzo said. "Fortunately I never had many of them."

"I think she's in love with a minister."

"With a what?"

"Well, an *assistant* minister, actually."

"But even so," said Alonzo.

"She went to his church in Semple. She's religious, too. Did I mention that? She went to his young people's group on Sunday evenings. Then they started going out together to lectures and debates and educational slide shows—oh, very proper, but she's only seventeen! And she brought him to our house so we could meet him. It was terrible. We all sat in the living room. Duncan says she has a right to choose whoever she wants but he doesn't think she *chose* this man, she just accepted him. Like a compromise. What else could it be, with a man so meek and puny? He's one of those people with white shiny skin and five o'clock shadow. Duncan says—"

"But after all," said Alonzo, "better that than a motordrome rider. My first wife's girl married a motordrome rider."

"I would prefer a motordrome rider any day," Justine said. Then she sighed. "Oh well, I suppose nobody likes who their children go out with."

"It's true."

"When *I* was courting, my father locked me in my room one time."

"Oh?" said Alonzo. He squinted, following the arc of the baseball floating across the sun.

"I fell in love with my first cousin."

"Oh-ho."

"On top of that, my *shiftless* first cousin. He drank and ran around. For years he had a girlfriend named Glorietta, who always wore red. My aunts and my mother would whisper whenever they mentioned her, even her name. Glorietta de Merino."

"Ah, Glorietta," said Alonzo, and settled back with his

face tilted to the sky and his boots stretched out in front of him. "Go on."

"He made terrible grades all through school and dropped out the first year of college. Nobody could ever find him when they wanted him. While I! I was an only child. I tried to be as good as possible. Would you believe, until I was twenty years old I had never tasted liverwurst?"

"Liverwurst," said Alonzo, turning it over lazily.

"Because my family didn't happen to eat it. Not that there was anything wrong with it, of course, they just weren't in the habit of ordering it from the market. I didn't know there *was* such a thing as liverwurst! The first time I tasted it I ate a whole pound. But that was later. First I fell in love with my cousin, and went on trips with him and rode in his unsafe car and had to be locked in my room. *Then* I discovered liverwurst."

"But what became of him?" Alonzo asked.

"Who?"

"The first cousin."

"Oh," said Justine. "Why, I married him. Who did you think I was talking about?"

"Duncan?"

"Of *course* Duncan," said Justine, and she sat up again and shaded her eyes. "Cousin Duncan the Bad," she said, and laughed, and even Alonzo, drowsy and heavy in the sun, had to see how happy she looked when she located Duncan's spiky gold head glinting above the weeds.

4

Duncan and Justine Peck shared a great-grandfather named Justin Montague Peck, a sharp-eyed, humorless man who became very rich importing coffee, sugar, and guano during the last quarter of the nineteenth century. On any summer day in the 1870's, say, you could find him seated in the old Merchants' Exchange on Gay Street, smoking one of his long black cigars to ward off yellow fever, waiting for news of his ships to be relayed from the lookout tower on Federal Hill. Where he originally came from was uncertain, but the richer he grew the less it mattered. Although he was never welcomed into Baltimore society, which was narrow and ossified even then, he was treated with respect and men often asked his advice on financial issues. Once there was even a short street named after him, but it was changed later on to commemorate a politician.

When Justin Peck was fifty years old, he bought a sycamore-shaded lot in what was then the northern part of town. He built a gaunt house bristling with chimneys and lined with dark, oily wood. He filled it with golden oak furniture and Oriental screens, chandeliers dripping crystal, wine velvet loveseats with buttons up and down their backs, heavy paintings leaning out from the walls, curlicued urns, doilies, statuary, bric-a-brac, great globular lamps centered on tasseled scarves, and Persian rugs laid catty-corner and overlapping. Then he married Sarah Cantleigh, the sixteen-year-old daughter of another importer. Nothing is known of their courtship, if there was one, but her wedding portrait still looms in a Baltimore dining room: a child-faced girl with a look of reluctance, of hanging back, which is accentuated by the dress style of the day with its backward-swept lines and the flounce at the rear of the skirt.

In 1880, only nine months after the wedding, Sarah Cantleigh died giving birth to Daniel. In 1881 Justin Peck remarried, this time into stronger stock—a German cutler's daughter named Laura Baum, who rescued Daniel from the old freedwoman who had been tending him. Laura Baum's portrait was never painted, but she lived long enough to be known personally even by Meg, her great-great-step-grandchild. She was a shallow, straight-backed woman who wore her hair in a knot. Although she was twenty when she married, observers said she looked more like forty. But then she looked forty when she died, too, at the age of ninety-seven. And it was clear that she made an excellent mother for little Daniel. She taught him to read and cipher when he was only three years old, and she made certain that his manners were impeccable. When Justin suggested that she stop taking Daniel with her on visits to her father she agreed instantly, even ceasing her own visits although Justin had not asked that of her in so many words. (Her father was very obviously a foreigner, an undignified little man given to practical jokes. His dusty jumbled shop by the harbor was a hangout for seamen and other rough types.) "Always remember, Daniel," she said, straightening his collar, "that you must live up to your family's name." She never explained what she meant by that. Her darkies broke into hissing laughter on the kitchen stairs and asked each other in whispers, "What family? What name? *Peck?*" but she never heard them.

In 1885, Laura had a son of her own. They called him Caleb. He was blond like his half-brother, but his tilted brown eyes must have snuck in from the Baum side of the family, and he had his Grandpa Baum's delight in noise and crowds. Even as a baby, being wheeled along in his caramel-colored wicker carriage, he would go into fits of glee at the sight of passing strangers. He liked anything musical—church bells, hurdy-gurdies, the chants of the street vendors selling hot crabcakes. When he was a little older he took to the streets himself, riding an iron velocipede with a carpeted seat. He and Daniel were confined to the sidewalk in front of their house, but while Daniel obeyed instructions, leafing through *The Youth's Companion* on the front steps with his chick-yellow head bent low, Caleb would sooner or later be tugged southward by the fire bell or the gathering of a crowd or, of course, the sound of a street musician. He followed the blind harpist and the banjoist, the walking piano that cranked out Italian tunes, and the lady who sang "The Pardon Came Too Late." Then someone would think to ask, "Where's Caleb?" His mother came out on the front steps, a fan of creases rising up between her eyebrows. "Daniel, have *you* seen Caleb?" And search parties would have to be sent down all the streets running toward the harbor. Only everybody soon learned: if you wanted to find Caleb, hold still a minute and listen. Whenever you heard distant music somewhere in the town, maybe so faint you thought you imagined it, so thin you blamed the whistling of the streetcar wires, then you could track the sound down and find Caleb straddling his little velocipede, speechless with joy, his appleseed eyes dancing. The maid would touch his sleeve, or Daniel would take his hand, or Laura would grab him by the earlobe, muttering, "*This* is where I find you! Out with a bunch of . . . well, I don't know what your father is going to say. I don't know what he's going to think of you for this."

Only she never told his father. Perhaps she thought that she would be held to blame. Sometimes, from the way she acted, you would think she was afraid of Justin.

On Sundays the Pecks went to church, of course, and on Wednesday evenings Laura had her Ladies' Circle. On holidays there were the formal visitors: Justin's business associates and their wives, along with their starched, ruffled children. But you couldn't say that the Pecks had *friends*, exactly. They kept to themselves. They were suspicious of outsiders. After guests left, the family often remarked on the gentlemen's inferior brand of cigars, the children's poor manners, the wives' regrettable overuse of Pompeiian Bloom rouge. Daniel listened, memorizing their words. Caleb hung out the window to hear an Irish tenor sing ''Just a Lock of Hair for Mother.''

Daniel was a tall, cool, reflective boy, and from the beginning he planned to study law. Therefore Caleb would take over the importing business. In preparation for this Caleb attended the Salter Academy, walking there daily with his friend Paul and a few of the neighborhood boys. He worked very conscientiously, although sometimes his mother suspected that his heart wasn't in it. Coming home from school he could be waylaid by any passing stranger, he fell willingly into conversation with all sorts of riffraff. He had no discrimination. And he still followed organ grinders. With his pocket money he bought tawdry musical instruments, everything from pennywhistles to a cheap violin sold him by a sailor; he could make music out of anything. He played these instruments not only in his room but outdoors as well, if he wasn't caught and stopped. More than once he was mistakenly showered with coins from someone's window. When Laura heard about it she would grow dark in the face and order him to remember his name. She shut him in the parlor, where he continued to spill out his reckless, made-up tunes on the massive piano draped in fringed silk. Unfortunately the Creole gardener, Lafleur Boudrault, had taught him ragtime. A disreputable, *colored* kind of music. Justin, home in his study doing the accounts, would raise his head to listen for a minute and frown, but then he shrugged it off.

In 1903, Caleb graduated from the Salter Academy. The day after his graduation Justin took him down to his office to show him around. By now, of course, the importing business was very different from what it had been in the '70's. The old fullrigged steamers, which looked like brigantines with smokestacks, had given way to modern ships, and their spectacular journeys to Brazil and Peru and the West Indies had been discontinued in favor of the more profitable coastwise hauls, carrying manufactured goods south and raw materials north. The Merchants' Exchange had been torn down; Caleb would be spending his days in an office above a warehouse, behind a roll-top desk, dealing with ledgers and receipts and bills of lading. Still, it was a fine opportunity for a young man with ambition, Caleb. Caleb?

Caleb turned from the single, sooty window, through which he had been gazing even though it was impossible to see the harbor from there. He said that he would prefer to be a musician.

At first Justin couldn't take it in. He was politely interested. Musician? Whatever for?

Then the situation hit him in the face and he gasped and caved in. He felt for the chair behind him and sat down, preparing bitter, harmful words that would convey all his horror and disgust and contempt. But music was so—no young man would ever seriously—music was for women! For parlors! He felt nauseated by the sight of this boy's intense brown eyes. He could hardly wait to chew him up and spit him out and stamp on what was left.

Instead, all that came from his mouth were strange vowel sounds over which he had no control.

He had to be carried away in his office chair by two men from the warehouse. They laid him in his buggy and folded both arms across his chest, as if he were already dead, and then Caleb drove him home. When Laura came to the door she found Caleb on the topmost step with his father curled in his arms like a baby. But Justin's eyes were two hard, glittering pebbles, and she could feel his rage. "What *happened?*" she asked, and Caleb told her, straight out, while struggling upstairs with his burden to Justin's high carved bed. Laura's face grew as dark as coffee but she said not a word. She had the kitchen maid fetch the doctor from down the street, and she listened stonily to the doctor's diagnosis: apoplexy, brought on by a shock of some sort. He did not hold out much hope for recovery. If Justin lived, he said, one side would likely be paralyzed, although it was too soon to say for certain.

Then Laura went downstairs to the parlor where Caleb stood waiting. "You have killed your half of your father," she said.

On Monday, Caleb started work behind the roll-top desk.

Daniel, meanwhile, had finished his courses at the University in record time and was now preparing himself further by working at the offices of Norris & Wiggen, a fine old respectable law firm. He lived at home and often relieved Laura at his father's sickbed, reading aloud to him from the newspaper or from Laura's enormous Bible. Justin would lie very still with one fist clenched, his flinty blue eyes glaring at the wall. He had not recovered the use of his left side. It was apparent suddenly that he was a very old man, with liver spots across his dry forehead and claws for hands. Half of his face seemed to be melting and running downward. He spoke only with difficulty, and when people misunderstood he would fly into a rage. Because he could not bear to have his weakness observed by the outside world (which would take advantage immediately, he was certain of it), he had determined to stay in his bedroom until he was fully recovered. For he assumed that he was suffering only a brief, treatable illness, his convalescence hampered by a worse-than-useless doctor and a half-wit wife. Therefore he undertook his own cure. He had all the panes in his windows replaced with amethyst glass, which was believed to promote healing. He drank his water from a quassia cup and ordered Laura to send away for various nostrums advertised in the newspaper—celery tonic, pectoral syrup, a revitalizing electric battery worn on a chain around the neck. His only meat was squirrel, easiest on the digestive tract. Yet still he remained flat on his back, whitening and shriveling like a beached fish.

On Friday nights Caleb came and summarized the week's business in a gentle, even voice, directing his statements to the foot of the bed. Justin looked at the wall, pretending not to hear. As a matter of fact it seemed that Caleb was handling everything quite adequately, but it was too late now. The time for that was past, there was no undoing what had been done. Justin went on looking at the wall until Caleb left.

Laura brought out an old busybody she had—a mirror arrangement placed to reflect passers-by on the street below. She thought he might like to keep in touch with things. But when Justin turned his face to the busybody he saw Caleb just descending the front steps, turned faded and remote and long-ago by the blue glass of the windowpanes. He told Laura to take her nonsense elsewhere.

In February, 1904, the Great Fire burned out the heart of Baltimore, sweeping away every tall building in the city and most major businesses, including Justin Peck's. When it was over Justin insisted upon being taken to see the damage for himself. His sons carried him to the buggy and drove him downtown, through the peculiar yellowish light that hung over everything. It was the first trip Justin had made since his illness. From the satisfied look he gave to the rubble and the littered streets and the jagged remains of walls, it seemed that he credited the destruction not to fire but to his own absence. Without him Baltimore had gone up in smoke. Under Caleb's care the warehouse had caved in, the office had disappeared, the roll-top desk had dissolved into ashes. He turned to Daniel with a crooked, bitter smile and waved his good hand to be taken home again.

Now he developed a new obsession: he wanted to leave this combustible city entirely and build further north, way out on Falls Road. He dreamed his room was alight with flames and not a member of his family would come to rescue him. He called in the night for Laura, whose bed he had left some fifteen years ago following her third miscarriage, and he made her sleep by his side with her hand on a brass bell from India. He jarred her awake periodically and sent her out to the hall to sniff for fire. And Caleb, who was working around the clock to rebuild the warehouse, had to come to his father's room every evening and listen to interminable garbled, stammered instructions for the buying of land in Roland Park. Nowadays Caleb always smelled of smoke from the city and he moved in a deep, tired daze. He would rest his cheek against the doorframe and slump until his sooty white shirt appeared to have nothing inside it, while his father wove his tangled mat of words: builders, masons, two fire, two fireproof houses.

Two?

Well, Justin figured Daniel would be marrying Margaret Rose Bell.

Now Margaret Rose Bell was a Washington girl who had come to spend the winter with her cousins, the Edmund Bells. And although it was true that she and Daniel were often seen together, the fact was that she was not yet eighteen years old, and Daniel was still working at Norris & Wiggen. Customarily a man would wait till he was able to buy and furnish a house by himself before he would take a wife.

Yes, but Justin planned to have a great many descendants and he was anxious to get them started.

Land was purchased in Roland Park. Master builders were hired to supervise the construction of two large houses set side by side, with almost no space between them, although great stretches of land lay all about. And meanwhile Margaret Rose was fitted for a complicated ivory satin wedding dress with one hundred and eight pearl buttons running down the back. They were married in the summer. Because the houses were not yet finished Margaret moved into Daniel's boyhood room, where his wooden-wheeled roller skates sat next to his shelf of lawbooks. She was a small, vivid girl who generally wore dresses of soft material like flower petals, and at any moment of the day she could be seen running up and down the stairs, or flinging open windows to watch some excitement in the streets, or darting into Justin's room to see if he needed anything. At the sight of her Justin would begin blinking and nodding in his doddering old man's way, and he would go on nodding and nodding and nodding long after she had kissed the top of his head and left again. Oh, he hadn't been mistaken, Margaret Rose was what this house had needed. And she would be certain to provide descendants. Why, by the fall of 1905, when Justin Peck's golden oak and wine-colored household set off on a caravan of wagons to Roland Park, Margaret Rose was already holding a baby in her lap and expecting another. Things were working out just fine. Everything was going according to plan.

By 1908 they had bought a snorting black Model T Ford with a left-hand steering wheel and splashless flower vases. Each morning the two brothers rode off to work in it—handsome young men in hats and high white collars. Daniel had his own law office now, a walnut-paneled suite of rooms with an oil portrait of his father over the mantel. He was taking on no partners because, he said, he wanted to have his sons for partners, not just anyone. And Caleb had rebuilt his father's warehouse, bigger and better than before. He had a brand new roll-top desk with twice as many cubbyholes.

Whenever Caleb chose to marry, another house would be built beside the first two, but meanwhile he lived at home with his parents. He was a quiet man who became quieter every year. It was a known fact that he drank sometimes, but he never troubled anyone and he never became rowdy or noisy. In fact Margaret Rose said she wished he *would* get noisy, once in a while. She was fond of Caleb. Between them they had a few old jokes, which would cause Margaret to laugh in her low, chuckly way until Caleb, in spite of himself, would let his own mouth turn up shyly at the corners. He would come talk to her in her shady back yard, waiting patiently through all her children's interruptions and requests and minor accidents. And several times she gave evening parties expressly to introduce Caleb to one or another of her pretty cousins. Girls always liked Caleb. But though he might dance with them or take them for a drive, he didn't seem interested in marriage. More often now he stayed home in his room, or he toured the taverns, or he went someplace else, no one knew where. Really, not even Margaret Rose could say for sure what Caleb did with himself.

For Christmas one year, Margaret persuaded Daniel to buy Caleb a Graphophone. She thought it would be the perfect gift for someone so musical. Along with it came disc recordings of Caruso, Arturo Toscanini, and Jan Kubelik on the violin. But these discs affected Caleb the way formal concerts did; he became restless and absent-minded and unhappy. He started pacing across the carpet and up and down the hall and eventually straight through the front door and out of sight, and was not seen again for the remainder of the day. So the Graphophone was never taken up to his bedroom, as Margaret had intended, but drifted into Justin's room instead, where it amused the old man for hours on end. He seemed particularly fond of Caruso. He would order Margaret to stand beside his bed cranking the machine and changing the heavy black discs. Margaret was surprised. If this was the way he felt, why had he forbidden Caleb's music in the house?

For Caleb continued to spend all his money on musical instruments—wooden flutes and harmonicas and cellos and even stringed gourds that only colored people would think of playing. He kept them in his room, but he was not allowed to sound a note on them where Justin could hear. In fact, even the piano was forbidden now, and had been exiled to Daniel's house, where Margaret Rose could tinkle out Czerny without disturbing her father-in-law. If Caleb wanted to make music he had to go far away, usually to the old Samson stable on the other side of a field. He would sit in the loft door blowing whistles or sawing out stringy little street tunes, and only wisps of his music drifted up to the house, never as far as Justin's densely curtained sickroom. Yet Justin always seemed to know when Caleb had been playing, and he would turn his face away irritably when Caleb stopped by later to offer his meticulous, patient account of the previous week's business.

Meanwhile Daniel's house was filling up with children,

and his practice was swelling, and he already had it in the back of his mind to become a judge someday while his sons carried on with the law firm. When he came home evenings, and Margaret ran up in her rustling, flowery dress to fling her arms around him, he would be remote and sometimes annoyed. His head was still crowded with torts and claims and statutes. He would set her gently aside and continue toward his study at the rear of the house. So for someone to talk to, Margaret tried giving afternoon tea parties. She invited her cousins and her girlfriends, who came tumbling in crying, "Maggie! Maggie Rose!" and kissing both her cheeks in the new way they had learned from Aunt Alice Bell, who had recently been to Paris. But Daniel said that he was not partial to these affairs. Oh, in the evening maybe, clients or business friends occasionally . . . he didn't want to be unreasonable, he said, but actually he expected his home to be a refuge from the outside world. And nowadays when he came in from a hard day's work he would be sure to find some unknown lady sitting on his leather chair, or a spectacular feather hat on the dining room buffet beneath Sarah Cantleigh's portrait, and once even the brass paperweight moved to the other side of his blotter, when everyone knew that his desk was forbidden territory. Besides, didn't she think she would be better off devoting those hours to her children?

They had six children. In 1905 Justin II was born, in 1906 Sarah, in 1907 Daniel Jr., in 1908 Marcus, in 1909 Laura May, in 1910 Caroline.

In 1911, Margaret Rose left home.

She had wanted to take the children to Washington on the train for her mother's birthday. Daniel didn't think she ought to. After all, she was a Peck now. What did she want with the Bells? Who at any rate were an undisciplined, frivolous, giggling lot. She said she would go anyway. Daniel pointed out that she was her own mistress, certainly, as everyone in his family had noticed more than once, but the children were *his*. And sure enough, there sat Daniel's children in a little bundle staring up at her, all Peck, blue Peck eyes and hair that matched their skin, solemn measuring Peck expressions, not a trace of Margaret Rose. She could go, Daniel said, but she couldn't take the children. And he expected her back on Saturday evening, as there was church to attend Sunday morning.

She went.

Saturday evening Caleb met the train but Margaret was not on it. When Daniel found out he merely pressed his lips together and walked away. Later he was heard telling his mother's servant Sulie to put the children to bed. Apparently no inquiries were going to be made.

On Wednesday Daniel received a letter from Margaret's father. He wrote in brown ink. Everyone knew that ink, because when Margaret's father wrote she would race through the house reading passages to different people and laughing at the funny parts. But Daniel read this letter in silence, and then went up to his room. When he came down again nothing at all was said about it.

In a month the children stopped asking for their mother. The baby stopped crying and the older ones went back to their games and nursery rhymes. Only Caleb seemed to remember Margaret Rose. He went up to Daniel one day and asked him point blank why he didn't go after her. Or Caleb himself would, though Daniel would be better. Daniel looked straight through him. Then Caleb went to Justin, who certainly loved Margaret Rose too and used to wait every day for the fluttering of her petal skirts against the banister. Now Justin merely closed his eyes and pretended not to hear. "But why?" Caleb asked him. "Don't you care? Life is not the same here when Maggie Rose is gone."

In all the accounts of the family history, told by all the aunts and uncles and upstairs maids, that was the only direct quotation of Caleb's that was ever handed down. Two generations later it was to ring in Justine's ears like poetry, taking on more depth and meaning than Caleb had probably intended. But Justin was not moved at all, and he kept his eyes shut very tightly and waited for his son to leave.

Now Laura ran both households, upright and energetic as ever in her ugly brown dresses with her hair screwed back so tightly it stretched her eyes. To the Peck children she was the center of the universe, sometimes the only family member they saw for days. Justin was too old and sick to be bothered, and Daniel hardly ever came home before their bedtime. As for Caleb, he kept to himself. They might catch sight of him striking out across the field toward the Samson stable, the sunlight pale on his Panama hat; or leaving for work in the morning, already tired and beaten-looking; or returning late in the evening with his manner of walking curiously careful. He never played with them. Sometimes on those extra-careful evenings he even got their names confused. He did nothing to earn their attention. So they failed to notice how he appeared to be dimming and wearing through, almost transparent; and how his only friends now were the questionable types in taverns, and how the music from the stable had thinned and shredded until you almost couldn't hear it. Laura noticed. But what could it mean? She pondered over his long, unbreakable silences, the likes of which she had not seen before and would not again until the days of Caleb's greatnephew Duncan, as yet unborn and unthought of. She tried to shame him into more normal behavior. "Where is your common *courtesy*? At least think of the family." But he would only wander off, not hearing, and sometimes he would not reappear for days.

On a Saturday afternoon in the spring of 1912, Daniel was standing at the bay window watching Justin Two ride his bicycle. It was a heavy black iron one, hard for Two to manage, but he had just got the hang of it and he teetered proudly down the driveway. From out of nowhere, Daniel saw a small, clear picture of Caleb on his velocipede merrily pedaling after a flutist on a sidewalk in old Baltimore. The memory was so distinct that he left his house and crossed the yard to his mother's and climbed the stairway to Caleb's room. But Caleb was not there. Nor was he in the kitchen, where he most often ate his meals; nor anywhere else in the house, nor outdoors nor in the stable. And the Ford was parked in the side yard; he wouldn't be downtown. Daniel felt uneasy. He asked the others—the children and Laura. They didn't know. In fact, the last time anyone could remember for sure he had been walking off down the driveway three days earlier, carrying his fiddle. The children saw him go. "Goodbye now," he called to them.

"Goodbye, Uncle Caleb."

But of course that didn't mean a thing, he would surely have . . . Daniel went to Justin's room. "I can't find Caleb," he said. Justin turned his face away. "Father? I can't—"

A long, glittering tear slid down Justin's stony cheek.

Really, the old man was beginning to let his mind go.

Years later, whenever he was fixing some family event in its proper time slot, Daniel Peck would pause and consider the importance of 1912. Could there be such a thing as an unlucky number? (Justine would look up briefly, but say nothing.) For in 1912 it seemed that the Peck family suddenly cracked and flew apart like an old china teacup. First there was Caleb's disappearance, without a trace except for a bedroom full of hollow, ringing musical instruments and a rolltop desk with an empty whisky bottle in the bottom drawer. So then they had to sell the business, Justin's last link with the outside world. And after that Justin started dying, leaving his family in the same gradual, fading way that Caleb had until it was almost no shock at all to find him lifeless in his bed one morning with his bluish nose pointing heavenward.

In the winter of 1912 there was another envelope from Washington addressed in brown ink. After Daniel read it, he told his children that Margaret Rose had been killed in a fire. They were to pray for her to be forgiven. Now her children wore brown to school and could properly be called poor motherless orphans, although they continued to look surprised whenever some well-meaning lady told them so. They were calm, docile children, a little lacking in imagination but they did well in their lessons. They did not seem to have suffered from all that had happened. Nor did Laura, who continued as spry and capable as ever. Nor Daniel, of course—a man of even temper. Although sometimes, late at night, he would take the Ford and drive aimlessly over the moonlit roads, often ending up in the old section of the city where he had no business any more, and knew no one, and heard nothing but the faint, musical whistling of the streetcar wires in the dark sky overhead.

5

Justine's childhood was dark and velvety and it smelled of dust. There were bearded men under all the furniture, particularly her bed. When her door was shut at night blue worms squiggled through the blackness, but when it was open the knob stuck out exactly like a shotgun barrel sidling through to aim at her head, and she would have to lie motionless for hours pretending to be a wrinkle in the blankets.

In the mornings her father was away, either at the office or out of town, and her mother was in bed with a sick headache, and Justine sat in the living room with the curtains shut so that even to herself she was only a pale glimmer. She was waiting for the maid. First there was the scrabbling of the key in the apartment door and then light, air, motion, the rustle of Claudia's shopping bag and her thin cross mosquito voice. "Now what you doing sitting there? What you up to? What you doing sitting in that chair?" She would yank the curtains open and there was the city of Philadelphia, a wide expanse of blackened brick apartment houses and dying trees in cages and distant factory smokestacks. Then she would dress Justine in a little smocked dress and braid the two skinny braids that she called plaits. "Don't you *go* getting that dress dirty. Don't you *go* messing yourself up, I'll tell Miss Caroline on you." By that time maybe her mother's headache would be lifting, at least enough so that her parched voice could trail out from the bedroom. "Justine? Aren't you even going to say good morning?" Although not an hour ago she had buried her face in the pillow and waved Justine away with one shaky, pearl-studded hand.

Justine's mother wore fluffy nightgowns with eyelet ruffles at the neck. Her hair was the color of Justine's but tightly curled. She was the youngest of Daniel Peck's six children, the baby. Even total strangers could guess that, somehow, from her small, pursed mouth and her habit of ducking her chin when talking to people. Unfortunately she tended to put on weight when unhappy, and she had become a plump, powdery, pouchy woman with her rings permanently embedded in her fingers. Her unhappiness was due to being exiled in Philadelphia. She had never guessed, when agreeing to marry Sam Mayhew, that the Depression would close down the Baltimore branch of his company just six months after the wedding. If she had had any inkling, she said—but she didn't finish the sentence. She just reached for another chocolate, or a petit-four, or one of the pink-frosted cupcakes she grew more and more to resemble.

But Justine loved her mother's soft skin and her puffy bosom and the dimples on the backs of her hands. She liked to huddle beneath the drooping velvet canopy of the bed, which was her mother's real home, surrounded by a circle of chocolate boxes, empty teacups, ladies' magazines, and cream-colored letters from Baltimore. Of course there were days when her mother was up and about, but Justine pictured her only in the dim rosy glow of the bedside lamp. She dwelt on the suspense of entering that room: was she welcome this time, or wasn't she? Some days her mother said, "Oh Justine, can't you let me be?" or wept into her pillow and wouldn't speak at all; but other days she called, "Is that my Justine? Is that my fairy angel? Don't you have one tiny kiss for your poor mama?" And she would sit up and scoop Justine into a spongy, perfumed embrace, depriving her of breathing room for a moment, not that it mattered. Then she flung back the ruffled pink sleeves of her bedjacket and taught Justine the games she had played when *she* was a child—cat's cradle and Miss Fancy's Come to Town and the doodle story, where you drew a map that turned out to be a goose. Or she would have Justine fetch scissors and she would cut, from the Baltimore newspaper, folded stars and paper dolls with pigtails and standing angels made from a circle cleverly slashed here and there as only she knew how. She would tell true stories, better than anything in books: How Uncle Two Scared the Hobo Away, How Grandfather Peck Fooled the Burglar, How the Mayhews' Ugly Dog Buttons Ate My Wedding Dress. She told how Justine was born in Baltimore thanks to split-second timing and not in Philadelphia as everyone had feared. "Well, luckily I had my way," she said. "You know how your daddy is. He didn't understand at all. When you started coming two months early I said, 'Sam, put me on that train,' but he wouldn't do it. I said, 'Sam, what will Father say, he's made all the arrangements at Johns Hopkins!' 'I just hope he didn't lay down a deposit,' your daddy said. So I picked up my suitcase that I had all ready and waiting and I said, 'Listen here, Sam Mayhew . . .' "

At six in the evening Claudia would leave, slamming the door behind her, and Justine's mother would look at the clock and her fingers would fly to her mouth. "How in the world did the time pass?" she would ask, and she would slide to the edge of the bed and feel for her pink satin slippers. "We can't let your daddy catch us lazing about like this." She would put on a navy blue dress with shoulder pads, and cover her rosebud mouth with dark lipstick, turning instantly from pink-and-gold to a heavy, crisply defined stranger like the ones hurrying down the sidewalk five stories below. "Of course my headache hasn't improved one bit," she would say. "I'd go back to bed but your daddy would never understand. He doesn't believe in headaches. He *certainly* doesn't believe in going to bed for them. It just is not his custom, I suppose."

To hear her talk, you would think Sam Mayhew was as different and exotic as an Asian prince, but he was only a small pudgy man with a Baltimore accent.

Then there were days in a row when Justine was not allowed in her mother's room at all, when she would puzzle and puzzle over what magic password had given her entry before. No one could go in but Claudia, carrying the latest string-tied box from the Parisian Pastry Co. Justine was marooned on a scratchy brocade chair in the living room and the bearded men beneath it were only waiting for her to lower one foot so that they could snatch her by the ankle and drag her down. Even Sam Mayhew's homecoming could not rouse his wife from bed. "Oh, go away, Sam, let me be, can't you see a crack is running down in front of my ears?" Sam and Justine ate supper alone, on the gold-rimmed plates that Claudia had laid out in the dining room. "Well, now, Justine, what have you been doing with yourself?" Sam would ask. "Did Claudia take you to the playground? Did you have a nice time on the swings?"

But he would quickly flounder and drown in her blank, astonished stare.

Day after day Justine on her brocade island looked at her mother's old *Books of Knowledge*—tattered maroon volumes with brittle pages, the only things she could reach without setting a foot to the floor. She lost herself in a picture of a train heading through outer space. It had been explained to her that this picture demonstrated the impossibility of man's ever reaching the moon. See how long it would take to cover the distance, even by rail? But to Justine it appeared all too easy, and she felt herself lightening and dwindling and growing dizzy whenever she saw that tiny lone train curving through the endless blackness.

Finally a time would come when she could raise her eyes from a page and find the air parting expectantly to make way for some change; she could always tell when change was coming. And not long afterward the telephone would ring, and Claudia would carry it from the foyer to the bedroom and rouse Justine's mother to shout long distance to Baltimore. "Hello? Oh, Father! Why are you—did Sam tell you to call me? What? Oh, not too well, I'm afraid. I said, not too *well*. Everything just seems to be going wrong, I can't quite . . .''

Justine would listen carefully, trying to discover exactly what had caused her world to collapse. She heard that her mother's nerves were acting up, her headaches were ferocious and no doctor could do a thing, the chandelier had fallen smack out of the ceiling, the landlord was impossible, Claudia showed no respect, there had been a very depressing story in the paper Sunday, Justine was turning sulky, Sam was out of town too much, and really it was entirely the fault of the City of Philadelphia. If he had any feeling, if he cared even a little, she knew it was asking a lot but she wished he would come and straighten things out.

He always came. She was his youngest daughter after all and very far from home, the only one of his children to leave the safety of Roland Park. Which was not to say that he approved of her. Oh, no. As soon as he stepped in the door, late that very night, he was curling his mouth downwards at the welter of pastry boxes and her crumb-littered, used-looking bed, and he was telling her outright that she had grown too fat.

''Yes, Father,'' Caroline said meekly, and she sat a little straighter and sucked in her stomach.

The next morning, when Justine got up unusually late after an unusually calm, dreamless sleep, she would find the apartment bright with sun and all the curtains open. Claudia was wearing a crisp white scarf and briskly attacking the dust in the cushions. Her mother sat in the dining room fully dressed, eating fresh grapefruit. And in the foyer her grandfather stood at the telephone announcing that he, Judge Peck, would personally drag the landlord through the entire United States judiciary system if that chandelier were not replaced by twelve noon sharp. Then he hung up and cupped Justine's head with his right hand, which was his way of greeting her. He was a bony man in a three-piece pinstriped suit, with fading hair like aged gardenia petals and a gold wafer of a watch that he let her wind. He had brought her a sack of horehound drops. He always did. Justine was certain that no matter what, even if he had rushed here through fires and floods and train wrecks, he would not forget to stop at Lexington Market first for a sack of horehound drops and he would not fail to cup her head in that considering way of his when he had arrived.

Generally during those visits Sam Mayhew would vanish, or if he did come home he wore a gentle, foolish smile and tried to keep out of the way. At any rate, the grandfather was never there for very long. He was a busy man. He came up over the weekend usually, just long enough to get his daughter to her feet again, and he left Sunday evening. Only once did he come on a working day. That was for Justine. She was supposed to be starting kindergarten, the first time she would ever be away from home alone. She refused to go. She wouldn't even get dressed. She became very white and sharp-faced and her mother gave in, sensing that there was no use arguing with her. The next morning when Justine awoke her grandfather Peck was standing by her bed carrying her plaid dress, her ruffled underpants with "Tuesday" embroidered on them and her lace-edged socks. He dressed her very slowly and carefully. Justine would have refused even her grandfather but his hands were so thick and clumsy, untying the bow of her nightgown, and when he stopped to pick up her shoes she could see the pink scalp through his thin pale hair. He even did her braids, though not very well. He even sat across from her and waited with perfect patience while she dawdled over breakfast. Then he helped her with her coat and they left, passing her mother, who wrung her hands in the doorway. They went down streets that were bitterly familiar, where she had shopped with her mother in the dear, safe days before school was ever thought of. At a square brick building her grandfather stopped. He pointed out where Claudia would meet her in the afternoon. He cupped her head briefly and then, after some fumbling and rustling, pushed a sack of horehound drops at her and gave her a little nudge in the direction of the brick building. When she had climbed the steps she looked back and found him still waiting there, squinting against the sunlight. Forever after that, the dark, homely, virtuous taste of horehound drops reminded her of the love and sorrow that ached in the back of her throat on that first day in the outside world.

In summer the leather suitcases would come up in the elevator to be packed, and Justine and her parents would board the evening train to Baltimore. Their arrival was never clear to Justine. She was half asleep, carried off the train and laid in the arms of some white-suited uncle. But when she awoke the next day there she was in Roland Park, all rustling with trees and twittering with birds, in her great-grandmother's white brick house, and if she went to the window she knew that all the houses within her view belonged to Pecks and so did the fleet of shiny black V-8 Fords lining one side of the street, and all the little blond heads dotting the lawn were Peck cousins waiting for her to come out and play.

Her mother would be talking in the dining room, but such a different mother—twinkling and dimpling and telling terrible giggling stories about Philadelphia. Aunts would be grouped around her, drinking their fifth and sixth cups of coffee. Aunt Sarah and Aunt Laura May were spinsters and still lived next door in the grandfather's house along with the bachelor Uncle Dan. Uncle Two's wife Lucy and Uncle Mark's wife Bea were Pecks by marriage only, and lived in the other two houses. They were not as important as the true Peck aunts, but then they *were* the mothers of the cousins. And of course, presiding over everyone was the great-grandma, a tidy, brownish woman. The white rims showing beneath her irises gave her a look of reproach, but as soon as she saw Justine she smiled and the rims disappeared. She offered Justine an enormous Baltimore breakfast—two kinds of meat, three kinds of pastry, and a platter of scrambled eggs—but Justine wasn't hungry. "Naturally," her mother said, laughing her summer laugh, "she's anxious to see her

cousins,'' and she tied Justine's sash and gave her a pat and
sent her off.

Justine had six cousins. All of them looked like her and
talked like her, all of them knew the story of how Grandfather Peck had fooled the burglar. It was very different from
Philadelphia, where her mother, coming to the school play,
referred to ''that *dark* little boy'' and asked, ''Who was the
child who spoke with such a nasal twang?'' With her cousins, there was no need to worry. Baltimore was the only place
on earth where Justine would not be going over to the enemy
if she agreed to play Prisoner's Base.

Yet even here, wasn't she an outsider of sorts? Her last
name was Mayhew. She lived in Philadelphia. She did not
always understand her cousins' jokes. And though they drew
her into every game, she had the feeling that they were trying
to slow down for her in some way. She envied them their
quick, bubbling laughter and their golden tans. Occasionally,
for one split second, she allowed herself to imagine her parents painlessly dead and some uncle or other adopting her,
changing her name to Peck and taking her to live forever in
Roland Park with its deep curly shadows and its pools of
sunlight.

At such times Aunt Bea, coming out to the front porch to
shade her eyes and check the children, would smile and sigh
over poor little plain Justine, whose pointed face was wisped
with anxiety so that it looked like crazed china or something
cobwebbed or netted. And who ran so artificially, so hopefully, at the edge of the other children's games, kicking her
heels up too high behind her.

In the evening they all went home. The four houses gave
the illusion of belonging to four separate families. But after
supper they came out again and sat on Great-Grandma's lawn,
the men in their shirtsleeves and the women in fresh print
dresses. The children grew over-excited rolling down the
slope together. They quarreled and were threatened with an
early bedtime, and finally they had to come sit with the
grownups until they had calmed down. Sweaty and panting,

choking back giggles, itchy from the grass blades that stuck to their skin, they dropped to the ground beside their parents and looked up at the stars while low measured voices murmured all around them. The oldest cousin, Uncle Mark's daughter Esther, held her little brother Richard on her lap and tickled him secretly with a dandelion clock. Nearby, Esther's twin sisters, Alice and Sally, were curled together like puppies with Justine in the middle because she was new and special. And Uncle Two's boys, Claude and Duncan, wrestled without a sound and without a perceptible movement so they wouldn't be caught and sent to bed. Not that the grownups really cared. They were piecing together some memory now, each contributing his own little patch and then sitting back to see how it would turn out. Long after the children had grown calm and loose and dropped off to sleep, one by one, the grownups were still weaving family history in the darkness.

In the winter of 1942, when Justine was nine, her father left for the war. The apartment was dismantled, a moving van came, and Justine and her mother took the train to Baltimore. Her mother cried all the way down. When they arrived she spilled out of the train and into her sisters' arms, still weeping, with her curls plastered to her face and her nose as pink as a rabbit's. Her sisters looked flustered and kept searching their purses for fresh hankies. The situation was new to them; no Peck had ever gone to war. It was believed that old Justin had mysteriously avoided the Civil War altogether, while every member of the family after him had possessed a heart murmur of such obviousness that they had been excused from even the mildest sports, the women cautioned against childbirth and the men saved from combat and long marches and the violence of travel by the unique, hollow stutter in their chests. Which did not prevent them from standing in a semicircle, bright-eyed and healthy and embarrassed, around their baby sister in the railroad station. It was their father who finally took charge. "Come, come," he said, and he herded them out of the station and into the line of Fords at the curb. Justine and her mother rode in his car, at the head of the procession. Justine's mother kept sniffing. Nothing irritated Grandfather Peck more than the sound of someone sniffing. "Look here, Caroline. We people don't *cry*. Get a hold of yourself," he said.

"I can't help it, Father. I just can't help it. I keep thinking of ways I could have been nicer to him. I mean I was never exactly—and I'm just certain he's going to be killed."

"He won't be killed," said Justine.

But nobody was listening.

They settled in Great-Grandma's house, since it had the most room. Justine was entered in the girls' school that Esther and the twins attended. Bit by bit she forgot almost completely the dark, bearded world of Philadelphia, and her mother grew carefree and girlish. Her mother seldom mentioned Sam Mayhew any more but she wrote him dutifully once a week, saying everyone was fine and sent him best regards. Only Justine, looking up sometimes from *The Five Little Peppers* or a game of backgammon, had a sudden picture of Sam Mayhew's sad, kind face and wondered if she had not missed out on something, choosing to be her mother's child alone.

Yet there were her cousins, always embarked on some new project. Esther wrote plays and her twin sisters shared a single role, speaking in unison. Justine played the princess in Aunt Laura May's blood-red lipstick. Little Richard would take any part you gave him, he was so happy to be included. And Uncle Two's son Claude was fat and studious; he was fine for rainy days, when he told horror stories in a hair-raising whisper in the gloom of the pantry stairwell.

But Duncan Peck was an evil, evil boy, and all his cousins worshipped him.

Duncan was prankish and reckless and wild. He had a habit of disappearing. (Long after she was grown, Justine could still close her eyes and hear his mother calling him—a soft-voiced lady from southern Virginia but my, couldn't she

sing out when she had to! "Dun-KUNN? Dun-KUNN?"
floated across the twilit lawn, with no more response than a
mysterious rustle far away or a gleam of yellow behind the
trees, rapidly departing.) While the rest of the cousins seemed
content to have only one another for friends, Duncan was
always dragging in strangers and the wrong kind of strangers
at that, ten-year-old boys with tobacco breath and BB guns
and very poor grammar. His cousins took piano lessons and
hammered out "Country Gardens" faithfully for one half
hour a day, but all Duncan would play was a dented Hohner
harmonica—"Chattanooga Choo Choo" complete with
whistles and a chucka-chucka and a country-sounding twang
that delighted the children and made the grownups flinch.
His great-grandma complained that he was impudent and
dishonest. It was perfectly obvious that he was lying to any
adult who asked him a question, and his lies were extreme,
an insult to the intelligence. Also he was accident-prone. To
his cousins that was the best part of all. How did he find so
many accidents to get into? And such gory ones! He never
just broke a bone, no, he had to have the bone sticking *out*,
and all his cousins crowding around making sick noises and
asking if they could touch it. He was always having a finger
dangle by one thread, a concussion that allowed him to talk
strangely and draw absolutely perfect freehand circles for
one entire day, a purple eye or an artery opened or a tooth
knocked horizontal and turning black. And on top of all that,
he was never at a loss for something to do. You would never
see *him* lolling about the house asking his mother for ideas;
he had his own ideas, none of which she approved of. His
mind was a flash of light. He knew how to make the electric
fan drive Richard's little tin car, he could build traps for
animals of all kinds including humans, he had invented a
dive-proof kite and a written code that looked like nothing
but slants and uprights. Tangled designs for every kind of
machine littered his bedroom floor, and he had all those
cousins just doting on him and anxious to do the manual
labor required. If he had been a cruel boy, or a bully, they

never would have felt that way, but he wasn't. At least not to them. It was the grownups he was cruel to.

Justine once saw him hanging from a tree limb, upside down, when the family was out on a picnic. He was safe but Aunt Lucy fretted away. "Dun-KUNN? I want you down from there!" she called. All Duncan did was unwrap one leg from the limb. Now he hung precariously, at an impossible angle, with his arms folded. Aunt Lucy rose and began running in ridiculous circles just beneath him, holding out her hands. Duncan grabbed the limb again—was he going to give in? What a disappointment!—but no, he was only readjusting himself so that now he could hang by his feet. All that supported him were his insteps, and it was not the kind of limb you could do that from. He folded his arms again and looked at his mother with a cool, taunting, upside-down stare that gave Justine a sudden chill. Yet wasn't Aunt Lucy laughable— flitting here and there crying, "Oh! Oh!" in a rusty scream. All the cousins had to giggle. Their grandfather set down his deviled egg and rose. "Duncan Peck!" he shouted. "Come down here this *instant*!"

Duncan came down on the top of his head and had to go to the emergency room.

Aunt Lucy, knitting soldiers' socks with her sisters-in-law, wondered and wondered what had made her son turn out this way. She considered all his flaws of character, his disgraceful report cards and the teachers' complaints. (He couldn't spell worth beans, they said, and had never learned that neatness counted. As for his papers, while there was no denying that they were ah, imaginative, at least what parts were readable, his hasty scrawl and his lack of organization and his wild swooping digressions left serious doubts as to his mental stability.) Now, where did all that come from? She reflected on her pregnancy: during her afternoon naps, she and the unborn Duncan had had, why, *battles!* for a comfortable position. Whenever she lay on her back, so the baby rested on the knobs of her spine, he would kick and protest until she gave in and shifted to her side. Of course she had only Claude to compare him with, but she had wondered even at the time: wouldn't the average baby merely have moved to a more comfortable position and let her rest?

The sisters sighed and shook their heads. The cousins, who had been eavesdropping in a row beneath the window, were very interested in pregnancy, but Duncan had a plan to weld all their bicycles together in a gigantic tandem and they couldn't stay to hear more.

When Sam Mayhew returned, his manufacturing company had reopened its Baltimore offices. There was no need to move back to Philadelphia. There was no need even to buy a place of their own, as his wife pointed out. Why bother, when Great-Grandma had three full stories in which she rattled around with no one but old Sulie the maid for company? So they stayed on in the white brick house in Roland Park, and Sam Mayhew rode downtown every day in a V-8 Ford behind his brothers-in-law. The Ford was a homecoming gift from the grandfather, who always had owned Fords and always would. To tell the truth, Sam Mayhew would have preferred a DeSoto. And he would have liked to buy a house in Guilford, which was where his parents lived. Somehow he never got to see his parents any more. But he was not a stubborn man and in the end he agreed to everything, only fading more and more into the background and working longer and longer hours. Once he took a three-day business trip and when he came home, only Sulie noticed he had been away. And *that* was because she had to count out the place settings for dinner every night.

His daughter, Justine, who had been undersized and pathetic when he left, was now a tall narrow beige girl. She had changed into one of those damned Pecks, clannish and secretive with a veiled look in her eyes, some sort of private amusement showing when she watched an outsider. And Sam was an outsider. Not that she was *rude* to him. All the Peck girls had excellent manners. But he knew that he had lost her, all right.

"What do those damned kids do all day? Don't they have any outside friends?" he asked his wife.

"Oh, they're all right. *We* were that way," she said serenely.

And she smiled out across the lawn at her brittle spinster sisters and her stuffy brothers who were all dressed alike, all lawyers as their father had wished them to be, and at the two wives who might have been chosen merely for their ability to be assimilated. Who *were* chosen for that. He looked down suddenly at his own colorless suit, so baggy that it seemed to be uninhabited. Then he sighed and walked away. Nobody noticed him leaving.

None of the girl cousins dated much in high school. At the mixers that were held with the boys' school up the road they were thought to be standoffish. Especially Justine, whose tense, pinched face stopped most of the boys from asking her to dance. Sometimes Sally, the prettier of the twins, might circle the floor with someone, but she tipped her pelvis away stiffly and seemed relieved when the music was over. As for the boy cousins, only Duncan had a steady girlfriend.

Duncan's girlfriend was a dimestore clerk named Glorietta de Merino. In an age when nice girls wore short skirts, Glorietta's swirled just above her ankles. She had a tumbling waterfall of black hair and a beautiful vivid face. There appeared to be sugar crystals on her eyelashes. Her waist was tiny and her breasts precisely cone-shaped, like the radio speakers Duncan was constructing in his basement. Anyone who talked to her appeared to be talking into the speakers—Grandfather Peck included, as Justine noticed when Glorietta came for Sunday dinner. Duncan was the only one who enjoyed that dinner. Even Glorietta must have suspected that things were not going exactly right. For afterwards, she never was seen in any Peck house again. Instead she took up residence in Duncan's car, a forty-dollar 1933 Graham Paige that smelled suspiciously of beer. Whenever the Graham Paige was parked outside, a green blemish in the row of Fords,

you could glimpse a flash of Glorietta's red dress through the
window. When Duncan taught Justine to drive, Glorietta rode
in the back like a lap robe or a Thermos bottle, part of the
car. She hummed and popped her chewing gum, ignoring
the shrieking gears and the quarrels and near accidents. Later,
when Justine had learned the rudiments of driving, Duncan
sat in the back as well. Justine could look in the rear view
mirror and see his arm cocked carelessly around Glorietta's
neck, his face peaceful as he watched the passing scenery.
She did not think *she* could ever be so relaxed with someone
outside the family.

Once for a school bazaar Justine was asked to run the
fortune-telling booth, which she knew nothing about. A very
peculiar old biology teacher sent her to a seeress named Olita.
"She is *my* fortune teller," she said, as if everyone should
have one, "and she'll teach you enough to get by." Duncan
and Glorietta drove Justine to a cleaner's in east Baltimore
and parked to wait for her. Olita had a room upstairs, behind
a plate glass window reading MADAME OLITA, YOUR DESTINY
DISCOVERED. Justine began to think that wasn't such a good
idea. She turned back toward the car, planning to tell Duncan
she had changed her mind, but she found that Duncan was
looking squarely at her, half smiling, with a spark in his eyes.
It reminded her of the time he had hung from the tree limb.
She went on up the stairs.

Madame Olita was a large, sloping woman with a stubby
gray haircut, wearing a grandmotherly dress and a cardigan.
Her room, which was bare except for two stools and a table,
smelled of steam from the cleaner's. Since the biology teacher
had called ahead, she already knew what Justine wanted. She
had written out a list of things to tell people. "Palms will be
simplest," she said. "Palms take much less time than cards,
and for a bazaar that's all that counts. Just sound sure of
yourself. Take their hands, like so." She reached for Justine's hand and turned it upward, smartly. "Start with the—
you could be telling fortunes yourself, if you wanted," she
said.

"But I will be," said Justine.

"I mean *seriously* telling fortunes. You have the knack."

"Oh," said Justine. "Well, I don't think I—"

"Do you ever have flashes when you know something is going to happen?"

"No! Really," said Justine. She pulled her hand away.

"All right, all right. Here's the list, then, of the major lines of the palm. Life, mind, heart, fate . . ."

But later when she had heaved herself up to see Justine to the door, she said, "This is really not a parlor game, you realize."

"No, I'm sure it isn't," Justine said politely.

"*You* know it isn't."

Justine couldn't think what was expected of her. She went on buttoning her coat. Madame Olita leaned forward and jabbed the back of Justine's left hand with one stubby finger. "You have a curved ring of Solomon, a solid line of intuition, and a mystic cross," she said.

"I do?"

"Even one of those denotes a superior fortune teller."

Justine straightened her hat.

"I have a mystic cross too," said Madame Olita, "but I've never found one on anybody else. They are very rare. May I see your right palm, please?"

Justine held it out, unwillingly. Madame Olita's hands felt like warm sandpaper.

"Well?" Justine said finally.

"You are very young," Madame Olita told her.

Justine opened the door to go.

"But you're going to enter into a marriage that will disrupt everything and break your parents' hearts," said Madame Olita, and when Justine spun around Madame Olita gave her a small, yellow smile and lifted a hand in farewell.

Out in the car, Duncan and Glorietta were kissing in broad daylight. "Stop that," Justine said irritably, and Duncan broke away and looked up at her, surprised.

Justine wondered if some aura of Duncan's had rubbed off

on her, so that Madame Olita had told the wrong person's fortune.

In the church hall after the sermon one Sunday a boy named Neely Carpenter asked Justine what time it was. "It's approximately twelve thirteen and a half," she told him.

"*Approximately* twelve thirteen and a *half?*"

"My watch says that, you see, but my watch is a little off," said Justine. "It's logical, really." She started laughing. Neely Carpenter who had always thought of her as a spinster-faced girl, looked surprised for a moment and then asked if she would like a ride home from church.

After that he gave her a ride every Sunday, and he took her to the movies every Saturday night. Justine's mother said she thought that was very sweet. It was the fall of Justine's senior year, after all; she was seventeen. It was about time she had a steady boyfriend. And Neely was a doctor's son recently moved to Roland Park, a serious-looking boy with very straight black hair and excellent manners. "Why don't you invite this Neely boy for Sunday dinner?" Justine's mother asked her.

Sunday dinner was always held at Great-Grandma's house, with four leaves extending the table so that everyone could sit around it. Neely looked a little stunned when he saw how many Pecks there were, but he found a seat between Aunt Sarah and Uncle Dan and did his best to keep his place in the conversation. "Yes, ma'am. No, ma'am," he kept saying. Justine thought he was doing fine. She was proud of her family, too—her aunts in their new rust-colored fall outfits, her handsome cousins, her stately grandfather with his hair turned silvery white and his face puzzled-looking from the effort he had started having to make in order to hear. So she was surprised when later, after Neely had gone home, Duncan said, "You'll never see *him* again."

They were out on Great-Grandma's lawn, where Justine had gone to see Neely off and where Duncan, up to some project or other, was unrolling a gigantic reel of baling wire across the grass. When he raised his head to speak to her Justine was struck by his expression, which was almost the same as his grandfather's. "Why do you say that?" she asked him.

"Nobody takes Sunday dinner with the Pecks and comes back for more."

"Well! Just because *Glorietta!* And besides, you're wrong. He's already asked me to Sue Pope's birthday dance."

"Then he's a fool," said Duncan. "No, I don't mean because of you, Justine. I mean, who would willingly mix with that crowd in the dining room?"

"I would," said Justine. "I thought they were very nice to him."

"Ah, yes! 'Ask if your little friend there would like another potato, Justine.' Little friend! And, 'Tell me, is it true that you go to public school? How *are* the public schools?' And, 'I understand your father is a doctor, um, Reilly. How nice! It's a very rewarding profession, I hear, though a little— mechanical, don't you think? *We* are all lawyers, I suppose you know—' "

"What's wrong with that? They were only showing an interest," Justine said.

"Ho! And then when he asked Great-Grandma if he could help to clear the dishes. *Then* he got it *twice!* 'Oh, my, no, we have a servant, dear.' And, 'Besides,' Aunt Caroline says, 'it's the very best china.' "

"Well?" said Justine. "We do have a servant. And it was the best china."

Duncan stopped unreeling the baling wire. He straightened up and wiped his face on his sleeve. "You really don't see it, do you," he said.

But Justine wouldn't answer. She folded her arms against an autumn wind and looked instead at the four brick houses behind them, where everybody was getting comfortable now with newspapers and needlework and cups of spiced tea. "You know what those houses remind me of?" Duncan said, following her gaze. "Hamsters. Or baby mice, or gerbils. Any of those little animals that cluster in one corner piled on top of each other even when they have a great big cage they are free to spread out in.''

"Oh, Duncan," Justine said.

She knew he only talked that way because he was going through a difficult time. Next year he would enter college and he wanted to go to Hopkins instead of the University and study science instead of law. But Grandfather Peck and the uncles kept arguing with him, nagging, pushing him. Of course he could study science, it was a free country, they said, but all the same there was something so *materialistic* about science, whereas law . . . "Peck, Peck, Peck & Peck," said Duncan, referring to the family firm, which was actually called Peck & Sons. "What a perfect name for them." And he would shut himself away in his room, or go riding aimlessly with Glorietta so close beside him that if the Graham Paige were a matchbox (which it almost appeared to be) they would have tipped over long ago.

So Justine didn't worry when he spoke so bitterly. And sure enough, Neely kept on asking her out. He never came to Sunday dinner again but that was because he really had to eat with his *own* family, he said. He did take her to movies and dances and birthday parties. He drove her home the long way around and parked some distance from the Pecks' in order to kiss her good night. He asked if she would like to move to the back seat where they would be more comfortable. "Oh well, oh no—" said Justine, uncertain of the proper answer. She really didn't know what she was supposed to do in this situation. None of her girl cousins could help her, either. All they knew about sex was what Duncan had told them when he was eight; that and the vague, horticultural-sounding information their mothers had given out. So Justine would flutter and debate with herself, but she always ended up saying, "Well actually I'm very comfortable where I am but thank you just the—" Neely, who might have been uncertain too, would look almost relieved. Going home he hummed along with "Good Night, Irene" on the radio.

He was starting to talk about their getting married someday, after he was through with medical school. Justine thought he was the best-looking boy in Roland Park and she liked his eyes, which were gray and translucent like quartz, and his quiet, level way of speaking. It was possible that she might even love him, but she didn't know what her mother would say.

By the fall of 1951, Justine had started attending a girls' junior college nearby. She thought she would do English or preschool education or something. It didn't much matter. Although she had always been a fair student she didn't have any real curiosity and she couldn't think of any career she wanted to aim for. So she and Esther drifted off to college every day in the Ford their grandfather had bought them for commuting, their bright kerchiefs flickering and their hair whipping in the wind. Almost every evening Neely would come over (he was at Hopkins now) to study in the dining room with her. And there were still the Sunday dinners, the cousins alternating with grownups around the table to discourage mischief, and Claude's round face shining with the relief of being home from the University even if just for a day.

But Duncan!

Something came over Duncan that year. No one could quite put a finger on it. He had what he wanted, didn't he? He was studying science at Hopkins, wasn't he? Yet it seemed sometimes that he was more dissatisfied than ever, almost as if he regretted winning. He complained about living at home, which he had to do because Hopkins was so expensive. He said the expense was an excuse; this was just the family's way of punishing him. Punishing! To live at home with your own close family? He was morose and difficult to talk to. He did not appear to have any friends at all, at least none that he would introduce, and Glorietta was no longer to be seen. Well, of course he had always been somewhat of a problem. Surely this was just another of his stages, the aunts told his mother.

But then he started reading Dostoevsky.

Naturally they had all read Dostoevsky—or at least the uncles had, in college. Or *Crime and Punishment*, at any rate. At least in the abridged edition. But this was different. Duncan didn't just *read* Dostoevsky; he sank in, he buried himself in Dostoevsky, he stopped attending classes entirely and stayed in his room devouring obscure novels and diaries none of the rest of the family had heard of. On a soft spring evening, in the midst of a peaceful discussion on the merits of buying a home freezer, Uncle Two's branch of the family might be startled by the crash of enormous footsteps down the stairs and Duncan's wild, wiry figure exploding into the living room to wave a book at them. "Listen! Listen!" and he would read out some passage too loudly and too quickly for them to follow. A jumble of extravagant Russian prose, where emotions were stated outright in a surprising way and a great many extreme adjectives were used and feverish fancies kept darting and flashing. Paragraphs were layered and dense and complicated like chunks of mica. "Did you *hear?*" he shouted. His parents nodded and smiled, their embarrassed expressions giving them the look of sleepers dazzled by bright light. "*Well* then!" he would say, and off he spun, up the stairs. His parents stared at each other. His father went to talk to the grandfather, who understood it no better. "But I thought he was scientific!" he said. "What is he reading for?" And then, "Ah well, never mind. At least it's the classics, they surely can't hurt him."

But that was before Easter Sunday. On Easter Sunday, at the dinner table, the aunts were discussing Mrs. Norman Worth's extensive collection of eggshell miniatures. The uncles were arguing the details of a hypothetical legal problem: If a farmer, while turning on the water to irrigate the fields, accidentally startled another farmer's mule, which, in turn, kicked down the fence enclosing a prize-winning Angus bull, who thereupon . . .

"Neither of these subjects is fit table conversation," Duncan said.

Everybody thought about that for a minute.

"But what's wrong with them, dear?" his mother said finally.

"They're not real."

Great-Grandma, who had lived longest and was hardest to shock, poured more ice water into her tumbler. "To you they may *not* be," she said, "but I myself find eggshell miniatures fascinating and if I didn't have this tremor I would take them up myself."

"You owe us an apology, Duncan boy," said Uncle Two.

"You owe *me* an apology," said Duncan. "I've spent eighteen years here growing deader and deader, listening to you skate across the surface. Watching you dodge around what matters like painting blue sea around boats, with white spaces left for safety's sake—"

"What?"

"Can't you say something that *means* something?" Duncan asked.

"About what?" said his mother.

"I don't care. Anything. Anything but featherstitch and the statute of limitations. Don't you want to get to the bottom of things? Talk about whether there's a God or not."

"But we already know," said his mother.

What was so terrible about that? None of them could see it. But Duncan stood up, as wild-eyed as any Russian, and said, "I'm leaving. I'm going for good."

He slammed out of the dining room. Justine jumped up to follow him, but then she stopped in the doorway, undecided. *"He'll* be back," Uncle Two said comfortably. "It's only growing pains. Ten years from now he'll talk the same as all the rest of us."

"Go after him," the grandfather said.

"What, Father?"

"Well, don't just—*somebody* go. You go, Justine. Go after him, hurry."

Justine went. She flew out the front of Great-Grandma's house and paused, thinking she had already lost him, but then she saw him just coming from Uncle Two's with a card-board box. He crossed the lawn and heaved the box into the back seat of the Graham Paige. Then he climbed in himself. "Duncan! Wait!" Justine called.

Surprisingly, he waited. She ran up out of breath, clutch-ing her dinner napkin. "Where are you going?" she asked him.

"I'm moving."

"You are?"

She looked at the back seat. It was like him to leave his clothes behind and take his box of tools and scrap metal.

"But Duncan," she said, "what are we going to do with-out you?"

"You'll manage."

"What if we need you for something? Where will we find you?"

By now other members of the family were straggling onto Great-Grandma's porch. She could tell by the look he flashed over her shoulder. "Bye, Justine," he said. "I've already got a place, beside that bookstore on St. Paul, but don't tell the others."

"But *Duncan*—"

"Bye, Justine."

"Bye, Duncan."

At first the family assumed he would be home in no time. It was only his age. Everybody eighteen expected deep things of people, but it never *lasted*. Yet the days stretched on and there was no word of him. They began to question Justine more closely. "He's all right, he's got a place to stay," was what she had said earlier, but now that wasn't enough. Had he told her where? Because this was not some childhood game any more, surely she was mature enough to realize that. Wasn't she?

But she had promised Duncan.

Aunt Lucy said Justine was cruel and selfish. Justine's mother said there was no call for *that* sort of talk, and then

Aunt Lucy broke down and cried. "Now look here. Get a hold of yourself," the grandfather said, which made her turn on him. Why couldn't a person let loose a little, after all? Where was the sin? How come a forty-four-year-old woman didn't have a right to cry in her own house, and state her feelings as she pleased, without a bunch of Pecks crowding around telling her she was not sufficiently dignified, and elegant, and tasteful, and respectable?

"Why, Lucy Hodges!" said Aunt Sarah.

Aunt Lucy gave her a look of pure hatred, there was no other way you could put it.

Justine was miserable. She would much rather tell and be done with it. But even if the grownup rules *were* different, Duncan was still playing by the old ones and he would be furious if she told. She hoped he would come home by himself—"turn himself in" was how she thought of it. Or that Uncle Two, strolling the Hopkins campus with false nonchalance during class break, would run across Duncan on his own. But Duncan didn't come and he wasn't seen on campus, and Uncle Two didn't want to ask at the Dean's office outright and involve other people in family matters. "You owe it to us to tell, Justine," he said. His face was tired and gaunt and there were shadows under his eyes. Aunt Lucy wasn't speaking. Even the cousins looked at Justine with a new edginess. How had she got herself into this? All she wanted was for the family to be happy together. That was the only reason she had run after Duncan in the first place.

She felt like someone who takes a single short step on solid ice and then hears a crack. She was halfway onto a drifting floe, one foot pulling out to sea and the other still on shore.

Then her grandfather said, "Have *you* been to see him?"

"Oh, I don't think he'd like me to, Grandfather."

"Why not? You're his cousin."

"I know."

"Yes, well," her grandfather said, and he pulled at his nose. "Well, never mind that. Go anyway. It's the only way we'll get any peace around here."

"Go visit him?"

"You didn't promise not to do *that*, did you? Go ahead. Don't worry, nobody will follow you."

But Justine half hoped someone *would* follow. Then life could get back to normal.

She knew the address because she had often gone with Duncan to the bookshop he mentioned—a cluttered place with creaky floorboards and great tilting stacks of used technical books. To the left of the shop was a paper sign, orange on black, saying ROOMS. When she opened the door she found narrow wooden steps, and at the top of the steps a dark hall with a toilet at the end. The doors reminded her of school, all thickly painted with scuffproof brown and marked off with curly metal numbers. But she should have brought a flashlight to read the nameplates by. She moved down the hall very slowly, hunching her shoulders against a feeling of unknown things at the back of her neck, peering at the names scrawled on scraps of ruled paper or adhesive tape: Jones, Brown, Linthicum, T. Jones. No Peck. Only a door to her right with nothing at all, no name in the slot. And that, of course, would be Duncan.

She knocked. When he opened the door she held onto her hat, like someone who has just pressed a fun-house button with no notion of what to expect. But all Duncan said was, "Justine."

"Hello," she said.

"Was there something you wanted?"

"I'm supposed to see if you're all right."

"Well, now you've seen."

"Okay," she said, and turned to go.

"But you might as well come in, I guess. Since you're here."

His room was small and dingy, with stained wallpaper, a flapping torn shade, a speckled mirror, and a metal bed with a sagging mattress. Over in one corner was his cardboard box. He wore the clothes he had left home in, brown suit pants and a white shirt without a tie. He seemed thinner. "It doesn't look as if you're eating right," Justine said.

"Is that what you came to tell me?"

"No."

She sat down very delicately on the edge of the bed. She lifted both hands to her hat, making sure it was perfectly level. For some reason, Duncan smiled.

"Well!" she said finally.

Duncan sat down next to her.

"Your mother is really taking on, Duncan. She's crying where everyone can see her. Your father is—"

"I don't want to hear about that."

"Oh. Well—"

"*I* know what they're doing. I always know, I can tell, I can see as if I'm sitting there. They're talking about someone in the outside world. They're digging the moat a little deeper. They're pointing out all the neighbors' flaws and their slipping dentures and mispronunciations, they're drawing in tighter to keep the enemy out. Why do you think my mother's crying? Because she misses me? Did she say that? Think a minute. Did she? Did any of them? No. They're worried I might be with the wrong kind of people. They're upset to think a Peck is out there in the world someplace. I've lowered the drawbridge."

"Oh *no*, Duncan—" Justine said.

"Everything they do is calculated to keep others at a safe distance. Everything. Look at your hat!"

Justine's hands went up again, uncertainly.

"No, no, it's fine. It's a fine hat," he told her. "But what are you wearing it for?"

"Why, I *always*—"

"Yes, but why? Did you ever take a good look around you? Only old ladies wear hats any more, outside of church. But every woman in our family, even little girls, they all wear hats even if they're just off to the side yard for a breath of air. 'A lady doesn't *go* without a hat, my dear. Only common people.' Common! What's so uncommon about us? We're not famous, we're not society, we haven't been rich since 1930 and we aren't known for brains or beauty. But our ladies wear hats, by God! And we all have perfect manners! We may not ever talk to outsiders about anything more interesting than the weather but at least we do it politely! And we've all been taught that we disapprove of sports cars, golf, women in slacks, chewing gum, the color chartreuse, emotional displays, ranch houses, bridge, mascara, household pets, religious discussions, plastic, politics, nail polish, transparent gems of any color, jewelry shaped like animals, checkered prints . . . we're all told from birth on that no Peck has had a cavity in all recorded history or lost a single tooth; that we're unfailingly punctual even when we're supposed to come late; that we write our bread-and-butter notes no more than an hour after every visit; that we always say 'Baltimore' instead of 'Balmer'; that even when we're wearing our ragged old gardening clothes you can peek down our collars and see 'Brooks Brothers' on the label, and our boots are English and meant for riding though none of us has ever sat on a horse . . . ''

He wound down like Great-Grandma's old Graphophone, and slumped forward suddenly with his long hands drooping between his knees.

"But Uncle Two is so *sad*," said Justine. "He wanders around the Homewood campus all day hoping to—"

"Justine. Will you please get *out?*"

She rose immediately, clutching her little suede purse. But in the doorway Duncan said, "Anyhow, thanks for coming."

"Oh, you're welcome."

"I meant it, Justine. I'm sorry I . . . really, if you wanted to come back sometime I wouldn't mind."

"Well, all right," Justine said.

Then of course when she got home everyone was furious with her, because she hadn't found out one concrete fact. What was he living on? Where was he eating? Was he going to school? Who were his companions?

"I just know he's taken up with some—trash, he does have such peculiar taste in friends," Aunt Lucy said.

And all of them wondered at Justine's sudden look of sorrow.

What Duncan was living on was a pittance paid him by a Hopkins professor. He was double-checking dry facts in a library, and then writing them into the blanks the professor had left in a very long, tedious book on paleobotany. He was eating saltines and peanut butter, washed down with a quart bottle of milk in his room. He had no companions at all, not even Glorietta, with whom he had had a terrible fight several months ago over her habit of saying "between you and I." Eventually he was going to go very far away, perhaps to British Columbia, but at the moment it seemed he just couldn't get up the energy. And no, he was not attending school any more. He was not even reading Dostoevsky, whose writing suddenly appeared to have the squirmy, eye-straining texture of plant cells. As a matter of fact, he thought he might be going crazy. He even *liked* the idea of going crazy. He waited for insanity as if it were some colorful character his parents had always warned him against, but every morning when he woke up his mind was the same efficient piece of machinery it had always been and he felt disappointed.

Several times a week, his cousin Justine would come bringing irritating, endearing gifts—a ridiculous pair of slippers, his striped bedspread from home, once his old blue toothbrush with Ipana caked in the bristles. Whenever he opened the door to her he felt deeply happy to see her thin, sweet face and her streamered hat, but before she had been there five minutes he wanted to throw her out. She had such a gift for saying the wrong thing. "Can I tell the cousins where you are? They want to come, too."

"No. God."

"Do you need any money?"

"I can take care of myself, Justine."

"Grandfather gave me some to bring to you."

"Tell him I can take care of myself."

"But I can't give it back to him, Duncan. He was so—he just pushed it into my hand all clumsy and secret. He pretended he wasn't doing anything."

"Change the subject."

"Like in the old days when he gave out horehound drops."

"Justine, I wish you would go now."

She always went. But she always came back, too, and when she stood in his doorway again a few days later he was all the more touched by her stupid, comical persistence. From earliest childhood she had been his favorite cousin—maybe because she was a little more removed, a Mayhew, a Philadelphian, not quite so easy to know. But he was surprised that she would brave his dark stairs and his rudeness. Here she had always seemed so docile! He made a special effort for her, smoothing the spread and offering saltines from his roach-proof tin and suggesting she take her hat off, which of course she would not do. "Justine, I'm glad you came back," he said.

"Why, thank you."

"You may get on my nerves sometimes but at least you show things, you say things outright, you don't feel it's a sin. You were the only one to ask me not to go, the Sunday I left."

"But Grandfather told me to do that," Justine said.

Right away she had managed to get on his nerves again.

She always had an answer. She drove him up a wall. He reached the point where he would turn on her the moment she entered, letting loose a flood of arguments that he had been storing up. "You know what they're like?" (There was no need to say whom he meant.) "You know who they remind me of? People choosing a number on a radio dial. The way they ignore anything that isn't Peck, like flicking past stations that don't concern them, just a split second of jazz or ballgames or revivalist ministers and they wince and move on, and settle finally on the one acceptable station that plays

Mantovani. Nothing uncomfortable, nothing extreme, nothing they can't tolerate . . .''

"They tolerate you at the Sunday dinner," Justine said. "Really you were as rude as can be and they tried to see your side of it and act reasonable. Who are you to say they can't talk about eggshells?"

Duncan said, "Nothing outside the family matters. Nobody counts if they're not Pecks. Not even neighbors, not even Sulie. Why, Sulie's been with us since our parents were children, but does anybody know her last name?"

"Boudrault."

"Hmm?"

"She married old Lafleur Boudrault, the gardener."

"Oh, details," said Duncan.

"He died in nineteen forty."

"Little church-lady Emily Post details and nothing underneath. And you're just like them, Justine, you always will be. Who asked you to come here and clutter up my life?"

But when she was gone, her smell of warm grass hung in the air and the memory of her imperturbable Peck face. At night her chilly little voice ran on and on, arguing, reasoning, imposing logic, even in his dreams. He would wake and punch his flattened pillow and toss beneath the spread that carried her smell too, even from its brief stay in her arms. He wished she were there to argue with; then he wished she were there to apologize to; then he wished she were there to lay her long cool body next to his on the sagging mattress and hold him close all through the deep, steamy Baltimore night.

Justine was not herself; everybody noticed it. Even summer vacation didn't seem to relax her any. She was strange and distant with her family. She began watching her aunts and uncles in a measuring way that made them uncomfortable. "What's the *matter* with her?" her father said once, but his in-laws only smiled blankly; they did not believe in asking too many questions.

It seemed that they accepted Duncan's absence now. Sometimes when Justine came back from visiting him they would forget to ask how he was. Or they would say, "See Duncan, did you?" and go on about their business. Even Aunt Lucy appeared resigned. But one day in August, a particularly hot Saturday morning, Aunt Lucy appeared on Great-Grandma's front steps with a small electric fan. Justine was drying her hair outdoors and reading *Mademoiselle*. "Justine, dear," said Aunt Lucy.

Justine looked up, with her mind still on her magazine. Her aunt wore the expression of a lady heading calm and smiling toward disaster.

"Justine, this is for Duncan," Aunt Lucy said.

"What? Oh, a fan. He could use it."

"Oh, I knew it! I'm so glad I—well, whenever you go to see him, then. Are you going today?"

"Today I'm going on a picnic with Neely. Tomorrow I might, though."

"Don't you think you might stop by this morning? Wouldn't you be able to work it in?"

Aunt Lucy's smile hesitated.

"Of course I could," Justine said, and she took the fan from her aunt's shaky hands.

It was not until she had parked in front of the bookshop that she noticed the little envelope dangling from the fan's grid.

Duncan's room was blasting with heat and he was so hot he seemed to have been oiled. He wore a grayish undershirt. His trousers were creased and limp. "Oh, it's you," was all he said, and then he sat back down on his bed and wiped his face with his balled-up shirt.

"Duncan, I brought you a fan from your mother."

"You've been telling her about my room."

"No, I haven't. She just *guessed* you would need this."

"What's that in the envelope?"

"I don't know."

He broke the string that tied it and pulled out a folded

note. First he read it silently and then he groaned and read it aloud.

Dear Duncan,

I am taking the liberty of sending you the fan from my bedroom, now that it is so warm.

Everyone is well although I myself have had a recurrence of those headaches. Just a little tension, the doctor says, so I keep my chin up!

Your father has been working very . . .

"What about the fan from *my* room?" Duncan said. "There is one, you know."

"She gave you her own to show she cares, she didn't know how else to put it," said Justine.

"None of them do. Oh, you can tell who she married into. She's just like all the rest of them now. Too little said and too much communicated, so that if you fight back they can say, 'But why? What did *I* do?' and you won't have any answer. It all takes place in their secret language, they would never say a thing straight out."

"But that's tact. They don't want to embarrass you."

"They don't want to embarrass themselves," Duncan told her.

She said nothing.

"Isn't that right?"

"Probably it is," she said. "But so is the other. There *isn't* any right and wrong. I keep looking at them, trying to decide. Well, everything you say is true but then so is everything I say. And what does it matter, after all? They're your family."

"You know who you sound like? Aunt Sarah, Justine. You're going to grow up an old maid. Or you'll marry a stick like Neely and have him change his name to Peck. I can see it coming. I can see it in that flat straight face of yours, just watch."

But he had gone too far. Even he must have known that.

When Justine turned away from him, fumbling for something in her purse, he said, "Anyway!" He jumped up and started pacing the floor. "Well, anyway, tell me all the news," he said.

"Oh . . ."

"Come on!"

"There's nothing much."

"Nothing? Nothing in all those four enormous houses?"

"Well, Aunt Bea has had to get glasses," Justine said.

"Ah."

"She's very shy about them, she wears them on a string tucked inside her blouse. She takes them off between sentences in a newspaper even."

"So Aunt Bea has glasses."

"And Mama's bought a TV."

"A TV. I might have known it would come to that."

"Oh, it's not so bad, Duncan. It's very convenient, don't you think, having a moving talking picture in your home that way? I wonder how they do it."

"Actually it's quite simple," said Duncan. "The *principle's* been around for decades. Have you got a pencil? I'll show you."

"Oh, I wouldn't understand," Justine said.

"Of course you would."

"But I'm not scientific. I don't see how you know those things."

"Those things are nothing," he said, "it's the others I don't get. The ones you take for granted. Like mirrors, for instance," and he stopped his pacing to wave at the mirror on the opposite wall. "I lay awake the other night going crazy over that. I spent hours trying to figure out the laws of reflected images. I couldn't measure the angles of refraction. Do you understand it? Look."

She stood up and looked. She saw herself in the speckled glass, nothing surprising.

"How come it shows my image and not yours?" he asked her. "How come yours and not mine? How come eyes can meet in a mirror when you're not looking at each other in real life? Do you understand the principle?''

In the glass their eyes met, equally blue and distant, as if the mirror were reflecting images already mirrored.

Duncan turned around and set his hands on her shoulders and kissed her on the mouth. He smelled of salt and sunlight. His grip on her was weightless, as if he were holding something back. When she drew away, he let his hands drop to his sides. When she ran out of the room he didn't try to stop her.

Justine wouldn't visit Duncan any more. Her grandfather kept coming around, pressing twenty-dollar bills into her hand, but she didn't know what to tell him and so she took the money in silence. She stuffed it haphazardly into her jewelry box, feeling like a thief even though she never spent it. She quarreled with her mother over a print dress, saying it was old-ladyish, although before she had worn whatever her mother picked out. When school started she studied indifferently and had trouble getting to class on time. Esther had graduated and was teaching nursery school, but now the twins were commuting with Justine and they objected to her late starts. "Is that what you call the point of life?" Justine asked them. "Getting to a class on the dot of nine o'clock?"

The twins looked at each other. Certainly they had never meant to imply that it was the *point* of life, exactly.

On a Saturday night in October, Justine was watching television with Neely in her great-grandma's study. Neely was stroking her neck up and down in a particularly rasping way, but she had been so short-tempered with him lately that she didn't want to protest. Instead she concentrated on the television: a mahogany box with a snowy blue postage stamp in its center, showing a girl who had become engaged due to cleansing her face with cold cream twice a night. She flashed a diamond ring at her girlfriends. "*Your* diamond's going to be *twice* as big," said Neely. "My father's already promised me the money."

"I don't like diamonds," said Justine.

"Why not?"

"I don't like stones that are transparent."

On the television, a man held up a watch that would keep running steadily through everything, even a cycle in a washing machine.

"How about me?" Neely asked.

"What?"

"Do you like *me?*"

His finger kept annoying her neck. Justine winced and drew away.

A man in downtown Baltimore was interviewing people coming out of a movie theater. He wanted to see if they had heard of his product, an antibacterial toothpaste. "Goodness, no," said a lady.

"Well, think a minute. Say you have a cold and get over it. You wouldn't want to catch it right back again from your toothbrush, would you?"

"Goodness, no."

He stopped a man in a raincoat.

"Sir? Have you ever thought how risky it is, using the toothbrush you used when you were sick?"

"Why, no, now I never considered that. But you got a point there."

He stopped Duncan.

"Say!" said Neely. "Isn't that your cousin?"

Duncan was wearing some dark shade of jacket that Justine had never seen before. His face was clamped against the cold. There was no one in the world with such a pure, unwavering face. He stooped a little to hear the question, concentrating courteously with his eyes focused on something in the distance. When the man was finished Duncan straightened and thought a moment.

"Actually," he said, "once your body's built up enough resistance to overcome those bacteria in the first place it's very doubtful if—"

The man discontinued the conversation and ran after a fat lady.

Justine went to the front hall for her coat. "Justine?" Neely called. She ignored him. Probably he thought she was out of hearing, maybe gone to the kitchen for soft drinks. At any rate, he didn't call again.

All she told herself was that she owed Duncan a visit. He was her cousin, wasn't he? And she really should give him their grandfather's money. (Which was still crammed in her jewelry box at home.) She had herself convinced. But Duncan must have known exactly how her mind worked, because when he opened the door he stood looking at her for a minute, and then he drew her in and kissed her, and then he said, "Look, I can see the layers sliding across your eyes like shutters until you can properly explain this away." Then he laid her on his bed, with its hollow center that rolled her toward him so that she could feel his warm bones through the thin white fabric of his shirt. He took off her clothes and his. Still she didn't make a single objection, she said none of the things that she had said to Neely. She felt happy and certain, as if everything they did was already familiar. She seemed to be glinting with some secret laughter at this newer, more joyous mischief that they were just inventing, or at Duncan's Puckish face turned suddenly gentle, or at her own self in his mirror eyes, a naked girl wearing a Breton hat.

6

Duncan came home in March of 1953. He walked into his great-grandma's dining room one Sunday at dinnertime. "Duncan!" his mother said, half rising. Then, "What on earth is that you're wearing?"

He was wearing a peajacket he had bought from Navy surplus. His hair needed cutting. He had been gone nearly a year and in that time his face had changed in some indefinable way that made him an outsider. The grownups stared and his cousins gave him self-conscious, sidelong glances. All but Justine, who raised her face like a beacon and smiled across the room at him. He smiled back.

"Well, my boy," his grandfather said. "So you're home."

"No," said Duncan, looking at Justine.

But they didn't believe him. "Pull up a chair," his mother said. "Take mine. Get yourself a plate. Have you had one decent meal since you left us?"

"I'm going to get married," Duncan said.

"Married?"

The ghost of Glorietta flashed scarlet through their minds. All the grownups shifted uneasily.

"I'm marrying Justine."

First they thought it was a joke. A tasteless one, but just like him. Then they saw how grave and still the two of them were. "My God," said Justine's mother. She clutched suddenly at a handful of ruffles on her chest. "My God, who would have thought of such a thing?"

Though it seemed to all of them, now, that they should

102

have thought of it long ago. Those visits Justine had paid him! Those trips! Everyone knew she hated traveling as much as any other Peck. Yet day after day this winter she had packed a lunch in Sulie's kitchen and said she wouldn't be home till night. "I'm going on a trip with Duncan. Out to the country somewhere." "Yes, yes, go," they told her. "Keep an eye on him for us." She had cut classes, missed important family gatherings, stopped seeing Neely, grown distant from her cousins—"But it's good she's with Duncan," they told each other. "She's sure to be a good influence on him." How she had deceived them!

Only Sam Mayhew, slow of mind, seemed unable to make the mental leap the Pecks had just accomplished. He looked all around the table, from one person to the other, with his face set to laugh as soon as he saw the joke. "What? What's that?" he said.

The others waved him aside, too busy adjusting to the shock. But Duncan came over and stood squarely in front of him and spoke very quietly, as if to a child.

"Uncle Sam, I'm marrying Justine."

"But—you can't!"

"I'm telling you I am. I'm telling you, not asking you. Nothing is going to make me change my mind."

"You can't."

"Why, it must not even be legal!" said Caroline.

"Yes, it is," Duncan told her.

"*Oh* yes," his grandfather said.

"But—" said Caroline.

"Who's the lawyer here, you or me? Boy's right. It's true. And yes, I know, there's a lot to be said against it. But look at it this way. What nicer girl could he have picked? She's sure to settle him down some. And this way there's no adjustment for them to make, no in-law problems—"

"You ought to be locked up," Sam Mayhew said.

"Sir!" said Grandfather Peck.

"Haven't you heard of inbreeding?"

"Not at the table, Sam."

"Haven't you heard of *genes*?"

"Now, we come of good solid stock," the grandfather said. "No worries there." He picked up the carving knife. "Care for a slice of ham, Duncan boy?"

"He's a blood relative," said Sam Mayhew. "And he's only twenty years old, and he hasn't got a responsible bone in his body. Well, I'm not going to allow it. Justine won't marry Duncan or any other Peck."

"Then we'll elope," Duncan said.

"Elope!" cried Justine's mother. "Oh, anything but that!"

"You are a fool, Caroline," Sam Mayhew said. Then he stood and took Justine by the wrist and pulled her up and toward the door. But she was still calm and so was Duncan. Nothing seemed to disturb them. As Justine passed Duncan he gave her a slow, deep stare that caused the rest of the family to avert their eyes. "*Come*, Justine," her father said. He led her through the living room and up to her bedroom. She went without a protest. He set her in her room and shut her door and locked it, and put the key up on the ledge again before he went back to the others.

In her ruffled rocker, Justine sat and waited. The pointlessness of being locked in her room seemed more comical than annoying, and she was not worried about her family. Hadn't Duncan predicted everything? "Your father's the one who'll be upset. The others will get over it. Anyway, it's always been a bother adapting outside wives. Then your father will give in because he has to. There won't be any problems."

"I know there won't."

"There would be even less if you would just run away with me."

"I want to do this right, I said."

"Does it matter that much? Justine, why does it matter? They're just a bunch of *people*, just some yellow-haired, ordinary people. Why do you have to ask for their approval?"

"Because I love them," Justine said.

He didn't have any answer for that. Love was not a word he used, even to her.

She rocked and gazed at the wintry gray sky, while downstairs the battle went on and on. Great-Grandma soothed everyone, a dry thread weaving in and out. She thought this marriage was a wonderful idea; she had never heard of genes. When Sam Mayhew stormed, Grandfather snapped and cut him short. Uncles rumbled and aunts chirped and burbled. And over it all rode Duncan's level voice, sensible and confident. Justine could tell when he began to win. He continued alone, the others fell behind. The worst of the battle was over. All that was left was for the losers to regain face.

Justine felt suddenly stifled and bored. She went into her bathroom for her toothbrush, and took a pack of matches from her bureau drawer. She had not grown up with Duncan for nothing: heating the toothbrush handle very slowly, she pushed it little by little into the lock of her door and then turned it and walked out free. When she re-entered the dining room, they didn't seem surprised to see her. Only Duncan, noticing the toothbrush in her hand, tipped back in his chair and looked amused, but he sobered up when Justine's father rose and came around the table to face her.

"Justine," he said.

"Yes, Daddy."

"It has been pointed out to me that there's nothing I can really do to stop you. All I can hope is that you'll listen to reason. Justine, look. Don't you see why you're doing this? It's merely proximity, the two of you had no one else, *no* one in this family has anyone else. You were thrown too much together, at an age when naturally . . . and you were afraid to turn to some outsider. Admit it. Isn't that correct?"

Justine thought it over. "Well," she said finally, "it does sound correct, yes."

"Well, then."

"But then, *both* sides sound correct. I always agree with who I'm listening to."

He waited, expecting more. All she did was smile. "Aah!"

he said suddenly, and turned away, throwing up his hands. "You even *sound* like him. You're a puppet. I've learned something today: set a bad and a good person down together and the bad wins every time. I always wondered."

"Say that again?" said Aunt Lucy. "Is it Duncan you're calling bad?"

"Who else?"

"*Duncan's* not a bad boy."

Even Duncan looked surprised.

"*Justine's* the one who kept the rest of us away from him. *Justine* wouldn't tell his own mother where he was staying! Blame your daughter!"

"Why, Lucy!" Justine's mother said.

Duncan let his chair tip forward. This might turn out to be interesting. But no, they were distracted by a new development: Sam Mayhew buttoning his suit coat. He worked with his elbows out and his clock-shaped face set impassively toward some point above their heads. They knew at once that something important was going on.

"I won't be attending this wedding," he said finally.

"Oh, Sam!" his wife cried.

"And I won't be living here."

"What?"

"I'm moving out to my parents'. I'm going to look for a house in Guilford."

He finished the buttons. He began pulling his shirt cuffs down, neat bands of white above his chubby red hands. "You may come too, of course, Caroline. And Justine if she decides against this marriage. But I warn you: if you come, we will only be visiting your family once a month."

"Once a *month?*"

"The first Sunday of every month, for dinner. We'll go home at three."

"But *Sam—*" his wife said.

"Make your choice, Caroline."

He continued to gaze above her head. Caroline turned to her family. She was still baby-faced, although the years had worked like gravity pulling on her cheeks. Her weight had settled in upon itself. She looked like a cake that had collapsed. To each brother and sister, to her father and her grandmother, she turned a round lost stare while twisting the pearls on her fingers.

"What's your decision, Caroline?"

"I can't just *leave* them like that."

"All right."

"Sam?" she said.

He walked over to Justine. Duncan rose instantly to his feet. "Justine," Sam Mayhew said, "you have been a disappointing daughter in every way, all your life."

Then Justine rocked back as if she had been hit, but Duncan already stood behind her braced to steady her.

The wedding was to be held in a church. All the family insisted on that. Duncan had not been to church in several years and detested Reverend Didicott, a fat man who came from Aunt Lucy's hometown and had a Southern accent that would surely double the length of the ceremony; but he said he would do whatever Justine wanted. And Justine, half willing anyway, went along with the others, submitting to a long satin dress, Sarah Cantleigh's ivory veil, and a little old lady consultant with an emergency cigar box full of pins, white thread, spirits of ammonia, and a stick of chalk for stains. "Oh, Duncan!" Justine said, as she sped by him on the way to the photographer. "I'm sorry! I know how you must hate this!" But he was surprisingly tolerant. He had agreed to give up his room and move home for the month preceding the wedding; he went without a word to buy a black suit that turned him stern and unfamiliar. During lulls in the excitement, he seemed to be observing Justine very closely. Did he think she would change her mind? Reading *Bride's* magazine, she felt his eyes upon her, weighing her, watching for something. "What is it?" she asked him, but he never would say.

Her mother was everywhere. She bustled and darted, giving commands, trilling out fitting schedules in a voice so gay it seemed about to break off and fly. "Really, no one would guess her husband's left her," Justine told Duncan.

"Don't speak too soon."

"Why?"

"Now she's got the wedding to keep her busy. What about later?"

Later Justine would be far away. One thing Duncan would not agree to was living in Roland Park. Nor even in Baltimore, not even long enough for Justine to finish school. And he would not go back to school himself. So they were renting a little house and a plot of land an hour's drive out in the country, where they used to go on their trips. Duncan planned to start a goat farm. It was what he had always wanted, he said. It was? Justine had never heard him mention it before. But he couldn't go on forever looking up facts for professors; and anyway, he kept losing those jobs, he gave in to a temptation to rewrite their material, making it more colorful, adding his own startling scraps of knowledge and a few untruths. And he and Justine each had a share of old Justin's trust fund. Because of the proliferation of heirs it amounted to almost nothing, but they could manage till the dairy started paying off. "You're strapping yourself in, boy," his grandfather said. "You want an education. And *renting's* no good, it's a shoddy way to do things."

"Sure, Grandfather."

But Duncan went on reading the *Dairy Goat Journal*, rummaging through his shocks of hair as he always did when he was absorbed in something. And a week before the wedding he helped supervise the loading of a Mayflower van containing ancient, massive furniture from the relatives and rolled-up rugs, crates of crystal stemware, gifts of silver and china, linens monogrammed by Aunt Laura May and heavy damask curtains, all meant for their three-room cabin. Justine wasn't entirely sure that everything was suitable, but how else would you furnish a place? She didn't know. Duncan made no comment, only watched without surprise as she directed the movers toward a claw-footed bureau, a tasseled floor lamp, a bedstead with pineapple knobs.

"Prepare your mother, now," he told her. "I mean it. Get her ready for doing without you, because it's going to be a shock for her once it happens."

"I will."

"Prepare *yourself*, Justine."

"Prepare for what?"

"Do you really understand that you'll be leaving here?"

"Of course I do," she said.

Well, naturally she would rather *not* be leaving. It made her sad just to think about it. But nothing mattered as much as the lurch in her stomach when she saw him. When they sat apart in Great-Grandma's study, some inner selves seemed to rise up and meet while their bodies remained seated. In halls and pantries and stairwells, they kissed until they were sick and dizzy. She missed Duncan's room downtown: his jingling bed, the warm pulse in the hollow of his throat, the leathery arch of his right foot curving exactly to the shape of her calf when they fell asleep.

"Still," Duncan said, "I wish I could be sure you know what you're getting into."

At the rehearsal, Esther took the part of the bride for good luck. It was terrible to see her up there so close to Duncan. Her emerald-green sheath showed off her figure, which was better than Justine's. "Tell me," Justine said to Duncan later. "Did you ever think of marrying Esther?"

"No."

"But why me?" she asked.

"Why *me*, for that matter?"

"I don't know," she said.

"Why are you marrying me, Justine?"

"Oh, well, Claude is too fat and Richard's too young."

She didn't understand the strange look he gave her.

* * *

On Justine's wedding morning, a pale cool day in April, her mother woke her by pulling open the curtains in her bedroom. "Justine," she said, "listen. Are you awake?"

"Yes."

"I want you to listen a minute."

She was wearing a slithery pink silk dressing gown and already her doll-like face was made up perfectly, her curls precisely flattened. She carried a torn scrap of paper. She sat on Justine's bed and held the paper out to her, smiling a coaxing smile like someone offering medicine. "Your daddy's telephone number," she said.

"My what?"

"Hear what I say, now. I want you to go out in the hall to the phone. I want you to dial this number. It's your grandmother Mayhew's. Ask to speak to your daddy. Say, 'Daddy, today is my wedding day.' "

"Oh, Mama."

"Listen! Say, 'Daddy, this is supposed to be the happiest day of my life. Won't you make it perfect and come give me away?' "

"But I can't talk like that," Justine said.

"Of course you can. And he has that fine suit that's still in the cleaner's bag, I know he took it with him. Why, it wouldn't be any trouble at all! Justine? I beg you, Justine."

"Mama—"

"Please, I've been counting on it. I know it will work. See, I've written the number so neatly? Take it. Take it."

She pressed it into her hands. Justine climbed out of bed, still unwilling.

"Go on, Justine."

In the hall, the telephone sat on a piecrust table. The window above it was party open, so that Justine in her flimsy cotton nightgown shivered while she dialed.

"Hello," Sam Mayhew said.

She had been expecting her grandmother, a static-voiced old lady she hardly knew. She wasn't prepared for her father yet.

"*Hello,*" he said.

"Daddy?"

There was a pause. Then he said, "Hello, Justine."

"Daddy, I—today is my wedding day."

"Yes, I saw it in the paper."

She was silent. She was taking in his soft, questioning voice, which reminded her of his baffled attempts at conversation long ago in Philadelphia. For the first time she realized that he had actually left. Everything had broken and altered and would not ever be the same.

"Honey," he said. "You can always change your mind."

"No, Daddy, I don't want to change my mind."

"I'm about to buy a house in Guilford. Wouldn't you like that? There's a room for you with blue wallpaper. I know you like blue. You could go away to college, someplace good. Why, you used to be a high-B student! Those Pecks think girls go to college to mark time but—it's not too late. You know that. You can still call it off."

"Daddy, will you come give me away at the wedding?"

"No. I can't lend myself to such a thing."

"I'd really like you to."

"I'm sorry."

Her mother tugged at Justine's nightgown. "Tell about the happiest day of your life!" she hissed.

"Wait—"

"Who's that?" her father asked.

"It's Mama."

"What's she doing there?"

"She says to tell you—"

"Did your mother put you up to this?"

"No, I—she just—"

"Oh," her father said. "I thought it was you that was asking. I wish it had been."

"I *am* asking."

"Justine, I'm not going to come to your wedding. Don't bring it up again. But listen, because these are the last sensible words you'll hear all day, or maybe all the rest of your life: you've got to get out of there."

"*Out*, Daddy . . ."

"You think you *are* getting out, don't you. You're going to farm chickens or something."

"Goats."

"But you're not really leaving at all, and anyway you'll be back within a year."

"But we're going to—"

"I know why you're marrying Duncan. You think I don't. But have you ever asked yourself why Duncan is marrying *you*? Why is he marrying his first cousin?"

"Because we—"

"It's one of two reasons. Either he wants a Peck along to torment, or to lean on. Either he's going to give you hell or else he's knotted tighter to his family than he thinks he is. But whichever, Justine. Whichever. It's not a business you'd care to get involved in."

"I can't talk any more," Justine said.

"What? Hold on there, now—"

But she hung up. Her teeth were chattering. "What happened?" her mother asked. "What *happened*, isn't he coming?"

"No."

"Oh! I see. Well."

"I feel sick."

"That's wedding jitters, it's perfectly natural," her mother said. "Oh, I never should have asked you to call in the first place. It was only for *his* sake."

Then she led Justine back to her room, and covered her with the quilt handstitched by Great-Grandma, and sat with her a while. The quilt gave off a deep, solid warmth. There was a smell of coffee and cinnamon toast floating up from the kitchen, and a soft hymn of Sulie's with a wandering tune. Justine's jaw muscles loosened and she felt herself easing and thawing.

"We're going to do without him just fine," her mother said. "I only wanted to make him think he was a part of things."

* * *

Later the minister, Reverend Didicott, told the assistant minister that the Peck–Mayhew wedding was the darnedest business he had ever seen. First of all the way they sat the guests, who were not numerous to begin with: friends clumped in back, and the bride's and groom's joint family up front. There was something dreamlike in the fact that almost everyone in the front section had the same fair, rather expressionless face—over and over again, exactly the same face, distinguished only a little by age or sex. Then the groom, who seemed unsuitably light of heart, followed him around before the ceremony insisting that Christianity was a dying religion. ("It's the only case I know of where *mental* sins count too; it'll never sell," he said. "Take it from me, get out while the getting's good." Right then Reverend Didicott should have refused to marry them, but he couldn't do that to Lucy Hodges Peck, whose family he had known down South.) The bride was given away by her grandfather, an unsmiling man with a mighty snappy way of speaking to people, although so far as was known the bride's father was in excellent health. The groom refused to kiss the bride in public. But the bride's mother was the strangest. Perfectly sedate all through the ceremony, if a little trembly of mouth, gay and flirtatious at the reception afterwards, she chose to fall apart at the going away. Just as the groom was enclosing the bride in his car (which was another whole story, a disgraceful greenish object with a stunted rear end), the mother let out with a scream. "No!" she screamed. "No! How can you just leave me all alone? It's *your* fault your father's gone! How can you drive off like this without a heart?" The bride started to get out but the groom laid a hand on her arm and stopped her, and then they took off in their automobile, which appeared to be led by its nose. The mother threw herself in the grandfather's arms and wept out loud. "We people don't *cry*, Caroline," he said. The most ancient Mrs. Peck of all put on a genteel smile and started humming, and Reverend

Didicott looked inside the envelope the groom had given him and found fifty dollars in Confederate money.

Duncan told everyone they would be away on a honeymoon, but they weren't; he just liked to lie. Instead they went straight to the farm. For two weeks they were left to themselves. Duncan worked uninterrupted, settling in eight Toggenburg does and a purebred buck who smelled like a circus, transporting bales of hay and sacks of Purina goat chow, a block of pink salt and a vat of blackstrap molasses he claimed would increase milk production when added to the goats' drinking water. The weather had turned suddenly warm and he went about in his undershirt, whistling "The Wabash Cannonball," while in their little house Justine threw open all the windows and tied the damask curtains back so they wouldn't hinder the breeze. She had made the place a replica of Great-Grandma's house, if you ignored the green paper walls and the yellowed ceilings. Rugs covered the flowered linoleum, and the four-poster bed hid the fungus growing beneath one window. She fought the foreign smells of kerosene and fatback by hanging Great-Grandma's china pomander ball in the hall. She worked for hours every day constructing meals from Fannie Farmer's cookbook, the one her aunts all used. In the evenings, the two of them sat side by side on the front porch in cane-seated rockers that used to be their grandfather's. They looked out across their scrubby, scraggly land, past the slant-roofed shed where the does stood swaybacked. Like an old country couple they rocked and watched the gravel road, where they might see an occasional pick-up truck bound for the Jordans' farm on the hill or a string of children carrying switches and weedy flowers, dawdling home. Justine thought she would like to stay this way forever: isolated, motionless, barely breathing, cut loose from everyone else. They were like people under glass. They rocked in unison side by side, almost touching but not quite, as if thin wires were stretched between them.

Then the letters started coming. "I keep busy, I go for a

lot of walks,'' her mother said. ''Not far, of course. Just up and down your great-grandma's side yard, up and down again.'' Aunt Lucy said, ''We think of you often. Especially Caroline does, you can tell although you know she wouldn't mention it for anything.'' ''Last Sunday,'' Great-Grandma said, ''we laid two places for you supposing you might be back from your honeymoon and would think to come for dinner, as it would do Caroline a world of good, but it seems you couldn't make it.''

Justine felt stabbed in the chest. ''Dear Mama,'' she wrote, ''I miss you very much. I want to come home for a visit. Duncan says we will just as soon as we can, although of course goats are not something you can just walk off and leave. They have to be milked twice a day and watered, and Duncan has to stay pretty close by anyway because he has to put an ad in the paper and soon customers will be coming . . .''

''Dear Ma,'' Duncan said on a postcard. ''High! We're doing fine. Say hello to everybody. Sincerely, Duncan.''

The family's ink was black, their envelopes cream. Nearly every morning a cream-colored accordion lay waiting in the mailbox at the end of the driveway. Once Duncan got there before Justine and he scooped the letters out of the box and flung them over his head. ''Hoo!'' he said, and tipped back his face like a child in a snowstorm while the envelopes tumbled all around him. Justine came running, and bent at the edge of the gravel to gather them up. ''Oh, Duncan, I wish you wouldn't do things like this,'' she told him. ''How will I know I've got them all?''

''What does it matter? Each one is just like the next.''

It was true. Still she read them closely, often stirring or starting to speak, while Duncan watched her face. Each envelope let out a little gust of Ivory soap, the smell of home. She could imagine the leafy shadows endlessly rearranging themselves outside her bedroom window, and her grandfather's slow, fond smile when he met her at the start of a day. She missed her grandfather very much.

"If you like," Duncan said, "I'll take you this Sunday for dinner. Is that what you want?"

"Yes, it is," she told him.

But somehow they didn't go. Duncan became involved in cleaning the barn, or wiring the new electric fence. Or they simply overslept, waking too slowly with their legs tangled together and their blue eyes opening simultaneously to stare at each other across the pillow, and then the unmilked goats were bleating and there were always so many chores to do. "Maybe next Sunday," Justine would write. When the new sheaf of envelopes arrived she felt chastened and sorry even before she had opened them. But when she took the letters to Duncan out in the barn he only laughed. Like a teacher with a pointer, he would poke a stalk of timothy at stray sentences here and there—reproaches, transparent braveries, phrases with double and triple and quadruple meanings. " 'Of course we're sorry you didn't make it but we understand perfectly, as I had already told your aunts that perhaps we shouldn't expect you.' Ha!" he said.

Justine's face, then, would slowly ease, but she reclaimed the letters and stacked them carefully before she went back to the house.

Then one day a truck rattled up their driveway and a man climbed out, carrying a telephone on the palm of his hand. "Phone," he said, as if Justine should lift the receiver to answer it. But he swung on by her and up the porch steps, with a beltful of tools clanking around his hips. Duncan met him in the doorway. "*We* didn't order that," he said.

"Somebody did."

"Not us."

The man pulled a folded sheet of paper from his pocket and shook it open. "Peck and Sons," he said.

"That's someone else."

"Your name Duncan Peck?"

"Yes."

"This phone is for you, then. Don't complain. Bill goes to Peck and Sons. Wished *I* got presents like that."

"If we had wanted a telephone we would have ordered it on our own," Duncan said.

But Justine said, "Oh, Duncan, it's a *gift!* We can't hurt their feelings."

Duncan studied her a minute. Then he said, "All right."

Now the phone rang once, twice, three times a day even, and Justine would come running in from the fields or the barn to answer it. "Justine," her mother said, "I am upstairs. I'm standing in the hall here looking into your room and your shelf of dolls along the wall, the Spanish lady with her real lace mantilla that your grandfather gave you in Philadelphia when you were only four, remember? She has the sweetest, saddest face."

"Mama, I'm helping Duncan dehorn a goat."

"Do you remember when Grandfather gave you the Spanish lady? You insisted on taking her to bed with you, though she wasn't a cuddly kind of doll. Your daddy and I came into your room every night after you were asleep and put her up on the bureau again. Oh, you looked so innocent and peaceful! We would stand there a while just watching you. Your daddy didn't have to travel so often then and it seemed we had so much more time together."

"Oh, Mama," Justine would say, "I wish I could be there with you. Don't take on so, please don't cry."

Aunt Sarah called, with Aunt Laura May on the upstairs extension. "She's started staying in bed, Justine, she never gets out of her bathrobe. She has these awful headaches. I called your daddy but I believe that man is possessed. He said he wouldn't come, she should come stay in *his* house and of course that is just not possible, he only has a weekly cleaning lady. Of course she would need more than that, it's all we can do to see to her wants even with Sulie helping out. We're running our feet off."

"We bring all her meals on a tray," Aunt Laura May said.

"We've moved the television up to her bedroom."

"The radio for daytime. *Stella Dallas.*"

Justine said, "We'll come on Sunday."

"Do my ears deceive me?"

"We'll be there around noon," said Justine. "But we can't stay the night, you know, the goats are—"

"The goats, yes."

"Goodbye till then."

She went back out to the field. "Duncan," she said, "I think we'd better go for dinner this Sunday."

"You do, do you."

"It's been six weeks, you know. And they say that Mama is—"

"You don't have to keep harping on it, we'll go."

But in bed that night, when he had just stretched out alongside her and taken her head in his hands, the phone rang again and he said, "Bulls-eye."

"I'll get it," she said.

"Oh, your mother and her X-ray vision. She's worked on this, she's got it timed. She couldn't call when you were just reading *Woman's Day*, no—"

"Let me up, I'll answer," said Justine.

"No, don't. We'll ignore it." But then he said, "How can we ignore a thing like that? Nine rings. Ten."

"I'll only be a minute."

"Eleven," Duncan said. He had laid one arm across her to hold her down but he kept his head raised and his eyes on the black shine of the telephone. "We'll go out and sleep in the field," he told her.

"The *field*, Duncan!"

"Where else? If we answer, she wins. If we lie here and listen she wins. Hear that? Four-letter rings. Come on, Justine."

"Well, just let me get a blanket."

"Here's a blanket."

"I'll need a bathrobe."

"What for?"

"Do you want your pillow?"

"*No* I don't want my pillow."

"And insect repellent."

"Oh, for—"

Then he was off the bed and out of the room. "Duncan?" she said. "Duncan, have you changed your mind?" But before she could follow him he was back, waving the huge iron clippers he used for trimming the goats' hooves. Justine heard a single click. The phone gave a whimper and died.

"Oh, Duncan," Justine said, but she was laughing when she lay back down.

All the next morning the telephone sat silent on the bureau with its comical stub of a tail sticking out. In the afternoon, when they were leaving to do some shopping in town, Duncan locked the front door so that no repairman could come while they were gone. "You *know* the family is going to let them hear about this," he said. "They'll be sending undercover men with their little bags of tools." And sure enough, when they got back there was a card hanging from the doorknob. "What a pity, our telephone representative has been and gone," he said. Still, Justine only laughed.

But in the evening, when they were sitting on the porch, something stopped her rocking. She straightened suddenly and frowned. "Duncan," she said.

"Hmm?"

"I have this funny feeling."

Duncan had been reading a book on how to start a chicken farm, sliding a flashlight down the page because it was already dark. He raised the flashlight now and shone it into her face.

"Something terrible is going on at home," she told him.

"Something terrible's always going on at home."

"I mean it. This is serious. I really mean it."

"What, have you turned psychic?"

"No, but I can tell if there's going to be a *change* of some kind."

He rocked and waited.

"We have to go there," she said.

The flashlight clicked off.

"I'm sorry, Duncan. I'll go alone if you'd rather. But I just feel I—"

"All right, all right."

While she packed an overnight case, he drove up the hill to ask Junior Jordan to tend the goats. They could have done that weeks ago! But then, Justine knew that as well as Duncan. She waited on the porch, clutching her case, shivering a little although the night was warm. When she saw his close-set headlights bobbing toward her she ran down the steps and opened the car door. "It's all set," Duncan told her. "Climb in."

The car seemed to be drawn down the road by two long yellow cones. Justine was reminded of other trips, before they were married, rushing home to beat a curfew. All through that silent drive she had the feeling that she was some younger, smaller self, anxiously chewing the ribbons of her hat while she wondered if she would be scolded for staying out so late.

In Guilford, at eight o'clock that morning, Sam Mayhew's cleaning lady had found him dead in his kitchen. He was wearing a bathrobe and there was a roll of Tums on the floor beside him. Apparently he had suffered a heart attack. By ten o'clock old Mr. Mayhew had called the Pecks, but at five o'clock that evening Caroline still knew nothing about it. Nobody wanted to tell her. Instead they huddled in small groups downstairs in Great-Grandma's house, whispering bulletins back and forth. "She's in bed eating the chocolates Marcus brought her." "She's watching a program on flower arranging." "She's trying to get Justine on the telephone again." "Oh, if only we could just never tell her and this would all blow over!"

Then the grandfather arrived from work. He was forcibly retired now but he liked to prowl around his sons' offices, checking up. "What's this?" he said, seeing clusters of women everywhere. When they told him he shook his head sharply, as if getting rid of a fly. "What? But how old was he? Not even out of his forties! And had a *heart* attack? What kind of stock did the man come from, for God's sake?''

Then he went to break the news to Caroline. The others stood around downstairs, pretending to talk but trailing off in the middle of sentences. One by one the uncles came to find out where everybody was, and they had to be told too. Richard arrived with a girlfriend who was asked politely to leave, as there had been an unfortunate occurrence. Aunt Lucy, who had double-dated with Sam and Caroline when they were young, became a little upset and kept hanging onto her husband's arm until Laura May suggested that she fetch her afghan squares to get her mind off things. Then down came the grandfather, sober and dignified, checking his flip-top watch. ''Well?'' they asked. ''How'd she take it?''

''Took it fine.''

''What'd she say?''

''Didn't say anything.''

''Shall we go up now?''

''Do what you like,'' he said, and then he went off to his own house, taking Esther with him to fix his supper.

The others tiptoed up the stairs. Caroline was sitting in her bed against stacks of pillows. When they came in she leaned over to lower the volume slightly on the television set. ''Caroline, we're so sorry,'' they said, and Caroline said, ''Why, thank you. It's so nice of you to take an interest.''

''If there's anything we could be doing now—''

''I can't think of a thing! But I do appreciate your asking.''

''Would you like to go over to the funeral home? Of course it's not as if you had still been *together* or anything, I'm not quite sure what is customary in this case but if you feel you—''

''Why, later, perhaps. Not just now.''

''It's probably not customary anyway.''

''No.''

''Well, if you want us, then—''

''Oh, certainly! I'll let you know first thing.''

They tiptoed down again. Although they should be going

to their homes for supper, they seemed inclined to churn about in Great-Grandma's living room instead. They weren't quite sure just how they should behave. The last death in the family had been in 1912, too long ago for most of them to remember. "Yet after all," Aunt Sarah said finally, "it's not as if Sam Mayhew were really—"

"No. No."

"And after all, he did actually—"

"Oh, he acted like a man possessed."

"Always trying to turn her against us."

"Making *no* effort to understand her."

"And Caroline's so sensitive. It's the way she is."

"Refusing to give his own daughter away."

"But still," said Aunt Lucy, who sometimes grew over-emotional, "Caroline loved him! I know she did, she must have, you could tell she was just torn. And now he's dead. Oh, what will she do now?"

"*Lucy,*" her husband said. "About time to feed me my supper, don't you think?"

"Well, all right."

"We'll try to call Justine from our house, Grandma. If the phone's not fixed, I'll drive out there in the morning."

"Oh, think of Justine. How will she ever forgive herself?"

Upstairs, cowboys sang lonesome songs around a campfire and the wind rolled tumbleweed across the desert with a howling sound.

At nine o'clock that evening, Caroline rose up in her pink silk gown and put on her feathered slippers. Before leaving the room she turned off the television set. She descended the stairs, stately and flowing; she crossed the front hall and went out the door. She drifted across the lawn and then onto the road, where she proceeded down the center with her arms out and her steps mincing and careful like a tightrope walker. To the first car that came, she appeared as monstrous and unexpected as a wad of pink bubble gum. The driver gasped and swerved at the last moment. The second driver was harder to surprise. "Do your drinking at *home*, lady!" he shouted out the window, and then he slid smoothly past.

She had to wait for six cars, all told, before she found one that would run her down.

Duncan brought Justine a cup of beef broth and a silver spoon and a linen napkin. He found her sitting in the living room of Great-Grandma's house, all alone, staring into space. "Oh. Thank you," she said. She set the cup on the coffee table.

"I made it myself."

"Thank you."

"Ma said coffee, but coffee has no food value."

She smoothed her dress.

"Broth has protein," Duncan told her. "You can go without protein for months and feel just fine, never notice, but underneath it's doing you harm that can never be repaired. Protein is made up of amino acids, the building blocks of the—"

"Duncan, I can't *believe* you're saying all this."

"I can't either," he told her.

He waited for her to try the broth. She didn't. He squatted beside her. "Justine—" he said.

But no, too late, the aunts had tracked them down again. "Justine? You mustn't sit like this, dear heart—"

They reminded him of ships. They traveled in fleets. Their wide summer skirts billowed and collapsed as they settled all around him, edging him out. But he didn't give in so easily. "We were just talking," he told them.

"She should be in bed."

"What for?"

"She doesn't look at *all* well."

She didn't. Even her hair seemed changed, hanging lank and lifeless around her face. In just four days she had developed a new deep hollow between her collarbones. She was already losing her country tan. If he could just carry her home, to the sunlit fields and their little house with its ridiculous damask curtains! But the aunts rustled and resettled, inching closer. "She ought to be left with us a while, Duncan. She just feels so *sorry*, you see. She's acting just like her poor dear mother did. You can't take her back to sit all alone in the middle of nowhere."

"Alone?"

"She needs looking after."

"*I* look after her," Duncan told them.

"Yes, but—and she could have her old room again, or maybe yours if hers would bring memories. You could go back to your cows or whatever and we would take good— Justine, do you like Duncan's room?"

"Duncan's? Yes."

"There, see?"

"Or she could come to us," Aunt Bea said. "At our house, you see, we have so much excitement, Esther and Richard rushing around and the twins so talkative, she'd just come out of herself in no time."

"Maybe she doesn't want to come out of herself," Duncan said.

"Oh, it helps to have a little company! All those young people making merry. Justine?"

Justine sat like a stone. The old secret, tucked-in smile she used to flash Duncan seemed gone forever. When he rose she didn't even look his way, and it seemed unlikely that she noticed when he left the room.

Now as she cruised through the darkening house she was aware of how everything here was attached to everything else. There was no such thing as a simple, meaningless teacup, even. It was always given by someone dear, commemorating some happy occasion, chipped during some moment of shock, the roses worn transparent by Sulie's scrubbing, a blond stain inside from tea that Sam Mayhew had once drunk, a crack where Caroline, trembling with a headache, had set it down too hard upon the saucer.

She went out the front door that was dented by Justin Peck's invalid's bed in the fall of 1905. She passed her grandfather's front porch, where Maggie Rose stood in the twilight waiting for a Model T. She climbed Uncle Two's front steps, surrounded by ghostly whispers and murmurs of love and scoldings and reproaches and laughter. Upstairs she found Duncan in his room among Erector Set machines he had built when he was twelve, a full-color poster of Princess Pet in the Land of the Ice Cream Star, the Monopoly board in which all seven cousins had played a thirty-eight-hour world series in the spring of 1944. But Duncan—oh, forever in the present!—was whistling "The Wabash Cannonball" and fiddling with a rectangle of lead-colored metal.

She didn't know how he could whistle.

When she came in the room he stopped. "Do you want to lie down?" he asked her. He began clearing his bed of everything on it, a jungle of wires and soldering irons, tubes of flux, glue, and paint. She sat on the edge of the mattress, but she didn't want to stretch out. It was barely eight o'clock. If she slept now she would lie awake for hours later on, as she had last night and the night before.

"Anything you wanted to say?" Duncan asked.

"No."

"Well." He went back to whatever he was doing, but he didn't whistle any more. "This is a wire-bending jig," he told her.

She didn't comment.

"These pegs can be moved, see? Then you bend the wire around them any way you want. There are all kinds of curves and angles. I could make you a bracelet. Want a bracelet? Or a necklace, if you like."

She laid her fingers across her eyes, cooling them.

"I've got it," he said. "A nose ring. Want a nose ring?"

When she opened her eyes she found a curve of wire nearly touching her nose, giving off a gray smell, sharp at one end.

She batted it away. "What are you trying to *do* to me?" she said.

He looked surprised.

"Are you trying to get me angry on purpose?" she asked him.

"Well, not on *purpose*, no—"

"Why are you acting this way?"

"Justine, *I'm* not acting any way."

"How can you play around with little pieces of wire when both my parents are dead, and you're the one that took me far off and cut the telephone cord and laughed at Mama's letters and wouldn't bring me to visit?"

"Justine."

"Daddy *warned* me," she said. "He told me straight out you were marrying me to torment me."

"Oh, did he?"

"Either that, he said, or to lean on me, but I don't picture *that* ever happening."

"Well, he certainly thought of *everything*, didn't he," Duncan said.

He went back to bending his wire. He adjusted a peg on the jig and turned a right angle.

"I'm sorry," Justine said finally.

"That's all right."

"I just feel so—"

"It's all *right*."

"Duncan, couldn't we just stay here a while?"

He looked up at her.

"We could live in Great-Grandma's house," she said. "Wouldn't that be nice?"

"No, it wouldn't."

"Please?"

"I should have known," he told her. "I didn't really believe you would come away with me in the first place."

"But I feel I'm getting *pulled*. I hate to just go away and leave them. And I can't stay here without you, but you wouldn't say a word against it when they brought it up.''

"*I* don't want to pull you, Justine.''

"But then they're the only ones doing it, and they'll win.''

"Is that the only way you go anywhere? Being pulled?''

She was silent.

"All right,'' said Duncan. "I'd like you to come with me. It's important. It's more important than they are.''

But she went on watching his face.

"Well, how am I supposed to do this?'' he asked her. "I was too well trained, I don't feel *comfortable* saying things straight out. They got to me a little too, you know.''

"Oh, Duncan,'' Justine said. "You've said everything straight out since you were four years old and told Aunt Bea she had hair like broccoli.''

"No,'' said Duncan. "I a Peck. I not talk so good but I give swell presents.''

Then he handed her his wire, a stick figure wearing Justine's flat hat and triangular dress, looking so straightbacked and light-hearted that even a tribesman in darkest Africa could tell that someone cared for her.

The family lined up to see them off, their faces papery in the morning sun. "I can't believe that you would be going like this,'' Aunt Lucy said. Justine kissed her. She kissed Aunt Sarah, who said, "Do you think your parents would have understood? Rushing off as if all that mattered was a pack of billy goats?'' Justine kissed her way down the entire row, not skipping even Richard, who ducked and blushed, and when she came to her grandfather she hung onto him hard for a moment as if this, not the wedding, were her real leavetaking. "Oh, um, now, Justine,'' her grandfather said.

"Goodbye, Grandfather.''

Duncan opened the car door and she climbed in. The seat covers had a fish-oil smell from the sunlight, and when she leaned out the window to wave the metal was pleasantly hot on her arm. In the trees above them, mockingbirds were singing. Even when the car roared up they didn't hush. "Scientists," said Duncan, "have been investigating the stimuli that cause birds to vocalize in the morning. So far they have determined only one. They sing because they're happy."

7

Duncan bought a dozen copper-colored hens and installed them in a shed he had built himself, complete with a box of oyster shells to assist in egg production and a zinc watering trough in which they all immediately drowned. But the goats flourished, and since only two customers had answered the newspaper ad there were quarts of surplus milk every day. Justine made butter and handcranked ice cream. Duncan boiled up kettles of Norwegian cheese. But no sooner had they finished one batch of milk than the goats gave more, and Justine dreamed at night of a white tide rising all around them. "Maybe we should cut down on the blackstrap molasses," she told Duncan.

"Well, I don't know if that would do much good. We seem to have started something we can't stop, here."

In the mornings Justine walked the gravel road with a basket of cheeses, peddling them to the neighbors, who bought them because they had grown to like her. Seeing her trudge up the driveway, in her country-looking hat and her plain cotton dress that was becoming a little faded, Mrs. Jordan would lumber out on her front steps and beam. "Why, it's Justine Peck! How are you, honey?" Justine smiled trustingly, holding out her basket. It was hard for her to ask people to buy things, but she did enjoy the visits. At each house she stopped for a few minutes to sit in the kitchen and talk, and gradually the smells of kerosene and fatback stopped seeming strange to her and she began to feel comfortable with the stooped, prematurely aged women who offered her buttermilk and ginger cake to put some meat on her bones.

Sometimes, though, alone at home, she felt a gust of sorrow blow through her like a wind and she would stop whatever she was doing, hands stilled, face stunned and gaze into space for several minutes. Once when she was trimming the weeds that drained the fence's current the smell of cut grass swung her back over years and years and she found herself sitting on a twilit lawn, nestled between her parents, listening to the murmur of her family all around her. She dropped the clippers and reached for the nearest object; she gripped the fence until her knuckles turned shiny. The throb of electricity caused a distant, dull ache. Duncan had to pry her fingers loose and say her name several times before she would look up.

They had not been back to Baltimore after that first visit, but she did write home weekly and one or another of the aunts would answer. Occasionally her grandfather composed a solemn, formal, nineteenth-century note saying that everyone was well and sent best regards. If only she could reach out and touch his knobby hand, as if by accident! But all she said in her own letters back was that Duncan was fine, the weather was fine, the goats were doing nicely.

If the sorrow went on too long she drove to Buskville, where she walked the streets for hours. She had been raised to believe that the best cure for grief was shopping, especially for things to wear. But there wasn't that much money and anyway, she discovered she was incapable of purchasing clothes for herself. Putting on a dress that her mother had not picked out was a betrayal. She was reduced to buying little domestic articles in the dimestore: lemon reamers, parsley choppers. It seemed very important to have everything that would make her house perfect.

One day in August, having exhausted all the dimestore's possibilities, she walked down a side street and discovered a hand-lettered cardboard sign reading MAGIC MARCIA. LOVE PROBLEMS. ADVICE. She swooped back through time and found herself on Madame Olita's doorstep, Duncan watching her teasingly with one arm hooked around Glorietta de Merino. After a moment she switched her Woolworth's bag to the other hand and rang Magic Marcia's bell.

The woman who answered was thin and dark, with a crimson slash of lipstick. She was not much older than Justine, but there were two little boys with runny noses hanging onto her skirt. Gray straps slid out from her scoop-necked blouse. Justine was sorry she had come, but it was too late to back out.

Then when she was settled at the kitchen table, over the remains of breakfast, it seemed she was expected to ask some specific question. She hadn't known that. "What is it?" the woman asked, flattening Justine's hand like a letter. "Husband? Boyfriend?"

"No, I—just general things, I wanted to know."

The woman sighed. She scratched her head and frowned at Justine's palm. Apparently she saw nothing unusual. "Well," she said finally, "you're going to live a long time, that's for sure."

"Yes," Justine said, bored. Really she had no particular interest in her future, which seemed certain to be happy and uneventful from here on out.

"Good marriage. Probably travel a little. Health is good. Probably have a lot of kids."

"I will?" Justine asked. Duncan didn't seem to want any children. But the woman said, "*Oh* yes."

A question began to tug at the edges of Justine's mind. She stared into space, not listening to the rest of her fortune. "Um, Magic Marcia," she said finally. "Could you tell me something? If your palm predicts a certain future, is there any way you can change it?"

"Huh?"

"If your future is having children, could you deliberately *not* have children? If your future is to cause someone pain, for instance, isn't there some way you could be very careful and *not* cause pain? Can't you escape your fortune?"

"What is written is written," said Magic Marcia, yawning.

"Oh," Justine said.

On Friday she went to Blainestown, having checked the yellow pages beforehand. She climbed the stairs to SERENA, MISSTRESS OF THE OCCULT. This time, she knew exactly what she wanted to ask.

"Could I have avoided my future if my future was to do somebody harm?"

"Man does not avoid the future," Serena said.

On Monday she went back to Blainestown, this time to MADAME AZUKI, ALL QUESTIONS ANSWERED.

"It's in the stars. There is no escape," said Madame Azuki.

"I see."

On Wednesday she went to Baltimore. Duncan was inventing an automatic bean stringer and he only nodded when she told him she would be out for a while. She drove directly to a cluttered section on the east side of town. She found the dry cleaner's, which was exactly the same even to its flyspecked, faded posters showing women in 1940's suits. But Madame Olita's sign on the window above had become a few flecks of paint, and there was a padlock on her door. Justine went into the cleaner's. A large gray man was lining up laundry tags on the counter. "Can you tell me anything about Madame Olita?" she asked him.

"Ah, Madame Olita. She's gone."

"What, is she dead?"

"No, retired. She's not feeling so well, you know? But was she a fortune teller! I don't mind telling you, I used to go to her myself. Okay, so it's mumbo-jumbo. You know why I went? Say you got a problem, some decision to make. You ask your minister. You ask your psychiatrist, psychologist, marriage counselor, lawyer—they all say, 'Well of course I can't decide *for* you and we want to look at all the angles here and I wouldn't want to be responsible for—' They hedge their bets, you see. But not Madame Olita. Not *any* good fortune teller. 'Do X,' they say. 'Forget Y.' 'Stop seeing Z.' It's wonderful, they take full responsibility. What more could we ask?''

"Well, do you know where she is now? Could I just visit her?''

"Sure, she's right down the block. But I don't know how much she's up to. Well, tell her I sent you, Joe sent you. Maybe she could use the company. Five eight three, apartment A.''

"Thank you very much,'' Justine told him.

"Hope you get the answer you want.''

She let the door tinkle shut and walked on down the street, passing more cleaners and cut-rate pharmacies and pawnshops. At the end of the block was a large Victorian frame house surrounded by a veranda, and on the veranda sat Madame Olita in a Polynesian wicker chair. Although it was hot, she wore a crocheted shawl. She still had her stubby haircut, but she had lost an enormous amount of weight. Her clothes flopped and her neck was so scrawny that her face appeared to be lunging forward, vulturelike. She looked hollowed out. While Justine climbed the steps she watched without interest, perhaps assuming this was somebody else's visitor. "Hello, Madame Olita,'' Justine said.

"Hmmm?''

Madame Olita pulled herself together, wrapping the shawl more tightly around her shoulders.

"Joe sent me,'' Justine said.

"Oh? Joe.''

"There's a question I wanted to ask. Would you mind?''

"Well, I'm feeling poorly these days, you see. I don't look into the future much.''

"No, it wasn't about the future.''

Madame Olita sighed. "Sit down,'' she said, pointing to the wicker chair beside her. She reached for Justine's hand, as if she hadn't understood.

"But I didn't want—''

Madame Olita bent Justine's palm back and frowned. "Oh, it's you," she said.

Justine felt pleased and shy, as if her unusual lines were her own accomplishment.

"Yes, I see," said Madame Olita, nodding and tapping her teeth with one finger.

"You said my marriage was going to disrupt everything," Justine reminded her.

"Did I."

"You said I would break my parents' hearts. How did you know that?"

"Oh, my dear," said Madame Olita, leaning back suddenly and dropping her hand. "Really, I don't remember. You were young and arrogant, and uncomfortable in my rooms, perhaps I just—"

"But it all came true!"

"Sometimes it does."

"Was that just luck?"

"It may have been. Sometimes it is, sometimes it isn't. Are you asking if I can truly see the future? I can. But more and more it seems to me that people are resisting change, digging in their heels against it. Which does make their futures easy to predict, but why bother? Fortune telling is only good when you forecast a *happening*. It falls flat when you say, 'Never fear, your life will continue in its present course forever . . .' "

She closed her eyes and then opened them and looked puzzled. "But I tend to go on and on," she said. "You had some question you wanted to ask."

Justine sat up straight and placed her hands together. "Madame Olita," she said, "if my fortune was to break my parents' hearts, is it true then that I had no way of avoiding it?"

"Oh, no."

"No?"

"Goodness, no. You can change your future. I have seen lines alter in a hand overnight. I have seen cards fall suddenly into places where they refused to appear at any earlier reading.''

''I see,'' said Justine, and then she sank back. It was the first answer that sounded right to her, but now she couldn't think why she had wanted to hear it. She felt limp and drained.

''Otherwise,'' said Madame Olita, ''why take any action at all? No, you can always choose to *some* extent. You can change your future a great deal. Also your past.''

''My past?''

''Not what's happened, no,'' Madame Olita said gently, ''but what hold it has on you.''

''Oh.''

''If you are so interested, I will teach you the art yourself if you like.''

''The—oh, well, I—''

''*Cards* would be your skill, I think.''

''Thank you anyway,'' Justine said.

''Never mind. You'll be back. I sit here every day of the week, taking the air. You can always find me. Shut the front gate going out, if you will.''

On Monday, Justine told Duncan that she was thinking of becoming a fortune teller. ''Oh, really?'' he said.

''Aren't you going to laugh?''

''Not yet,'' he said. ''First I have to see how good you are.''

So she drove off to Baltimore again, to the white frame house where Madame Olita nodded dimly in her Polynesian chair.

''These are ordinary playing cards,'' said Madame Olita, but to Justine they looked anything but. They were very old and the back of each was different: antique circus scenes of clowns, trapeze artists, dancing dogs, and bareback riders. ''They once belonged to my mother. Who, though you wouldn't believe it to look at me, was a genuine gypsy lady with seven ruffled petticoats and tiny brass cymbals that attached to her fingers for keeping time while she danced. She was raised in an abandoned candy store on Gay Street. Not exactly a painted *wagon*, but still . . . unfortunately she married my father, a high school civics teacher. She left her old life entirely, she cut off her long black hair, she had two daughters whom she sent to Radcliffe. However, I would rather have been raised a gypsy.''

She cut the cards. Justine sat across from her with her mouth open.

''It was my plan, after I graduated from Radcliffe, to join a caravan and marry a man with one gold earring. But it didn't work out that way. I looked then more or less as I do today. I never married anyone, let alone a gypsy. So I had to get a job in my father's high school, teaching algebra, but meanwhile I had learned fortune telling from my mother. Dancing I never mastered. I tried, though. My sister was quite good at it. But I bettered her at fortune telling. How I coveted these cards! My mother refused to give them to me. Cards like these are passed on only when the owner is dying, you see, and has no further use for them. Naturally I didn't want my mother to die. But shall I tell you? When she failed to wake from surgery at the age of fifty-seven, the first thing I thought was, 'Now I can have the cards.' I went home and got them out of her wooden chest, then I walked over to the school and resigned my position. I set up shop in east Baltimore, above the cleaner's. I have never laid eyes upon a caravan.''

She laid the cards out in concentric circles on a wicker table.

''My sister,'' she said, ''got the cymbals.''

Then she frowned and stabbed a card with her forefinger. ''But pay attention! These cards are not read like books, you know. They have meanings assigned that you can memorize in half an hour, but ambiguous meanings. The death card, for instance. So *called*. But whose death? The client's or someone's close to him? And when? Is it real or metaphorical? No, you must think of these cards as tags.''

"Tags," Justine said blankly.

"Tags with strings attached, like those surprise boxes at parties. The strings lead into your mind. These cards will pull out what you already know, but have failed to admit or recognize. Which is why palmistry works as well, or tea leaves or the Tarot or crystal ball. They all have validity, yes, but only when coupled with your own intuitions. You could take up astrology, even, but I already know: you haven't the scholarly mind for it.''

"I prefer cards," said Justine.

"Yes, yes, I know. But pay attention to *everything*. Watch your clients carefully. There will only be two kinds. Most are bored and merely hope to be told that something will happen. A very few lead eventful lives but cannot make decisions, which may be *why* they lead eventful lives; they will ask you to decide.''

"Which am I?" said Justine.

"Hmm? I don't know. Maybe neither. You have never asked me to read your fortune, after all.''

"Oh. I guess not," Justine said.

"You're still looking backward, anyway," Madame Olita told her.

"No, I'm not!"

"Suit yourself.''

After her lessons Justine drove straight home, but threads, strings, *ropes* pulled her in the direction of Roland Park and although she never gave in she had the feeling she was bleeding somewhere inside. "Well, you could go over for lunch," Duncan said, but she thought from the way he spoke that he dreaded her agreeing to it. And she knew that her family would be distressed if they heard about Madame Olita. Then her new accomplishment, which was still as thin and fragile as a freshly hatched egg, would never seem right to her again; that was the way her mind worked. She didn't go.

Did she believe in fortune telling herself? At Madame

Olita's she did. She was drawn in, impressed and fascinated by those no-nonsense hands dealing out the future. But then at home she felt compelled to test her faith with Duncan. She laid out her Bicycle playing cards self-consciously in front of him. "Today," she told him, "I learned the formation used by Mademoiselle Le Normand, back in Napoleon's time."

"Le Normand," he said, interested, cataloguing the name in his mind.

"We practiced on Madame Olita's landlady, who is eighty-four years old. I predicted she was going to get married."

He grinned.

"But!" said Justine. "She is! She told me afterward."

"Good for you. Good for *her*."

"Madame Olita says just a little longer and I can set up in business."

"We'll retire and live on your earnings," he said.

She was relieved that he didn't laugh. This was the only special skill she had ever possessed, the only thing she knew that he did not. Once he started memorizing her list of significations, but he got sidetracked while shuffling the cards and worked out a proof for Bernoulli's Law of Averages instead.

There were days when Madame Olita was sharp-tempered and nothing would satisfy her. "Really, Justine, I despair of you!" she said. "Your mind! You have every qualification to be a good fortune teller but you will never be great, you're mentally lazy. You coast along in intuition."

"You said intuition was everything."

"Never! I never said it was *everything*. You have to know a few facts as well, after all. These cards are like a doctor's instruments. A good doctor has intuition too but he would never throw his instruments away on the strength of it."

"But you said they were just tags, you said—"

"Enough!" And Madame Olita would fling up her hands and then slump in her chair. "You'll spend your life doing readings for housewives and lovesick schoolgirls," she said. "I don't know why I bother."

But other days she was as mild as milk. Then she would tell stories about her clients. "Will I ever forget that first year? All the Negroes came for clues on how to play the numbers. 'Madame Olita I dreamed of handcuffs last night, which is number five nine eight in my Eye of Egypt Dream Book, but also razors, there was a cutting, eight seven three. So which do I play?' 'My dear,' I told them, 'you leave those numbers alone,' and after a while they gave up on me and never came back. But how I tried! I wanted to have some influence, you see, on their lives. I would give them demonstrations of my psychic ability. I would have them choose a card and sight unseen I would tell them what it was."

"I can't do that," Justine said sadly. Duncan had tested her once after reading an article on J. B. Rhine.

"No, I doubt very much that you would be psychic."

"Then how come I can tell the future?"

"People who have led very still lives can often sense change before others can," Madame Olita said.

"My life isn't still," said Justine.

Madame Olita only sighed.

At the last lesson, she gave Justine a test. "It's time for you to read *my* fortune," she said. Justine had been wanting to do that. She settled down happily at the wicker table, while Olita gazed off toward the street. It was one of her irritable days. "Cut the cards," Justine told her, and she said, "Yes, yes, I know," and cut them without looking. Justine chose a very complicated formation. She wanted to do this thoroughly, not missing a thing. She laid each card out with precision, and then sat back and drummed her fingers on her chair arm. After a moment she moved one card a half inch to the left and resettled herself. She frowned. She stopped drumming her fingers.

Madame Olita looked over at her with cool interest. Still Justine didn't speak.

"Never mind," said Madame Olita. "You passed."

Then she became full of bustle, issuing last-minute instructions. "Did I tell you that strangers should pay ahead of time? If they don't like their fortunes they tend to walk out, they'll walk right out on you."

Justine only gathered the cards in silence, one by one.

"Watch where you work, too. Some places have license fees, sometimes hundreds of dollars. It isn't worth it. Are you listening?"

"What?"

"Don't go to Calvert County. Don't go to Cecil County, don't go to Charles."

"But we live on a farm, I'm not going anywhere."

"Ha."

Justine wrapped the cards and set them on the table. She came to stand in front of Madame Olita.

"Be a little mysterious, I didn't tell you *that*," said Madame Olita. "They'll have more faith. Don't let on where you come from or how you learned what you know. Make a point of ignoring personal questions when you're giving a reading. Will you remember all this? What else should you know?"

Then she gave up. "Well, goodbye, Justine," she said.

"Goodbye," said Justine. "Could I come back for a visit?"

"Oh . . . no. No, I'll be going into the hospital for a while, I think. But I wish you luck."

"Thank you," said Justine. She turned to go.

"Oh, and by the way."

Justine turned back. Madame Olita, sagging in her chair, waved one hand toward the cards. "You might as well take those along with you," she said.

When fall came Justine worked up the courage to offer her services at the high school homecoming fair. She donated her fees to the school. After that people began traveling all the way out to the farm, several a week, mostly women, asking if they should get married, or divorced, or sell their land or have a baby or move to California. Justine was astonished. "Duncan," she said, "I don't want to be *responsible* for people. For telling them who to marry and all."

"But I sort of thought you believed in this," Duncan said.

She wound a strand of hair around her finger.

"Well, never mind," he told her. "Just don't say anything that would cause somebody harm. But I don't think people take *bad* advice. They've got intuition too, you know. In fact I'd be surprised if they take any advice at all."

So she continued receiving people in her small, warm kitchen, laying Madame Olita's cards across the surface of Great-Grandma's rosewood table. She became a gatherer of secrets, a keeper of wishes and dreams and plans. Sometimes when people very young or very old came in, full of vague hopes, unable or unwilling to say what they would like to ask, she merely reassured them. But sometimes she was so explicit that her own daring amazed her. "Don't sell any family possessions, particularly jewelry, particularly your mother's," she would say.

"How did *you* know?"

She hadn't known she did know.

Then sometimes people came whose flat, frictionless lives offered Justine no foothold at all, and she slid into whatever general advice came to mind.

"Don't rely too heavily on a man who bites his finger-nails."

In the next room, Duncan snorted.

Justine charged three dollars for each reading. They needed it; their milk customers barely paid for the newspaper ad. Juggling the budget to meet the rent, scraping up money from half a dozen sources, Justine had the feeling that she had been through all this years and years ago. Then she remembered: Monopoly. When Duncan had wiped her out and she was selling back hotels and mortgaging her railroads and turning in her get-out-of-jail-free card, all to pay the rent on Boardwalk. Their present problems did not seem much more serious than that. She knew that Duncan would manage.

For Christmas they went home to Baltimore. The family

was very cautious and tactful, circling widely around all delicate subjects. It broke Justine's heart to see what an effort they made. She worried about Duncan—would he say something new to hurt them? She went to bed each night exhausted. But Duncan was meticulously polite. He passed around the gifts that Justine had made by hand and he even invited the family to come and visit some Sunday. ("Oh, well, but it's so much more comfortable for you to come here, don't you think?" everybody said.) On the fourth day, when he became very quiet, Justine was quick to agree that they should head back early. She felt sad saying goodbye, particularly to her grandfather, but each time now it seemed a little easier than before.

In February, when money was especially tight, Duncan got a part-time job in town reporting for the Buskville *Bugle*. "But you can't spell!" said Justine.

"Never mind, you can."

For three weeks he ricocheted around the countryside, attending cornerstone layings, turtle derbies, zoning meetings, a Future Farmers contest in parliamentary procedure, a lecture on crop rotation. He enjoyed everything he went to, indiscriminately, and came home full of new scraps of information. "Did you know you can call up earthworms by vibrating a stick in the ground? If you harvest crimson clover too late it will turn into balls in your horses' stomachs. I've learned a quilting pattern from the eighteenth century." But then writing articles made him irritable. He never did like going at something systematically. He would hand Justine great sheaves of yellow paper all scrawled over and crossed out, with doodles in the margins. When she ran through them with a red pencil, correcting his spelling and slashing through his long digressions, he lost his temper. "Occurrence, o-c-u-r-e-n-c-e," he said. "Why wreck it up adding extra c's and r's?"

"Because that's how it's spelled."

"A waste of letters. This language has no logic to it."

"I can't help that."

"Why'd you cross out my butterfly paragraph?"

"In an article on potato blight?"

"There happened to be a particularly fine great spangled fritillary sitting on the farm agent's shoulder, totally out of season, ignored by everybody, all the way through the lecture. You can't expect me to overlook a thing like that."

And he would type the article complete and hand it in to the office, where any reference to butterflies was immediately deleted.

"They have minds like a snake's intestinal tract," Duncan said.

The fourth week, he attended an amateur musicians' contest. His article that night began very well, describing the contest's history, its sponsors, and the instruments represented. The next paragraph switched suddenly to first person and related his own impromptu entry with a borrowed harmonica, playing "Chattanooga Choo Choo," for which he won fourth prize. In the third paragraph he reflected on the oddity of the "impromptu," which could easily be mistaken, he said, for the name of some obscure Rumanian composer.

The newspaper editor said that, actually, they didn't need a new reporter as much as they had thought they would.

By March, Duncan was becoming restless. Justine was not sure why. Everything was going well, six does had been dried off in preparation for their kidding in the spring. But Duncan rattled around the house like a bean in a box, staring out one window after another, starting inventions he didn't finish, sending off to the Department of Agriculture for pamphlets on all sorts of impulsive projects: angora rabbits, fruit trees, popcorn. He painted half the kitchen yellow and then quit. He brought home a carload of rhododendron bushes with their roots balled up in burlap and he planted them all around the yard. "But Duncan," Justine said, "do you think this is the proper time?" They were still wearing overcoats to bed; the ground was still cold and gray. "Why do I have to do everything *properly?*" he asked. "Don't worry, I've got a green thumb. A green hand. I'm a whole green *man.*"

And sure enough, the rhododendron took heart and started growing. But Duncan went off and forgot all about it; his strange mood hadn't eased in the least. "To tell the truth, Justine," he said, "this winter business is wearing thin. I imagined we'd be sitting by the stove oiling harness leather or something, but we don't *have* any harness leather. Don't you feel tired of it all?"

"No," Justine said.

She watched, frowning, while he measured the kitchen for some shelves. She didn't think he would ever finish them.

In April eight kids were born, all does. "Did you ever see such luck? We've got a whole damn *herd*," Duncan said. Justine was glad because the bucks would have had to be killed. She spent hours playing with the kids, running across the field so that they would frolic behind her. They kicked up their heels and turned awkward half cartwheels. She set her face next to their muscular little muzzles; their yellow, slashed-looking eyes looked softly back at her. After the first few days they were switched to bottle feedings, and then to milk from a pan, while Justine crouched beside them and stroked their tufted spines. She fed them handfuls of grass to accustom them to solid food, and for most of the day she kept them in her yard. Meanwhile Duncan carried in endless buckets of warm milk, which he filtered and ran through the great silvery separator. There was suddenly a stream of customers with indigestion, allergies, or colicky babies, all desperate for goat milk, and the grocery store in Buskville had shown an interest in carrying Duncan's cheeses. "There," said Justine. "I knew it would work out!"

"Well, yes," Duncan said.

In May, all the kids died in one night from eating rhododendron leaves.

Justine wandered around forlornly for days, mourning as if the kids had been human. But all Duncan would say was, "Isn't it peculiar? You would think if rhododendron was poisonous they'd know it."

"All those lovely little brown soft furry babies," Justine said.

"But then, goats are fairly intelligent. Are intelligence and instinct inversely related?"

"At least we have the nannies still," Justine said. "We don't have to start *completely* over."

"No."

"And there'll always be a new batch next year, and I won't let them in the yard at all."

Duncan picked up her hand. "Justine," he said, "what would you think of getting out of the goat business?"

"What? Oh, Duncan, you can't quit now. Not after one little setback!"

"No, that's not the reason. I've been considering this for some time. I mean, there's no challenge to it any more. Besides, it keeps you tied down, you always have to be around at milking time. It makes me feel *stuck*, I feel so—and I was thinking. You know what I enjoyed most this year? Building that hen house. Putting things together, fixing them up. Now Ma's brother Ed has a sort of cabinetworks down in Virginia, making unfinished furniture and so on. If he could take me in—"

"Virginia? But that's so far. And *I* never knew you wanted to make cabinets."

"Well, I do."

"We're so nice and settled!"

"But I don't like being settled."

"And we would never get back to Baltimore. Duncan, I've already gone far enough, I don't want to go farther. I couldn't stand going farther."

He waited a moment, looking down at her. Then he said, "All right."

They didn't talk about it again.

People came filing through Justine's kitchen for advice on their spring problems: love affairs, unexplainable bouts of wistfulness, sudden waves of grief over people and places they had not even thought they liked. Justine laid her cards on the rosewood table.

"It will work out."

"Just wait through this."

"You will feel better a week from now."

Duncan plodded through carrying buckets full of milk.

He had grown very silent, although if she spoke to him he always answered. He began drinking bourbon at night after supper. He drank from his great-grandfather's crystal stemware. After the second glass his face became radiant and serene and childlike, and he would switch on a lamp in slow motion and start reading paperbacks. The technical books that he usually liked grew a film of dust while he worked his way through a stack of moldy, tattered Westerns the previous tenants had left in the barn. Whenever Justine looked over his shoulder stubbled men were drawling threats and cowboys were reaching for their guns.

"Duncan," Justine said, "wouldn't you like to sit out on the porch with me?"

"Oh, no thank you. Later, maybe."

But later he went to bed, moving dreamily through the house, not asking if she were coming too. She sat alone at the kitchen table and shuffled her cards. Then she laid them in rows, idly, as if she were her own client. She yawned and looked to see what had shaped up.

She saw journeys, upheavals, surprises, new people, luck, crowds, hasty decisions, and unexpected arrivals.

Which meant, of course, that Madame Olita was right: it was not possible to tell your own fortune.

All the same, if she had had a client with these cards! She imagined how she would glance at him, interested for the first time, amazed at his quicksilver life after all the stale ones she had seen up till now. She imagined possessing such a future herself, having to consult the cards every day, so much was going on.

Then it seemed to her that she was not reading her fortune after all, but accepting little square papers that told her what was expected of her next. She had no choice but to stand up, and gather her cards, and wrap them in their piece of silk before she went to the bedroom to wake Duncan.

This time they moved in a rented truck, which was cheaper than Mayflower. They left behind Justine's beloved goats, Duncan's chewed-looking rhododendron bushes and his empty, echoing, beautifully built hen house. They took most of the Peck furniture as well as ten years' supply of Bag Balm, which turned out to be excellent for chapped hands. And all the way to Virginia, his truck following behind the apple-green Graham Paige, Duncan studied the back of Justine's head and wondered what was going on in her mind. He knew she hated this move. She had joined up with him, he thought, as easily as taking the hand of someone next to her on a sofa. How could she guess that immediately afterward she would be pulled not only off the sofa but also out of the house, out of the city, off to another *state*, even, clinging fast in bewilderment and asking herself what had happened? And now look: she was so bright and reckless, rattling down the highway, he was reminded of her mother's terrible gaiety at the wedding reception. He knew that sooner or later she was going to break down.

Yet in Virginia, in their shallow hot apartment above Uncle Ed Hodges's garage, Justine remained cheerful. She hummed as she settled their belongings in—only, perhaps, taking a little less care this time, leaving the damask curtains unhung and giving Aunt Marybelle, without a thought, the huge walnut breakfront when it wouldn't fit through the apartment door. She located a church bazaar, where she told fortunes, and after that there was a steady trickle of clients. To Duncan they were indistinguishable from her Buskville clients—mostly women, faded housewives and very young girls—and their lives were indistinguishable too, and their futures, which even he could have predicted, but Justine was patient and kind with them and it was plain they all loved her. In the afternoons if she had no readings, she came to the cabinetworks and watched Duncan build things. At first she was shy among the blunt, sawdusty carpenters, but she warmed up after a while. She made friends with them and told fortunes for their wives and kept their children. Sometimes she even helped out with the work, sitting on a board for someone or sanding down a tabletop. And always she was so joyous. How long could this last?

She said she wanted a baby. Duncan didn't. The idea of a family—a closed circle locking him in, some unlucky child whom *he* would lock in—made him feel desperate. Besides, he was not so sure that it was medically sound. Who knew what might be passed on? He pointed out their heredity: heart murmurs, premature births, their grandfather's deafness.

"But!" Justine said. "Look at our teeth! They're perfect, not a cavity in the lot. Nobody's ever lost one."

"Justine, if I hear one more word about those goddam teeth—"

But in the end he gave in. He agreed to a baby the way Justine, he imagined, had agreed to move to Virginia; he assumed it was necessary for her in some way that he would never understand. And all through her pregnancy he tried to take an interest. He listened to the details of every doctor's appointment, he practiced her breathing exercises with her until he grew light-headed. Twice he drove her to Baltimore for overlong visits with the aunts, who fussed and clucked around her while Duncan skulked nearby with his collar turned up and his hands jammed deep in his pockets. It seemed to him that his part in all this was so *incidental.* But when he steeled himself to suggest that she might want to go to Baltimore for the birth as well, Justine turned a sudden level gaze on him and said, "No, thank you. I'll have it here with you." How did her mind work?

By her seventh month she had started poring over old photographs in the evenings, particularly photographs of her mother. She sat squinting through a magnifying glass, her hard little knot of a stomach straining the faded dress she had worn since she was seventeen. For she hadn't bought any maternity clothes. Was she worried about the expense? In his experience, women *shopped*. He had expected a frilly layette to mount up in some bureau drawer, but the only things she had were what the aunts gave her. All the preparation she had made was to start building a cradle at the cabinetworks. And when he offered to get her a maternity dress himself her eyes spilled over with tears, something that almost never happened. "But I don't *want* anything. Nothing is right. I couldn't stand to buy anything in those stores," she said. Duncan was mystified. He did the only thing he could think of: he went out and bought three yards of flowered material and a Simplicity dress pattern. He assumed there was not much difference between reading a pattern and a blueprint: he could figure it out in no time and run it up on Aunt Marybelle's Singer. But when he got home Justine was in labor, and he had to take her straight to the hospital. It occurred to him during the trip that Justine was going to die. He thought he had known that all his life without admitting it: she would die at an early age because the world was so ironic. The sight of her calm face beside him—she was so *ignorant!*—made him furious. "You are *not* going to leave me with that baby to raise," he told her, and she turned and looked at him gently, from a distance. "No, of course not," she said.

She was right, of course. The birth was easy. Justine didn't die, she didn't come close to dying. He had been angry for nothing, and on top of that he had an eighty-five-cent pattern now which would never be used, because he'd be damned if they would ever go through this again.

Justine wanted to name the baby Margaret Rose, which was fine with him. But he was a little surprised. He had expected to have to argue against Caroline, or Lucy or Laura or Sarah, none of which he could stand. How long had Justine's fancy been taken by her runaway grandmother? Who was never mentioned, not ever, except by Sulie, who had loved Margaret Rose since first arriving to work for the Pecks at age thirteen. Certainly their grandfather never spoke of her. Duncan was curious as to what the old man would say now. Would he object? But no, when he came for a visit and they told him (Justine shouting it fearlessly into his good ear, which was turning bad like the other), he only nodded as if it meant nothing. Duncan should have guessed. *Justine* knew. In that family wrongdoers vanished without a trace, not even a hole to show where they had been.

They called the baby Meg for short. She was a blond, stocky, serious baby whose silvery eyebrows were quirked in a permanent frown. When she learned to walk, she *trudged*; if she laughed, it was only after a moment of study. Everything she did was laborious, even stringing wooden beads or feeding a doll or lugging around the large cardboard boxes that for several years she insisted on taking wherever she went. It touched Duncan to see her heaving her toys back into the toy chest every evening, unasked. As she grew older, as life became more hurried and scattered, she developed into a housewifely, competent little soul who always knew where things were, and what had been forgotten, and when they were supposed to be somewhere. By the age of six she had her own alarm clock, the only one in the house. For her seventh birthday she asked for a pop-up toaster. (She wanted to make toast like other people, she said, not in the oven.) She fixed her own breakfast, rinsed her own dishes, and hunted her own socks. Every afternoon when school was over she did her entire homework assignment without being told, her soft yellow head bent low, a pencil clutched tight in her fist. She asked to go both to Sunday school and church, neither of which her parents ever attended; she went alone, dressed in clothes from her grandmother, a bonnet and white gloves, clutching a quarter for the collection plate. Saturday afternoons she read her Bible assignment. "Meggie!" Justine would say, swooping down on her. "Come outside! Come play!" But Meg would have to finish and put everything away before she came. Then Justine took her out visiting other children, or hopscotching, or roller skating. If

Justine stretched Meg's skates to the largest size she could wear them herself, and she demonstrated all she remembered from the old days. In a strong wind she stood still and was blown backwards, with her skirts pressed wide and flat. She leaned on the air like a figurehead, laughing, but Meg watched dubiously with her thumb in her mouth.

"This is a cricket," Duncan told Meg.

"Ooh."

"Do you want to know how he chirps?"

"No."

"Many people suppose that he does it with his legs but actually—"

Meg looked not at the cricket but at Duncan. Her eyes were transparent, and flat at the bottom.

He had not expected to feel like a father, but he did. Just the curve of her cheek could give him a wrench, or the blue veins inside her wrist or the stolid way she stood watching other children playing. But he was clearer-sighted than Justine, who thought Meg was perfect. He knew, for instance, that although Meg was of normal intelligence she had a mind that plodded and toiled, with narrow borders; that she was fiercely anxious for regularity, permanence, order. It seemed to him that he was the object of an enormous joke: he had feared all the genetic defects but the obvious one, total Peckness. She was more Peck than anybody, more even than stodgy Claude or the soft, placid twins. When she went to Baltimore for a visit she was the darling. There was not one facet of her that was foreign in any way. It was Duncan who was foreign. As she grew older she seemed to realize that, and more and more often the two of them found fault with each other, bickering pointlessly, defending their two worlds. Then Meg, silenced finally by his quicker tongue, would take on a closed, sad look, and he would be reminded of Justine as a child. He remembered how hopefully Justine would follow her cousins, her eyes anxious, her smile hesitant, her dress as carefully kept as when her mother had buttoned it in the morning. He softened, and gently tweaked a sprig of Meg's hair until she gave in and smiled.

But where was the child Justine had been? There was nothing hesitant about her now. She had become fast-moving, kaleidoscopic. There was a sort of dash to everything she did that surprised and fascinated him. When she flew down a street people turned to look after her: an angular, frayed, pretty woman who looked as if she had no idea where she was going. She still wore the washed-out dresses from her girlhood, their hems adjusted belatedly half a dozen times, either raised to stand out like a spare tire around her knees or lowered and showing all previous levels like lines on ruled paper; and on her feet, Mary Janes with neat little straps; on her head that everlasting Breton, which Duncan had had to replace, twice, when the crown broke through from all the times she had clutched it to her head on her wild, careening journey through life. Her days consisted of a string of unexpected events. Passing a crazy man talking to himself, for instance (whom Duncan pretended not to hear), Justine stopped to answer whatever question he had asked the clouds and ended up involved for years in the man's Houdini-like escapes from asylums. She was the only person Duncan knew who had actually had a baby left on her doorstep. (Later the mother changed her mind, but Justine had been prepared to keep him.) At any moment of the day he might catch sight of her driving seventeen third-graders in a fire engine down Main Street, or picketing a whites-only movie theater with the day's groceries still in her arms, or zipping past his shop window towed by two gigantic St. Bernards when an hour ago she had owned no dogs at all. And she moved so easily from town to town! Oh, at first, of course, she was always a little reluctant. "But I like it here. We were just getting settled." (She could get settled anywhere, he thought, in a cave or a coal mine even; she was like a cat.) "I don't want to leave all our friends," she would say. (*Her* friends, generally; Justine made friends by leaps and bounds while Duncan was more gradual. It seemed he had barely started getting close to people when it was time to leave a place.) "What do we have to go for, Duncan?" But it was plain what they had to go for—there he was, ever grimmer and bleaker, slogging through the days. "Oh, well," she always said in the end. "We'll move. We'll just move, what's wrong with that?" Then the two of them grew light-headed, as if spared from some disaster they had been dreading for weeks. Justine went off too far ahead of time to pack—her favorite occupation, which became easier every year as they left more and more things behind. She had very nearly stopped cooking, stopped cleaning; she had given away her wedding saucepans as if just *being* were enough to take all her time and attention. For dinner she served whatever came to mind, forgetting to eat herself and opening a window instead to beg a street Arab to let Meg have a ride on his horse. "Oh, *Mama*," said Meg, who would not think of riding such an animal and wished that her mother would not embarrass her by hanging out windows. But Duncan drifted on this turbulence happily; during lulls he felt something was missing. When he came home and Justine was out the air seemed empty and dead. He plowed through the rooms calling her name. He went to neighbors. "Is Justine with you? She's not at home, I don't see her anywhere." Until having tracked her down, he could heave a long sigh and sink onto the nearest flat surface. "I couldn't find you. I didn't know where you were. I didn't know what had happened to you." Then life zoomed into full speed again, the unexpected fluttered all around them like confetti, and Duncan felt peaceful.

Sometimes he remembered that she had not always been this way, though he couldn't put his finger on just when she had changed. Then he wondered if she only *pretended* to be happy, for his sake. Or if she were deliberately cutting across her own grain, like an acrophobe who takes up sky diving. He became suddenly thoughtful, offering her perhaps a visit to Baltimore, although still, after all these years, the mere thought of his family filled him with a contrariness he seemed unable to control. Justine was still very fond of the family.

When he pointed out for her the meaning beneath their words, the sharp edge beneath their sweet, trite phrases, Justine pointed out the meaning beneath *that* meaning, and he would have to admit some truth in what she said. She had the pathetic alertness of a child who has had to depend too much on adults; she picked up every inflection, every gesture and untied ribbon and wandering eye, and turned it over and over to study its significance. (Was that how she could read the future? She had foretold Great-Grandma's death, she said, when she noticed her buying all her lotions in very tiny bottles.) So with Justine's words fresh in his mind he would drive to Baltimore feeling charitable and enlightened, though that never lasted past the moment of entering staid chilly Roland Park with its damp trees and gloomy houses and its reluctant maids floating almost motionlessly up the hill from the bus stop, following their slow flat feet while their heads held back. And once they had arrived he kept watching her, trying to see if deep down she hated him for taking her away. But Justine was no different here from any other place. She gave everybody sudden kisses, knocked Aunt Bea's spectacles askew, swooped through the house causing all the fairy lamps and figurines to tremble on the tables, and once at supper she accidentally ate the little glass spoon from her salt dish. All the aunts jumped up and wrung their hands, but Duncan smiled and his forehead smoothed and he rested back upon the white, tumbling waters of life with Justine.

Now the aunts and uncles were old, the grandfather wore a hearing aid, and the cousins (Sally divorced, the rest unmarried, all childless) were developing lines and sags in their curiously innocent faces like aging midgets. The lawns had grown meager and the fleet of Fords was outdated. The only servant was old Sulie, who shuffled around angry about something, as she had been for years, stirring the dust back and forth with a wilted gray rag. Great-Grandma's house was inhabited by Esther and the twins, but Justine was the legal owner. Someday, everyone said, Justine and Duncan would want to come home bringing their sweet Meg, and when they did this house would be ready. Justine only smiled. Of course they would never live there. Yet always in the backs of their minds it waited as a last resort, if all else failed, if they ever were forced to admit defeat. It figured in back-up plans; it moved in on them, inch by inch, whenever money was tight and jobs were scarce, and over the years it had come to contain an imaginary life parallel to their own, advancing when theirs did. They knew what nursery school they would have sent Meg to if they had lived here, and then what grammar school; what pharmacy they would have patronized and where they would have gone for their groceries. Yet only one glance at that house, where it loomed beneath the oaks, was enough to make Duncan grow dark and hollow and he would suddenly lay a hand on Justine's thigh as if she were a square of sunlight on a windowseat, and he just in from the cold.

8

An inferior class of people tended to travel by bus. Daniel Peck glared at them: three sailors, a colored boy in a crocheted cap, and a sallow, weasely woman with four children whom she kept slapping and pinching. One of the children stuck out his tongue. "Look at there. Did you see that?" Daniel asked his granddaughter.

She glanced up from her magazine.

"Child made a face at me."

She smiled.

"Well, there's nothing funny about it, Justine."

Whatever she said, he didn't quite catch. It bothered him to go motoring with his hearing aid on.

They were returning from Parthenon, Delaware, where finally after a great deal of tedious correspondence, he had located the youngest son of the past headmaster of Salter Academy. A Mr. Dillard. Mr. Dillard had already informed him by letter that he had never kept in touch with any of his father's students (who were older than he and not likely to be among the living anyway, he said tactlessly), but Daniel Peck knew that memory was not such a well-ordered affair. Sometimes little things could jog it, he knew, sometimes so small a thing as the smell of clover or the sight of a boy wobbling on a bicycle. So he had come in person, bringing his photograph of Caleb and prepared to offer any detail he could think of, a whole wealth of detail flattened and dried in his mind. "He was a tardy boy, always tardy. Perhaps your father mentioned having a student with a tardiness prob-

156

lem. And let's see, he was extremely sociable. Surely if there had ever been a class reunion of any sort he would have attended. Or just come visiting, don't you know. Perhaps come visiting your father years later, he would do that sort of thing. Can you remember such a visitor? Tall boy, blond, this picture doesn't quite show. He had a habit of tilting his head when listening to people. If you were a child he passed on his way to your father's study, for instance, he would most surely have spoken to you. Though he was not a *smiling* person. Did you see him? Do you know?"

But Mr. Dillard did not know. A stooped, red-faced man who wouldn't speak up. There were cartoon fishes all over his bathroom wallpaper. His wife was nice, though. Lovely lady. She offered them homemade butter mints, the first he had tasted in years, and gave Justine the recipe on an index card.

He set his face toward Justine, waiting till she would feel it and raise her head again. "Yes, Grandfather," she said.

"What'd you do with that recipe?"

She looked blank.

"Recipe card Mrs. Dillard gave you."

"Oh!"

"Don't tell me you lost it."

"Oh no. No, I—"

He didn't know the rest of what she said but he could *see* her plainly enough, rummaging through her crushed straw bag and then her dress pockets, one of which was torn halfway off. Gone, then. He would never have those fine butter mints again.

He removed a large leather wallet from the inner breast pocket of his suit coat. He took out a cream-colored envelope and a sheet of stationery. The envelope was already stamped and addressed. He was very well organized. His stepmother had taught him years ago: compose your card of thanks on the carriage ride home. Never allow an hour to elapse before writing a bread-and-butter note. "Then why," Duncan had asked as a child, "don't we write the whole *letter* ahead of time?'' But no, that wouldn't do at all. You had to mention something personal that had occurred during the visit, don't you see. As Daniel did now, after frowning a moment at his pen.

Dear Mrs. Dillard,   March 5, 1973
   I write to express my appreciation for your hospitality. Your butter mints were extremely tasty, and it was very kind of you to take the time to see us. We shall remember our visit to you with a great deal of pleasure.
                                        Respectfully,
                                   Daniel J. Peck, Sr.

When he got back to Caro Mill or wherever he would type a copy of this note for his files. He liked to keep a record of all correspondence, particularly that regarding Caleb. His old Underwood typewriter, with its metal keys and high black forehead, was forever set up on the bureau by his bed; his file cabinet was packed solid with letters of inquiry, thank you letters, follow-up letters, for how many years back? How many years?

Well, his stepmother died in 1958. *That* was a hard time. She was the last person on this earth who called him Daniel. He had not realized that until she died. She had journeyed through all his life with him, minus the first few months: seventy-seven years. The only person who remembered his kid soldier doll, and his father's way of widening his eyes when displeased, and the rough warm Belgian blocks that used to pave the streets downtown. She left her house to Justine, and he knew why. (She was uneasy in her mind about that girl, the sweetest of his granddaughters and the most defenseless, dragged from pillar to post by harum-scarum Duncan, whom marriage had not toned down in the least.) But for months after her death Daniel would not enter her house or look at it, and although he allowed Esther and the twins to move in he told them to stay out of her bedroom. He would sort her things later, he said; he was just a little busy right now. He walked around feeling wounded, struck as if for the first time by the fact that the world kept progressing and people aged and died and nothing in life was reversible. Where had it all gone to? Whatever happened to that little brown German step-grandfather he used to have? Or Sarah Cantleigh's family, who cried whenever they saw him, were they all dead by now? Where was that silent, musical brother of his with the tilted head?

But he was a sensible man, and in time he recovered. Then he sent for Sulie with her ring of keys. They went to sort Laura's belongings. "Oh, my soul," Sulie kept saying. "My soul." She had been mad at Laura for decades, but she looked stricken as she gazed around the dark, stale room. Her eyes were triangular and the cords stood out in her neck. She had a wrinkled face like a yellow paper kite. "So this is what it all come to," she said.

"Now if you don't stop that," Daniel told her, "you can just go on back to the kitchen, hear?"

He left the clothes for the women to deal with; that was none of his business. What concerned him were her desk drawers, jewelry boxes, and knick-knack shelves, which held little mementos that should be parceled out among the family. He opened drawers guiltily, shamed by the puffs of lavender scent that rose from everything as if she were still in the room somewhere. "Well, I just don't know," he said to each new object they found, and then when he had laid it aside Sulie would pick it up and say, "Miss *Sarah* always admire this," or "Miss Bea always saying how she wish she had one like it."

"Take it to her then. Fine. Fine," said Daniel.

He kept nothing for himself. Those neat drawers, with everything arranged so precisely and all for nothing, took away his interest in life. And maybe Sulie's, too. At any rate, when he offered her the oval brooch that contained a plait of Laura's mother's hair and had only one little thing wrong with the clasp, Sulie's mouth turned downward. "I don't want it," she said.

"Suit yourself," he told her. Not everyone would put up with Sulie's rudeness the way he did.

In a desk drawer behind a stack of stationery he found an ancient brittle advertisement for Baum's Fine Cutlery. Beneath it, an envelope that looked as if it had been handled a great deal. Inside was a photograph of Caleb playing the cello in a stable loft.

Now, where did that come from?

He had never seen it before, but from the poor focus and the haphazard composition he guessed that it was the work of Margaret Rose that summer she got her Brownie. For a few months she had wandered everywhere, photographing the most unlikely things: Sulie stringing beans, Sarah on her rocking horse, Lafleur Boudrault playing cigar-box guitar and Mark with a mouthful of honeysuckle blossoms. (Daniel had known she was gone for good when he found all her photos of the children missing. But enough of that.) He peered at Caleb's blurred, sharp-featured face. So far as he knew this was the only picture of Caleb in existence. Not counting the one in the album: age two, wearing a ruffled dress and holding an open book he could not possibly have read. And of course all traces of Margaret Rose had been systematically destroyed long ago. Yet in a sense this was a picture of her too, a permanent record of her hasty way of doing things; and her presence could be inferred from the head-on, quizzical look Caleb directed to the camera holder—an expression he reserved for Margaret Rose. Daniel passed a hand over his eyes. "I believe that will be all for today, Sulie," he said.

"What, you quitting?"

"For now."

"Leaving this mess any which old way?"

"*Later* I'll tend to it."

When he left she was poking the piles of belongings with angry, crabbed hands, muttering beneath her breath. He didn't care to hear what she was saying.

Then for several evenings in a row he sat alone in his

bedroom studying the photograph, testing the new feeling of sorrow that drove straight through his ribcage. And when that was absorbed (not lessened, just adjusted to) he became, he admitted, a little crazy. He began wondering if this photo didn't have some secret message to it. It was impossible for such an object just to *be*, wasn't it? He studied the angle of Caleb's hat, the set of his cello, the shreds left on the stable wall by some old poster. What was the significance? Meanwhile his bachelor son and his two spinster daughters whispered downstairs, wondering what he could be doing. When Laura May knocked on his door, he jumped and shoved the photo into his pocket. All she found was her father in his easy chair with his arms folded unnaturally across his front.

Then he went to Lucy, who played a little piano still. He pulled her aside one day when she was counting Mason jars in the pantry. "Lucy," he said, "*you* know music."

"Oh, Father Peck, I—"

"Look here. What note is this man playing?"

He showed her the photo. Surprise set little sharp pleats across her forehead. "Why, who—" she said.

"What note is he playing?"

"Oh, well, I don't—actually, it doesn't look to me as if he's playing *any* note."

"What? Speak up."

"Not any note."

"Why, how is that possible? No note at all? I never heard of such a thing."

"It looks to me as if he's just resting his bow on the strings, Father Peck."

"But that would be ridiculous."

"Oh, no, it's really quite—"

"I never heard of such a thing," he said, and then he slammed out of the pantry.

Already he knew he had made a mistake. For Lucy, of course, had to go and tell Two, and Two out of all the family was the most certain to recognize a description of Caleb. Then everybody knew, and everybody asked him what he thought he was up to. Caleb was best forgotten. He was surely dead by now. What did it matter what note he had played on a summer's day in 1910?

When Justine visited home that August, she came to where he sat in his slat chair beneath an oak tree. She kissed his cheek and drew back and looked at him. He could tell she had heard something. They had all been discussing him behind his back. He snorted. "You know, of course, that I am *non compos mentis*," he told her.

She went on studying him, as if she took what he had said seriously. A literal-minded girl, Justine. Always had been.

"Could I see Caleb?" she asked finally.

"Pardon?"

He thought he had heard wrong.

"Your picture of Caleb."

"The others are asking *not* to see it."

"But I don't even know what he looks like," she said.

He frowned at her. Well, no, of course she wouldn't. Probably didn't know much of *anything* about him. Laura never let his name cross her lips; he seldom had himself; and to the others Caleb was nearly forgotten, a distant grownup uncle whom they had never found very interesting.

"Well," Daniel said.

He drew out the photograph, protected now by glass.

"My brother," he said.

"I see," said Justine.

"Generally he did not go about in his shirtsleeves, however."

Justine bent over the photograph. Her lowered eyelids reminded him of wings. "He looks like you," she said.

"But his eyes were brown."

"His face is the same."

"Yes, I know," said Daniel, and he sighed. He took back the picture. "The others, you see, they don't count him any more. To them he's a deserter."

Justine said something he couldn't catch.

"Eh? To me," he said, "he is still a member here. He

goes back to nearly as long ago as I can recollect. I just like to think of him, is all. What's wrong with that?"

"Not a thing," Justine said.

"I would give all the remaining years of my life if I could set eyes on him again."

She said something else. He took a swipe at the air, protesting the curtain of muffled sound that separated them.

"If I could just walk to church with him once more," he told her, "only this time, paying closer *attention*, don't you see. If I could pass by the Salter Academy and look in the window and see him wave, or hear him play that foolish messy music of his on the piano in the parlor—if they could just give me back one little scrap of time, that's all I ask!"

"Oh, well," said Justine. "Come around to the front, Grandfather, see how Meg's grown." And then she took him by the hand, so that he had to rise and follow. In a way, he was a little disappointed in Justine. He had thought she might understand his viewpoint, but if she did she didn't let on.

In November of that year, on a cold, waterlogged day, he received an envelope postmarked Honora, Maryland, where Justine was living at the time. There was no letter, only a clipping from the Honora *Herald*, a whole page devoted to education. He was puzzled. Education did not much interest him. But wait: at the bottom was a very old-fashioned photograph of rows and rows of young boys. The caption said:

The Good Old Days

Above, the author's own school, Salter Academy in Baltimore, around the turn of the century. Note gaslights along the walls. Author is in seated row, second from left.

Daniel took off for Honora within the hour, driving his V-8 Ford. He arrived at Justine's house waving the clipping. Justine was in the kitchen reading some lady's future—an occupation he and all the family preferred to ignore. "Never mind that," he told her. "I want to see Ashley Higham."

"Who's Ashley Higham?"

"The man who wrote this piece, of course."

"Oh, then you *do* know him!" Justine said.

"No I don't know him, don't know him from Adam, but it says right here he went to Salter Academy, doesn't it? Says this is him seated, second from left, and not an arm's length away from him is my own brother Caleb isn't it?"

"Is that right?" said Justine. She set down her cards and got up to have a look. So did the lady, not that it was any of her business.

"Now all I've got to do is find Ashley Higham," Daniel said.

"Oh, well, Grandfather, I don't really know where—"

"*I* know," said the lady.

So it was the lady who led the way to Ashley Higham. And Mr. Higham did, in fact, remember Caleb well, but had not seen him since graduation day in 1903. However, he had a remarkable mind and could reel off the name of every boy, his shaky white index finger slowly traversing the rows of faces. Daniel recorded each name on a sheet of paper. Later he would copy them into a pocket-sized ring notebook that he carried with him everywhere, gradually stuffing it fatter and fatter. For one thing led to another, one man remembered another who had been a friend of Caleb's and *that* man remembered Caleb's elocution teacher, who turned out to be deceased but his grandson in Pennsylvania had saved all his correspondence and from that Daniel found the name of the geography teacher, and so on. His files began filling up. His Ford clocked more miles in a year than it had in all its past life. And bit by bit, as the rest of the family grew more disapproving (first arguing reasonably, then trying to distract him with television and scrapbooks and homemade pie, finally stealing his car keys whenever his back was turned) he began staying for longer periods of time with Justine. Only visiting, of course. It would never do for Caleb to come home unexpectedly and find him vanished without a trace. His house still waited for him in Baltimore, his daughters still kept his room made up. But Justine was the only one who would hop into the car with him at a moment's notice, and go anywhere, and talk to anyone and interpret all the mumbled answers. And when he was discouraged, Justine was the one who bolstered his confidence again.

For he did get discouraged, at first. At first he was in such a hurry. He thought he was right around the corner from success, that was why. Then when he traveled clear across the state to find Caleb's oldest, dearest friend and learned that he had last seen Caleb in 1909, he grew morose and bitter. "I always assumed," he told Justine, "that people keep in touch, that if they lost touch they go back and pick it up again, don't you know. Of course I am more a *family* man myself, family's been my social life. But I would suppose that if you just watched a man's best friend long enough, you would be certain to see the man himself eventually. Well, not Caleb. In fifty years he has not once gone back to pay a call, and his friend has never done a thing about it. What do you make of that?"

Justine said, "Never mind, Grandfather. It will work out." (Was she speaking *professionally?*) And the next morning she was perfectly willing to set off again, cheerful as ever, never losing patience. So there was no need to hurry after all. He began to relax. He began to enjoy the search itself, the endless rattling rides, the motionless blue sky outside the window of his train. (For they had quickly switched to railroad, as his deafness had caused several near accidents and Justine's driving terrified him.) In the old days, merely a business trip to New York had made him feel like a ball of yarn rolling down the road, unwinding his tail of homesickness behind him in a straight line back to Roland Park. But now he learned to concentrate solely on the act of traveling. He liked to imagine that Caleb himself had ridden this very train. He bobbled along on the Southern Railroad Line or the B & O, on dusty plush seats, occasionally stretching his legs on some small-town platform where, perhaps, Caleb had stood before him. And he returned home as confident as when he left, for there was always time to search further, next week or next month or whenever he felt up to it.

If Duncan minded this permanent visit, he never said so. In the beginning Daniel had asked him outright. (Well, as outright as he could get.) "Nowadays, people seem to prefer a minimum of adults in one household, have you noticed?" he had said. But Duncan only smiled. "Some do, some don't," he said. Another of those unexplained remarks of his. He did it on *purpose*. Daniel mulled for several days, and then he went to Justine. "Duncan of course has never kept close family ties," he told her, and waited, trustingly, for her to understand. She did.

"That's true," she said, "but he hasn't said anything so far."

And Daniel was careful to see that he never gave Duncan reason to. He held back from advice (which Lord knows the boy could have used) and praise and criticism. He accepted every change of address without question, although none of them were the least bit necessary. Didn't it occur to Duncan that other people had low periods too, and just sat them out instead of packing up bag and baggage? You endure, you manage to survive, he had never heard of someone so consistently refusing to. But never mind, he didn't say a word. He went uncomplainingly to each new town, he accepted Justine's half-hearted cooking and cleaning, which were, he assumed, the natural result of failing to give a woman any permanence in her life. Why should she bother, in those shabby, limp houses that looked flung down, that seemed to be cowering in expectation of the next disaster? And meanwhile Laura's fine place was sitting empty. (He didn't count Esther and the twins living there, for really they belonged at home with their parents.) But leave it be, leave it be. The only change he made in their lives was to deed his Ford to them once he quit driving. It made him nervous to ride about in the Graham Paige, for which Duncan had to haunt antique shows every time a part wore out. "But I don't like Fords," Duncan said. "I have a deep-seated *hatred* of Fords," and for half a year they had been a two-car family, Justine darting about in the Ford and Duncan in the Graham Paige, whistling cheerfully and looking down from time to time to watch the highway skating along beneath the hole in the floorboards. The engine, he said, was in fine shape, and no doubt it was, for Duncan was an excellent mechanic. But you have to have something to put an engine *in*, not this collection of green metal lace and sprung springs; and on moving day that year, without a word, Duncan had left it sitting in front of the house and driven off in the U-Haul. His grandfather pretended not to notice. He was a tactful man.

He lived in his own tiny, circular world within their larger one. While they moved up and down the eastern seaboard, made their unaccountable decisions, took up their strange acquaintances and then lost them and forgot them, Daniel Peck buttoned his collarless shirt and fastened his pearl-gray suspenders and surveyed his white, impassive face in the bedroom mirror. He wound his gold watch. He tidied his bed. He transformed even his journeys, the most uncertain part of his life, into models of order and routine and predictability. For Justine was always with him, he always had the window seat, she read her *National Geographic*, they carried on their spasmodic, elliptical conversations over the noise of the road. Now they had to ride the buses more and more often, since that was all most towns had these days. They would take long circuitous routes in order to join up someplace, somehow, with a railroad, and even *then* it was usually Amtrak, a garish untrainlike train where nothing went right, where certainly Caleb had never set foot in his life. But still Daniel traveled calm and expressionless, his hands on his knees, a ten-dollar bill pinned inside his undershirt, and his granddaughter's hat brim comfortingly steadfast in the righthand corner of his vision.

They were drawing close to what's-its-name, Caro Mill. He noticed people rising to put their coats on, and lifting suitcases down from the rack. He noticed within himself a sudden feeling of emptiness. So they were back again, were they? He sighed. Justine looked up again from her magazine.

"We didn't get much done," he told her.

"Why, no."

To her it didn't matter. She thought he felt the same, he had ridden content beside her for so many years now. But lately he had had a sense of impatience, as in the old days when he first began his search. Did that mean he was drawing close to Caleb? Once he almost asked her outright for a reading from her cards—ridiculous business. Of course he had stopped himself in time. Now he stared bleakly out the window at a jumble of service stations and doughnut shops. "So *this* is where we're headed," he said.

"What?"

"It's not much of a place to come back to."

"Oh—" said Justine, and then something else he couldn't catch, but he knew it would be cheerful. Justine did not seem to be easily disappointed. Which was fortunate. Whereas he himself was leaden with disappointment, sinking fast. He felt there was something hopeless about the deep orange sunset glowing beyond an auto junkyard. "Grandfather?" Justine asked, in her most carrying tone. "Are you all right?"

"Yes, certainly."

The bus wheezed past a dismal hotel with tattered windowshades. It stopped in front of the Caro Mill Diner. Place couldn't have a regular terminal, no. Out they had to climb, in the middle of the street. The driver did not so much as give Justine a hand down the steps, or either of the other ladies; Daniel had to do it. He touched his temple for each one in turn as he let go of her arm. "Why, thank you," one lady told him. The other didn't say a word, or else he missed it.

In front of the diner sat the Ford, three feet from a hydrant, battered and dusty and bearing a long new dent in the rear bumper. He studied the damage. In the old days people left notes about such things, giving their names and telephone numbers. Not any more. When he finally climbed into the car he said, "Conscience has vanished."

"Excuse me?"

Justine looked at him, one hand outstretched toward her own door which was flapping open and snarling traffic. "*What's* vanished?"

"Conscience, I said. They dent your bumper and don't even leave a note."

"Perhaps *I*," said Justine, and something else.

"No, if you had done it I would have noticed. Besides, you've *had* this week's accident." His little joke. He laughed, covering his mouth with his fist to turn it into a cough.

Then, *wham!* He was jarred and knocked into the windshield. Aches and pains started up all over, instantly. It seemed that someone had reached down a gigantic hand and flung him like a doll. "Grandfather?" Justine asked. There was a long red welt on the inside of her arm, and a few dots of blood. Just past her, a car had stopped and a man was climbing out. And where the door had been swinging open there was nothing now at all, just clear blank air and then the man's angry face. The man was shouting but all his words were a blur. It didn't matter; Daniel was just relieved to see the cause of his shake-up. Of course, a door torn off! Yet he continued to feel disoriented. When the man had driven away, and Justine stepped out to drag the door to the trunk and heave it in, he was still so dazed that he didn't offer to help. He watched numbly as she slid behind the wheel again. "At least we're well ventilated," she told him. A strange thing to say, or perhaps he had misunderstood. He wished he were home. He raced through the hallways of his mind calling out for Laura, his father, Caleb, Margaret Rose. But really he should never have married Margaret Rose. A shared background was the important thing. If he had not been such a fool for her chuckling laugh and the tender, subtle curve at the small of her back he would have made a more sensible choice, a person he had known all his life. Who was that little girl who used to come visiting with her parents? Melissa, Melinda? But he had wanted someone new and surprising. A terrible mistake. How he hated Margaret Rose! The thought of her made him grind his teeth. He would like to know where she was now so that he could do something dreadful to her, humiliate her in front of all her fancy, tinkling friends. But no, she was dead. He was so disappointed to remember. As usual she had done something first, run ahead of him laughing and looking back at him over her shoulder, and for once he could not refuse to follow.

"Once you're alive, there's no way out but dying," he told Justine.

She looked over at him.

"You've set a thing in motion, you see."

"It's like being pregnant," said Justine. Of course she couldn't *really* have said that. His ears were bad. His mind was bad. He was going to have to get a hold of himself. He straightened his back and looked out the window, a respectable elderly gentleman admiring the view as they rattled homeward.

Meg Peck and the Reverend Arthur Milsom were sitting in the living room waiting for Meg's parents. Or Arthur was sitting; Meg kept moving around. First she chose the armchair because she wanted to look proper and adult. Then she thought it was more natural to sit next to Arthur on the couch. They were about to ask permission to get married; what would they be doing across the room from each other?

Arthur had on his clerical collar, which wasn't absolutely required but it looked very nice. He was a young, pale, tense man, small but wiry. When he was nervous he cracked his knuckles and his brown eyes grew so dark and sober that he seemed to be glaring. "*Don't* be nervous," Meg told him sitting back down on the couch. She reached over and took his damp hand.

This visit had been planned for weeks. The first Monday after she turned eighteen, he said, he would come talk to her parents. (Monday was a slow day at the church.) They had worked it out by letter. It was Arthur's feeling that Duncan was the important one, but as Meg pointed out they needed Justine there to smooth things over. For certainly Duncan would be at his sharpest. He didn't like Arthur. (How could anyone not like Arthur?) What they hadn't counted on was Justine's vanishing, taking Grandfather on one of his trips. Now there was no telling when she would be back, and meanwhile Duncan was coming home from work at any minute. They would have to handle him alone after all.

Meg always thought of her parents as Duncan and Justine, although she didn't call them that. It might have been due to the way they acted. They were not very parent-like. She loved them both, but she had developed a permanent inner cringe from wondering how they would embarrass her next. They were so—*extreme*. So irresponsible! They led such angular, slap-dash lives, always going off on some tangent, calling over their shoulders for her to come too. And for as long as Meg could remember she had been stumbling after, picking up the trail of cast-off belongings and abandoned projects. All she really wanted was to live like other people. She tried to keep the house neat, like her friends' houses, and to put flowers in the vases and to hide, somehow, whatever tangle of tubes and electrical wires Duncan was working on at the moment. But then it seemed so hopeless when she knew how soon they would be moving on. "We're nomads," Justine told her, "think of it that way"—as if making it sound romantic would help. But there was nothing romantic about this tedious round of utility deposits, rental contracts, high school transcripts and interrupted magazine subscriptions. "He's ruining our *lives!*" she told Justine. Justine looked astonished. "But Meggie darling, *we* can't be the ones to say—" Then Meg's anger would extend to her mother, too, who was so gullible and so quick to give in, and she closed herself up in her room (if they were in a house where she *had* a room) and said no more.

She kept herself occupied with sewing, or pasting pictures in her scrapbook full of model homes—French windows and carpeted kitchens and white velvet couches. She straightened up her closet with all her shoes set side by side and pointing in the same direction. She ironed her own dresses, as she had since she was nine. (Justine thought there was no point to ironing, as long as things were clean.) At the age of ten she had baked her first cake, which everyone admired but no one ate because they were too busy rushing off somewhere; they seemed to live on potato chips from vending machines. Nothing ever worked on a schedule. She was encouraged to bring her friends home at any hour of the day or night. "This family is not a closed unit," Duncan told her—apparently his only rule, if you could call it that. But how could she bring friends when her parents were so certain to make fools of themselves? "Oh, I just love your folks," girls were always saying, little dreaming what agony it would be to have them for their own. For Justine might be found barefoot and waving her dirty playing cards, or sitting at the kitchen table with three or four unsuitable friends, or racing about looking for her broken straw carry-all in order to go to the diner whose food she preferred to her own. She had a high-handed, boisterous way of acting sometimes and she was likely to refer to Duncan publicly as "Meg's second cousin," her idea of a joke. And Duncan! Spouting irrelevant, useless facts, thinking out loud in startling ways, leaving her friends stunned and stupid-looking. *His* idea of a joke was to hang idiotic newspaper and ladies' magazine pages all over the house, bearing what he thought were appropriate messages. On Justine's birthday he pasted up a bank ad saying WE'RE INCREASING OUR INTEREST, and after Meg spent too much money on a dress (only because she wanted to look like the other girls for a change, not all homemade and tacked together) she found a page Scotch-taped to her closet door:

HAVE YOU EVER HAD
A BAD TIME IN LEVI'S?

Then she had snatched up the page and stalked in to where Duncan sat inventing a new keyboard arrangement for the typewriter. "Act your *age!*" she told him. But when he looked up his face was so surprised and unguarded, and she saw that he really *was* aging, there were dry lines around his eyes and two tiny crescents left by his wide, dippy smile. So she laid the paper down gently, after all, and went away defeated.

Now she sighed, remembering, and Arthur squeezed her fingers. "In an hour this will all be over," he told her.

"It will never be over."

"I don't understand."

"We're going to be demolished," she said. "I feel it."

But now she had insulted him. He straightened up, which made him look smaller. He said, "Don't you think I can have a reasonable discussion with my own girl's parents?"

"Yes but—"

"You forget, I'm a minister. I've convinced families who swore they'd cut off their daughters without a penny. I've convinced fathers who claimed that—"

"But it wasn't you their daughters were marrying."

"Now don't *worry*. If worst comes to worst we'll just go away quietly and have the ceremony in my own church."

But neither of them wanted that. They wanted everything perfect. Arthur wanted her to be happy, and Meg would only be happy with a white dress that dipped to a point at the waist, Sarah Cantleigh's veil, and a bouquet of baby's breath. She wanted to walk down the aisle of the family's church in Baltimore where her mother had been married; she would like to be guarded by rows and rows of aunts and uncles and second cousins, grave Peck eyes approving her choice. Bridal showers, long-grained rice, Great-Grandma's sixpence in her shoe. Arthur waiting beside the minister, turning his pale, shiny face to watch her procession. Whenever he looked at her, she felt queenly. All right, so he was not a handsome man, but would a handsome man treat her as adoringly as Arthur Milsom did? When they went to lectures she looked at the lecturer and Arthur looked at her. She felt the thin moon of his face turned upon her. He assisted her in and out of cars, through doorways, up the shallowest steps, his hands just barely brushing her. (The aunts would love his manners.) He devoted his entire attention to her, so much so that sometimes, he said, he worried about his jealous God. Nobody had ever, in all her life, felt that way about her before.

A car drove up in front of the house, chugging and grinding familiarly. "There's Mama now!" Meg said. "Look, she beat him home after all." She rose and went out to the porch. Justine was still seated behind the wheel, straightbacked and prim, unguarded by even the vestige of a door. The car looked like a cross-section of something. But, "Certainly makes it easier to get in and out!" she called to Meg, and she waved gaily and stepped onto the sidewalk. "Coming, Grandfather?"

"Mama, I want to talk to you," Meg said.

But then up spoke Dorcas Britt, the lady next door, calling over the hedge in a large, rich voice that seemed to mock Meg's. "Justine, honey! I got to talk to you."

"A man came along doing eighty and flung Grandfather into the windshield," Justine said.

"Mama."

The house was swept suddenly with a variety of colors and shapes—the white, tottering grandfather, Justine flicking back her yellow hair, Dorcas all chartreuse and magenta on red patent-leather spike-heeled sandals. Arthur stood up with his fingers laced in front of him, as he did when greeting church members after the sermon. He wore a determined smile. Meg felt a twist; was she doomed to be embarrassed by *everyone*, all her life, even Arthur? "Mama, Grandfather, you remember Arthur," she said. "Mrs. Britt, this is Arthur, my—Arthur Milsom."

"My baby has been kidnapped," Dorcas told him.

Her baby was nine years old and she was kidnapped regularly, always by her father, who did not have visiting rights, but Arthur didn't know that and he grew white around the lips. "Oh, my heavens!" he cried.

"Arthur. It's all *right*," Meg told him.

"All right?" said Dorcas. "To you, maybe."

"Grandfather was zonked in the forehead," Justine said.

Which caused Arthur to spin next in the grandfather's direction, full of a new supply of horror and sympathy. He hadn't learned yet. Such an expenditure of emotion would drain you in no time, living here. *"Arthur,"* Meg said.

"The man was going eighty, at least," said Justine. "How else could he have ripped a door clean off like that?"

"It was already hanging by one hinge, Mama."

" 'You were going eighty,' I told him, but guess what he said? It's against the law to open a car door on the street side. Did you know that? How are we supposed to get into our cars?"

"Perhaps from the sidewalk side," Arthur said carefully.

Justine paused, in the middle of removing her hat, and looked over at him. "Oh. Arthur," she said. "Why, how are you?"

"I'm just *fine*, thank you, Mrs. Peck. How are *you?*"

"And Meg! Meggie, did you find my note? I forgot to tell you I was going off today. Did you have anything to eat when you came home from school?"

She didn't wait for an answer. She kissed Meg on the cheek—a breath of Luden's cough drops. Whenever she kissed people she gave them quick little pats on the shoulder. Meg drew away, trying to regather her dignity. "Mama, when you get a moment," she said.

"But I *have* a moment. All the time in the world. What can I do for you?"

"Don't you have to start supper?"

She meant, Can't you come out in the kitchen and talk without Dorcas? But Justine said, "Oh, I thought we would just have pick-ups tonight." The only one who understood Meg was Dorcas, who drew herself in while remaining, somehow, as billowy and bosomy as a featherbed. A fat blonde with tiny hands and feet. *"You* are not a mother," she said. "You have never had your baby kidnapped. This is not something I can just go home and forget until a more convenient time.''

''Perhaps if you called the police,'' said Arthur.

''Police! Ha!''

''Mama, I want to talk to you a second.''

''All right.''

''I mean, privately.''

''Honey, can't you talk here? Dorcas is a friend, we don't have to be private from *her*.''

''I should say not,'' said Dorcas.

''Well, I'll wait till Daddy comes home,'' Meg said.

''Oh, Duncan! Where is he? Shouldn't he be here by now?''

And off she flew to the window, with Dorcas tripping behind her on her ridiculous shoes. ''Look here, Justine, you got to help. Won't you lay the cards? I got to know where Ann-Campbell is.''

''Oh, well, I'm sure she's all right.''

Ann-Campbell would be all right anywhere. Meg pitied her kidnapper. But Justine gave in, soft-hearted as usual. ''But maybe just a *quick* reading,'' she said. And off they went to the kitchen for the cards. Grandfather Peck stood teetering from heel to toe, peering after them. ''Are they going to make supper?'' he asked Meg.

''They're doing a reading, Grandfather.''

''A what?''

''*Reading.*''

''What would they be reading *now*? It's suppertime.''

He sat down suddenly in the armchair. There was a long knot growing on his forehead. ''Grandfather, you're turning purple,'' Meg said.

''Ah?''

''Perhaps he needs medical attention,'' Arthur whispered.

But the grandfather, who could sometimes hear astonishing things, slapped his knee and said, ''Nonsense!''

Then there was a blue-and-yellow flash in the door—Duncan, wearing the jeans Mr. Amsel had asked him not to.

He sprinted across the hall and into the coat closet. "Daddy?" Meg said.

"Meg, where is that magazine I was reading last night?"

"I don't know."

"Do you have to put everything away all the time?"

"*I* didn't put it anywhere."

"Never mind, I found it."

Off he went again. The door slammed. Arthur began stroking his chin thoughtfully.

"Was that Duncan?" the grandfather asked.

"Yes, Grandfather."

"*You're* a pastor," he told Arthur.

"Assistant pastor, yes sir."

"Here's an idea for a sermon."

"Grandfather."

"All our misery comes from the length of our childhood. Ever thought of that?"

"No, sir, I don't believe I have."

"Look at it this way. Everything arises from boredom, right? Irritation, loneliness, violence, stupidity—all from boredom. Now. Why are we bored? Because the human childhood is so durned lengthy, that's why. Because it takes us so durned long to get grown. Years. Years and years just hanging around waiting. Why, after that just *anything* would be an anticlimax."

"Sugar," Duncan called, crossing the front hall again.

"How's that?"

"Eat more sugar."

"*What'd* he say?"

Duncan stuck his head in the living room door. "Sugar hastens puberty," he said. "All the Eskimos are growing up faster now they've switched to carbohydrates."

Grandfather Peck scratched his head.

"Daddy," said Meg, "we want to talk to you."

"Ah so, Meggie." But then he saw Arthur. "Why, looky there, a man of the cloth."

"Daddy, when Mama gets through—"

"Where *is* your mother?"

"She's reading the cards for Dorcas."

Arthur stood up. Next to Duncan he looked very small and stalwart. "Actually, Mr. Peck," he said, "I feel it would be quite enough just to talk to you."

"Oh, more than enough," said Duncan.

"When I became a man," the grandfather said, "I caught myself thinking, many times, so this is what it's like to be grown up! Plodding back and forth, between work and home. Even being a judge was not what I had hoped. Really you don't make judgments at all; you simply relate what happens today to what has happened yesterday, all the precedents and statutes and amendments. And when you've waded through that, what next? You get old. And you're old for years and years and years. Your hearing goes and your knees go. Some people's teeth go. I myself have kept all my teeth but I wouldn't say it has done much good. After all, whatever I eat I ate a thousand times before. In addition I have become more and more conscious of where the food comes from. Pork tastes like pigs, beef like cows, lamb like sheep's wool, and so forth. Milk chocolate, which I used to consider a treat, nauseates me now. I taste the smell of cow barns."

"I wonder," said Duncan. "If we ran some experiments with *goat's* milk chocolate—"

"The Chinese venerate age. If I were in China people would come to me and say, '*You're* old and wise. What's the meaning of it all?' "

"What *is* the meaning of it all?" Duncan asked.

"I don't know," his grandfather told him.

"Mr. Peck," said Arthur, "I would like to marry your daughter."

The grandfather said, "My daughter?"

But Duncan understood. He gave Arthur a long, clear, untroubled look, as if nothing such a man could say would bother him. Then he said, "She's seventeen."

"Eighteen," said Meg.

"Eighteen? Oh yes."

"And Arthur's twenty-six."

"Well, that's ridiculous," said Duncan. "When you're seventy he'll be seventy-eight."

"So?"

"And you're still in school."

"We're planning a June wedding," said Arthur. "She'll be graduated by then."

"And Daddy, you know I'm not the college type."

"Who is? Who cares about college? Did I ever say I wanted you to go to college? But I didn't say I wanted you to get married right off the bat, either, and go live in Simper, Virginia, sitting in the front pew every Sunday nodding all the flowers off your hat. It's a trap. Do you want to be trapped? I thought you would go off and do something, Meggie, travel somewhere. Leave old Caramel behind if you like, we're not trying to keep you for ourselves. Hitch-hike to California. Take a freight train. Take a *bus*. Learn to surf. Marry somebody unpredictable. Join the Foreign Legion."

"But I can't be that way."

"Try! Anything but this. Just settling for it doesn't matter who, any pale fish in a suit—"

"Mr. Peck," said Arthur, "I understand, of course, that in the heat of the moment—"

"How will you have babies, Reverend Mildew, osmosis?"

"Mama!" Meg called.

"Don't trouble your mother, Meg, I'll see him out myself."

"Unfortunately I am not that easy to discourage," Arthur said.

"That *is* unfortunate." But Duncan was guiding him toward the door anyway, and Arthur was allowing it. "Now," said Duncan, "if by any strange chance Meg still feels the same when she is of a decent age, Reverend, I admit there is nothing I can do about it. Meanwhile, goodbye."

"But I am of age!" Meg said.

The front screen slammed.

Meg looked at her great-grandfather, who smiled a weary

smile showing every one of his perfect teeth. She crossed to the kitchen door and opened it.

"Meg," said Dorcas, "your mother's a marvel. My cards say Ann-Campbell is with Joe Pete and I'm to enjoy the rest while she's gone."

"Mama, listen."

Justine looked up. She was seated at the kitchen table, holding both hands rigid. Between each finger were long sprays of raw spaghetti. "Look, Meg!" she said. "I'm learning the I Ching!"

"Is that all you have to do?"

"Well, we should use yarrow stalks but we don't know what they are."

"I just want to tell you this," Meg said. "I blame you as much as him."

"What, Meggie dear?"

"The two of you are as closed as a unit can get, I don't care *what* he says."

"Closed? What?" said Justine, looking bewildered. She rose, holding out two spaghetti whiskbrooms. "Wait, Meggie darling, I don't—"

But Meg was gone. She ran across the hall and out of the house. There was no sign of Arthur or Duncan in the yard. Only the Ford, melting into the twilight, with a magazine page flapping in the space where the door should have been: WOULDN'T YOU REALLY RATHER HAVE A BUICK?

9

For the Polk Valley church's April bazaar Justine wore her very best dress—an A-line shift that Duncan had bought her five years ago at a nearly-new sale. She pulled her hair into a sprout on top of her head, covered it over with her hat, and dabbed at her mouth with a pink Tangee lipstick from high school. On her feet she wore her black Mary Janes, on her arm a gypsy bracelet borrowed from the Blue Bottle. Generally speaking, she thought she looked very presentable.

Because the car was in the body shop, Justine had to ask for a lift in Dorcas's baby-blue Cadillac. And Ann-Campbell had to come along, jouncing in the back seat, periodically nosing her sharp little freckled face between the two women to eavesdrop. Justine liked Ann-Campbell. She was certain she was going to lead a very interesting life.

On the way to Polk Valley Dorcas talked about her ex-husband, Joe Pete, whom she had married and divorced three times now. Every time she married him she had a large church wedding all over again, with Ann-Campbell as flower girl in a floor-length organdy dress to cover the scabs, scars, scrapes, bruises, and Band-Aids on her bony knees. Lately relatives had stopped attending, and the gifts had thinned out. "But," said Dorcas, "he's still my first husband, isn't he? I've never been married to anybody else, and neither has he. Why can't I have a wedding like I choose?"

Justine didn't want to think about weddings. They reminded her of Meg. She was worried sick about Meg, who had become very quiet the last few weeks, and whenever she talked it over with Duncan he acted so cross and stubborn that he was no help at all. He said Meg could marry anyone she chose, a Congo chieftain if she cared to, but not a man whose only quality was harmlessness. "Maybe she loves him," Justine said, but doubtfully. She *tried* to believe it. Whenever she saw Arthur she worked at being interested in him. She observed that he was kindhearted, steady, polite . . . and then her mind would trail off to some other subject and she forgot he was there. She watched Meg, who appeared as placid as ever. But then Meg didn't show emotions, that was all. Of course she loved him or she wouldn't say she wanted to marry him.

Oh, the things she had prepared herself for, when Meg was born! Merely the fact of having a new person in the world implied a stream of unforeseen events endlessly branching and dividing. As Meg grew into her teens Justine was braced for long-haired suitors, LSD, shoplifting, pregnancy, revolutionists, firearms in the closet—anything, for her daughter's sake she could deal with anything! She just hadn't expected Arthur Milsom, exactly.

"Thursday night Joe Pete calls up. 'Will you be at home a while?' Where would I go to? On no alimony at all and six months behind in child support. And Joe Pete's a rich man, Britt Texaco. 'Joe Pete,' I told him, I said, 'all in the world that's left for me to do tonight is read my November seventy-two *Modern Movies*,' and he says, 'Fine, for I'm bringing back your daughter and you owe me forty-eight ninety-five for my new emerald rug which she dribble-bleached with a gallon of Clorox. I won't charge for the Clorox,' he says. 'Well and good,' I tell him, 'you can take that up with the FBI when they haul you in for kidnap.' *I'm* no fool.''

"When he brought me back he stayed all night," said Ann-Campbell.

"It's his English Leather aftershave," said Dorcas.

Justine laughed.

The church parking lot was packed with cars, flashing the afternoon sunlight off their chrome, and ladies were swarming in the front yard and spilling down the hill as far as the cemetery. "I want to get a hot dog," Ann-Campbell said, "and you owe me a balloon from that time at the shopping center, and I need a caramel apple. If they have cotton candy, can I have some? If they're selling lemon sticks—"

"Ann-Campbell, you promised me you would act nice now if I let you stay out of school today."

"In school we do this math," Ann-Campbell told Justine.

"*Oh* yes," said Justine, who had disliked math.

"If five mothers are fighting over ten blond wigs, how many does each of them get? They want me to say two, but how can I be sure? Maybe one wig's ugly and nobody takes it. Maybe one mother's stronger than the rest and she gets five. Or one's got a head that's too big for the—"

"Ann-Campbell Britt, you are sending a shooting sharp pain right down between my shoulder blades," her mother told her.

If Justine had had to choose what child would most likely be Duncan's in all the world, she would have said Ann-Campbell. Never Meg.

The bazaar was in the church basement, down a flight of linoleum steps. It took Justine's eyes a minute to get used to the dimness. Then she saw rows of booths covered with crêpe paper, and more ladies bustling around in pantsuits and varnished hairdos. Justine hated pantsuits. Whenever she saw one she had an urge to tell the owner some scandalous fortune, loudly enough to be heard everywhere: "The father of your next-to-last baby has run off with a cigar-smoking redhead." But she kept her bright smile and waited, clutching her bag, until the woman in charge noticed she was there. Mrs. Edge's pantsuit was pale aqua, Justine's least favorite color. Oh, but she would have to get over this mood she was in. She widened her smile another inch. "I'm Justine Peck," she said. "I promised to come tell fortunes."

"Mrs. Peck? Why, I thought you would be darker. We've heard such amazing things about you, dear. Now *somewhere*, let me see now . . ."

Mrs. Edge led the way toward a card table. It was covered

with a white cloth to which stars and crescent moons had been pinned. Justine followed and behind her came Dorcas, wobbling on her spike heels and humming. There was no telling where Ann-Campbell had got to.

"Now dear, this is your cashbox. I've laid a few dollar bills in for change. Is there anything else you'll be wanting? I do hope you won't be chilly. Perhaps you should have brought a wrap."

"Oh no, I'll be fine," said Justine, who was always burning up.

"Why! Here's Mrs. Linthicum, our pastor's wife. Mrs. Peck here is just a *wizard* telling fortunes, Mrs. L."

"Oh, then you can start on me," Mrs. Linthicum said. *She* was wearing a dress, and a little brown mushroom of a hat. She was a tall wispy woman with freckles seeping through her pink face powder. When she sat down in the folding chair she arranged herself so graciously, smoothing her skirt beneath her and then patting her bosom as if to make certain it was there, that Justine felt an unexplainable rush of sorrow. She reached over without planning to and touched Mrs. Linthicum's freckled hand. "Oh, is it the *left* palm you read?" asked Mrs. Linthicum.

"No, no, I don't read palms," said Justine, withdrawing her hand.

But she could easily have read that one, with its lengthwise groove and the worn wedding ring no wider than a thread.

She took out her cards and unwrapped them. "Why, how fascinating," said Mrs. Linthicum.

"Is there anything in particular you want to know?" Justine asked.

"Oh, nothing I can think of."

Dorcas leaned closer, giving off waves of Tabu, while Justine laid the cards down very, very gently. Madame Olita used to snap them down, but that was before they had started falling apart. When these went, where would she get more? She gazed into space, considering.

"I'm not afraid to hear, if it's bad," said Mrs. Linthicum.

Justine pulled her eyes back to the cards. "Oh, it's not bad, not at all," she said. "You're going to do just fine."

"I am?"

"You'll continue to have money worries, but not serious ones. You shouldn't be so concerned about your children. They will turn out all right. No trips in sight. No illness. You have true friends and a loving husband."

"Well, of course," said Mrs. Linthicum.

"All in all it's a very good life," Justine said. She cleared her throat and steadied her voice. "Anybody would be happy to have a formation like this one."

"Why, thank you very much," said Mrs. Linthicum. Then when the silence had stretched on a while she gave a little laugh and rose to pay her fee, pressing Justine's palm briefly with her cool, wilted fingers. When she left, Justine gazed after her for so long that Dorcas waggled a hand in front of her face and said, "You in there?"

Then others came, woman after woman, giggling a little in front of their friends. "No tall dark strangers? No ocean trips?" Several young girls filed through, a little boy in a baseball suit, a man in platform heels, an old lady. Justine tried to pin her mind to what she was doing. This was how she attracted future clients, after all. "You will have a minor car accident," she told one girl, relieved to see something concrete.

"Even if I drive slower?"

"No, maybe not."

"Then what's the point of all this?"

"I don't know."

"To warn you to *start* driving slower, Miss!" Dorcas cried. "Honestly, Justine! Where are you today?"

Oh, beautiful Dorcas, with her watery silk dress showing dimpled knees and her jangling bracelets and creamy throat! *Her* fortune altered from week to week. Which gave Justine a greater likelihood of error, but at least she enjoyed doing it.

During a lull they captured Ann-Campbell, who was winning too many prizes anyway tossing nickels into ashtrays,

and Justine read her cards. Ann-Campbell leaned over her
with a cone of cotton candy, smelling of burnt sugar and
money. "You'll have to travel your whole life to use up all
the travel cards I'm seeing," Justine told her.

"*I* know that."

Then Dorcas, who had learned palmistry in high school,
examined Ann-Campbell's little square hand—a mass of
warts and deep, soiled lines. "I find travel too," she said,
"but I don't know, Ann-Campbell gets carsick. Let me see
yours, Justine."

Justine turned her palm up. Secretly she had become as
addicted to the future as Alonzo Divich, now that life moved
so quickly.

"Oh, talk about *travel!*" said Dorcas.

"What do you see?"

"Lots of trips. Oh, well, there's much too much to read
here. You have an indecisive nature, there are lots of . . . but
I'm not too sure what *this* means. And then a frequent change
in surroundings and tendency to—"

"But is it a *good* palm?"

"I'm telling you, Justine! Of course it is, it's just full of
things."

"No, I mean—"

Dorcas raised her head.

"Oh well, it doesn't matter," Justine told her finally.

She never did say what she had meant. She sat silent,
frowning at the cracked square of silk in her lap, while beside
her Ann-Campbell started firmly, grimly patting her arm with
the hand that wasn't holding the cotton candy.

Duncan looked up from polishing a Cinderella pastry cutter
and found Justine staring at him through the plate glass window, directly beneath his hand-lettered sign, ANTIC TOOLS
WANTED. She was wearing her fanciest church bazaar outfit
and there was a chain of safety pins dangling from the tip of
her left breast. When he waved she waved back, but she kept
on standing there. He rose and came close to the glass, pop-

ping his mouth like a goldfish. She smiled. "Come *in!*" he shouted.

So she came, leaving the door swinging open behind her. "I was just passing," she told him.

"You want to hear about my movie?"

"Yes."

"I'm going to buy a camera and walk around filming to one side of things, wherever the action isn't. Say there's a touchdown at a football game, I'll narrow in on one straggling player at the other end of the field. If I see a purse-snatcher I'll find someone reading a newspaper just to the right of the victim."

"What's the point?" Justine asked.

"Point? It'll be the first realistic movie ever made. In true life you're *never* focused on where the action is. Or not so often. Not so finely." He stopped and looked at her. "Point?" he said. "You don't usually ask me that."

"Duncan, I wish I knew what we should be doing about Meg."

"Oh. School called. She cut all her afternoon classes, they said. Is she sick?"

"Why, I don't know. I haven't been home."

"Every day this week she's had a headache."

"See there? No wonder I worry," Justine said. "I ought to go look in on her." But instead she sat down on a knobby piano stool he had been trying to get rid of for months. "I am forty and one-third years old," she said.

Duncan blew on the pastry cutter and started polishing it again.

"Doesn't it seem to you that things are going by very fast?"

"I have always thought everything moved too slowly," he said. "But I know I'm in the minority."

"How did we *get* here?"

But when Duncan looked up, she had her eyes fixed on the opposite wall as if she didn't want an answer.

He set down his work and rose to walk around the shop,

passing his rows of polished tools and utensils. They did his heart good. He ignored what Silas had brought in from his tours of the auction sales—the china and scrolled furniture, which he allowed to pile up in dim corners. He paused beside a nineteenth-century pressure scale and laid his hand upon it gradually, delighting in its intricate, precise design. Behind him he heard the familiar *plop, plop* of Justine's cards. What would she be asking, all alone? But when he turned he saw that she was laying the cards absent-mindedly, the way another person might doodle or chew a pencil. Her eyes were on something far away; she smoothed each card blindly as she set it on the sewing chest beside her.

While he watched, she frowned and collected her thoughts. She looked down at what she had laid out. "Why, Duncan," she said.

"What is it?"

"Why—"

"What is it, Justine?"

"Never mind, don't worry. Don't worry."

"Who says I'm worried?"

But she was already out the door, running down the street with her hat streamers fluttering. It was the first time Duncan had ever known her to leave her cards behind.

Daniel Peck was on the front porch, rearranging a sheaf of correspondence, when Justine came dashing up the walk between the rows of sprouting vegetables. She looked wild-eyed and flustered, but then she often did. "Grandfather," she called, "have you seen Meg?"

He tried to think.

"Meg."

"Well, now I wonder where she could be," he said.

"What time is it?"

He fumbled in his pocket and hauled out lengths of gold chain hand over hand, raising his eyebrows when his fingers met up with a watch. "Ah! Five twelve," he said.

She spun past him, into the house, clattering the screen

door behind her. He felt the noise rather than heard it. He felt his bones jar. Then there was peace, and he returned to a letter dated April 10, 1973. He squinted in the twilight at a ragged blue script.

> Dear Mr. Peck:
>
> In response to your query of March 17, I am sorry to say that I do not recall my grandmother's ever mentioning a Caleb Peck or, for that matter, any other young man she used to dance with. I was not aware that she danced. However my cousin Amabel Perce (Mrs. John M.) of Duluth, Minnesota may know more. I myself was never at all close to my grandmother and am certainly not the one to . . .

He sighed. Long white fingers entered his vision, fluttering another letter on top of the first.

> Dear Mama,
>
> I have gone to be married in Arthur's church. We will be living with Arthur's mother. Don't worry about me, I'll finish school in Semple. I will keep in touch.
>
> Love,
> Meg

"Eh? What's this?" he asked Justine.

She merely lifted an arm and dropped it, as if she couldn't speak.

"Why," he said, "*I* didn't know it was proper for ministers to elope."

Justine went down the porch steps, back through the vegetables toward the street, drifting along slower than he had seen her in years.

"Justine? Wasn't that fellow a minister?"

She didn't answer. In the end he simply filed the letter away among his other correspondence and went on with what he had been doing before.

10

By May the whole front yard was a tangle of cucumber vines and little green stalks of corn. Neighbors began knocking on the door. "Justine, of course, it's your lawn to plant as you please although frankly it seems . . . but never mind, what is that smell? What we want to know is, that *smell!*"

"Oh, just things from the blender."

"The—? When you turn down this street it's the first thing you notice. It smells like a zoo. A city dump. A *slaughter*-house."

"I'll mention it to Duncan," Justine said. But her face was lit up and her eyes all curly, she was so happy to see somebody. She would reach out to touch visitors on the wrist or shoulder, drawing them in. "Since you're here, why don't you stay?"

"Oh, well . . ."

"We can sit out back. You won't smell a thing."

"Oh, well, maybe for a minute."

"I'll make you lemonade, or coffee. Anything. What would you like?"

The fact was, Justine hated to be alone. She had felt so restless and unhappy lately, wandering from room to room, trying to start up conversations with her grandfather when he was too busy with his own thoughts to answer. "Grandfather, isn't there any place you'd like to go?"

"How's that?"

"Do you want to *go* somewhere, I said."

"No, no."

She sank back and twisted a piece of her hair. It was impossible to drive off on her own; a car was so private. Like a sealed black box. She would end up speeding just to get her isolation over with, or she would run a stop sign because even horns and curses were better than silence. So instead of driving she walked to Duncan's shop, missing no opportunity to speak to passers-by. "Hello, Mr. Hill, did you get the money I said you would? Where's *Mrs.* Hill? Wait, Red Emma, I'll walk along with you," and she would run to catch up and travel three blocks out of her way, pausing at each house while Red Emma delivered the mail. She parted from people with difficulty, dragging it out, loitering on the sidewalk fiddling with a button and finding new things to say to them. She dreaded walking even half a block with only her own thoughts for company. And when finally she arrived at the Blue Bottle she would be full of pent-up words that exploded from her before she was fully in the door. "Duncan, Red Emma told me . . . Bertha Miller asked . . . oh, Duncan, I just had a thought, can we borrow a wayward girl from the police station?"

"A *what's* that?"

"Surely they must have some, wouldn't you think? We could leave our name and the next time the police arrest somebody they could bring her to us. I mean the house seems so—"

"Well now, wait a minute."

But she would be off to something new, picking up merchandise and putting it down. "Oh look, a locket like Aunt Bea's almost. And Aunt Sarah's dinner ring but the stone's a different color. Isn't it funny they call these antiques? They're only what our aunts wear every day of their lives. What's this thing, Duncan?"

"A Victorian slide pendant," Duncan said glumly. "If you ask me, it's junk. All this stuff is junk. Yesterday Silas brought in a whole carton full, he'd been to some flea market. 'Here, take this,' he said, 'and get rid of that mess on the table, it doesn't look nice.' Do you know what he called *mess?* A genuine chromatrope I bought from old Mrs. Milhauser, and a Boston bathing pan with a pump that still works . . . where is it now? I wanted to show you. He dumped it in some corner or other. He doesn't like tools and things with moving parts, he says they clutter the shop. We spend all our time shifting each other's merchandise into hiding places and out again, in and out. Look at that chair! He likes it. He wants me to ask a hundred and fifty dollars for it.''

Justine looked at a chair with a curved spine that was all pointed leaves and flowers and little sharp berries. On one of its finials Duncan had impaled a liniment ad. ''I've a good mind to quit this job,'' he said, but she didn't bother answering that. He would never quit in the middle of a fight.

She wanted him to come with her somewhere. ''Maybe we could take a trip,'' she told him.

''All right.''

''Just spur of the moment.''

''All right.''

''We might even stop and see Meg.''

But then his face grew cold and stubborn. ''Not a chance. Not until we're asked, Justine.''

''But she *said*. She said in her letters.''

'' 'We'll have you over sometime soon,' is what she said. Pay attention.''

He knew Meg's letters by heart, the same as Justine. It was all an act, his unconcern. (''Duncan,'' she had told him, ''Meg has gone to marry Alfred, I mean Arthur,'' and he had grown motionless for one split second before continuing to close up shop.) ''As long as we don't come for a meal,'' she said now, ''why do we have to wait to be invited?''

''We're not going till we are, I tell you.''

''Oh, that's ridiculous. She's our *daughter*.''

''So what?''

''Remember when she was colicky, all those evenings you walked up and down with Meggie on your shoulder? You sang 'Blues in the Night.' Her head was straight up and wobbling, her forehead would get all wrinkled from trying not to miss a word."

"Merely singing 'Blues in the Night' to someone does not obligate me to pay them an uninvited visit seventeen years later."

"Eighteen," said Justine.

"Eighteen."

"You used to take her to the circus when she was too little to hold down a spring-up seat. For three straight hours you leaned on it for her so she wouldn't pop right up again."

"There was an intermission."

"Even so."

"Merely leaning on a spring-up seat for someone—"

"And she's not just *someone*. She's not just any old person that you would treat so formally the minute she hurt your feelings."

"Who's hurt?" Duncan said.

"Look at Grandfather. Do you know what I found him doing the other day? He was at the kitchen table all hunched over with his head in his hands. I thought something was wrong. Then he sat up and I saw he'd been studying this world map in the Hammond atlas. Not Maryland, not the United States, the *world*, Duncan. That's how far he let Caleb run before he would go after him. Are we going to do that too?"

"We're never going to forget that man, are we," Duncan said. "The one that got away." He set down a crimping iron. "However, we're wandering off the subject here. Meg has not vanished. We know exactly where she is. She writes us a letter once a week. All I'm saying is don't repeat history, give her a little breathing space. Let her ask us first."

"Oh, there's always some excuse."

"I'm just telling you what I think."

"Do you wish I hadn't come after *you*, when you left home?"

"No."

"Well, I wish it sometimes, Duncan Peck."

"No doubt you do," said Duncan.

"And if you ever walk off again, you realize I won't follow. I'll have them declare you legally dead, I'll remarry right away."

"Of course," he said serenely.

There was no way to win a fight with that man.

She stormed out of the shop and then stood on the sidewalk, wondering what to do with herself. Everything seemed irritating. The sunlight was too sharp for her eyes. The traffic was too noisy, a swarm of gigantic glaring station wagons. She hated the way the women drivers were poised at the Main Street traffic light, all lifting their arms simultaneously to orchestrate their hairdos. She turned in the other direction, toward home, which was not where she wanted to be but she couldn't think of any place else.

In the kitchen, her grandfather was washing the dishes. Periodically he had these spells of trying to make the house look cared for. He wore around his waist a striped linen dishtowel with an enormous charred hole in its center. He bent over the sink, unaware of Justine's presence, doggedly scrubbing a saucepan with a piece of dried gourd that Duncan had grown two years ago after reading about its scouring properties. The gourd looked like a chunk of hardened beige seaweed. From time to time he stopped scrubbing and examined it, frowning, as if he found it difficult to believe. Then he rinsed the saucepan and plodded over to the table with it, head bowed, shoulders hunched. "Hello, Grandfather," Justine said. "Grandfather?"

He started and looked up. "Eh?"

"You don't have to wash the dishes."

"I'd like to know what we'd eat off tonight if I didn't."

"We could always go to the diner," Justine said.

"Ha."

He dried the saucepan on a corner of his apron. Then he set it on a stack of meticulously cleaned, polished plates and trudged back to the sink. He was so stooped that, from behind, his head seemed to disappear. All Justine saw was his rounded shoulders, the elastic X of his suspenders in the hollow of his spine, and his trousers draped and formless as if he had no seat. Nowadays, everywhere Justine looked she found something to make her sad.

She would have liked to write Meg another letter, but she had sent one just this morning. So she went instead to Meg's bedroom, to open her closet and stare at the row of shirt-dresses that seemed to be leading a gentle muted life of their own. Someday soon, Meg said in her letters, she would stop by for the rest of her things or her parents could bring them when they came to visit. But Justine felt comforted by what was left behind and she would be sorry to see the room stripped. She took a deep breath of Meg's clean smell: Ivory soap and fresh-ironed fabric. She stroked the collar of the nearest dress, with its precise top-stitching, and then she lifted the cover of the sewing machine to admire Meg's mastery of such a complex, wheeled invention. She would have opened bureau drawers, but Meg was particular about her privacy.

When Meg was a baby, Justine had realized for the first time that it was possible to die. She had felt suddenly fragile under the responsibility of staying alive to raise her daughter. (In those days, she expected to do it perfectly; she thought no one else could manage.) She developed a fear of fire that was so unfounded she couldn't even tell Duncan because of course he would laugh at her. Over and over again she imagined the salty smell of smoke in the air, or a flickering red glow reflected on the wall. If Duncan were home he could get them out of anything, but what if it happened in the daytime while he was at work? By herself she was so young and skinny and incompetent. Then gradually, she developed an escape plan. They were living in Uncle Ed Hodges's garage apartment at the time. If fire broke out she could snatch up the baby, climb out on the kitchen window ledge, and make a long, desperate leap to the roof of Uncle Ed's back porch. Once she had pictured all this she relaxed, and eventually she forgot her fear completely. It was not till years

later, returning to Uncle Ed's for a visit, that she saw that
such a leap would have been insane. It was not only too far,
it was also upward. She would have had to soar through the
air like some surrealistic figure in a painting by Chagall, feet
set neatly together and arms primly clasping the baby. But in
those days, she might have managed anything. She was so
necessary. Even when Meg had left infancy, given up first
Justine's breast and then her lap and finally gone to play in
other rooms altogether, Justine had to *be* there. She had to
be the feeder, the fixer, the sounding board for an endless
stream of announcements. "Mama my dress is dirty, Sammy
hit me, the violets are out. Mama there's a spider in my
chocolate milk, a moth in my bath, a ladybug on the windowscreen. My stomach aches. My mosquito bites itch. Janie
has a hamster, Edwin's in the asparagus, I broke the handle
off my teapot, Melissa has a music box you can watch right
through the glass." Justine nodded, barely listening; the only
answer required was, "Yes, dear." Then Meg was satisfied,
as if things came into existence only when she was certain
her mother knew about them. And now what? Justine had
raised her daughter without dying after all; she was freed
from her fears. But at night she woke up shaky and sad, and
she pressed her face against Duncan's chest and said, "I'm
not necessary any more."

"To me you are," he said.

He didn't see what she meant. He hadn't had that feeling
of being essential to Meg in the first place; he couldn't know
how it felt to lose it.

She wandered to other rooms, to hers and Duncan's with
its unmade bed and scattered clothing, to the hall where she
tripped over a stack of lumber. Everything looked dusty and
stale. She hung out the living room window to be revived by
Ann-Campbell, who was taunting a playmate among the cucumber vines:

> Little boy your teeth are green
> And your tongue it is rotting away.

Better gargle with some gasoline,
Brush with Comet and vomit today.

She returned to the kitchen, feeling more cheerful. "Grandfather, let's take a trip," she said.

"A what?"

"A trip."

"But we don't have any leads right now, Justine."

"Why wait for leads? Oh, why won't anyone *do* anything? Are we just going to sit here? Am I going to get rooted to the living room couch?"

Her grandfather watched her, with his eyes wide and blank and his hands endlessly drying an Exxon coffee mug on the corner of his apron.

Justine took her grandfather to an afternoon concert in Palmfield, although she did not like classical music and her grandfather couldn't hear it. The two of them sat rigid in their seats, directing unblinking blue stares toward the outline of a set of car keys in the violin's soloist's trouser pocket. Then they went home by bus with Justine as dissatisfied as ever, bored and melancholy. Each time strangers rose to leave she mourned them. Who knew in what way they might have affected her life?

She took Duncan, her grandfather, and Ann-Campbell Britt to the funeral of a chihuahua belonging to an old lady client. "*What* is this? *Where* are we going?" her grandfather kept asking. "Don't worry, just come," said Justine. "Why do you care? Just grab up your hearing aid and come, Grandfather. If you want things to happen you have to run a few blind errands, you know." So he came, grumbling, and they sat on folding chairs in a cow pasture that had recently been turned into a pets' memorial garden. "The casket cost one hundred and forty-five dollars," Justine whispered to Duncan. "It's all metal. But they could have settled for wood: thirty-two ninety-eight. Mrs. Bazley told me. She selected the hymns herself. The minister is fully ordained."

"Oh, excellent," said Duncan. "I wonder if he needs an assistant," and after the service he went up and offered Arthur Milsom's address to the minister. But Grandfather Peck wandered among the wreaths and urns looking baffled. Why had he been brought here? Justine could no longer tell him. She rode home beside Duncan without a word, swinging one foot and rapidly chewing coffee beans that she had taken to keeping in a tin container at the bottom of her bag.

On Sundays she drove her grandfather to Plankhurst for Quaker meetings, which used to be something she tried to get out of because she didn't like sitting still so long. Now she would go anywhere. Grandfather Peck was not, of course, a Quaker and had no intention of becoming one, but he resented regular church services because he claimed the minister wouldn't speak up. It made him feel left out, he said. Even the Quakers would sometimes take it into their heads to rise and mumble, perversely keeping their faces turned away so that he couldn't read their lips. Then he whispered, "What? What?"—a harsh sound sawing through the air. He made Justine write everything down for him on a 3 × 5 memo pad he kept in his breast pocket. Justine would click the retractable point of his ballpoint pen in and out, in and out, waiting for a five-minute speech to be over, and then she wrote, "He says that God must have made even Nixon," or "Peace is not possible as long as neighbors can still argue over a lawn mower."

"*That* took him five minutes?"

"Ssh."

"But what was he up there working his mouth all that time for?"

"Ssh, Grandfather. Later."

"You must have left something out," he told her.

She would hand back his pen and pad, and sigh, and check the Seth Thomas clock on the mantel and run her eyes once more down the rows of straight-backed radiant adults and fidgety children lining the wooden benches. After twenty minutes the children were excused, rising like chirping, squeaking mice to follow the pied piper First-Day School teacher out of the room, breaking into a storm of whistles and shouts and stamping feet before the door was properly shut again. She should have gone with them, she always thought. The silence that followed was deep enough to drown in. She would plow desperately through her straw bag, rustling and jingling, coming up finally with her tin container of coffee beans. When she bit into them, she filled the meetinghouse with the smell of breakfast.

Once her grandfather wrote on the pad himself, several lines of hurried spiky handwriting that he passed to her. "Read this out when no one else is talking," he whispered. She struggled to her feet, hanging onto her hat. Anything to break the silence. "My grandfather wants me to read this," she said. " 'I used to think that heaven was—palatable? Palatial. I was told it had pearly gates and was paved with gold. But now I hope they are wrong about that. I would prefer to find that heaven was a small town with a bandstand in the park and a great many trees, and I would know everybody in it and none of them would ever die or move away or age or alter.' "

She sat down and gave him back the memo pad. She took the top off her coffee beans but then she put it on again, and kept the container cupped in her hands while she gazed steadily out the window into the sunlit trees.

One afternoon toward the end of May the doorbell rang and Justine, flying to answer it, found Alonzo Divich standing on the porch. Although it was hot he wore a very woolly sheepskin vest. He carried a cowboy hat, swinging by a soiled string. "Alonzo!" Justine said.

"I was afraid you might have moved," he told her.

"Oh no. Come in."

He followed her into the hall, shaking the floor with each step. Grandfather Peck was on the living room couch writing a letter to his daughters. "Don't get up," Alonzo called to him, although the grandfather was still firmly seated, giving him that stare of shocked disbelief he always wore for Alonzo. "How's the heart, eh?" Alonzo asked. "How's the heart?"

"Hearth?"

"Nothing's wrong with his heart," said Justine. "Come into the kitchen, Alonzo, if you want your cards read. You know I can't do it right with Grandfather watching."

While she cleared the remains of breakfast from the table, Alonzo wandered around the kitchen examining things and whistling. "Your calendar is two months ahead," he told Justine.

"Is it?"

"Most people's would be behind."

"Yes, well."

She went to the living room for her carry-all. When she returned Alonzo was standing at the open refrigerator, looking into a bowl of moldy strawberries. "How is my friend Duncan?" he asked her.

"He's fine."

"Maybe I'll drop by and see him. Is Meg out of school yet?"

"She's married."

"Married."

"She eloped with that minister."

"I'm sorry, Justine."

He shut the refrigerator and sat down at the table to watch her shuffle the cards. He looked tired and hot, and the grooves alongside his mustache were silvered with sweat. A disk with Arabic lettering gleamed in the opening of his shirt. Last time it had been a turquoise cross. She didn't ask why; he wouldn't have answered. "Alonzo," was all she said, "you have no idea how it gladdens my heart to see you. Cut, please." He cut the cards. She laid them out, one by one. Then she looked up. "Well?" she asked.

Alonzo said, "You realize, last time I took your advice."

"You did?"

"When you told me not to sell the business."

"Oh yes. Well, I should hope so," said Justine.

"It was the first time you ever said to keep on with something I was already doing."

She stopped swinging her foot.

"But I was tempted to disobey you anyway," he told her. "I admit. I went to see my friend, the one in merchandising. He has these clients, you understand, department stores and such, they come to him for ideas on . . . but anyway. I said I might join up with him. 'Oh, fine,' he tells me. But then he starts suggesting I wear a different style of clothes. Well, that I can follow. I am practical, I know how the world works. But he doesn't see, he's still trying to convince me. 'Face it, Alonzo,' he says, 'we all have to give in in little ways. Look at *me*. I'm a tall man,' he says. And he is, a fine tall man. 'Well,' he says, 'when important clients come, know what I do? I try to stay seated as much as possible, and if I stand I kind of squinch down. I don't *stoop*,' he says, 'that's too obvious. Just bend at the knees a little. Understand, it's not something I think of so consciously. But you can see a client, important fellow like that, he wouldn't feel right if I was to tower over him. You got to keep a watch for such things, Alonzo.' "

He shook his head, and pulled his great silver belt buckle around to where it wouldn't cut into his stomach so.

"Justine," he said, "do you know that I have never before done what you told me to do?"

"I'm not surprised," she said.

"I mean it. You're always right, but only because I go against instructions and things turn out badly just the way you said they would. Now I discover things turn out badly anyhow. Is that your secret? I've found it, ha? You give people advice they'll be sure not to follow. Right?"

She laughed. "No, Alonzo," she said. "And I'm glad you didn't sell the carnival. *Whatever's* gone wrong."

"My mechanic's been arrested."

"Lem?"

"He robbed a bank in nineteen sixty-nine. They *say*."

"Oh, I see."

"Now, here's what I want to know. Is he coming back, or not? I mean if he's coming soon I'll hold the machines together somehow and wait it out, but if he's guilty, on the other hand—"

"Well, I don't think I'm supposed to say if someone's *guilty* or not."

"Look here! What do I care about guilt? All they lost was two hundred dollars, let him keep it. Besides a little matter of a shooting. I want to know about my *business*. I want to know if I should just give up, because to tell the truth this fellow Lem was a man I relied on. He saw to everything. Now, merchandising is out but there is always something else, and the jodhpur lady still wants my carnival. Shall I sell, after all? Is the man gone forever?"

Justine frowned at a card.

"You see what I've fallen to," Alonzo said. "I used to ask about beautiful women. Now it's financial matters."

"Well, Lem is not coming back," said Justine.

"I knew it."

"But you shouldn't sell the carnival."

"How can you keep saying such a stupid thing?"

"Don't argue with me, argue with the cards. Have you ever seen anything like it? I've turned up every jack in the deck, you'll have all the mechanics you want."

"Oh, of course," Alonzo said. "One after the other. The first one drinks, the second leaves with my ponies—"

"And look at the women! Look, Alonzo, you're not paying attention. See? Here you are, the king of hearts. And here's the queen of hearts, the queen of clubs, the queen of diamonds . . ."

Alonzo sat forward, peering at the cards, resting his hand upon his knees.

"Here is the good luck card, the card of friendship, the celebration card . . ."

"All right, all *right!*" Alonzo said.

She sat back and smiled at him.

"Oh, Justine," he told her sadly, "sometimes I think I

would like to go live in a cabin in the woods, all alone. I'd take a lifetime supply of slivovitz, my accordion, plenty of food, perhaps some books. Do you know I've never read an entire book? Just the good parts. I think about hibernating like a bear, just eating and drinking and sleeping. No tax, insurance, electric bills, alimony, repairs or repainting or Rustoleum, no women to mess up my life, no one shooting bank guards, no children. Then here you come galloping along in your terrible hat and your two sharp hipbones like pebbles in your pockets and you tell me all these things I may expect, a life full of surprises. How can I refuse? I feel curious all over again, I like to know what will happen next.''

And he shook his head, stroking downward on his mustache, but he did not look so tired as when he had arrived. All his tiredness seemed to have passed to Justine, who sat slumped in her chair with her hands limp on the cards.

Duncan and Justine were on the front steps, watching the fireflies spark all around them. ''Today I sold an antique garden engine,'' Duncan said.

''What's a garden engine?''

''It's this big wheeled thing to spray water on your flowers. What a relief! I bought it with my own money in a moment of weakness. I kept it sitting in the back room; I had to open the double doors to get it in and then I was afraid it would go right through the floorboards. A man named Newton Norton bought it. He's just started reconstructing this old-time farmhouse out in the country.''

''Well, that's nice,'' said Justine.

''He also bought some fuller's shears, and all my carpentry tools.''

''That's nice.''

He looked over at her.

''When I went into Meg's room,'' she said, ''and found her note telling me she'd gone, I never read anything that hurt so. But then I looked up, and there I was reflected in the window that was just starting to go dark outside. There were these deep black shadows in my eyes and cheekbones. I thought, 'My, don't I look interesting? Like someone who has had something *dramatic* happen.' I thought that!''

She laid her face against Duncan's sleeve. Duncan put his arm around her and pulled her closer, but he didn't say anything.

11

Lucy Peck had to ride in the suicide seat, beside her husband Two, who was driving. Laura May and Sarah got to sit in back. Lucy had to put up with the hot air rushing in Two's open window and Mantovani playing much too loudly on the radio. She had to say what roads to take when she couldn't even *fold* a map right, much less read it. "Now the next thing is you're going to turn left, about a quarter-inch after Seven Stone Road. Or, I don't know. What would a little bitty broken blue line seem to mean?" Her husband set his front teeth together very, very delicately, not a good sign at all. A bumble bee flew in past his nose, causing Lucy to cry out and fling her road map into the air. And meanwhile there sat Laura May and Sarah, protected by layered hats with brown veils, contemplating two separate views peacefully like children being taken for a drive.

It was the sixth of June and they were on their way to Caro Mill, Maryland, to celebrate their father's ninety-third birthday. Unfortunately his birthday fell on a Wednesday this year, which meant that no one who worked could come along. And Bea was confined to her bed with lower back pain. It was up to them: Lucy and the maiden aunts, and Two, who was now retired. Between them they had loaded the car with presents and fruit, a Thermos of Sanka, Laura May's needlework, Sarah's knitting, insect repellent, sunscreen, Bufferin, Gelusil, a Triple-A tour guide, a can of Fix-a-Flat, a fire extinguisher, six emergency flares, and a white banner reading SEND HELP. They had had the Texaco man check the gas, oil, water, brake fluid, transmission fluid, tire pressure, and windshield cleaner. Then Two nosed the car out into traffic and they were on their way, with enough horns honking behind them to remind Lucy of an orchestra tuning up. Young people nowadays were so impatient. Luckily Two was not a man who could be fussed, and he went on driving at his same stately tempo. In his old age he had shrunk somewhat, and was made to seem even smaller by his habit of tipping his head back as he peered through the windshield. His eyes were narrow blue hyphens. His mouth was pulled downward by two ropes in his neck. When he decided to turn left from the right-hand lane he signaled imperiously out the window, still facing front, maintaining his cool Apache profile for Lucy to marvel at while behind them more horns honked. "Kindly check the odometer, Lucy," was all he said. "I would be interested in knowing our mileage on this trip."

"Yes, dear."

Once they hit the open road they were dazzled by too much sunshine and too wide an expanse of fields. It was some time since they had been in the country. (One year ago today, to be exact.) Lucy longed for her wing chair in which she could sit encircled, almost, with the wings working like a mule's blinders to confine her gaze to the latest historical romance. The upholstery was embroidered in satin-stitch, which she loved to stroke absently as she read. Then in the back yard her Sea Foam roses were just opening; there were going to be more this year than ever before and she was missing one entire day's worth. And it was so much cooler and greener at home, so shadowy, so thickly treed that when you spoke outdoors your voice came echoing back, clear and close, as if reflected from a vaulted green ceiling not far above your head. Here the sun turned everything pale. Pinkish barns sped past and bleached gray roadbanks, and beige creeks spanned by wooden bridges like dried-up whitening bones. Lucy turned and sought out her sisters-in-law—a double pair of webbed eyes reluctantly drawn to hers. "Really, traveling makes me sad," Lucy told them. But they didn't answer

(Lucy always said such *personal* things), so she faced front again.

At Plankhurst there was a very confusing crossroads and she sent Two thirteen miles out of the way before the mistake was realized. "Oh, I'm just so—I just can't tell you how badly I feel about this," she said. Two grunted. In the back seat her sisters-in-law gave her disappointed looks that made her want to cry. "I just seem to do everything wrong," she said. Nobody denied it.

Two hours out of Baltimore they began to encounter signs for Caro Mill, although still it seemed they were in the depths of the country. The only buildings were farmhouses, widely scattered, and occasionally a little grocery store patched with soft drink ads. Then they swooped over a hill and there was the town all spread out before them, a clutter of untidy buildings. They had traveled this Main Street annually for years, although each time in a different location. They had passed this very Woolworth's, diner, pizza parlor, fabric store displaying dingy bolts of cloth turning gray along the creases. Still, Lucy sat up straighter and began perking the lace at the neck of her dress. Two pressed his thin white hair flat against his head, and in back there were rustles and whispers. "Oh, I do hope Father likes the—" "Remind me to ask Father if he wouldn't care to—" But Duncan was the one Lucy thought of, not her father-in-law at all. It was for Duncan she had bought this hat (only wouldn't he think the wooden cherries were—old-ladyish, maybe?) and put on these coins of rouge and her eighteen-hour girdle and the Sunday pearls. (Only come to think of it, hadn't he always laughed at the family's fondness for pearls?) She twisted her rings. "Perhaps he won't be home," she said.

"Who?" Two asked, although of course he knew.

"It *is* a working day. Though Justine said he comes home for lunch. But perhaps he won't. I mean, one time—"

One time when they visited he had gone fishing with a friend. A *plumber* or something. Another time he had wandered around the house all afternoon wearing earphones on a very long cord, following a baseball game. You could only grasp the depth of the insult when you remembered that Duncan did not like sports and would prefer to do almost anything but listen to a game. "*One* time—" she said, but Two's voice cracked across hers like a whip.

"Leave it," he said. "What'd you do with Justine's letter?"

"Letter?"

"Her *letter*, Lucy. Telling us how to get to their house."

"Oh. Oh, why I—"

She remembered suddenly that she had left the letter at home on the dining room buffet, but she didn't want to say so. "Why, *someplace* here," she said, riffling through her pocketbook. Two let out a long puff of air. He slowed and beckoned from the window, startling a fat lady standing on the median line. "Pardon me," he said. "We are looking for Watchmaker Street. For twenty-one Watchmaker Street."

"Oh, *Justine*," the lady said.

Everyone flinched. Justine's name was always bandied about so. Like common property.

"Why, you just turn left at the next light," she said, "go two blocks and turn left again. That's Watchmaker Street."

"Thank you."

He rolled the window all the way up.

Now they were silent, concentrating on the view, wondering what sort of house they were headed for. Hoping, just this once, for something really fine. But no. Of course: there it was, a flimsy, no-account little place. Tacked to the screen was what appeared to be a magazine ad for traveler's checks. YOU ARE FAR, FAR FROM HOME, it said, IN UNFAMILIAR TERRITORY . . . But then out flew Justine, barefoot, glowing, in a dress with a lopsided hem. "Uncle Two!" she cried. "Aunt Lucy! You got here!" She hugged them—some of them twice over. She called for her grandfather, who naturally couldn't hear. She showed Laura May and Sarah up the rickety steps and into the house to find him, and then she ran out again to help Two and Lucy unload the trunk. "Duncan will be here in a minute," she said. "He's coming for lunch. Oh look! This is Aunt Bea's gift, I know the wrapping. Will you look at that bow?" But then she dropped it. Fortunately it was not breakable. Lucy had often wondered: was accident-proneness *catching*? Justine had been such a careful little girl. "I wrote and asked Meg to come too but they're having final exams," Justine said. "It seems to me these birthday parties get smaller every year. She sent her love to all of you."

"Oh, bless her heart," Lucy said. "Well, some of these things are her wedding presents. Did we tell you we're giving her your great-grandma's silver?"

Not a one of them was tactless enough to comment on Meg's manner of marrying.

"Now," said Two. "Tell me straight. How's Duncan's business going?"

"Oh, fine, Uncle Two. Just fine."

"What is it again? Jewelry?"

But then Grandfather Peck came down the steps, bending in an odd flimsy way at the knees, and he had to be greeted and fussed over. Lucy kissed his bristly white cheek, Two shook his hand. "Happy birthday!" Lucy shouted.

"How's the what?"

"Happy birthday!"

He looked at her for a moment, considering. "Oh, very well, thank you," he said finally.

"You don't have to shout, Aunt Lucy," Justine told her. "Only narrow *in*. You know what I mean?"

"Oh yes," said Lucy, although she didn't. They went through this on every visit.

Once they were inside the house, there was the usual difficulty in knowing what to say about it. Certainly *some* comment seemed called for. But the rooms were small and dark. The windows were curtained only by great tangles of plants all merging and mingling and sending long runners clear across the floor. There were not nearly enough places to sit. In one of the little back bedrooms, Lucy was horrified to glimpse an absolutely bare, rust-stained mattress, striped blue and white. It reminded her of the time her church group had toured a flophouse for their social service project. "Justine, dear heart," she said, "have we interrupted your bedmaking?"

"My what? Oh no, I'm going to run the sheets down to the laundromat this evening."

"Perhaps I could help you put the fresh ones on."

"But I don't have any others," Justine said.

Lucy sat down very suddenly on a chrome-legged chair that had been dragged out of the kitchen.

Grandfather Peck never would open his presents until after lunch. He had them taken to the table, and meanwhile he and Two settled themselves in the living room and discussed business affairs. Since both of them were retired, it was a vague, wistful, second-hand sort of discussion. "Dan I believe is very much involved with that Kingham matter," Two said. "*You* remember Kingham."

"Oh yes. What was that again?"

"Well, let's see, I'm not quite . . . but he says it's moving just fine."

"Fine, is it."

Perhaps Two should not have retired just yet. But he would feel better when his brothers joined him—Dan in two years, Marcus the year after that. (Sixty-eight was the age they had agreed upon.) Then Claude and Richard could run things on their own. There was no point in working yourself straight into the grave. Still, Two seemed bored and listless as he sat sunk in a corner of the threadbare couch. His father nodded opposite him. His father was so aged that he had reached a saturation point; no new wrinkles had been added in years. He looked not much different from the way he had at seventy. Not much different from Two, as a matter of fact. They might have been brothers. This was how they all ended up, then: arriving at some sort of barrier and sitting down to wait for death, joined eventually by others who had started out later. In the end, the quarter-century that divided their generations amounted to nothing and was swept away. Lucy passed a hand over her own wispy, corrugated forehead. She looked at Two, a handsome man whom she had determined to call Justin back when they were courting, but finally she had given in and called him what his family did. They won, as they always had. Everything was leveled, there were no extremes of joy or sorrow any more but only habit, routine, ancient family names and rites and customs, slow careful old people moving cautiously around furniture that had sat in the same positions for fifty years.

But just as she felt herself sinking into a marsh of despair, she heard Duncan's light quick step across the porch. She saw him fling the screen door open—such a tall boy, or man rather, with his eyes lit from within and that awning of fair hair flopping over his high, pure, untouched forehead. She rose and smoothed her skirt down and held her purse more tightly to her stomach. "Duncan, darling," she said. His kiss was as hurried as ever, brief and light as a raindrop, but she felt her heart floating softly upward and she was certain that this time everything was going to go wonderfully.

For lunch Justine served baked ham, potatoes, and snap beans. Everyone was pleasantly surprised. "Why, Justine," said Two, "this is excellent. This ham is very tasty."

"Oh, Grandfather did that."

"Hmm?"

They stared at her. She seemed perfectly serious. Her grandfather was absorbed in salting his beans and could not be contacted.

For dessert they had a layer cake with nine large candles on it and three small ones. Lucy watched closely while it was sliced. "Is it a mix, dear?" she asked.

"Oh, no."

"You made it from scratch?"

"Grandfather made it."

This time, he looked up. He gave them a shy, crooked smile and then lowered his white eyelashes. "Why, Father Peck!" Lucy said.

"I did the ham too," he said. "She tell you that?"

"Yes, she did."

"Also the potatoes. I baked them first, you see, then scooped them out . . . found it in Fannie Farmer. Some people call them potato boats."

Two looked at his watch.

"The cake is what is known as a war cake," said the grandfather. "It makes do with considerably less butter and eggs than we would normally use, you see. After all, we're living in reduced circumstances."

He seemed to savor the last two words: reduced circumstances. Lucy thought they sounded smugly technical, like devaluated currency or municipal bonds. For a very brief moment she wondered if he didn't almost *enjoy* this life—these dismal houses, weird friends, separations from the family, this moving about and fortune telling. If he weren't almost proud of the queer situations he found himself in. But then Sarah said, "Remember Grandma's orange peel cake?" and his face became suddenly thin and lost.

"Oh. Oh yes," he said.

"She used to mix it secretly in the pantry. Remember? She said she would give the recipe to Sulie but Sulie says she never did. Although of course we can't be too sure of that."

"I wonder what was in it," Justine said dreamily, and she paused so long with her knife in mid-air that Two grew impatient.

"*Come* on," he said. He looked at his watch again. "It's one thirty-two. Do you always have dinner so late?"

"Mostly we don't have dinner at all," Justine said.

"I ask because last year we ate around noon. Dessert was served shortly before one."

"Was it?"

"The year *before* that, we ate even earlier."

"Did we?"

"Is this a new hobby of yours?" Duncan asked Two. "Are you planning to graph us?"

"To—no. No, it's just a little matter of timing, you understand. I thought the presents would be opened by one o'clock. Maybe we could do them before dessert.''

''But I had counted on enjoying my cake,'' the grandfather said.

He and Two stared at each other, a pair of old, cross men. ''This is a matter of timing, Father,'' Two told him.

''Of what?''

''Timing!''

''Speak up.''

Two groaned.

''The worst of it is,'' Lucy whispered to Justine, ''now Two is growing a teensy bit deaf himself.''

''I most certainly am *not*,'' Two said.

''Sorry, dear.''

Two picked up a small flat package. ''From Sarah,'' he said. ''Happy birthday.''

Two's father took the package and turned it over. How many times had Lucy watched him painfully untie a bow, peel off the Scotch tape, remove the paper and fold it carefully for future use before he would look to see what he had been given? Year after year he received this cascade of shirts and socks and monogrammed handkerchiefs, all in glossy white boxes and handsome paper, tied with loopy satin bows. To each gift he said, ''Why, thank you. Thank you very much,'' after which he replaced it in its box. Probably none of these things would ever be used. Except, of course, Justine's: a crumpled white sack of horehound drops that honestly seemed to delight him, although that had been her gift for as long as anyone could remember. ''Can you figure it out?'' he said. ''Stuff's practically impossible to find any more but every year she manages. Expensive, too. *Justine* makes do with Luden's cough drops but I fail to see the resemblance myself.'' He popped a lozenge in his mouth and passed the sack around. Only Justine took one. Nobody else could stand them. ''Last chance till next year,'' he told Lucy, flooding her with his pharmaceutical breath. Lucy shook her head.

Duncan of course gave nothing at all, and would never allow Justine to pencil his name beside hers on the sack of horehound drops. He didn't believe in celebrating birthdays. He would give presents any time, to anyone, sudden surprising *touching* presents, but not when the rules said he was supposed to. And this year there was no gift from Meg either. Lucy was watching. No so much as a tie clasp or a bureau top organizer. She felt a brief surge of wicked joy: now Duncan himself knew the pain of having an ungrateful child. Perhaps he had thought, when Meg eloped, So this is what it feels like! This is what my parents have had to put up with all my life! But then she was ashamed of herself, and she felt truly sorry that her granddaughter had somehow forgotten such an important occasion.

Next to last came Laura May's gift: needlework, as usual. This year a family tree, embroidered on natural linen with a wooden frame. "Why, thank you," said her father. "Thank you very much." But instead of setting it back down, he held it in both hands and looked at it for a long, silent moment. A diamond shape, that was what it was. Lucy had never noticed before. Justin alone began it and Meg alone ended it. In between there was a sudden glorious spread of children, but what had they come to? Nothing. Claude, Esther, the twins, and Richard stood alone, unmarried, without descendants. (Laura May had tactfully left off all record of Sally's divorce and Richard's annulment.) Only Duncan on the far left, son of the oldest child, and Justine on her far right, daughter of the youngest child, were connected by a V-shaped line that spilled out their single offspring at the bottom of the diamond. There was no room for anyone below Meg's name. Lucy shook her head. "But," said Justine, "maybe Meg will have six children and things will start all over again!"

Maybe so. Lucy pictured the diamond shape endlessly repeated, like the design on the border of a blanket. But the thought failed to cheer her up.

Then came the last gift, the largest, a gigantic cube two feet square. The card was the largest too. It had to be.

*Birthday greetings and many happy returns from your sons
Justin II, Daniel Jr., and Marcus.*

"*Well* now," said Grandfather Peck.

Two began chuckling. The wrapping was a joke.

First the striped paper, then a large white box. A slightly
smaller box inside, then fleur-de-lis paper covering another
box, then another, another . . .

Grandfather Peck grew bewildered. Mountains of ribbon
and tissue rose around him. "What's all this?" he kept asking. "What's . . . I don't understand."

"Keep going," Two said.

He and his brothers had spent an entire evening working
on the wrapping. Ordinarily they were not humorous men,
but while fitting cartons inside cartons on Lucy's dining room
table they had chortled like schoolboys, and Lucy had had
to smile. She smiled now, seeing Two's face all squeezed
together to keep the laughter in. "Go on, go on," he kept
saying.

A hatbox, containing a shoebox, containing a stationery
box, containing a playing card box, containing a matchbox.
And finally the gift itself, wrapped in white paper. Two was
laughing so hard that the corners of his eyes were damp. "It's
a joke," he explained to Duncan. "See?"

"Typical," said Duncan.

"No, see? They did it at this office party, when Dan's
secretary got married. They wrapped a little tiny present in
a great big box, funniest thing you ever saw."

"It would be funnier if they had wrapped a great big present in a little *tiny* box," said Duncan.

"No, see—"

Grandfather Peck removed the Scotch tape from the minute rectangle of paper. He opened the paper carefully, but
for once did not fold it and set it aside. Perhaps because it
was too small. Perhaps because he was too shocked: his
present was a single calling card.

" 'Worth and Everjohn, Inc.,' " he read out. " 'Your Local Domestic Investigation Agency. 19 Main Street, Caro

Mill, Maryland. Why Stay in Doubt? Call Us and Find Out. All Reports in Strictest . . .' " He looked up at Two. "I don't quite understand," he said.

But instead of answering Two rose and left the room. They heard him open the front screen door. "All right now!" he shouted.

The man he brought back with him looked like Abe Lincoln, even to the narrow border of beard along his jawline. He wore a black suit, a very starched white shirt, and a string tie. Probably he was in his thirties, but his weary, hungry expression made him seem older. Runlets of sweat streaked his temples. There was a pulse in the hollow of one cheek. "Sorry to have kept you out there so long," Two was saying. "I know you must be hot."

"Oh, I didn't have nothing else to do."

"Father, this is Mr. Eli Everjohn," Two said.

Mr. Everjohn held out his hand, which seemed to have an unusual number of bones in it. Grandfather Peck peered into his face. "I don't understand," he said.

"Your birthday present, Father."

"Oh, naturally," Duncan said to no one. "I'm surprised they didn't gift-wrap the man himself."

"Well, they thought of it," Lucy told him.

"Father, Mr. Everjohn's a detective," said Two.

"Yes?"

"He tracks people down."

"Yes, of course," said Grandfather Peck. He waited patiently, ready to smile as soon as he saw the point.

"He's going to track Uncle Caleb for you."

"How's that?"

"See, Dan and Mark and I pooled together and hired him. We thought, why not get this thing settled? I mean determine, once and for all, that Uncle Caleb is . . . I mean *you're* not getting anywhere, Father. Now we'll spare no expense. We've picked a man who's located here so that you can keep tabs, help out in any way that's needed, and no matter how long it takes we're prepared to foot the bill. Understand? That's our little gift to you. Happy birthday."

His father stared at him.

"Didn't you hear?" Two asked.

"But I don't . . ."

Mr. Everjohn's hand remained outstretched, motionless. You would think that he went through this every day.

"I don't believe I require any assistance, thank you just the same," Grandfather Peck told him.

"But Father! It's your birthday present."

"Then it's his to refuse," Duncan said.

"Stay out of this, Duncan."

Duncan rose and came around the table. He shook Mr. Everjohn's hand. "I believe," he said, "that my grandfather likes to track his own people."

"Certainly, for fifteen *years!*" Two shouted.

But he was not a shouting man. Even his sisters, fluttering their hands toward their ears, couldn't hold it against him. This was all Duncan's doing, some germ he spread. "Two, dear," Lucy told him, and right away he lowered his voice.

"Oh," he said, "don't think I don't know why you've let him live here, Duncan. You *like* to see this happening, your grandfather chasing rainbows on the Greyhound bus line. But consider him, for once. At the present rate, how long will it be before he's successful?"

"Forever, probably," Duncan said. "But at least he's happier than most other Pecks I know."

Everyone looked at the grandfather. He stared blandly back, not giving away a thing.

"And I doubt if success is what we want here," said Duncan. "What would you do with Caleb now? Where would you fit him in? In the end you'd just have to let him run on, like a fox after a foxhunt."

"Oh, was he a sportsman?" Mr. Everjohn asked.

"What? I don't know. No."

"Of course not," said Two.

Mr. Everjohn took a spiral notebook from his shirt pocket. He uncapped a Bic pen and wrote something down. In the sudden silence Justine said, "Maybe you'd like a seat."

"What for?" Duncan asked. "He's not staying."

And his grandfather said, "Yes, actually *Justine* and I—"

"That's just what we're trying to spare you," Two told him. "These endless, fruitless searches, wandering about the country like a pair of—let a professional do it." He turned to Duncan. "As for what to do with Caleb," he said, speaking very low and fast, "I seriously doubt that that problem will arise. If you follow me."

"What, do you imagine he's dead?"

Two gave his father a sidelong glance.

"You can't stand to think he's alive and well and staying away on *purpose*," Duncan said. "Can you? But he's a Peck and he's not even ninety, barely in his prime. I'll bet you a bottle of bourbon he's sitting in an old folks' home this very minute watching *The Dating Game*."

Grandfather Peck slammed a hand down on the table. Everybody stared.

"I've stood a lot from you, Duncan," he said, "but not this. *I do not have a brother in an old folks' home.*"

If he had spoken to Lucy that way she would have crumbled and died, but Duncan only raised his eyebrows. (And though she blushed for him, she felt a little thrill that nothing these Pecks could do would ever really touch him.)

"Mr. Everjohn," said the grandfather, "I'll tell you all I know, and then you get to work. I am not a drinking man but I want to collect a bottle of bourbon from my grandson here."

Then he stood up and led Mr. Everjohn to the living room. Two went with them but the others stayed in the kitchen, gazing down at their slices of cake, which no one had the appetite for. Lucy tore her napkin to shreds and wondered where the Gelusil was. Sarah fanned herself with a sheaf of folded wrapping paper. Justine was chewing on a birthday candle and Laura May had picked up the family tree to admire her own embroidery. Only Duncan, circling the table aimlessly, seemed to have any energy left. He whistled something unfamiliar. He touched a strand of Justine's hair as he passed. He looked over Laura May's shoulder at the family tree. "Has it occurred to you," he asked her, "that someone somewhere may still be searching for Justin?"

By four o'clock Two still hadn't made a move to go. And he was the one who hated night driving! He said he had to get everything straight with the detective first. Lucy could tell he was beginning to regret his choice, not that there *was* much choice in a town like Caro Mill. This Mr. Everjohn was turning out to be a little peculiar. The more peculiar he got the grimmer Two's face grew, and the gayer Duncan's. Justine became downright hospitable and offered Mr. Everjohn root beer and birthday cake. By now they were all in the living room, the aunts in a row on the couch and the others in kitchen chairs, having been lured there one after another by the goings-on. Grandfather Peck was giving Mr. Everjohn the names of every classmate Uncle Caleb had ever had. Every teacher, friend, and business associate. Where did he get them all? Then Uncle Caleb's church, school, barber, tailor, doctor, tavern . . . she had never known a Peck to frequent a tavern. But Mr. Everjohn did not look surprised. He continued filling his spiral notebook, scribbling away at unexpected moments for unexplainable lengths of time. He requested and pocketed the grandfather's treasured photo, saying he would have a copy made, but why, when it was half a century out of date? He listened to a recital of the entire attendance sheet of a vacation Bible school that had opened, and closed forever, in the summer of 1893. Whole strings of names were allowed to slip by, but then he would pounce on one and fill two pages. What was he writing? Lucy sat up very straight, but she couldn't see into his lap.

Now another peculiar thing was, how a man of business could spare so many hours. Naturally a detective was not like a *lawyer* or anything, but still you would think he had appointments and commitments. Mr. Everjohn seemed ready to give the Pecks the rest of his life. He sat without fidgeting, keeping his sharp knees clamped together and his elbows close to his body. One trouser leg was rucked up to show a shin like a stick of timber. He wrote with his pen held so awkwardly that it made Lucy's hand ache. When he asked questions, they were always the least likely. For instance, he wanted to know Uncle Caleb's smoking habits, the name of his childhood nursemaid, his mother's birthday, and his preference in shoes. He asked about Laura's reading matter and Justin's will, about religious beliefs and shipping schedules. The stranger the questions, the more excited Grandfather Peck became. It was like going to the doctor for a headache and having him examine your toenails. What undreamed-of things he must know! Even when Mr. Everjohn asked about Margaret Rose, Grandfather Peck barely flinched. "Of course, that's something I never think about," he said. "I've forgotten her entirely."

"Ah," said Mr. Everjohn. When he opened his mouth like that, his face became impossibly long and his cheeks sank in.

"Anyway, she left before Caleb did," said the grandfather.

"Now where was it she went to?"

You could have heard a pin drop.

"Washington," said the grandfather.

"Oh yes."

"She got a job. But she died."

"What kind of job?"

"There's not much point in going into this," the grandfather said.

"I got to know anyway, Mr. Peck."

"Uh, she laundered money."

"Money."

"She worked for the U.S. Treasury. She washed old bills."

Mr. Everjohn's deep, bruised-looking eyes searched mournfully around the room.

"It's perfectly possible," Duncan told him. "They used to wash them and coat them with rosin. For crispness. In the past they weren't so quick to throw things away. They had a machine that—"

"I see," said Mr. Everjohn. "Cause of death?"

"Boardinghouse fire," said Grandfather Peck.

"She lived in a boardinghouse?"

"Her parents wouldn't *let* her stay with them, you see. In those days women were expected to be better behaved. They tried to make her come back to Baltimore. Her father wrote and told me."

"Now. You sure she really died."

"They buried her, didn't they?"

"I was thinking maybe that was where your brother went to: Washington. Maybe the *two* of them. You ever consider that?"

Lucy had. But Grandfather Peck was merely impatient. "If he were such a scoundrel, why would I be looking for him?" he asked.

"*Oh* yes," said Mr. Everjohn, and he seemed perfectly satisfied. He slipped the notebook and pencil back into his pocket. "Well, I think I got something here to start on."

"We certainly appreciate your making a housecall, Mr. Everjohn," Two said.

"Why, that's all right."

"I never expected to take so much of your time, but of course I am fully prepared to—"

"Think nothing of it," Mr. Everjohn said. "To be honest, this town don't keep a man very busy." He felt beneath his chair for his hat and then rose, unfolding foot by foot. With a hat on he looked more like Lincoln than ever. The crown was even slightly squared, the brim oddly curved. "There's so little call for us, me and my partner have to shadow each other's wives for practice," he said.

"Really," said Two.

"Women's lives are right dull, I've found. My partner's

wife goes to one store for toothpaste and another for mouth-wash, just to get herself two outings."

"Well, I know you have to be getting back," said Two.

"Now *my* wife takes *lessons*. She will sign up for any-thing. You wouldn't believe the places Joe has got to follow her to."

"May I expect your bill on a monthly basis?"

"Pet grooming. Exotic dance. Kung-fu. Stretch-'n-Sew."

"Oh, Eli!" cried Justine, making one of her shocking leaps to a first-name friendship. "Won't you take your wife a piece of birthday cake?"

"She's on this diet," Mr. Everjohn said gloomily. "She goes to Weight Watchers and Slenderella, and every Thurs-day from two to four she's got her this class in low-carbohydrate food preparation." He shook Justine's hand too hard. "I'll keep in touch," he told her.

"Well, drop in any time. Grandfather will want to hear."

"And thank you again for your patience," Two said.

But the minute Mr. Everjohn was out the door, Two col-lapsed in his chair. "I knew we should have used a Baltimore man," he told Lucy.

"Well, there, dear."

"I must have the names of twenty good detectives back home. But no, Marcus said it had to be a Caro Mill fellow. That way Father could handle things, he said. Otherwise *we'd* be the ones to—"

'Well, I thought he was very nice," Justine said, returning from the front door.

"If you children would live in a civilized area, Justine—"

"Caro Mill is civilized."

Two turned to Duncan, who was playing with what looked to be an auto part over by the window. "You need to come back to Baltimore, boy," he said. "What's stopping you? Jobs? You know there's lots to do in a law office that wouldn't take a degree. Your cousins could fix you up. Quick mind like yours, there's *lots* to—"

"Thanks anyway," Duncan said.

"Do Justine good. See there? She's looking a little tired."

Lucy glanced over at her. Why, she was. It was true. Now that she was not running or laughing or talking too much, her face seemed strained and pale. Blame Meg, that's who. Children! She shifted her gaze to Duncan, an aging little boy. Secretly her favorite son, and she had always imagined what a fine man he would be once he was grown and mellowed. But that had never happened. He was preserved forever as he had been at ten, reckless and inconsiderate, not kind at all, not even willing to make allowance for other people's weaknesses. He had needed a good strong wife to settle him down and round his sharp edges, but he hadn't got one. Only Justine. Was Justine the way she was *deliberately?* Had she just flat out decided one day that she would refuse to take responsibility, that Duncan could go caroming straight to hell taking wife and daughter along before she would say a word? Something made Lucy speak up suddenly, when she hadn't even known she was going to. "Oh," she said, "if only poor dear Caroline could have been with us today!"

The look Duncan gave her was as cold and hard as glass, but Lucy felt her little triumph warming all her bones when she saw how still Justine grew.

By the time they were back in the car it was very nearly twilight. Even so, Lucy took the preaddressed envelope out of her purse and unfolded a sheet of stationery and wrote, as Two had taught her to:

Dear Justine,   June 6, 1973

Thank you so much for the lovely time! As always you made a perfectly charming hostess, and the War Cake was delicious. We shall remember our visit with a great deal of pleasure.

                                                        Love,
                                                    Aunt Lucy

She placed the note in the envelope and sealed it. ''Whenever you notice a mailbox, Two . . .'' she said, but then she trailed off, bleakly tapping the letter against her purse. Two moved his lips as he drove. In back, Laura May and Sarah sat side by side beneath veiled brown hats and looked out the windows at their separate views.

12

Now Justine and her grandfather had no place to go. At first they hardly noticed; they traveled less during the summer months anyway. But as June dragged on, hot and humid, and then July took over, Justine grew unhappier. She didn't have enough to do with herself. There was some troubled feeling gnawing at the back of her mind. Uneasiness drove her into quarreling with Duncan, snapping at her grandfather, telling skimpy, half-hearted fortunes for her clients. She spoke with an unplaceable foreign accent for days at a time. She insulted Dorcas. The cat moved out of the house and into the crawlspace behind the rose bushes. Her grandfather sat on the porch, unusually still, with his face slack and vacant.

"Look, Grandfather," Justine said, "isn't there someone you would like to look up? How about that man in Delaware? Maybe he's remembered something new."

"It wouldn't be any use," her grandfather said.

"Well, I don't see why not."

"That detective fellow didn't even take his name down. Took hardly *any* of those names. Seemed to think they would serve no purpose whatsoever."

"Oh, what does *he* know," Justine said.

She had begun to resent Eli's odd, probing questions and the mysterious silence that followed all answers. After each of his visits she felt tampered with. He had a way of arriving when no one was home and settling himself to wait on the front porch. When she and her grandfather returned he would loom up, tall and black as a raven, with his squared-off hat centered over his chest. "Eli!" she always cried, but her heart grew thick, as if preparing against invasion. And her grandfather, who made a point of remembering every passing name, said, "Mr.—ah," and stood scowling down at his shoes like a forgetful schoolboy. But Eli was humble and awkward, and he began by discussing something harmless— his shadowing practice, his wife's calligraphy lessons. After all, he was in no hurry. Then Justine warmed to him all over again, to his absurd fringe of a beard as precise as the brush on a typewriter eraser and his preposterously long, multiple-jointed fingers fumbling at his hat; and her grandfather relaxed enough to grow politely bored. "Come inside, Eli," Justine would say. "I'll make you some iced tea." But at that very moment his face would narrow, his fingers would grow still. "What all were the records your family owned?" he might ask.

"What?"

"*Recordings*. For that old-timey phonograph."

She had to turn to her grandfather, who scuffed the porch floorboards petulantly. "Caruso, I remember," he said finally. "Other things. Red Label discs."

"Oh yes. Red Seal."

"In the beginning they were called Red Label."

"Ah," said Eli.

"Don't you know *anything*?"

"But what besides Caruso? Any more?"

"I don't recall."

"It's something I got to find out," said Eli, but he wouldn't say why. "Well, I reckon I'll just have to go to Baltimore again. You've kept them, now."

"We've kept everything," said Grandfather Peck. And when he went inside he would slam the screen door. Yet it was plain that Eli's questions intrigued him. For the remainder of the day he would be thinking hard, frowning until his eyebrows met. "Can you tell me why he would ask such a thing? What has he got up his sleeve? That fellow must know something we just have no idea of, Justine.''

But for the grandfather, after all, finding Caleb was the only goal. For Justine the point of the search had been the trips themselves, and now she felt bereft and useless. She wandered from room to room, absently carrying her straw bag around with her as if she were a visitor, long after her grandfather had settled himself in the armchair to plan what he would say first when he and Caleb met.

Meanwhile Duncan was selling antique tools by the dozen, by the gross, faster than he could stock them. Why did things always work out this way? Newton Norton, the man who had bought the garden engine, was reconstructing his ancient farm down to the last pitchfork in the barn. He haunted the Blue Bottle, seizing on old rusty pliers and milking lanterns, blacksmith's implements, kitchen utensils. ''If you could see Silas's face!'' Duncan told Justine. ''Sometimes Newton Norton has to call for a truck just to take his purchases home.''

''He must be crazy,'' said Justine. ''What if he has to move someday?''

They were on the front porch, Duncan sitting on a stool while Justine gave him a haircut with the kitchen shears. His hair was thick and straight, audible when it fell. She cut it in layers down the back like a shingled roof, and then when she combed it the layers sifted magically together and evened out. She combed again, floating off into a trance among the shimmering yellow ribbons. She cut another inch off. ''Maybe I should have been a barber,'' she said.

''Let's not get carried away here,'' Duncan told her.

By now it was August and their corn was so tall it blocked their view of the street. Cars swished by unseen, almost unheard. (Duncan was interested in the effect of greenery upon the decibel count.) People walking past were no more than disembodied voices.

''Hello!'' they called, apparently taking it on faith that

someone was there to answer. "Well, hi!" said Justine. She waved her flashing shears in the air. Duncan didn't look up. He had his mind on other things.

"I told Silas, 'See there?' He wouldn't let me buy that old sewing machine of Mrs. Farnsworth's, now he's sorry. Newton Norton tracked it down himself and gave her twice what it was worth. But you know Silas. 'Yes,' he said, 'but once he's got this farm of his set up, what then? Hmm?' Well, yesterday Newton Norton opened his place to the public, a fully working nineteenth-century farm. Admission two dollars. Fifty cents for children. *Plus*. Cooking lessons. A six-week course in old-time American cooking. You learn in this kitchen that has a wood stove and a fireplace big enough to roast an ox. You make cabbage custard and codfish cakes—well, to tell the truth, none of it sounded edible. But *somebody* must like it. All this morning women were coming in asking for sausage guns. Bird's-eye maple sauerkraut mashers. They snatched up these hand-cranked machines that I hadn't even quite figured out yet, things to pare cucumbers and strip corncobs and peel potatoes. By noon I'd sold every utensil in the place."

"Think of that! You're a success," said Justine, trimming around his ears.

"That's what they call it."

But he spoke through a yawn, and then sneezed when a snippet of hair landed on his nose. His face glinted all over with stray blond sparks. He didn't *look* like a success.

On the fourth Sunday in August, the three of them drove to Semple to visit Meg. They were supposed to go earlier but always at the last minute Duncan claimed that something had come up. He had to attend an auction, or a special flea market, now that Silas was urging him to buy more tools. Yet he returned without any tools whatsoever—only, once, a carton of Rusty Prince Albert tobacco tins. "These are antiques?" Justine asked. "Imagine, they used to be garbage. I used to see them in the weeds along Roland Avenue. But where are the tools? What about the kitchen utensils?''

"None of them appealed to me," said Duncan. "Only Prince Albert."

"In the end, the silliest things get valuable. We shouldn't throw *anything* out."

"It doesn't seem to me that we do," said Duncan.

Now he wanted to cancel the trip yet another time (he said there was a Tailgate Treasures near Washington) but Justine had caught on to him. "It's not possible," she said. "You know how long we waited for Meg to invite us. Now we've put her off twice. What will she think?"

"Maybe just you and Grandfather could go. I could go to Washington alone."

"What on, bicycle?"

"I could borrow Silas's station wagon," he said.

"Besides, I don't want to go just with Grandfather. I'd really like you with me this time."

"Maybe in the fall, when things are quieter."

"I don't understand you, Duncan," Justine told him. "What is it you have against this visit?"

But then he grew touchy. He always did object to the way she dragged his secret feelings into the open.

Still, on the fourth Sunday in August there he was, maybe a little grimmer than usual but resigned to the trip, heading the Ford along a gritty two-lane highway toward Semple with Justine sitting beside him and Grandfather Peck next to the window. On the rear seat was a stack of Meg's summer dresses and a paper bag containing a dozen ears of corn. ("But the corn will be wasted," Duncan said. "Reverend Mildew will try to eat it with a knife and fork.") Meg's other belongings—her set of Nancy Drew mysteries and her pennants and bottles of cologne—remained in her room. Duncan had thought they should bring everything in one fell swoop but Justine preferred not to. "All she asked for were her summer dresses," she said. "Maybe she doesn't have space yet for the rest."

Duncan, who never dragged anyone's secret feelings into the open if he could possibly help it, merely nodded and let her have her way.

They reached the outskirts of Semple at two in the afternoon. WELCOME TO SEMPLE, VA., "PRETTIEST LITTLE TOWN IN THE SOUTH," the sign said, looming above a stack of pine boards weathering in a lumberyard. They bounced over railroad tracks, past rusty, gaping boxcars. "Now *there* was a town," said Grandfather Peck. "Had its own train."

"Only freight trains, Grandfather," Justine said.

"Pardon? Freight? Didn't we go to Nashville once from here?"

"That was from Fredericksburg. Three years back."

"Oh yes."

"Here we had to take a bus to Richmond and *then* catch a train."

"Nashville was where that boy played the banjo," said her grandfather. "His great-uncle taught Caleb how to work a stringed instrument when they were both fourteen."

"That's the place," Justine said.

He slumped, as if the conversation had taken everything out of him.

On Main Street Justine saw someone she knew—old Miss Wheeler, who used to ask the cards whether she should put her father in a nursing home—and she wanted to stop and speak to her, but Duncan wouldn't hear of it. "I'd like to get this over with, Justine," he said. Going back to places always did make him cross. When they passed the Wayfarer's Diner and then the Whole Self Health Food Store, whose tattered awning and baggy screens leapt out like familiar faces, Justine could feel the edginess in the skin of his arm. "Never mind, we're only visiting," she told him. But she had trespassed again and he drew himself in, moving slightly away from her so that their arms no longer touched and there was a sudden coolness along her left thigh.

Arthur Milsom's church was a large brick building on the other side of town. Justine had never attended it, but of course

Meg had pointed it out to her—she remembered how the steeple had seemed sharper than necessary, barbed with some glittery metal at the tip. The rectory was brick also, but the house of the assistant pastor, next door to the rectory, was a small white cottage without trees or shrubs, set on a square of artificial-looking grass. There was a bald picture window with a double-globed, rosebud-painted lamp centered in it, and beside the front walk a hitching post in the shape of a small boy with a newly whitened face and black hands. Duncan stopped to study it, but Justine took her grandfather by the elbow and hurried him up the steps. "*Where* is this?" he asked her.

"This is Meg's, Grandfather. We're visiting Meg."

"Yes, yes, but—" And he revolved slowly, staring all about him. Justine pressed the doorbell, which was centered in a brass cross with scalloped edges. From somewhere far away she heard a whole melody ringing out in slow, measured, golden tones. Then the door opened and there was Meg, thinner and more poised, with longer hair. "Hello, Mama," she said. She kissed Justine's cheek, and then her great-grandfather's. When Duncan had turned from the hitching post and climbed the steps she kissed his cheek as well. "Hello, Daddy," she said.

"Well, Meggums."

"I thought you might change your mind and not come."

"Would I do a thing like that?"

She didn't smile.

She led them across sculptured blue carpeting into the living room, where Christ gazed out of gilt frames on every wall. Most of the furniture seemed to come in twos—two identical tables flanking the sofa, two beaded lamps, two ice-blue satin easy chairs with skirted ottomans. On the spinet piano in the corner there were two framed photographs, one of Arthur in a clerical robe and the other of Meg with some sort of shiny drapery across her bare shoulders—but so retouched, so flawlessly complexioned, her hair so lacquered, that it took Justine a moment to recognize her. Besides, what right did some unknown woman have to set Meg's photo in her living room? Justine picked it up and studied it. Meg said, "Oh, that's my—that's just the picture we put in the paper when we—" She snatched the photo away and set it down. "I'll get Mother Milsom," she said.

Justine sought out Duncan, who was slouched on the sofa leafing through a *Lady's Circle*. His feet, in enormous grease-spattered desert boots, were resting on the coffee table. "Duncan!" she said, slapping his knee. He looked up and then moved his feet carefully, picking his way between china rabbits and birds, candles shaped like angels, a nativity scene in a seashell and a green glass shoe full of sourballs. Justine let out a long breath and settled down beside him. Across the room, her grandfather paced the carpet with his hands clasped behind his back. He did not like to sit when he would have to struggle up again so soon for the entrance of a lady. He paused before first one Christ and then another, peering closely at a series of melancholy brown eyes and lily-white necks. "Religious art in the *living* room?" he said.

"Ssh," Justine told him.

"But I was always taught that that was in poor taste," he said. "Unless it was an original."

"Grandfather."

She looked at the door where Meg had disappeared. There was no telling how much could be heard. "Grandfather," she said, "wouldn't you like to—"

"They've got him in the dining room too," said Duncan, peering through the other doorway. "Praying in the garden."

"Oh, Duncan, what do you care? When did you ever give a thought to interior decorating?"

He frowned at her. "So you're going to take their side," he said.

"I didn't know there were sides."

"How's that?" asked her grandfather.

"Duncan thinks I'm defecting."

"Hmm?"

"Defecting."

"Nonsense," said her grandfather. "You're as smart as anybody."

Duncan laughed. Justine turned on him. "Duncan," she said, "I certainly hope you're not going to go into one of your silly fits here. Duncan, I mean this. For Meg's sake, now, can't we just try to—"

But then whispery footsteps crossed the carpet, and a lady in white entered the room with Meg just behind her. "Mother Milsom, I'd like you to meet my mother," Meg said. "And my father, and my great-grandfather Peck." Meg's face was stern and her forehead was tweaked together in the center; she was warning her family not to disgrace her. So Duncan rose to his full height, keeping one thumb in his magazine, while the grandfather touched his temple and Justine stood up and held out her hand. Mrs. Milsom's fingers felt like damp spaghetti. She was a long, wilted lady with light-brown hair parted in the center and crimped tightly to her head, a pale tragic face, eyes as black and precisely lidded as a playing-card queen's. Her dress, which was made of something crêpey, hung limp over her flat chest, billowed hollowly at the waist and wrists, and dripped in layers to her skinny sharp legs. She wore pointed silver pumps from the Sixties. When she smiled her eyes remained wide and lusterless, as if she were keeping in mind some secret sorrow. "So finally we meet," she said.

"We would have come before but Duncan was buying Prince Albert tins," Justine told her. Nervousness always did make her talk too much.

"*I* understand. Won't you be seated? Margaret, darling, would you care to serve the iced tea."

Meg looked at her mother. Then she left the room. Mrs. Milsom floated slowly downward into one of the satin chairs, parts of her appearing to settle whole minutes after other parts. She laid her hands delicately together. "Arthur I hope will be joining us shortly," she said. "At the moment he's napping."

"Arthur naps?" said Duncan.

"It's a fourth Sunday. His day to preach. Preaching takes so much out of him. Naturally we had been hoping that you would be here in time to hear his sermon, but apparently things did not fall out that way." She gave Justine a deep, mournful look.

"Oh well—" said Justine. They would have come for the sermon, even Duncan—anything for Meg—but Meg had specifically told them not to arrive till after lunch.

"Generally on fourth Sundays he awakes with a headache," said Mrs. Milsom, "and sustains it during the entire service and even afterward, until he admits that I am right and takes to his bed. He suffers real pain. This is not some ordinary headache."

"Maybe he should switch to *fifth* Sundays," Duncan said. "Sixth, even."

Justine shot him a look.

"Where's the minister?" asked Grandfather Peck, settling creakily into an armchair.

"*Grandfather*, turn on your—"

"Arthur is napping, Mr. Peck," said Mrs. Milsom. Her voice was thinned to just the right pitch. "I know all about the deaf," she told Justine. "My father was afflicted. In his later years he would go so far as to sing the 'Doxology' while his congregation was on 'Bringing in the Sheaves.' "

"Oh, your father was a minister too," Justine said.

"Oh yes. *Oh* yes. All my family."

"And your husband?"

"No, ah—he was in construction."

"I see."

"But *my* family, now they have been clergy for a great many years. I myself am a healer."

"Is that right?" said Duncan. He stopped rolling up his magazine. "You heal by faith?"

"I certainly do."

She smiled at him, her eyes like black pools. Then Meg came tinkling and clinking through the doorway with a tray, and Justine tensed because she herself, of course, would have spilled ice cubes into Mrs. Milsom's snowy lap or tripped over the veins in the carpet. She forgot that Meg was as graceful and confident as her maiden aunts. The tray paused at each person, dipping neatly, holding steady. Mrs. Milsom watched its progress with her lower lip caught between her teeth. She was tense too, as if Meg were *her* daughter. It wasn't fair. She had no right. Justine snatched a tumbler off the tray and a disk of tea flew onto the sofa cushion, but Duncan instantly covered it with his *Lady's Circle*. "Mama. It's sweetened," Meg whispered.

"What?" Justine said aloud.

"It's *sweetened*."

"The tea is sweetened," said Mrs. Milsom. "Thank you, Margaret. Won't you take some yourself?"

"I was thinking I might go see if Arthur's awake."

"Oh no, dear, I wouldn't do that just yet."

"He did say to wake him when they came."

"If we do he'll have his head till tomorrow, believe me," said Mrs. Milsom. "I know him." She smiled and patted the arm of her chair. "Come sit with us a while."

So Meg came to perch at Mrs. Milsom's side, and Justine averted her eyes and concentrated on her tea. It was a fact that the only thing she couldn't stand was sweetened tea. It made her gag. She would feel sick and heavy for the rest of the day. Still she drank it, searching with her tongue for the nearest ice cube to dilute the sugary taste. Duncan, who didn't care one way or the other, finished his own drink in one breath and set the glass down upon the polished table. "Well," he said. "So you've got your diploma, Meggie."

She nodded. Her hair touched her collar, a little less neat than it used to be. Maybe she was trying to look older.

"So what next?" Duncan asked her.

"Oh, I don't know."

"Going to get some kind of a job?"

"Mr. Peck," said Mrs. Milsom, "being a minister's wife *is* a job."

Duncan looked over at her. Justine grew worried, but in the end all he said was, "I meant, *besides* that."

"Oh, there's nothing besides that. Believe me, I know. I'm a minister's daughter. And I've been standing behind Arthur all this time filling in until he found himself a wife: attending teas and sewing circles, helping at bazaars, fixing casseroles—"

"Meggie, your mother must know people," Duncan said. "All sorts of people with jobs to offer, I'm sure of it. How about Pooch Sims? The veterinarian." He turned to Justine. "*She* could use someone."

"Oh, Mr. Peck," said Mrs. Milsom. She laughed and her ice cubes rattled. "Margaret wouldn't want to do that."

Everyone looked at Meg. She stared down into her glass.

"Would you, Meg?" Duncan asked.

"No," said Meg, "I guess I wouldn't."

"Well, then, what?"

"Oh, I don't know, Daddy. Mother Milsom's right, I do have a lot to do already. I've taken over the nursery at church and I have so many calls to pay and everything."

Justine's teeth seemed to be growing fur, and still she hadn't made a dent in her drink. She longed for something sour or salty. She had a craving for pickles, lemon rind, a potato chip even. But Mrs. Milsom gazed at her so reproachfully that she raised the glass and took another swallow.

"Mainly of course the minister's wife is a *buffer*," said Mrs. Milsom. "She filters his calls, tries to handle the little things that so clutter his day—oh, Margaret can tell you. We've been teaching her all about it. Arthur is not terribly strong, you see. He's allergic to so much. And he has these headaches."

"But I thought you were a healer," Duncan said.

"A healer, yes! I have a little group that meets on Sunday evenings. Anyone can come. I inherited the gift from my father, who once gave sight to a blind man."

"But your father was deaf."

"He still had the *gift*, Mr. Peck."

"I meant—"

"Of course the gift must be kept alive by prayer and faith, it has to be nurtured along. That's what I tell Arthur. I feel that Arthur very definitely has the gift. I am working with him on it now. So far there has seemed to be some—I don't know, some sort of *resistance*, I'm just not—but we're working, I'm sure we'll get there."

"How about Grandfather here?" Duncan asked. "*He* could use some help."

She hesitated.

"Think you could just clap a couple of hands on his ears to oblige us?"

"Well, I'm not—is it nerve deafness, or what?"

"Oh, if faith only heals certain *kinds*," said Duncan.

Both Meg and Justine stirred, uneasily. Duncan gave them a wide, innocent smile that did not reassure them. "But never mind," he said, "my real interest was headaches."

"Headaches, Mr. Peck? Do you suffer from headaches?"

"No, your son does."

"My son."

"Arthur."

"Oh, *Arthur*," she said blankly.

"Didn't you say that Arthur got headaches?"

"Why, yes."

Duncan looked at her for a moment, honestly puzzled. "But then," he said, "why can't you heal him?"

Mrs. Milsom clasped her hands tightly. Her mouth became blurred and her eyes filled with what must surely be black tears; but no, when they spilled over they were clear and they made white tracks down her hollow white cheeks.

"Oh, Duncan," Justine said. But what had he done, after all? Nobody understood, except perhaps Meg, who quickly buried her nose in her tea glass. Then Mrs. Milsom straightened and darted an index finger beneath each eye, quick as a frog's tongue. "Well!" she said. "Haven't we had nice weather for August?"

"It's been very nice," Duncan told her gently. And he

must have been planning to stay that way to the end, sober and courteous; he would never willingly hurt anybody. Except that Justine chose that moment to reach toward the green glass shoe on the coffee table—sourballs! right under her nose!—and choose a lemony yellow globe and pop it into her mouth, where she instantly discovered that she had eaten a marble. While everyone watched in silence she plucked it out delicately between thumb and forefinger and replaced it, only a little shinier than before, in the green glass shoe. "*I* thought we could have used more rain," she told the ring of faces.

Duncan made a peculiar sound. So he *was* going to have a silly fit after all. Justine had to sit as straight as a statue, dignified enough for the two of them, while at intervals Duncan steamed and chortled like an electric percolator on the couch beside her.

When Arthur was up (pale and rumpled, inadequate-looking in a short-sleeved Hawaiian shirt) they moved out to the back yard to admire Mrs. Milsom's flowerbeds, then over to the church to see the new red carpet just recently installed in the aisles. They tiptoed through the vaulted, echoing nave with their faces very serious. They were all particularly careful of one another, if you didn't count Duncan's pinching Justine when he didn't know Mrs. Milsom was looking. They were so appreciative, so soft-voiced and attentive, that by the time they had assembled beside the Ford to say their good-byes everyone was exhausted. But Mrs. Milsom held out both hands bravely for the sack of sun-baked corn, and Arthur insisted on taking the entire burden of wedding silver from the trunk. He staggered off, stringy-armed, sway-backed beneath his load. Meg remained beside the car with her pile of shirtwaist dresses. "Well," said Justine, "I suppose we'll be seeing you soon." She felt bruised by disappointment. She had imagined that this visit might, in some way, wrap things up—that whatever had gone wrong in their family might finally be straightened out, or at least understood; and that having seen Meg settled and happy she could let her go at last. She had supposed that care and responsibility could be shucked like old skin, leaving her cool and smooth and lightweight. But Meg's face was screwed so tight it made her ache, and she would never be free of Meg's old, anxious eyes. "Meggie, is there anything you need?" she asked. "I mean, if you think of something, anything at all—"

"I'm sorry about the tea," Meg said.

"Tea?"

"I told her you didn't drink it sweetened."

"Oh, that's all right, honey."

"She was making it after lunch and I said, 'Don't put sugar in it, Mama likes hers with just lemon.' But she said, 'Oh, everybody likes their tea with sugar, it's so refreshing.' I said, 'But—' "

"Meg, I don't care," said Justine.

"I said I would mix a separate glass then," Meg told Duncan, "but she doesn't really like me in her kitchen."

Duncan studied her. Grandfather Peck stroked his chin.

"She does everything, even makes our bed up. She says I don't know hospital corners. You never taught me about hospital corners, Mama."

"I'm sorry, honey."

"I wanted to have you for lunch today, I said I would cook it myself. You know I can cook. Simple things, at least. Fannie Farmer. But she said it wasn't possible because her group was coming over for supper, these people in her healing group. She had to have the kitchen to herself. The people in her healing group are all old and strange, they have chronic illnesses and they think she helps, and then sometimes they bring her someone new and they all pray together holding hands."

"Does it work?" Justine asked.

"What? No. I don't know. I thought when I got married we would be so—regular. I thought finally we—I didn't know all this would be going on. When I met her she was like anybody else. Except for wearing white. She did wear white all the time. But I didn't know then about this healing. She wants Arthur to learn healing too and she even wanted to look at *my* hands, she wondered if I have the gift.''

"Do you?" Justine asked.

"Mama! I wouldn't go along with a thing like that."

"Well, I don't know, at least it would be a new experience."

"I don't want new experiences, I want a normal happy life. But Arthur just won't stand up to her, really he—and now she wants him to develop his gift because hers is going. She thinks it's because of her age. At the meetings they pray and cry, you can hear them everywhere in the house. She reminds God of what she used to accomplish: once she stopped a man in the middle of a heart attack.''

"She did?"

"She says she has so much left to do, she should be allowed to keep her gift. She says it's unjust. There are people sick just everywhere, she says, and blind and crippled and suffering pain, and there she is powerless and she can't even stop her own son's headaches any more. She goes on and on about it, calling out so everyone can hear: just because a little time has passed, she says, *that's* no reason to let her dwindle down this way.''

"Well, I should say not," said Justine.

Meg paused and gave her a look. "Are you listening?" she asked.

"Certainly I'm listening."

"I live among *crazy* people!"

"You should leave," Duncan told her.

"Oh, Duncan," said Justine. She turned to Meg. "Meggie darling, maybe you could just—or look at it this way. Imagine you were handed a stack of instructions. Things that you should undertake. Blind errands, peculiar invitations . . . things you're supposed to go through, and come out different on the other side. Living with a faith healer. *I* never got to live with a faith healer.''

"That's what you're going to tell your daughter?" Duncan said. "Just accept whatever comes along? Endure? Adapt?"

"Well—"

"And how would people end up if they all did that?"

Justine hesitated.

"Never mind, Mama," Meg told her. "I didn't mean to mention it, anyway."

So Justine got into the car, but untidily and with backward glances because so much seemed still unsettled. The troubled feeling was nagging at her mind again. She couldn't quite put her finger on it. She felt as if she had mislaid an object somewhere, something important that would thread through all her thoughts until she found it. But she sat forward briskly and called out the window, "Meggie darling!"

"What is it?"

"If you do have to do bazaar work, you know, if you need any help, I'll be happy to drive down any time and tell fortunes."

"Thank you, Mama."

"You know I have a lot of steady clients here."

"Well, that's very nice of you, Mama," Meg said. But Justine could tell that she had made a mistake. She should have offered something plainer and sturdier—anything but more gifts from heaven.

By the time they reached Caro Mill it was night, and the streets had a dismal abandoned look. The only place open was the diner, eerily lit and vacant except for Black Emma swabbing the counter. "Maybe we could stop for coffee," said Justine. But the car slid by, and neither Duncan nor her grandfather answered. (They had not spoken all the way home, either one of them. Only Justine had chattered on and on until she wondered herself when she would shut up.) "Duncan?" she said. "Couldn't we stop for coffee?"

"We have coffee at home."

"I don't want to go home," she said. "I have this peculiar

feeling. I wouldn't mind staying the *night* somewhere, even. Duncan?''

But he said, *"Endure,"* and turned sharply down Watchmaker Street. She blinked and looked at him.

In front of their house, when the engine had died and the headlights had faded, the three of them sat motionless for a moment gazing through the windshield, as if being borne along on some darker, more silent journey. Then Justine touched her grandfather's arm. "Here we are," she said.

"Eh?"

He stumbled out, latching the door inconclusively behind him, and Justine slid after Duncan out the driver's side. They went single file up the walk between looming rustling cornstalks. At the porch, they stopped short. A shadow unfolded itself from the steps. "Eli!" Justine said.

"Eh?" said her grandfather.

And Duncan said, "Well, Eli. What have you found for us?"

"Caleb Peck," said Eli.

13

Eli Everjohn drank his coffee white, preferred Jane Parker angel food cake to taco chips, and was perfectly comfortable sitting on a chrome-legged chair in the kitchen. He had to make all that clear before they would let him get on with his report. "Listen here," he kept saying. "Listen. It struck me right off—" But Justine would interrupt to ask, couldn't she take his hat? wouldn't he be cooler in his shirtsleeves? And old Mr. Peck trudged around and around him, thinking hard, occasionally offering interruptions of his own. "I believe I ought to fetch my notebook, Justine."

"Yes, Grandfather, I would do that."

"I believe that windowscreen is torn. Where else would these mosquitoes be coming from?"

"I'll find the swatter."

"Oh, leave it, leave it. Mr. Everjohn here has something he wants to say to us."

But when Eli took a breath Justine halted him. "Wait, I've been wanting something sour all *day*. Don't start without me."

"Justine—" Duncan said.

Eli Everjohn was a patient man. (In his business, he had to be.) Still, he had been dreaming of this moment for a good long time now. He had come over on a Sunday evening expressly to bring this news, which he thought might cause him to burst if he left it till Monday: in just under three months, he had accomplished what a whole family could not do in sixty-one years. He had performed a spectacular piece of

243

deduction, and now he wanted to tell about it in his own slantwise, gradual way so that everyone could admire how one clue had built upon another, one path led to the next, with sudden inspired leaps of the imagination to bridge them. True detective work was an art. *Finding* was an art. He was grateful to the Peck family for handing him this assignment. (How could he ever again settle for guarding anniversary gifts or pretending to read *Newsweek* in front of beauty parlors?) So he cleared his throat, and pushed his coffee cup a certain distance away, and plaited his long fingers on the table before him and began as he had planned. "It struck me right off," he said, "that there was one thing the same in all accounts of Caleb Peck."

"You'll have to speak up," said the old man.

"Oh. Sorry. It *struck* me—"

"Justine, I think my battery's going."

"Will you let the man *speak*?" Duncan said.

So that Eli, with the last of his patience worn away, ended up blurting it out after all and ruining the moment he had planned for so long. "Mr. Caleb Peck," he said, "is in Box Hill, Louisiana, alive and well."

It had struck Eli right off that there was one thing the same in all accounts of Caleb Peck: he was a musical man. To his family that was only a detail, like the color of his eyes or his tendency to wear a Panama hat just a little past the season. But to Caleb, wasn't it more? Eli pondered, sifting what he had heard and endlessly rearranging it. He traveled a few blind alleys. He scanned the alumni lists of several well-known music schools, including Baltimore's Peabody Institute. He checked the family's old phonograph records for performers whom Caleb might have been moved to seek out. He inquired as to Caleb's piano teacher—someone young and pretty, maybe? Someone inspirational, to teach him those Czerny exercises he found crumbling away on top of the piano in old Mr. Peck's Baltimore parlor? But no, the Czerny was Margaret Rose's, said Mr. Peck. Caleb had not liked

Czerny. He was not, to tell the truth, very fond of the classical mode. And he had never had a music teacher of any kind. Only little Billy Pope passing on his fiddle lessons, and a leatherbound book telling how to play the woodwinds (which in those days were really made of wood—see the ebony flute in Caleb's old bedroom?) and for the piano, Lafleur Boudrault, who taught him ragtime.

Was this Lafleur Boudrault young and pretty, by any chance?

But Lafleur Boudrault was the Creole gardener, not pretty at all—a scar down one cheek and a permanent wink. Long dead now. Survived by his wife Sulie. He wouldn't have helped out anyway: a cross-grained sort.

Eli traveled once again to Baltimore and sought out Sulie, who was moving a dustcloth around and around the attic. Nowadays all she did was dust. She would not give up her cloth, which had to be pried from her fingers in her sleep as you would pry a pet blanket from a child in order to wash it. And what she dusted was not helpful at all—never the furniture, which Lord knows could *use* a dusting, all those bulbs and scallops and crevices; but only the hidden places that didn't count, the undersides of drawers and the backs of picture frames and now these trunks and cartons in the attic, which she had been on for weeks and weeks. They couldn't get her to stop. They wanted to pension her off; didn't she have family somewhere? They were almost certain there had been a daughter. But Sulie only laughed her cracked, rapid laugh and said, ''*Now* you wants to do it. Now you wants.'' Oh, she was mad, no question about it. But Eli needed Caleb's contemporaries and there were not all that many to pick and choose from. He climbed the narrow, hollow, pine-smelling steps to Laura's attic, submerging first his head and then his shoulders and then his wool-wrapped body in a heat so intense that it seemed to be liquid, and at the last he was merely floating upward in a throbbing dull haze. He swam between crazed china hurricane lamps and slanted portraits, across rugs rolled and stacked like logs, toward the spindly figure briskly polishing an empty Pears soap box down where the dusty light fingered its way through the louvers. "Mrs. Sulie Boudrault?" he asked, and without looking up she nodded and hummed and went on polishing.

"Widow of Lafleur Boudrault?"

She nodded.

"You wouldn't happen to know where Mr. Caleb Peck has got to."

Then she stopped polishing.

"Well, I thought they wouldn't never ask," she said.

She settled him on a china barrel, and she herself sat on a stack of *St. Nicholas* magazines with her dustcloth clutched daintily in her lap. She was a very small woman with stretched-looking skin and yellow eyes. Her manner of speaking was clear and reasonable, and her story proceeded in a well-ordered way. No wonder: she had had over half a century in which to arrange it.

"When first Mr. Caleb had left us," she said, "I told Lafleur, 'Lafleur, what do I say?' For I know where he had went to yet I would hate to give him away. 'Lafleur, do I lie?' 'That ain't never going to come up,' he say. 'Them folks don't think you know *nothing*.' Well, I was certain he was wrong. I waited for old Mrs. Laura to fix me with her little eyes. She the one to watch for. Mr. Justin the First couldn't do nothing, maybe wouldn't have anyhow, but he had that Mrs. Laura so scared she would do it for him and more besides. She was one scared lady, and it had turned her mean and spiteful. Watch out for Mrs. Laura, I told myself, and so I watch and waited and plan how to answer what she ask. But she never do. Never once. Never even, 'Sulie, do you recollect if you served Mr. Caleb breakfast that day?' Never a word."

Sulie set her skirt out all about her—a long draggled white eyelet affair that hit halfway down her skinny calves, with ankle-high copper-toed work shoes swinging below them. After thinking a moment, she dug down into her pocket and came up with a handful of Oreos, mashed and limp. "Have you a cookie," she said.

"Thank you," said Eli.

"She never ask. Nor none of the others. Took me some time to see they never would. 'Why, looky there!' I say to Lafleur at last, and he say, 'Told you so. They don't reckon just old us would know *nothing*,' he say. So my eyes was opened. That was how. I made up my mind I wouldn't tell till they say straight out, 'Sulie, do you know?' And Mrs. Laura I wouldn't give the time of *day* even. I never did. She live forty-six years after Mr. Caleb had went and I never spoken to her once, but I don't fool myself she realize that. 'Sulie is getting so *sullen*,' was what she say. Even that tooken her five or so years to notice good."

Eli finished the Oreo and dusted off his hands. From his pocket he took a spiral notebook and a Bic pen. He opened to a blank page.

"Now," said Sulie.

She stood up, as if to recite.

"Mr. Caleb was a musical man," she said.

"I had heard he was."

"He like *most* music, but colored best. He like ragtime and he copied everything Lafleur do on the piano. He like stories about them musicians in New Orleans, which is where Lafleur come from. Lafleur had got his self in a speck of trouble down there and couldn't go back, but he would tell about the piano players in Storyville and what all went on. Understand this was back *long* time ago. Didn't many people know about such things.

"Then times got hard and Miss Maggie Rose left us. I had to move on over to Mr. Daniel's house and tend the babies. I was not but in my teens then. I had just did get married to old Lafleur. I didn't know much but I saw how Mr. Caleb was mighty quiet and maybe took a tad more to drink than was needed. But I never thought he'd leave. One night he come down cellar to our bedroom, me and Lafleur's. Knocks on our door. 'Lafleur,' he say, 'this fellow down at the tavern is talking about a trip to New Orleans.'

" 'Is that so,' say Lafleur.

" 'Wants me to go along.'

" 'That so.'

" 'Well, I'm thinking of doing it.'

" 'Why, sure,' Lafleur tell him.

" 'Permanent,' Mr. Caleb say. 'Unannounced.'

"But still, you see, we didn't have no notion he was serious.

"He ask Lafleur was there someplace to go, to stay a whiles. Lafleur mention this white folks' boardinghouse over near where his sister live at. Mr. Caleb wroten it down on a piece of paper and fold it careful and left. We didn't think a thing more about it. Come morning he arrive for breakfast, sometime he would do that. Eat in Mr. Daniel's kitchen. 'Fix me a lot now, Sulie,' he say. 'Can't travel far on an empty stomach.' Well, I thought he meant travel to *town*. I fix him hotcakes. I set out his breakfast and when he had done finished he thank me politely and left. I never did see him again."

She considered her fingernails, ridged and yellowed like old piano keys.

"Could I have that boardinghouse address?" Eli asked her.

"Yes, why surely," she said, and she gave it to him, slowly and clearly, having saved it up on purpose all these years, and he wrote it in his notebook. Then she faded off, so that Eli thought she had forgotten him. He rose with care and tiptoed to the attic steps. He had already dipped one ankle into the coolness below when she called him. "Mr. Whoever-you-are!"

"Ma'am?"

"When you tell how you found him," she said, "make certain you put in that Sulie known the answer all along."

* * *

So now he had an address, but it was sixty-one years old. He knew he couldn't expect too much. He caught a plane to New Orleans that night. He took a cab to where a boarding-house had stood in the spring of 1912. All he saw was a supermarket, lit inside with ghostly blue night lights, hulking on an asphalt parking lot.

"I reckon there's no sense hanging around," he told the cab driver.

Eli registered at a small hotel from which immediately, despite the hour, he called every Peck in the telephone book. No one had an ancestor named Caleb. He went to bed and slept a sound, dreamless sleep. On the following day, he set out walking. He picked his way past suspicious-looking hidden courtyards and lacy balconies, secret fountains splashing, leprous scaly stucco, monstrous greenery and live oaks dripping beards of moss, through surprising pockets of light where the air seemed to lie like colored veils. In various echoing buildings, archives both official and unofficial, he wandered gloomily with his hands in his pockets peering at yellowed sheet music, clippings, menus, and sporting-house directories under glass, as well as cases full of dented trumpets and valve trombones that appeared to have come from the dime-store. In the evenings he attended nightclubs, where, wincing against the clatter of brass and drums, he sidled between the tables to stare at the curling photographs on the walls and the programs once handed out during Fourth of July celebrations. There was no Caleb Peck. There was never that stiff, old-fashioned white man's face or Panama hat.

Eli's wife called, sounding lank and dragged out with the heat. "But it's hotter here," he told her. "And you ought to see the bugs." She didn't care; she wanted him home. What was he doing there, anyhow?

"I'll be back in another week," he told her. "In a week I'm going to have this thing wrapped up."

It was August eighteenth. Although he did not have a single new clue, he was beginning to feel excited.

Now he started shadowing the gaudy, sunglassed tourists, who seemed to know something he did not. They were always in possession of secret addresses: the lodgings of palsied old saxhornists, clarinetists, past employees of the Streckfus Excursion Lines and granddaughters of Buddy Bolden's girlfriends. (Who was Buddy Bolden?) Eli slipped in behind them through narrow doors, into dingy parlors or taverns or bedrooms. Sometimes he was ushered out again. Sometimes he would pass unnoticed. Then he introduced questions of his own, all of them out of place:

"You wouldn't know a jazz *cellist*, by some chance."

"Any good musicians out of Baltimore?"

"Whereabouts were you in the spring of nineteen twelve?"

Ancient, dusty eyes peered back at him, but never ancient enough. "Nineteen twelve? What kind of memory do you think I got, boy?"

By imperceptible degrees the Pecks had altered Eli. He had begun to ignore the passage of time, as if it were somehow *common*. He felt irritated that ordinary people could not do the same.

Days were tiresome, yes, and hard on the feet, but nights were worse. The string of clubs, bars, cafés, dance halls, and strip joints went on forever, and all the music sounded the same to him: badly organized. Eli slipped into a place and out again, into the next. He ducked away at any mention of cover charge, waved off waiters and hostesses. When pressed, he ordered Dr. Pepper; mostly he left before things had gone that far. The scent of success discouraged him. He wanted failure, spooky little hole-in-the-wall cafés. For surely, he was thinking now, Caleb himself was a failure. Whatever he had ended up doing, it had not left any mark upon this town.

He entered bars that smelled of mildewed wood, that had names like The High Note or Sportin' Life, where a few musicians played raggedly and without much interest. A black man sang above a guitar:

My train done left, Lord, done left me by the track,
My train done left, Lord, done left me by the track.
Tell the folks in Whisky Alley
I ain't never coming back : . .

Eli shook his head. He slid past a drunkard and returned to the sidewalk, where he milled among the tourists in a greasy, neon-lit, garlic-smelling night.

The following morning, he was up unusually early. He ate breakfast in a coffee shop near where he had been the night before, and he strolled past the same bars, but they were closed now. Farther down, an aproned man was sweeping the entrance of a strip joint that looked cheerful and homely by daylight. "Tell me," Eli said to him. "You know that little old bar back there? Easy Livin'?"

The man squinted. "What about it?"

"You know what time it opens?"

"Most likely not till evening," said the man. "You got a wait, fellow."

"Well, thank you," Eli said.

This morning he did not delve any further into the archives of jazz. He bought a paper and read it in a park. He had a second cup of coffee and a glazed doughnut. Then when the movies opened, he toured the city catching Jimmy Stewart films. Eli very much admired Jimmy Stewart.

At six o'clock he had a plate of scrambled eggs in a diner, followed by another cup of coffee and apple pie à la mode. Then he set off toward Easy Livin'—on foot, since it wasn't far. He took his time. He nodded soberly as he walked and he looked about him with a well-meaning expression such as Jimmy Stewart might have worn. When he reached his destination, he straightened his string tie before stepping through the battered door.

Easy Livin' was dark even now, when it was barely twilight. There was a bar with a brass rail, a few scarred tables, and at the end of the room a raw wooden platform for the entertainers. At the moment, there were no other customers.

Only a boy behind the bar, and on the platform the black man who had sung the night before. He was squatting to hitch up some sort of electrical wire. He didn't even look around when Eli came up behind him.

"Say," said Eli. "Could I ask about a song?"

The singer grunted and then rose, brushing off his dungarees. He said, "This here is not one of them jazz joints, baby. Go on up the street."

"Last *night* you were singing," Eli said.

"Only the blues."

"Ah," said Eli, who did not see the difference. He pondered a moment. The singer looked down at him with his hands on his hips. "Well," Eli said, "you were singing this here song I was wondering about."

"Which."

"Song about a train."

"*All* songs got trains," the singer said patiently.

"Song about Whisky Alley."

"Mm-*hmm*."

"You recall it?" Eli asked.

"I sung it, didn't I?"

"You know who wrote it?"

"Now how would I know that?" the singer said, but then, all of a sudden: "Stringtail Man."

"Who?"

"The Stringtail Man."

"Well, who was that?"

"*I* don't know. White fellow."

"But he's got to have a name," Eli said.

"Naw. Not that I ever knew of. White fellow with a fiddle."

"A fiddle," said Eli. "Well—I mean, ain't that a little peculiar for jazz?"

"Blues," said the singer.

"Blues, then."

"Now I don't know a thing more than what I told you," said the singer. But he hunkered down, anyway, getting closer to Eli's level. "This fellow was *away* back, long before my time. He was lead man for White-Eye, old colored guitar man that used to play the streets. Now White-Eye was blind and the fiddler would lead him around. But whenever he fiddled, looked like the music just got *into* him somewhat and he would commence to dancing. Old White-Eye would hear the notes hopping to one side and then to the other and sometimes roaming off entirely if the music was fast and the fiddler dancing fast to match. So White-Eye hitched his self to the fiddler's belt by means of a string, which is how we come by the Stringtail Man. *Any body* roundabouts can tell you *that* much.''

''I see,'' said Eli.

''How come you to ask?''

''Well, there used to be this tavern in Baltimore, Maryland, called Whisky Alley,'' Eli said. ''Close by the waterfront.''

''So?''

''You don't recollect where this Stringtail fellow was *from*, by any chance.''

''Naw.''

''Well, how about White-Eye?''

''Him neither.''

''No, his name. Didn't he have a name?''

''White-Eye. White-Eye. White-Eye—Ramford!'' said the singer, snapping his fingers. ''Didn't know I could do it.''

''I'm very much obliged,'' Eli said. He dug down in his trousers pocket. ''Can I buy you a Dr. Pepper?''

The singer looked at him for a moment. ''Naw, baby,'' he said finally.

''Well, thanks, then.''

''Nothing to it.''

By noon the following day, Eli had contacted every Ramford in the telephone book. He had located White-Eye Ramford's great-granddaughter, a waitress; from there he had gone to see a Mrs. Clarine Ramford Tucker, who was residing in the Lydia Lockford Nursing Home for the Colored and Indigent; and from there to a Baptist cemetery in a swampy-smelling section outside the city. The sight of Abel Ramford's crumbling headstone, a small Gothic arch over a sunken grave obviously neglected for years, smothered by Queen Anne's lace and chicory, brought Eli up short, and for a long time he stood silent with his hat in his hands, wondering if this were the end of his road. Then he took heart and went to see the caretaker. He learned that Mr. Ramford's site had no visitors at all, so far as was known; but that every year on All Saints' Day a bouquet of white carnations was brought by Altona Florists, a very high-class flower shop with lavender delivery trucks.

And Altona Florists said yes, they did have a standing order for that date: a dozen white carnations delivered to this little colored cemetery way the hell and gone; and the bill was sent to Box Hill, Louisiana, to a Mr. Caleb Peck.

That was Saturday, August twenty-fifth. It had taken Eli exactly eighty-one days to complete his search.

Because he had been warned not to approach Caleb in person ("I want to do that much myself," Mr. Peck had said), Eli came home without that final satisfaction. But it was almost enough just to tell his story in Justine's kitchen and watch the old man's astonishment. "What? What?" he said, even when he had clearly heard. He started circling the table again, kneading his hands as if they were cold. "I don't understand."

"He's in Louisiana, Grandfather."

"But—we never did go anywhere near there. Did we, Justine?"

"We didn't know."

"We never thought of it," said Mr. Peck. "Louisiana is one you forget when you're trying to name all the states in the Union. What would he be doing there?"

"Eli says—"

"I always suspected that Sulie was no durn good."

"Now Grandfather, you didn't either, you know how you used to rely on her."

"She took advantage," he said. "Why, if we somehow missed asking her—and I don't believe for a minute that we did—it was an oversight. Just chance! How long are we going to be held accountable for every little slip and error?" He frowned at Eli. "And you say Caleb is a—"

"Fiddler."

"I don't understand."

"Fiddler."

"Yes, but I don't—" He turned to Justine. "That doesn't make sense," he told her.

"You always did say he was a musical man," she said.

"It's the wrong Caleb."

"No sir!" said Eli, lifting his head sharply. "No indeed, Mr. Peck."

"Bound to be."

"Would I come to you if I wasn't sure yet?" Eli fumbled in his breast pocket, brought out his notebook, and turned the curly, gray-rimmed pages. "Here. I checked this man out, listen here. Caleb Justin Peck, born February fourteenth, eighteen eighty-five, Baltimore, Maryland. Who else could it be?"

"How'd you learn all that? I told you not to go near him."

"I called and spoke to a nurse at the Home."

"Home?"

Eli flipped back one page in his notebook. "Evergreen County Home for the Elderly, two fourteen Hamilton Street, Box Hill, Louisiana."

Mr. Peck felt behind him for a chair and sat down very slowly.

"If you say a word," Justine whispered to Duncan, "I'll kill you. I'll kill you."

"I wasn't going to say anything."

Eli looked from one face to the other, confused.

"But of course he's not *in* the Home," said Mr. Peck.

"Why, yes."

"He just lives nearby. Or visits some acquaintance there."

"He's a resident."

"He is?"

"Room nineteen."

Mr. Peck rubbed his chin.

"I'm sorry," said Eli, although previously he hadn't felt one way or the other about it.

"My brother is in a Home."

"Well now, I'm sure it's—"

"My own brother in a Home." His eyes flashed suddenly over to Duncan, spiky blue eyes like burs. "You will want your bottle of bourbon or whatever."

"Forget it," said Duncan. He looked somehow tired, not himself at all.

"Why!" said Mr. Peck. "Why, Caleb must be *old!*"

Nobody spoke.

Mr. Peck thought a moment. "He is eighty-eight years old," he said at last.

Telling the news was not as much fun as Eli had expected it would be.

14

21 Watchmaker Street
Caro Mill, Maryland
August 27, 1973

Dear Caleb,
    I take pen in hand to

21 Watchmaker Street
Caro Mill, Maryland
August 27, 1973

Dear Caleb,
    When I heard you were alive, Caleb, my heart

21 Watchmaker Street
Caro Mill, Maryland
August 27, 1973

Dear Caleb,
    This is your brother writing. My name, in the very likely
event that you have forgotten, is

21 Watchmaker Street
Caro Mill, Maryland
August 27, 1973

Dear Caleb,
    I take pen in hand to express my hope that you are in
good health and spirits.
    Originally I had planned to visit unannounced, extend-
ing personally an invitation to stay with us here in Caro
Mill. However my grandson reminded me that perhaps

you had no wish to see your family again. I told him that of course this would not be the case. Is it?

A great deal of water has flowed under the bridge. Altogether now I have seven grandchildren and one great-grandchild. I regret to inform you that both of our parents passed on some time ago, as well as the baby, Caroline. My sons and two grandsons are running the firm etc.— but it is difficult to impart all this via the post. I am hoping that soon we shall be speaking face to face instead.

My grandchildren Duncan and Justine, who live at the above address and with whom I often visit, second my invitation and look forward to making your acquaintance. Should you find yourself short of cash at the moment I would be willing to provide the airplane ticket. I understand that one may fly from New Orleans, journeying from Box Hill by Greyhound bus which if I am correct is the only recourse in those parts.

I have flown by airplane myself on several occasions. Airplanes are now quite a common occurrence and what the Ford has developed into will be difficult for you to believe.

Of course it is no disgrace to find oneself residing in a Home, if alternatives are lacking and one's family has all passed on. In your case I do not know about the alternatives, but I do know that your family *has not all passed on*. They are mostly alive and would never consider allowing one of their number to enter a Home for any reason whatsoever. You must surely have guessed this and yet, by some manner of logic which utterly confounds me, chose not to call upon your own flesh and blood in an hour of need.

But we will let bygones be bygones.

But in what way did the family ever injure you? If our father was, perhaps, overmuch involved in business, our mother a trifle strict, was that so important that you must ruin your life for it and then, having completed the ruin, fail to turn to us for aid?

But there is no point in dwelling upon such things.

I neglected to mention that I was made a Judge, though now of course retired. It is my understanding that you entered the musical world in some capacity, which is not quite clear to me though I hope to hear more about it when we meet.

My grandson says that you have a right to be left alone, and that surely you would have contacted us long ago if you had any desire to see us. Of course it is not my intention to intrude where I am not wanted.

You could have sent us a telegram collect from anywhere in the country and we would have come immediately, yet you chose not to. This to me, Caleb, speaks of some *spitefulness*, for surely you knew that it would pain us to think of a Peck in any such Institution. You were always contrary, even as a child, and caused our mother much worry, due to your stubborn nature which, as I gather, you never managed to overcome.

But enough of that. It is all over now.

My grandson says that your whereabouts is your own secret, to keep or not as you see fit, and consequently I must not let the rest of the family know without your permission. He has instructed the friend who found you not to notify my sons until you allow it. He says we had no right to run you to the ground this way. I told my grandson that I did not believe you would view it in such a light. Surely you understand that my only desire was to see you once more and perhaps have a little talk, not about anything in particular, which there never seemed to be enough time for back in 1912.

To tell the truth, Caleb, it appears that my ties to the present have weakened. I cannot feel that what happens today is of any real importance to me. I am not overly connected to my own descendants, not even to my granddaughter. She means well of course but is so different from me and so unlike my earlier recollections of her, perhaps I would not know her if I came upon her unexpectedly in the street. Consequently it is my hope that you will answer this letter, and that you and I may soon meet to talk over those years which once seemed so long ago but now appear clearer than they were even while we lived them.

I remain

Your brother,
Daniel J. Peck, Sr.

15

Justine stood on her front walk, ignoring a shower that was more mist than rain, talking to Red Emma. "Say you mailed a letter August twenty-seventh," she said. "Or *I* don't know, it was afternoon; maybe it went out the twenty-eighth. No, because he sent it direct from the post office. He has stopped trusting the corner boxes ever since they changed to red and blue. Say you mailed a letter August twenty-seventh, and it was going to a little town in Louisiana. How long would it take?"

"Airmail?" asked Red Emma.

"He doesn't trust airmail."

"He doesn't trust *anything!*"

"There've been so many plane crashes lately."

"Well, I would give it three days," said Red Emma. "And considering he didn't mail early in the day and it's going to a little town, make it four."

"So it got there August thirtieth," Justine said.

Red Emma nodded. Tiny droplets clung to her curls like the dew on a cobweb, and her face was shiny and her mail pouch was growing speckled.

"Then how long back again?" Justine asked. "Four more?"

"I would say so."

"Plus a day in between for the answer to be written."

"Well, if it would *take* a whole day."

"September fourth," said Justine. "A week ago. I don't think Grandfather can stand to wait much longer."

261

"Really he ought to develop some other interest," Red Emma told her. "Join the Golden Age Club."

"Oh, I don't think he'd like it."

"But he would be so popular! With his fine head of hair and all his teeth."

"Maybe so," said Justine, "but I don't picture it."

She waved goodbye and went back to the house with her mail—a sample packet of salad dressing mix and a postcard from Meg. "Here," she said to Duncan. He was playing solitaire on the living room floor. When she tossed him the postcard he picked it up and squinted at the picture, which showed thousands of people stretched out nearly naked on a strip of sand. He turned the card over. " 'Dear Mama and Daddy and Grandfather,' " he read. " 'Here we are with the Young Marrieds Fellowship having just a wonderful time and wish you were . . .' " He passed the card to his grandfather, who was sitting on the couch doing nothing at all.

"What's this?" said his grandfather.

"Card from Meg."

"Oh, I see."

He set the card very carefully on the couch beside him and went back to staring into space.

"Grandfather, would you like to play cribbage?" Justine asked him.

"Cribbage? No."

"It's just as well, you always forget the rules," Duncan told her.

"Would you like a game of chess, Grandfather?"

He looked at her blankly.

"Or a trip in the car. You don't want to just *sit*."

"Why not?" he asked her.

Duncan laughed.

"It isn't funny," Justine told him. "Oh, when is this rain going to stop?" She swept tangles of plant vines aside in order to peer through the window. "I wish we had somewhere to go. I wish we could just get in the car and drive, or catch a train somewhere."

"You know," her grandfather said, "my feelings won't be hurt at all if he doesn't ever answer."

Justine turned to look at him.

"Anyhow, what was I thinking of? It would be so tiring, having to bring him up to date on all that's happened. Too much has gone on. I might not know him. He might not know *me*. I might look old to him. Now I recall we were often short-tempered. Why, we couldn't sit and talk five minutes without one or the other of us losing patience! And he never showed much interest in the children. And I wouldn't know *what* to say about his music and all. Then look at that place he's living in. Who knows what goes on there? Probably they have this schedule of activities, and special shelves to put your pajamas on and rules and medication and refreshment hours and seating arrangements that I would just have no inkling of. We have nothing in common. Know what I dreamed last night? No, maybe *two* nights ago. I dreamed that I saw Caleb driving down the street. Looking fine, just as fine as always. But his car! Peculiar little foreign station wagon, with a pinchy face and windows too big for it like one of those durned chihuahua dogs you see around. 'Caleb!' I called to him, 'what are you *doing* driving that thing?' and all he did was turn and wave. You would think that he belonged in it."

"Grandfather, it will work out," Justine told him. "All week I've had this feeling of change coming. He's going to write any day now. We'll send him a plane ticket and settle him in Meg's old room."

"Then what?"

"What?"

"*Then* what, I said. Then what will we do? 'Oh, it will work out, it will work out.' You're always so blasted cheerful, Justine. But where is your common sense?"

"Why, Grandfather—"

"Sometimes it gets too much for me," he told Duncan. "*You* expect me to have the patience of a saint."

"Not at all," Duncan said.

"You think I shouldn't say how I feel. Underneath, you think that."

"Do what you like, I don't care."

"In my childhood I was trained to hold things in, you see. But I thought I was holding them until a certain *time*. I assumed that someday, somewhere, I would again be given the opportunity to spend all that saved-up feeling. When will that be?"

Nobody answered. Justine stayed braced against the windowframe, Duncan lowered a three of spades and stared at him. Finally their grandfather rose and went off to his room, leaning on each piece of furniture as he passed it.

At noon Justine had to eat lunch alone. Duncan had left for the shop and her grandfather, when she knocked on his door, said that he was busy. From the sudden squawk of metal on metal she guessed that he was rearranging his file cabinet. "But maybe you could just come out and have some coffee," she called.

"Eh?"

"You could keep me company."

"How's that?"

She gave up and went back to the kitchen. She opened a bottle of pickled onions and set it on the table, went to the drawer for a fork, and then suddenly straightened and frowned. This premonition of hers was pressing now against her temples and the small of her back. She returned to her grandfather's room and knocked again. "I was wondering," she called. "Would you like a cup of tea, instead?"

"Justine."

"I asked if—"

"Justine, I don't feel so well."

She opened the door instantly. Her grandfather sat on his bed holding a sheaf of papers. His face was white and slick and the papers were trembling. "What is it?" she asked.

He passed a hand across his eyes. "I was standing over

there, you see," he said, "just rearranging my files a bit. I was just *standing* there when I felt so—"

He trailed off and looked at the shaking papers.

"Lie down," Justine told him. When he didn't seem to hear she touched his shoulder, pushing him gently backward until he gave in. She bent to scoop his feet up and set them on the bed. Now he lay half on his side, half on his back, breathing a little too quickly. "Are you sick to your stomach?" she asked him.

He nodded.

"*Oh*, then. Probably just . . . are you dizzy?"

He nodded.

"Well . . . but your chest doesn't hurt."

He nodded again.

"Does it? Say something."

"Yes."

"I see," Justine said.

She thought a moment. Then she went to the open window and leaned out. Next door, Ann-Campbell stood in a wading pool wearing bikini underpants, tilting her face into the rain and singing,

> We are fine mermaids of high pedigree,
> We eat baby sharks and we pee in the sea . . .

"Ann-Campbell!" Justine called. "Go get your mother. Hurry. I want her to call the ambulance in Plankhurst."

Ann-Campbell broke off her song.

"Hurry, Ann-Campbell! Tell her to call Duncan too. My grandfather's having a heart attack."

Ann-Campbell darted off, all flashing angles and freckles and patches of peeled skin. Justine turned back to her grandfather. "A what?" he said, bewildered. "Having a what?"

"Well, maybe not."

He pressed a hand to his chest.

"Is there anything I can get you?" she asked him. "Do

you want a drink of water? Or—I don't know, maybe you aren't supposed to. Just lie still, Grandfather."

He did not look capable of doing anything else. He seemed to be flattened, sinking into his mattress. Nevertheless, his neck was tightly strung as if he were determined to keep his head just slightly off the pillow; it was not dignified to be seen in a horizontal position. Perhaps he even wished she would leave him in privacy, but she couldn't. She paced around and around the tiny room, willing into him all her strength and her burning, aimless energy. She kept being drawn to the window, which opened onto the side yard and would not have shown her the ambulance even if it could come so soon. "Oh, I wish Caro Mill had a hospital of its own!" she cried.

"I would never agree to a hospital," her grandfather said. He closed his eyes.

Then the screen door slammed and Justine could breathe again. "Duncan?" she called. "Is that you?"

But it was only Dorcas, clattering across the floor on her spike-heeled sandals. She stuck her bubbly head in the door and rounded her eyes at Grandfather Peck, who pretended to be asleep. "Justine honey, I called right away," she said. "They're sending an ambulance. Now I'm going to stand on the corner and wave it down."

"And Duncan? Did you call Duncan?" Justine asked.

Dorcas was already leaving, but her voice floated back. "He's coming too, he'll be here in a minute."

Justine went back to the bed and sat down on the edge of it. She laid a hand on her grandfather's cold, damp forehead. His eyes flew open and he gave her a look she had not seen him wear before: he seemed to be asking something from her. "What is it?" she said.

"Justine, I—there seems to be a considerable amount of pain starting up."

"Oh, where is Duncan?"

"I believe that I'm having a heart attack."

She picked up both his hands, which passed on their shakiness to her. His eyes withdrew and he thought something over in the gray of the ceiling. "Well," he said finally, "I had certainly hoped for more than *this* out of life."

"Don't talk!" she told him. She jumped up and ran to the window again. "Oh, where is—"

Then something made her turn, some sound much smaller than a click, and she saw that her grandfather had let his head rest at last and his hands were still and his face was calm and dead.

While she waited for Duncan she went into the living room, but it made her sad to abandon her grandfather and she returned to the bedroom. Even now, after all, there was that pinstriped collarless shirt and the silvery slant of hair, those perfect teeth glinting between the thin Peck lips, the waxy gray cord of his hearing aid and the deep-socketed eyes, closed but still leaking their blueness into the white of the lids. There was more to him than soul; there was this body, which would have looked different worn by any other man. She memorized the single stark line running alongside each corner of his mouth, drawn by pride and firmness of purpose. She willed his gnarled hands to press into hers, one more time, a bitter oval of horehound, but she did not reach out to touch him. He was too much present still, and would not have approved. Instead she slightly altered the position of his pillow, causing his head to lie straighter; and when the movement set up a rustling of papers she pulled from beneath his shoulder the sheaf of letters he had held, his carbon copies on onionskin. Their new creases and the blurred gray softness of the type made them seem to have come from someone already long dead and forgotten. "Dear Caleb," she read, from the top page. "I take pen in hand to express my hope that . . ." Her eyes slid down, line by line. When she reached the end of the letter she lowered it and stared at her grandfather's closed, set face.

"Justine!" Duncan called.

She spun around.

''Justine? Dorcas says—''

He stopped in the doorway, and then walked in and picked up his grandfather's wrist. ''Well,'' he said after a moment, and when he set the wrist back down he was so gentle that there was no sound at all. Then he came to stand in front of Justine. ''I'm sorry,'' he told her.

She held the letter out to him, and he took it from her to read it. First he sighed, then he smiled; then he stopped reading and looked over at her.

''Oh, Duncan,'' Justine said, ''how could he write such a thing?''

But when he reached for her, she dodged his hands and went to the opposite side of the room.

16

Down the curved, gleaming staircase (which in her girl-hood she used to descend holding onto her chest, to prevent exercising off what little she had), across the porch where her great-grandmother had often sat listing the three permissible excuses for typing a note of condolence (paralytic stroke, severed tendons, and amputation) Justine moved dimly beside her husband, wearing the suit she had worn to her mother's funeral and clutching one frayed white glove. (She had not been able to find the other.) She entered her uncle Mark's car; she rode through Roland Park, alighted in front of the church, and climbed the steps leaning backward slightly as if she feared what she would find inside. But inside there was only a density of carpet and shadowy pastel light from the windows, and up front an anonymous coffin. Then a cemetery as flat and well mown as a golf course, rows upon rows of glazed granite headstones including PECK Justin Montague, PECK Laura Baum, MAYHEW Caroline Peck and finally an admirably well cut rectangular ditch beside which the coffin lay like something forgotten, abandoned at the brink, while more words were said. Afterwards the family went home to receive their callers, who had been streaming in for the past two days and continued even now that it was over—elderly gentlemen, ladies in hats and gloves and veils and crocheted shawls in spite of the heat. "My," they said to Justine, "are *you* that little girl of Caroline's? But you used to be so—well, you certainly have—now, this is your husband, isn't it? *Him* I recognize."

Him they recognized. From her new distance Justine turned and looked at him, at his boyish pointy chin and his gawky way of standing, twining one leg about the other and rocking slightly with his hands in his back pockets so that his elbows jutted out to spear passers-by. The upturned corners of his mouth made him appear to be smiling mysteriously, teasingly, and perhaps he was. "Why, Duncan!" said Justine, dropping her glove. "You haven't changed a bit!"

An old lady mumbled, embarrassed at her mistake. Plainly these two were not married and perhaps not even related, in spite of the resemblance. Then Duncan stooped for the glove and handed it formally to Justine, and Justine turned and went off alone.

Not only had Duncan remained the same but so had her aunts and uncles, solidified in their flowery dresses and summer suits, and her cluster of cousins passing trays of tea cakes as they had when they were children. Only Justine stood swaybacked, chewing the empty finger of her glove, in a distant corner of the room.

"You were that little girl who used to be so sweet," a spindle-shanked lady told her. "And still are, I'm sure. You used to bring me little handfuls of flowers. You would never stay and talk because you were too shy."

Justine removed the glove from her mouth and gave her a sweet, shy smile, but the lady was not deceived and moved on immediately.

When the guests were gone Duncan escaped to bed, but the rest of the family had a light supper in the kitchen, working around Sulie, who was dusting the pipes under the sink. They laid out memories of Grandfather Peck, one by one. Aunt Lucy cried a little. Aunt Sarah became irritable and informed Justine that there was no call to wear a hat in her own family's house. "Oh, I'm sorry," said Justine, removing it. Then she didn't know what to do with it. She balanced it on her lap, leaving her sandwich untouched. She was feeling very tired. Really she would have liked to go off to sleep. But she stayed on, and by the time the aunts and uncles had risen to go she had her second wind and remained in the kitchen with the cousins, who discussed memories of their own. *They* remembered their grandfather's expression at that picnic for which Duncan had made him a Noxzema and olive sandwich, and first they sputtered into their iced tea and then laughed outright. Justine looked around at each blond, lit-up face, remembering times when she had been a member here. When she and the girls were eleven and twelve and thirteen, what on earth had they all found so funny that it made them laugh until they squeaked?

Esther was now the supervisor of a nursery school. Alice was a librarian, while Sally, the prettier twin, had returned from her month-long marriage a little less outgoing than she used to be and now taught piano in the privacy of Great-Grandma's house, on a modern blond upright that looked peculiar in the wine-colored parlor. Richard had a high-rise apartment downtown, and Claude lived over the garage behind Uncle Two's and spent all his money on steel engravings that nobody liked. New little lines were pricked in all their faces and their hair was dryer and duller, their hands growing freckles; but still they were the same. Only Justine was different, and when she tried to talk to them she had the sense of swimming hard against a strong current. Frustration made her clumsy, and she spilled a glass of ice cubes into Claude's lap but everyone said it didn't matter a bit.

Upstairs, in her old pink-and-white bedroom, she undressed in the dark so as not to wake Duncan and lay down beside him. It was going to be one of those nights when she couldn't sleep. She felt a familiar alertness in her legs, as if she were tightrope-walking on a rubber band. Voices swam in and out of her hearing: Duncan at twelve, explaining shotgun poker; Richard asking if he could come too; Aunt Bea naming all the wedding gifts she had received in the summer of 1930; and her grandfather calling, "Wait for me, Justine! There's no need to rush so." But she had rushed anyway. She had been so quick and brash, so loud, so impatient, which must explain that constant look of puzzlement he had worn in his later years; for where was the old slow, tender Justine?

"Wait for me," she heard Meg say, and she clearly saw Meg's five-year-old face, apple-round, rosy with heat, in the shadows of a spiral staircase in a lighthouse on the New Jersey coastline. They had stopped there on the way back from an unsuccessful job interview. (Justine had always wanted to live in a lighthouse.) Justine had climbed up and up, tumbling over her feet in her haste to see what was at the top, while Meg trudged panting behind. There were two hundred and seventy-eight steps, a sign outside had said. But when Justine reached the top, she found the catwalk enclosed in clear plastic, which clouded the view. The only room was a small dark alcove in which a uniformed park guard sat tipping his chair, reading a paperback Mickey Spillane. So she didn't want to live there after all. She descended more slowly, still breathless from her upward run, and on the next to the last flight she found Meg sobbing on a windowsill while Duncan tried to comfort her. "Oh, *honey!*" Justine cried. "I forgot all about you!" But had that taught her anything? She had only speeded up with every year, gathering momentum. Racing toward some undefined future and letting the past roll up behind her, swooping Meg along under one arm but neglecting to listen to her or to ask if she wanted this trip at all. So Meg grew up alone, self-reared, and left home alone for a sad stunted life she had not really wanted; and Grandfather Peck became ever more lost and bewildered stumbling through a series of paper shanties. And Justine awoke one day to wonder how it had happened: what she had mislaid was Justine herself.

But Duncan, who had changed her whole life and taken all her past away from her, slept on as cool as ever, and on the crown of his head was the same little sprig of a cowlick he had had when he was four.

In the morning everyone suggested they stay a while, but Duncan said he was anxious to get going. He barely tolerated the lengthy discussion on traffic conditions, alternate routes, and whether or not to take a Thermos. He acted jittery and exasperated during the loading of the car trunk, while the uncles were padding more of Meg's wedding presents with the flowered sheets that Aunt Lucy had insisted they accept. ("I can't forget that bare mattress in your little home," she had said, shuddering. "*Nobody* just washes their linens and puts them right back on. You give them a rest in a cupboard first, which increases their life span by sixty-six percent.") Then there were the ritual cold drinks out on the porch, with Duncan finishing first and nervously rattling his ice cubes while waiting for Justine. Justine took extra long, to make up for him. She kept gazing around her at her family. "If only you could have got in touch with Meg!" Aunt Sarah told her.

"We'll call and break the news as soon as she gets back from the beach."

"She'll feel terrible, missing the funeral."

There was a quavering in the air, thin sad thoughts hovering among them. Uncle Two cleared his throat sharply. "Well!" he said. "I never asked how the health food business was going."

"Antiques," Duncan said.

"Antiques, then."

"It's okay." He looked off across the lawn and tapped his glass. "Justine, we have to get started if we want to beat the heat."

"Oh. All right," she said. But she would rather have stayed. It gave her a tearing feeling to have to rise and kiss each soft, kind face in turn.

The family descended the steps with elaborate care, proving their reluctance to say goodbye—except for Duncan, of course, who danced down the walk ahead of them tossing and catching a spangle of car keys. "Duncan, boy," said Uncle Mark, "if your grandfather left any unpaid bills, now, medical expenses and so on—"

"I'll let you know."

"And I suppose I'd better write those detective fellows, tell them to close their case." He opened the car door for Justine. "Durned people have been spending money like water anyway," he told her. "I'm glad to be shed of them."

Justine threw Duncan a glance, but he wouldn't meet it. He had made her promise to keep Caleb's secret forever, unless he changed his mind and wrote. So all she could say to her uncle was, "I'll tell Eli myself, if you like."

"His latest expenditures are downright *bizarre*," her uncle said. "Why would he want to bribe a florist?"

"I'll take care of it."

She climbed into the car, and Duncan started the motor. "Finally," he muttered. Then they were off, zooming down the road scattering a cloud of maple-seed propellers while Justine leaned out the window to wave. Aunt Lucy shouted something. "What?" Justine called. Aunt Lucy shouted again.

"Duncan, stop," said Justine. "Your mother's trying to tell us something."

Duncan slammed on the brakes. The car whined into reverse. "What?" Justine called.

"I said, *Don't forget to rest your linens!*"

Duncan clapped a hand to his head, but Justine only nodded and called, "Thank you, Aunt Lucy," and blew her a kiss, and then more kisses for all the others, until Duncan jerked the car into forward again and bore her away.

17

Duncan had been playing solitaire for months now, but nobody guessed it had been that long because at first he had kept it a secret. At first he always did. Like an alcoholic hiding his bottle while everyone else drinks in public, he had stashed decks of cards in out-of-the-way places and he played in uncomfortable and poorly lit corners. At the smallest sound he was ready to scoop his game together and look up with an innocent face and a smile. (He did not like to be caught depending on things.) But gradually, drugged with patience and canfield and accordion, he forgot his surroundings and forgot to hide the cards, then failed to notice when someone came upon him, then finally wandered into the living room absent-mindedly and laid out his game in the center of the floor where everyone had to stumble over the great spread V of his legs. He played throughout meals, visits, family quarrels, and his grandfather's wake. He returned from Baltimore carrying a suitcase in which a single deck of cards had scattered itself through everything—interleaving with the pleats of Justine's funeral skirt and standing upright among the bristles of her hairbrush. But he didn't bother collecting them. He took instead a double deck that had been waiting all this time behind a begonia pot, and he settled himself on the floor and laid out a hand of spider, which was his favorite, most absorbing game, requiring hours and days of deliberation and strategy and intricate plotting. He kept losing and laying out new set-ups. Justine wandered through the rooms still wearing her hat.

At the Blue Bottle, when he went, he played on a scarred wooden desk behind the counter. He swept away stacks of bills, circulars, and correspondence, clearing the large space that spider required. When the bell tinkled over the door he didn't hear. If he had to answer a question or ring up a purchase he was annoyed, and showed it. Couldn't they see he was busy? By now he despised antiques. He despised the people who collected them—artificial-looking ladies who had, no doubt, thirty years ago thrown away the identical beechwood rolling pins that they were now rebuying at such exorbitant prices. And to make it worse, Silas Amsel had become a nuisance. Once the shop had proved a success, he *expected* things of Duncan. He was always waiting to hear good news. Duncan couldn't stand to have things expected of him. Gradually he sold less and less, bought fewer tools, behaved more rudely toward the customers. Silas began to complain. He mentioned trivial lapses: the few times Duncan had forgotten to lock up, and the mornings he was slightly late. There was a misplaced bronze he claimed had been stolen. (As if anyone would bother stealing an object so ugly, or so heavy.) There were little spats and insults every time Silas came to the shop. And he came more and more often, and stayed longer, and meddled more. He would start grumbling even before he was fully inside. He would stand in the doorway, shaking his head. Duncan pretended not to see him. (Sometimes he *really* didn't see him.) He remained seated, pondering over a vast network of playing cards, one finger hooked in a bottle of Old Crow. He felt the air turning gluey with the weight of other people's disapproval, suspicions, hopes, preconceived notions. Only Justine allowed him to go unclassified.

Justine trailed through the shop and out again with the crumpled streamers of her hat fluttering indecisively.

"I'll be finished in a minute," he called, and she said, "Hmm?" and returned, vaguely. She did not shut doors behind her; so for her the antique sleighbell was forever still, a fact he appreciated. She lacked finality. She was the other shoe which never dropped. He looked up from his cards and sent her a smile so deep and sudden that it would surely have wiped all the forlornness off her face if she had seen it, but she didn't. She was studying a chipped paperweight. She looked lost. Nowadays all she would talk about was her grandfather, his wishes she had not granted and gifts she had not thanked him for. She did not mention Caleb. Duncan waited for her to, but she didn't. Now it was October and if she were disappointed, leafing through the mail every morning with her listless, uncertain fingers, she didn't show it. She merely returned to the same old subject: she unwrapped the past endlessly, untying the ribbons, removing the tissue, untying more ribbons. "Do you remember when he took us on the train? I don't know where to. He took all us children, it was some kind of outing. Some patriotic occasion of some sort. I believe he was sorry before we'd even left the depot but it was too late to back out and he didn't want—"

Duncan couldn't remember. He suspected that he had been left at home. But he didn't say so to Justine. He watched her turning the crystal paperweight, and peering into it, and then raising her eyes to examine without interest her own reflection in an ormolu mirror. "Look at me," she said, "I'm one of those eccentric old ladies you see on the street, with a beat-up hat and a shopping bag."

But to him she was an awkward girl-cousin wearing very long shoes, and the comical up-dip at the ends of her hair was enough to make him leave his cards and come set a kiss on her cool cheek.

"You might find me going through a trash basket," she said, still to the mirror. She ignored his kiss.

"Maybe we should take a trip," Duncan told her. "Somewhere we've never been."

"Children would make bets on what I carry in my string bag."

But her bag was straw, not string, and he *knew* what she carried. Coffee beans, and salty things to nibble on, and the future wrapped in a square of rotting silk. Hadn't she always?

She turned from the mirror, as if guessing his thoughts, and opened the bag to show him. He saw neither food nor cards but only sheaves of yellowed photographs belonging to her grandfather. Aunts and uncles standing around in the ocean, by waterfalls, beside new cars; cousins holding up fish and diplomas and Bible-study trophies; Grandfather Peck carefully posed, 8 × 10, behind an enormous empty desk, beneath a parade of *Maryland Digests* and *ALR* volumes; somebody's bride; somebody's baby; Duncan laughing; Great-Grandma guarding her soul against theft by camera; more uncles; more aunts at someone's garden party, clustered together with their faces frozen in surprise. (They would run to a mirror just beforehand and then run back, level, bearing their chosen expressions as carefully as jellies on a platter.) Justine snapped her bag shut again. She gave him a long measuring stare that turned him cold. "That's what I carry," she said, "but don't tell the children."

Then she walked out. The bell quivered but kept silent. Duncan thought of going after her—asking at least where she was headed, or whether she would be there to fill the house for him when he got home. Or most important: what he had done to make her look at him that way. The way other people had looked at him all his life. All his life they had marked him as thoughtless and mischievous, wicked even; yet he had continued to feel that somehow, underneath, he was a good man. With Justine, he *was* a good man. Had she changed her mind about him? He didn't want to know. He didn't want to ask, and have to hear her answer. In the end all he did was return to his game of solitaire.

In an airport waiting room, at eleven thirty in the morning, Justine sat in a vinyl chair with her straw bag balanced on her knees. She was watching a group of students on standby. The regular passengers had already filed through, and now an official took a stack of blue tickets from his podium and began calling out each standby's name. They cheered and came forward, one by one. They accepted their tickets like Oscars, smiling at the official and then waving triumphantly to their friends, who clapped. Justine clapped too. "Mr. Flagg!" the official called. "Mr. Brant!" Mr. Flagg beamed. Mr. Brant kissed his ticket. "Mrs. Peck!" And though Justine had no one with her, she was so carried away by all the gaiety that she beamed too, and turned back to bow to the empty row of chairs before she headed through the gate marked *New Orleans*.

18

At night, in his narrow white cot, with old men wheezing and snoring all around him, he lay flat on his back and smiled at the ceiling and hummed "Broken Yo-Yo" till the matron came and shut him up. "Just *what* do you think you're doing?" He didn't answer, but the humming stopped. A fellow at the end of the row called out for a bedpan. The matron left, on dull rubbery heels. The fellow went on calling for a while but without much interest, and eventually he fell silent and merely squeaked from time to time. Caleb continued smiling at the ceiling. What no one guessed was that "Broken Yo-Yo" was still tumbling note on note inside his head.

From four a.m. till five he slept, dreaming first of a cobbled street down which he ran, more agile than he had been in years; then of fields of black-eyed Susans; then of grim machinery grinding and crumpling his hands. He awoke massaging his fingers. The ache was always worse in the early morning hours. He lay watching the darkness lift, the ceiling whiten, the sky outside the one gigantic window grow opaque. The tossing forms around him stilled, signifying wakefulness, although none of them spoke. This was the hour when old men gave in to insomnia, which had been tracking them down all night. They would rather not admit their defeat. They lay gritting their gums together, tensed as if on guard, betraying themselves only by a dry cough or the occasional sandpapery sound of one foot rubbing against the other. Caleb was stillest of all, but now "Stone Pony Blues" was spinning between his ears.

At six o'clock the matron came to snap on a switch. Long after she had gone, fluorescent tubes were fluttering and pausing and collecting themselves to fill the room with glare. The sky appeared to darken again. Morning came later now; it was fall. In December he would have been here seven years and he knew every shadow and slant of light, all the sounds of night and morning and mealtimes, which he tabulated with a sense of contentment.

Those who could manage for themselves began to struggle out of bed and into their bathrobes. Caleb's bathrobe was a rubberized raincoat, whose belt he tied clumsily without moving his fingers. He had asked Roy's wife Luray for a real bathrobe this coming Christmas and he was fairly certain she would bring him one. He slipped his feet into paper scuffs and went off across the hall to the toilets. Already a line had formed. While he waited he hummed. The old men went on discussing their constipation, indigestion, leg cramps, and backaches. They were used to his humming.

For breakfast there were grits, shredded wheat biscuits, and coffee. The men sat on long wooden benches, eating from tin plates with compartments. The women sat on the other side of the dining hall. They could have mingled with the men if they wished but they didn't, perhaps preferring not to be seen in their flowered dusters, with their veiny white legs poking out and their scalps showing through the thin strands of hair. Caleb, however, bowed and smiled in their direction before taking his place on a bench.

After breakfast they went to the social room. Some watched television, most just stared into space. Those who were crippled were wheeled in and parked like grocery carts. A gin rummy game started up in one corner but lapsed, with the players merely holding their cards and sitting vacantly as if frozen. A man with a cane told another man how his son had done him out of a house and five acres. Caleb himself did not have anyone to talk to at the moment. His only friend had died in August. Jesse Dole, a horn player who had been recorded several times in the days when you blew into a large black morning glory and it came out of another morning glory in someone's parlor. They used to sit in this very spot between the radiator and the Formica coffee table, arguing the fine points of their different styles of music. Then one night Jesse died and they collected him in his bedsheet and swung him onto a stretcher, leaving Caleb to spend his days all alone with the vinyl chair beside him empty. The others thought he was a little odd. They didn't have much to do with him. But Caleb was accustomed to making friends with anyone, and he knew that sooner or later he would find somebody or somebody would find him, maybe some new man coming in with new stories to tell. Till then, Caleb sat tranquilly in the social room with his knotty hands resting on his knees and his eyes fixed upon the green linoleum floor. For lack of anything else he had begun thinking back on his memories, which wasn't like him. He had never been a man to dwell on the past. Leaving places, he forgot them, always looking ahead to the next; but he had supposed that someday he would have the time to sit down and take a look at where he had been and this must be it.

New Orleans in the early part of the century: jitney dances at the Okeh Pavilion and the faint strains of quadrilles, schottisches, and polkas, and musical beggars one to a block playing anything that made a fine noise. White-Eye Ramford bowling along the sidewalk with his buckle-kneed gait, plucking notes like little golden fruits and singing and stumbling so you thought he was drunk, till you saw his flickering black paper eyelids and the blind, seeking roll of his head. He had lost his sight at twelve or maybe twenty, his stories differed; and by the time he reached middle age he should have learned how to navigate but he hadn't. He was hopeless. A plump, clumsy, hopeless man with a mild face, wincing when he stumbled and then moving on, resigned, plucking more notes from his cracked guitar. He wore a ragged white carnation in his buttonhole, and a derby on his head. It was the fall of 1914. Caleb was on his way home from the sugar refinery and he stopped and stared. Then he followed behind. Till the blind man called, "Who that?" and Caleb melted into a doorway. The next day, the same street, Caleb brought along his fiddle. When he heard the guitar he started playing. High haunting notes wailed and rose, commenting on the tune, climbing behind it. He had known immediately what this sort of music required. The guitar readjusted, making way for the fiddle, and the two of them continued down the street. Someone dropped a coin into a lard bucket hanging from the guitarist's belt. "Thank you," said Caleb, always well mannered. The guitarist spun around. "*White* man?" he cried. Caleb was so pleased at his surprise that he hardly noticed he was left standing foolishly alone. He was certain (because he wanted it so much) that the two of them would meet again, and that he would go on playing his fiddle behind the cracked guitar until he was accepted. Or tolerated, at least. Or recognized to be unavoidable.

In 1912 or 1913 you could run into Caleb Peck in just about any sporting house or dance hall in the city, always propped against the piano or the edge of the bandstand, puzzled and wistful, worn down from his menial daytime job, hoping to be allowed to fill in for some musician, though no one was that eager to have him. After all he did not play any brass, and most had no use for a fiddle. As for piano, he was a musical Rip Van Winkle. He had learned from a man who left New Orleans in the nineteenth century, when jazz was still spelled with two s's. So in 1912 and 1913 Caleb merely hung around the edges of places, with a thin strained face from so much listening, from absorbing so much, from trying to understand. But in 1914 he discovered the blues, which he understood instantly without the slightest effort, and for the next twenty years you could find him in the same small area of the Vieux Carré, linked to a blind man by a length of twine and playing a fiddle above a slippery song.

While he stared now at the streaks of detergent on the green linoleum, he could hear White-Eye's loopy thin voice and the twang he made sliding a bottleneck down the strings of his guitar. He sang "Careless Love" and "Mr. Crump."

He sang what Caleb made up—"Shut House" and "Whisky Alley" and "Cane Sugar Blues." Then "The Stringtail Blues," which some people credited to Caleb too but it was plainly White-Eye's, telling how a blind man felt leaning on other people. Caleb's fiddle shimmered and lilted, the guitar notes thrummed beneath it. Caleb had turned shabby, and not quite clean. It took money to be clean. He was surprised sometimes when he caught sight of himself in a window: the lanky man in a grimy frayed suit. Often he bore welts from the bedbugs in his rooming house, where he continued to live alone, unmarried, year after year. He had a great many friends but they were mostly transients, disappearing unexpectedly and resurfacing sometimes months later and sometimes never. Only White-Eye was permanent. Yet you could not say that they were friends, at least not in any visible way. They hardly talked at all. They never discussed their personal affairs. But some people noticed how their two stringed instruments spoke together continuously like old relations recollecting and nodding and agreeing, and how when Caleb and White-Eye parted for the night they stood silent a moment, as if wishing for something more to say, before turning and shambling off in their separate directions. At night White-Eye went to a wife he never named and an unknown number of descendants. Caleb went to work as watchman in a coffee warehouse; otherwise he would have starved. (He took no more than a deceptive jingle of coins from the lard bucket.) For twenty years he existed on four hours of sleep a night. He did it for the sake of a single body of music: those peculiarly prideful songs celebrating depression, a state he had once known very well. He could no longer imagine any other kind of life. If you asked where he came from, or who his family was, he would answer readily but without real thought. He never pictured the city he named or the people. His mind veered away from them, somehow. He preferred the present. He was happy where he was.

The other street musicians dwindled to a handful, and Storyville was closed and the jazz players went off to Chicago or the excursion boats or the artificial bands hired by debutantes' mothers. But White-Eye and the Stringtail Man continued, supporting themselves more or less even through the Crash of 1929. They had become a fixture. Though not famous, they were familiar; and the poorest people were willing to give up a coin in order to keep the world from changing any more than it already had.

In 1934, on a Monday morning very early in the year, Caleb set out searching as he always did for the first faint sound of White-Eye's guitar. (Their meetings were never prearranged. You would never suppose, at the close of a day, that they were planning to see each other tomorrow.) But he had not gone two blocks when a brown woman wearing a shawl came up and touched the scroll of his fiddle, and told him White-Eye was dead. She was his widow. On the very morning of the wake she had taken the trouble to locate Caleb and break the news and invite him to the funeral—a fact that he appreciated, though all he did was nod. Then he went home and sat for a long time on his bed. He wouldn't answer when his landlady called him. But he did attend the funeral the following afternoon and even accompanied the family to the cemetery, a remote little field outside the city. He stood at the edge of the swampy grave between two tea-colored girls who stared at him and giggled. Throughout the ceremony he kept brushing his hair off his forehead with the back of his hand. He was, by then, nearly fifty years old. It was the first time he had stopped to realize that.

Now Caleb traveled the streets alone. Since he had never been a singer he merely fiddled. (No one guessed that White-Eye's voice still rang inside his head.) The solitary strains of his music had a curious trick of blending with street sounds—with the voices of black women passing by or the hum of trolley lines or a huckster's call. First you heard nothing; then you wondered; then the music separated itself and soared away and you stood stock still with your mouth open. But when people offered him a coin, moved by what they thought they might have heard, they found no tin cup to drop it in.

They tucked it into his pockets instead. At night Caleb would find all his pockets lumpy and heavy and sometimes even a crumpled paper bill stuck into his belt. He could not always remember where it had come from. He merely piled it on top of his bureau. But as the months passed the dazed feeling left him, and one noon when he was sitting in a café eating red beans and rice he looked up at the waitress pouring coffee and realized that life was still going on.

He stayed in New Orleans two more years, and might have stayed forever if he had not fallen in with a pair of cornetists who talked him into taking a trip to Peacham. Peacham was a small, pretty town just to the north, still suffering like any-place else from hard times and unemployment. But the mayor had hit upon a solution: he planned to make it a resort. (No-body thought to ask him who would have the money to go there.) He published a three-color brochure claiming that Peacham had all the advantage of New Orleans with none of the crowds or city soot: fine food, lively bars, two full-sized nightclubs rocking with jazz, and musicians on every street corner. Then he set to work importing busloads of chefs, waitresses, and bartenders, as well as players of every known musical instrument. (In all the native population there were only three pianists—classical—and the minister's daughter, who played the harp.) References were unnecessary. So were auditions. In a creaky wooden hotel on the wrong side of town musicians were stacked on top of one another like crated chickens, venturing out each morning to look picturesque on designated corners. But there was no one to drop money in their cups. The only visitors to Peacham were the same as always—aging citizens' grown sons and daughters, come to spend a duty week in their parents' homes. One by one the new employees lost hope and left, claiming they had never thought it would work anyhow. Only Caleb stayed. He had landed there more or less by accident, reluctant to leave New Orleans, but as it turned out he happened to like Peacham just fine. He figured he could enjoy himself there as well as anyplace else.

Now he worked days as janitor for an elementary school, and in the evenings he played his fiddle on the corner he had been assigned. He ate his meals at Sam's Café, where a large red kind-faced waitress gave him double helpings of everything because she thought he was too skinny. This woman's name was Bess. She lived just behind the café with her two-year-old boy. It was her opinion that Caleb's hotel charged too much for his room, and bit by bit she persuaded him to move in with her instead. It wasn't hard. (He was so agreeable.) Before he knew it he found himself settled in her kerosene-lit shack, in her brown metal bed, beneath her thin puckered quilt, which smelled faintly of bacon grease. If she was, perhaps, not the one he would have chosen out of all the women in the world, at least she was cheerful and easygoing. Sometimes he even considered marrying her, in order to give her son Roy a last name, but they were already so comfortable together that he never got around to it.

By 1942 Bess had saved enough money to buy a café of her own in Box Hill, a town some twenty miles away. Caleb wasn't sure he wanted to go; he liked it where he was. But Bess had her mind made up and so he followed, amiably enough, lugging his fiddle and his pennywhistle and a flute and a change of clothes. This time he took a job as short-order cook in Bess's café. He found a park to do his fiddling in, a new crowd of children and courting couples to hear him in the evenings. Only nowadays more and more of the men wore uniforms, and the girls' clothes were too uniform-like—square-shouldered, economical of fabric—and he wondered sometimes, playing his same old music, whether people could really understand it any more. In his head, White-Eye Ramford still sang of despair and jealousy and cruel women and other rich, wasteful things. The couples who listened seemed too efficient for all that.

There was some trouble with Caleb's fingers—a little stiffness in the mornings. His bow hand could not get going at all if the weather was damp. And by now his hair was nearly white and his whiskers grew out silver whenever he went unshaven. On several occasions he was startled to find his father's face gazing at him from mirrors. Only his father, of course, would not have worn a dirty Panama hat, especially in the house, or a bibbed white apron stained with catsup or trousers fastened with a safety pin.

Bess's café was close to the freight tracks, between a seed store and a liquor store. There were some tough-looking men in those parts, but nothing that Bess couldn't handle. Or so she said. Till one evening in March of 1948 when two customers started arguing over a mule and one drew a gun and shot Bess through the heart by accident. Caleb was fiddling at the time. When he returned, he thought he had walked into a movie. These milling policemen, detectives, and ambulance attendants, this woman on the floor with a purple stain down her front, surely had nothing to do with the real world. In fact he had trouble believing she was dead, and never properly mourned her except in pieces—her good-natured smile, her warm hands, her stolid fat legs in white stockings, all of which occurred to him in unexpected flashes for many years afterward.

Of course now Caleb was free to go anywhere, but he had the responsibility of Bess's boy Roy, who was only thirteen or fourteen at the time. And besides, he liked Box Hill. He enjoyed his work as short-order cook, frying up masses of hash browns and lace-edged eggs in record time, and since the café now belonged to Roy what else could they do but stay on?

Year by year the café became more weathered, the sign saying "Bess's Place" flaked and buckled. Roy grew into a stooped, skinny young man with an anxious look to him. They took turns minding the business. Evenings Caleb could still go out and fiddle "Stack O'Lee" and "Jogo Blues." But his hands were knotted tighter and tighter now, and there were days when he had to leave the fiddle in its case. Then even the pennywhistle was beyond him; there was no way to tamp the airholes properly when his fingers stayed stiff and clenched. So he set about relearning the harmonica, which he had last played as a very young man. The warm metal in his hands and the smell of spit-dampened wood reminded him of home. He paused and looked out across the counter. Where were they all now? Dead? He wiped the harmonica on his trousers and went back to his song.

Roy said they needed a waitress. This was in 1963 or so. They had the same small group of customers they always had, railroad workers mostly and old men from the rooming houses nearby. Caleb couldn't see that they had any sudden need for a waitress. But Roy went and got one anyhow, and once he had then Caleb understood. This was a pretty little blond girl, name of Luray Spivey. Before six weeks had passed she was Mrs. Roy Pickett and there was a jukebox in the corner playing rock-and-roll, not to mention all the changes in the apartment upstairs, where he and Roy had lived alone for so many years. She covered the walls of Roy's bedroom with pictures of movie stars torn out of magazines, mainly Troy Donahue and Bobby Darin. She brightened the living room with curtains, cushions, plastic carnations and seashells. She followed Caleb around picking up his soiled clothes with little housewifely noises that amused him. "Hoo—*ee!*" she would say, holding an undershirt by the tips of her fingers. But she wasn't the kind to run a man down. She knew when to stop housekeeping, too, and sit with Roy and Caleb and a six-pack of beer in front of the second-hand television she had talked Roy into buying for her. In the café she cheered everybody up, with her little pert jokes and the way she would toss her head and the flippy short white skirt that spun around her when she moved off to the grill with an order. All the customers enjoyed having her around.

Then the twins were born, in the fall of 1964. Well, of course life is hard with twins; you can't expect a woman to be as easy-going as ever. Plus there was the financial angle. Certainly people require more money once they start having children. Luray was just *frazzled* with money worries, you could see it. She wanted so many things for her babies. She was always after Roy to take a second job, maybe driving a cab. "How we going to even eat?" she would ask him, standing there scared and fierce in her seersucker duster. (Once she had ordered her clothes off the back pages of movie magazines, all these sequined low-necked dresses and push-up bras.) So Roy took a job with the Prompt Taxi Company from six to twelve every night and Caleb ran the café alone. Not that he minded. There wasn't much business anyway and he had just about given up his evening fiddling now that the park was gone and his hands were so stubborn and contrary. (Besides, sometimes lately when he played he had the feeling that people thought of him as a—character, really. Someone colorful. He had never meant to be that, he only wanted to make a little music.) So he would putter around the café fixing special dishes and talking to the customers, most of whom were friends, and after the plates were rinsed he might pull out his harmonica and settle himself on a stool at the counter and give them a tune or two. "Pig Meat Papa" he played, and "Broke and Hungry Blues" and "Nobody Knows You When You're Down and Out." The old men listened and nodded heavily and, "Now that is so," they said when he was done—a much finer audience than any courting couple. Till Luray came down from upstairs with her hair in curlers and her duster clutched around her. "What all is going on here? Caleb, you have woken both babies when I had just slaved my butt off putting them down. What is everybody sitting here for? Shoo now! Shoo!" As if they were taking up seats that someone else wanted, when it was clear no more customers were coming; and anyway, they were having fun. There was no point to hurrying off when you were having fun.

Then Luray got back in her transparent white uniform and said she saw that she would have to start waiting tables again; men customers would leave her tips that they wouldn't leave Caleb. "Well, naturally," Caleb said. "They're personal friends, they wouldn't want to embarrass me." "It don't embarrass *me*," said Luray, tossing her head. She would open the stair door, listening for the babies. Caleb worried about her leaving them alone but she said they would be fine. She was saving up to buy them an electric bottle sterilizer. Caleb didn't think a sterilizer was all that necessary but he cold see that, to Luray, there was always the chance that some single magic object might be the one to guarantee that her babies would live happily forever; and maybe the sterilizer was that object. So he was not surprised when after the sterilizer was bought she started saving up for a double stroller, and after that a pair of collapsible canvas carbeds although they didn't own a car. And he didn't hold it against her when she started criticizing his work, although certainly there were times when she got him down. "What do I see you doing here? How come you to be using pure cream? What you got in mind for all them eggs?"

The fact was that Caleb was pretty much a custom chef by now. He had known his few patrons a very long time, and since he was not a man who easily showed his liking for people he chose to cook them their favorite foods instead— the comfort foods that every man turns to when he is feeling low. For Jim Bolt it was hot milk and whisky; for old Emmett Gray, fried garden-fresh tomatoes with just a sprinkle of sugar; and Mr. Ebsen the freight agent liked home-baked bread. The narrow aluminum shelves behind the counter, meant to hold only dry cereals, potato chips, and Hostess cream-filled cupcakes, were a jumble of condiments in Mason jars and Twinings tea from England, Scotch oatmeal tins, Old Bay crab spice, and Major Grey chutney. The café appeared, in fact, to be a kitchen in the home of a very large family. It had looked that way for years, but this was the first time Luray noticed. "What kind of a business *is* this?" she asked. "Do you want to send us all to the poor-house? Here am I with these two growing babies and lying awake at night just wondering will we manage and there you are cooking up French omelettes and rice pudding, things not even on the menu and I don't even want to know how much you're charging for them . . ."

Luray took over his job, whipping an apron around her

little tiny waist. She acted as if she thought Caleb had grown weak in the head. She sent him up to tend the babies. Caleb had never been good with children. The sight of them made him wretched; he was so sorry for humans in the state of childhood that he couldn't stand to be near them. When one of the babies cried his insides knotted up and he felt bleak and hopeless. So he tended them as if from a distance, holding himself aloof, and as soon as it was naptime he hurried downstairs to socialize with the customers. He sat turning on a stool, talking and laughing, a little silly with relief, plunking down money from his own pocket to pay for a cup of coffee so Luray wouldn't send him off. He would fish out his harmonica with stiff, thickened fingers and give the men "Shut House" or "Whisky Alley." Till Luray stopped in front of him with her hands on her hips and her head cocked. "Hear that? Hear what I hear? Hear them babies crying?" Then Caleb put away his harmonica and went back upstairs on slow, heavy feet.

In the fall of 1966, Luray found out she was pregnant again. She was not very happy about it. Money seemed scarcer than ever, the twins were getting to be a handful, and already the apartment was cramped. Caleb slept on the couch now, and the babies were in his old room. When he got up in the night he stumbled over blocks and wheeled toys and cold soggy diapers all the way to the bathroom, where likely as not Luray had shut herself in ahead of him. "Go away!" she would shout. "Go back to bed, you old skunk!"

One morning she went out all dressed up, leaving Roy to tend the café and Caleb to mind the babies. When she came back she told Caleb she had found him a place to move into. "Oh! Well," Caleb said.

He had thought a couple of times himself about moving, but not so concretely. And then there was the money. "This café just can't *support* two apartments, Luray," he said.

"It's not an apartment."

"Oh, a room? Well, fine, that'll be—"

"This is a place the county helps out with."

Then she flashed Roy a sudden look, and Roy hung his head in that bashful way he had and his face got red. But still Caleb didn't understand.

He understood only when they deposited him in the gray brick building with the concrete yard, with attendants squeaking in their rubber-soled shoes down the corridors. "But—Luray?" he said. Roy wandered off and looked at a bulletin board. The back of his neck was splotchy. Only Luray was willing to face Caleb. "Now you know they'll take good care of you," she told him. "Well, after all. It's not like you were any real relation or anything." She was balancing a baby on each arm, standing swaybacked against their weight—a thin, enormously pregnant woman with washed-out hair and cloudy skin. What could he say to her? There was no way he could even be angry, she was so dismal and pathetic. "Well," he said. "Never mind."

Though later, when the nurse told him he couldn't keep his harmonica here, he did feel one flash of rage that shook him from head to foot, and he wondered if he would be able to stand it after all.

Now he had to hum to make his music. Unfortunately he had a rather flat, toneless voice, and a tendency to hit the notes smack dab instead of slithering around on them as White-Eye Ramford used to. Still, it was better than nothing. And as time went by he made a few acquaintances, discovered a dogwood tree in the concrete yard, and began to enjoy the steady rhythm of bed, meals, social hour, nap. He had always liked to think that he could get along anywhere. Also he did have visitors. Some of these old men had no one. He had Roy and Luray coming by once a month or more with their four little towheaded boys—Roy as young as ever, somehow, Luray dried and hollowed out. But she was very kind now. When the clock struck four and the matron shooed them from the visitors' parlor Luray would reach forward to touch Caleb's hand, or sometimes peck his cheek. "Now we'll be coming back, you hear?" she said. She always said, "Don't see us out, you sit right where you're at and stay comfortable." But he came anyway, out the steel door and across the concrete yard, to where the gate would clang shut in his face. He would wave through the grille, and Luray would tell her boys to wave back. And maybe halfway up the street, heading toward the bus stop, she would turn to smile and her chin would lift just as it used to, as if she were letting him know that underneath, she was still that sweet perky Luray Spivey and she felt just as bewildered as he did by the way things had worked out.

In his patched vinyl chair in the social room he hummed old snatches of song, joyous mournful chants for St. Louis and East St. Louis, Memphis and Beale Street, Pratt City and Parchman Farm. But it was a fact that he never hummed the "Stringtail Blues" at all, though White-Eye Ramford sang it continually in the echoing streets of his mind:

> Once I walk proud, once I prance up and down,
> Now I holds to a string and they leads me around . . .

The morning the letter came he had been sitting like this in the social room. He remembered that when the attendant tossed the envelope into his lap he had expected a good half hour, perhaps, of studying pictures of floral arrangements. (Altona Florists were his only correspondents.) Bouquets named "Remembrance," "Friendly Thoughts," and "Elegance," which you could send clear across the continent without ever setting foot in a shop. But when he ripped open the envelope what he found instead was a typewritten letter of some sort. He checked the outside address. Mr. Caleb Peck, yes. All the postmark said was "U.S. Postal Service Md." Whatever had happened to postmarks?

Maryland.

He shook the letter open. "Dear Caleb," he read. He skipped to the signature. "Your brother, Daniel J. Peck, Sr." A stone seemed to drop on his chest. But he was glad, of course, that his brother was still alive. He remembered Daniel with affection, and there were certain flashing images

that could touch him even now, if he allowed them to—
Daniel's yellow head bent over a schoolbook; the brave,
scared look he sometimes gave his father; the embarrassed
pride on his face when Maggie Rose came down the aisle in
her wedding dress. Yet Caleb shrank in his vinyl chair, and
glanced about the room as if checking for intruders. Then he
read the rest of the letter.

It seemed that Daniel was inviting him to pay a visit. He
was asking him to come to a place called Caro Mill. Caleb
had never heard of Caro Mill. He found it difficult to imagine
his brother anywhere but Baltimore. And when he pictured
accepting the invitation he pictured Baltimore still, even with
this letter before him—a streetcar rattling toward the sandy,
shaded roads of Roland Park, a house with cloth dolls and
hobbyhorses scattered across the lawn. Daniel descending
the steps to welcome him, smiling with those clear, level
eyes that tended to squint a little as if dazzled by their own
blueness. Caleb smiled back, nodding gently. Then he started
and returned to the letter.

He learned that his parents were dead, which of course he
had assumed for many years. (Yet still he was stunned.) And
the baby, Caroline, whom he had forgotten all about. But
where was Maggie Rose, had she ever returned? Daniel neglected to say. Caleb raised his eyes and saw her small, dear,
laughing face beneath a ribboned hat. But she would be an
old lady now. She had grandchildren. Her sons were lawyers,
her husband a judge. It was 1973.

Yet the language in this letter came from an earlier age,
and the stiff, self-conscious voice of the young Daniel Peck
rang clearly in Caleb's ears. All the old burdens were dropped
upon him: reproaches, forgiveness, reproaches again. An
endless advancing and retreating and readvancing against
which no counter-attack was possible. "You must surely have
guessed . . ." "But we will let bygones be bygones." But,
"You were always contrary, even as a child, and caused our
mother much . . ." Then Caleb reached the final paragraph,
skimming rather than reading (so that none of it should really

soak in). "To tell the truth, Caleb," his brother said, and held out his hand and stood waiting. As in the old days, when after weeks of distance he would climb all the steps to Caleb's room simply to invite him for a walk; or some other member of the family would, for they were all alike, all advancing and retreating too, and Caleb had spent far too many years belatedly summoning up his defenses only to have them washed away by some loving touch on his shoulder, some words in that secret language which, perhaps, all families had, but this was the only one Caleb had ever been able to understand. He was angry and then regretful; he rebelled against them all, their niggling, narrow ways, but then some homeliness in the turned-down corners of their mouths would pull at him; then he reached out, and was drowned in their airless warmth and burdened with reminders of all the ways he had disappointed them.

So he asked an attendant for writing paper, chafing and excited for the three hours it took her to bring it, but once it came the stony feeling weighed him down again and he found it impossible to form the proper words. Besides, his hands ached. His fingers would not grasp the pencil firmly. He folded the blank page and stuffed it in his pocket, where Daniel's letter was. Days passed. Weeks passed. For a while his family infiltrated every thought he had, but eventually they faded, returning only occasionally when he put on the coat that served as bathrobe and a rustle in the pocket cast a brief shadow over his morning.

For lunch there was chicken á la king on toast. After lunch came naptime. Wheelchair patients were laid out like strips of bacon on their beds, but most of the others—rebelling in little ways—wandered in the aisles or stood at the window or sat upright in bed in nests of thin, patched blankets. Caleb himself lay down but did not sleep. He was mentally playing the fiddle. Anyone watching closely could have seen the fingers of his left hand twitch from time to time or his lips just faintly move, uttering no sound. He was playing the "Georgia Crawl'' and every note was coming just the way he wanted.

After naps they were supposed to stay in the social room till supper. Caleb, however, wandered out into the yard, and since he always went to the same place nobody tried to stop him. He sat on a bench beneath the little dogwood tree growing from a circle in the concrete. Its upper branches were dry and bare. Lower down, a few red leaves shook in a cold wind. Caleb turned up the collar of his raincoat and huddled into himself. Before long it would be winter and they wouldn't let him come here any more. By next spring the tree might have died. He was not much of a nature lover, but the thought of sitting in utter blankness, unsheltered by even this cluster of dry twigs, made him feel exposed. He glanced around, suddenly wary. All he saw was a woman in a flat hat picking her way across the concrete.

Now visiting hours were well under way and outsiders would be everywhere, their unexpected colors turning the Home drabber than its residents had realized. Perhaps this one was lost. She moved toward him as if fording a river full of slippery stones. Her straw-colored hair, hanging gracelessly to her shoulders, made him think of the very young girls of his youth, but when she came closer he saw that she was middle-aged. She looked directly at him with a peculiarly searching expression. She held out her hand. "Caleb Peck?" she asked.

"Why, yes."

He took the hand, although she was a stranger. He would go along with anything; he always had.

"I am Justine Peck."

"Oh."

He looked at her more closely, past the helter-skelter hat and the aging clothes to her sandy face, sharp nose, blue eyes. He would know her anywhere, he thought. (But he hadn't.) A sad kind of shock went through him. He continued holding onto her bony hand.

"I am Daniel Peck's granddaughter."

"Oh yes. His granddaughter."

"Whom he didn't feel connected to," she said.

"Yes, I seem to remember . . ."

He let go of her hand to reach toward his pocket, the one that rustled.

"I have bad news," he heard.

His—niece? Great-niece. Sat beside him on the bench, light as a bird. He knew what she was going to say. "Daniel is dead," he told her. How could he have awakened this morning so contented, not guessing what had happened?

"He had a heart attack," she said.

He felt cheated and bitter. A deep pain began flowering inside him. His hand continued automatically to his pocket, found the letter and pulled it out. "But I hadn't yet answered," he said. "*Eventually* I was going to."

"Well, of course."

Which was not what he had been afraid she would say.

He opened out the letter, blinking through a mist, and smoothed it on the bench between them. Daniel's typing was conscientious and stalwart and pathetic. This wasn't fair; it was like having him die twice. "It isn't fair," he told Justine.

"It's not. It's not at all."

She sat watching a pigeon while Caleb reread the letter. The margins wobbled and shimmered. Now everything came clear to him. He saw kinder, gentler meanings in Daniel's words; the other meanings were no longer there. He understood the effort involved, the hesitations, searches for the proper phrase, false beginnings tossed in wastebaskets.

"I should have written," he told Justine.

She went on watching the pigeon.

"It always seemed to work out with them that I didn't do what I should have. Did do what I shouldn't have."

Her gaze shifted to him, transparent blue eyes whose familiarity continued to confuse him.

"How did he find me?" he asked her. Before, he had barely wondered.

"A detective did it," said Justine," but we'd been hunting for years."

"I thought they would just forget about me."

She started to say something, and stopped. Then she said, "I used to read the cards for you."

"The—?"

"Fortune-telling cards."

"Oh yes," he said. .

"I asked, would Grandfather ever locate you? The cards said yes. However there was always room for error, because Grandfather didn't cut the cards himself. He wouldn't have approved. I never thought of asking would he actually *see* you."

Caleb folded the letter and put it back in his pocket. He was not sure what they were talking about.

"Uncle Caleb," said Justine, "will you come home with me?"

"Oh well I—that's very kind of you."

"You know we'd love to have you. Duncan and I. Duncan is another grandchild, I married him. You'd like him."

"Married him, did you," said Caleb, unsurprised. He sniffed, and then blotted both eyes on the sleeve of his raincoat. "*Well* now," he said. "Whose little girl are you?"

"Caroline's."

"Caroline's? I thought she was the baby, I thought she died."

"Only after she grew up," said Justine. "Duncan is Uncle Two's."

"Two's? Oh, Justin Two."

He contemplated the pigeon, whose feathers reminded him of a changeable taffeta dress that Maggie Rose had once worn. Justin Two was the most demanding of all her children, he seemed to remember; the loudest and the shrillest, the most likely to interrupt a conversation. "Tell me," he said, "is he still the same?"

"Yes," said Justine, as if she knew what he meant.

He laughed.

Justine said, "Listen. You can't stay here! I went to that office in there to ask for you and they said, 'He's out by the tree, but you've only got twenty minutes. Then visiting hours will be over,' they said. I said, 'But I've been traveling since yesterday! I am his great-niece Justine Peck and I've come all the way from Caro Mill, Maryland. I *have* to spend more than twenty *minutes!*' 'Sorry, Miss,' they said, 'rules are rules.' You can't stay in a place like this!"

"It's true," said Caleb, "they do like rules."

"Will you come? We could leave this evening."

"Oh, well you see they'd never let me do it," Caleb said. "No. You weren't the person who signed me in here, they'd never just let me . . . or if they did, there'd be so much paperwork. It would take some arranging. Perhaps several weeks before they would allow me to—"

"*Allow* you?" Justine said. "What, are you in prison?"

Caleb blinked and looked around him.

"Never mind, just come," said Justine. "You already have your coat on. There's nothing you want from inside, is there? We can go over the wall in back, where it's lowest. They won't even see us leave."

"You mean—*escape*?" said Caleb.

"Won't you just come away with me?"

People had been saying that to him all his life. He had still not learned to turn them down.

19

Every now and then Justine would catch a glimpse of Caleb—as he passed a doorway, or skimmed in and out of view in front windows while walking the porch—and she would mistake him for Grandfather Peck and her heart would leap. She had never managed to believe that some people truly will not be seen again. Look, there was that jutting head, the glint of silver hair, the long nose pinched white at the tip! But then she would notice his eyes. The shock of brown eyes in her grandfather's face. Or she would call and he would answer instantly, wincing if she spoke to him too loudly, which she was always doing, out of habit. Or his clothes gave him away—her grandfather's, yes, but on Caleb they looked scruffy and poorly cut. She sank back, wherever she was, and Duncan looked at her curiously but said nothing.

Duncan was playing Battue now, moving yellow plastic disks among a triangle of pegs. For him it appeared to be another game of solitaire, not a puzzle; he had solved the puzzle years ago. The disks clicked steadily like the beads of an abacus or a rosary, their rhythm dictated by the churning of private thoughts. What were Duncan's private thoughts? He wouldn't say. He kept the bourbon bottle beside him, always nearly empty, it seemed, its cheap wavery glass perfectly clear down to the inch or so of yellow in the bottom. Occasionally he smoked a doll-sized metal pipe containing foul-smelling leaves and seeds and stems. Then he would grow dreamy and whimsical, although the leaves were so old now (having been stored nearly forever in an oregano bottle in the kitchen) that Justine suspected they had lost all their potency. He suggested unusual projects—for instance, planting the little round seeds on some village green. "Once a year we could have a new ritual, the Burning of the Green. All the villagers could sit around breathing the smoke and getting happy on a specified day." Justine looked sideways at Caleb to see if he were shocked. He didn't seem to be. He was not above accepting a slug or two of bourbon himself (those rigid, grandfatherly lips poised at the rim of a bottle!) and perhaps would have tried the pipe as well, if smoke did not make him cough. Nevertheless, Justine continually felt the need to tell him, "You mustn't think Duncan's always like this."

"He's not?" said Caleb.

"No, really he's just—it will pass."

Then she wondered why she bothered explaining, for Caleb only looked disappointed. He had some sort of expectation of them that Justine couldn't understand. On the trip, for instance, his moods had kept shifting until she hadn't known what to think of him. First he was elated, almost all the way to New Orleans. It was her favorite view of Caleb so far: his face alight, looking much like Duncan's, just as she had always known it would. He was tense with excitement and his hands moved rapidly as he spoke. (Yet Justine had been taught that a Peck does not gesticulate.) He told her his whole life, everything that had happened to him since leaving Baltimore—*buckets* of life, torrents of names and places, snatches of song broken off and sentences left unfinished. She had the feeling that he had been saving it up for sixty years, until he could locate a family member. But then when he had finished and she questioned him on the fine points—"Whatever happened to the friend you went to New Orleans with?" "What sort of man was White-Eye Ramford?" "Did you ever think of coming home?"—he became morose and short of words. "I don't know. I don't know," he muttered. Thinking to cheer him up, she said "When we get to New Orleans we'll buy you some shoes. You can't get on a plane in paper slippers.'' But if anything, that only deepened his gloom. He looked out the window, his thumb and middle finger steadily stroking the corners of his mouth in a way that made her uncomfortable. But of course: he was mourning his brother. She should have thought. No doubt he had only been making an effort for her sake, earlier, and it had worn him out. So she let him sit in silence, and when they reached New Orleans she didn't mention his shoes again. He did, though. He became suddenly brisk. ''Say now!'' he said. ''Weren't we going to change out of these paper scuffs? We can't go back to the family looking unkempt.''

''Well, if you want to,'' Justine said carefully.

''Unfortunately I am out of funds at the moment but—''

''Oh, I'll take care of that.''

In that respect, at least, he showed his background. He did not make any sort of unseemly fuss over financial matters.

They had to stay overnight in a very poor hotel, for which Justine was apologetic, but Caleb didn't seem to mind. He retired early after eating a large quantity of salad; fresh fruits and vegetables were some sort of obsession with him. When he waved good night in the corridor he looked just fine, but the next morning on the plane he was up and down, up and down. Talkative, then moody. Mostly moody. He asked her unlikely questions. ''How many ships do you have?''

''Ships? What?''

''Do you own or lease them now?''

''*Ships!* Oh,'' said Justine. ''We're not importers any more.''

''You're not?''

''The family sold it all.''

''Why! When did they do that?''

''Right after you left,'' said Justine.

Then he sank into himself again, and hardly spoke until they had landed and caught the two connecting buses to Caro Mill. When she led him up Watchmaker Street she felt she was *laboring* with him, he looked so dismal. But at her front walk he stopped short. "Here?" he said. "Is this where you live?"

For the first time she noticed how unsteady the house appeared, how the screens bagged and the steps buckled. She wondered what that rusty motor was doing on the porch. "Yes, it is," she said.

She felt him staring at her. She focused on the tips of her shoes.

"This is your *house?*"

"Yes."

"And what is this yellow stuff in the yard?"

"Why, cornstalks."

"I mean—*eating* corn?"

"Well, Duncan wanted to grow some, you see, and he said the back didn't get enough sun. He said we could grind up the garbage for fertilizer and spread it on the—"

She felt herself growing desperate, trying to convince him that really their life was perfectly logical. But she shouldn't have bothered. For when finally she raised her eyes (just a glance at his face to see how she was doing) she found the corners of his mouth perked upwards like Duncan's, his expression bright and merry again. He was back to being cheerful. And he remained cheerful ever after, growing more light-hearted day by day. He fit right in. She couldn't understand him.

Sometimes Duncan let the Battue disks fall silent a moment while he read the newspapers. Help Wanted, of course. "Look, Justine, someone in Virginia wants a zoo keeper."

"You've never been a zoo keeper, Duncan."

"Right."

"I mean you don't know the first thing about it."

"Right."

"You have a job. Duncan, you *have* a job, and you should have been there three hours ago."

Then he would rise, steady on his feet but a little slow, his face luminous and calm and angelic as only bourbon could make it, and he would very, very carefully button himself into his jacket. "If you really want to know," he said (but speaking in Caleb's general direction), "I don't believe in people sacrificing themselves for the sake of other people."

"But neither do I, Duncan," she said.

He didn't have any answer for that.

So he would give a little salute to Caleb, and turn up his collar as if facing winter winds before he set off for the antique shop. Where there would be no customers anyway, now that opening hours were so uncertain. Where antiques lay in a jumble, dusty and neglected, and half the lightbulbs were out and the window was patched with adhesive tape. Look at this very newspaper column, spindled now on a Battue peg: WANTED *antique shop mgr. must be reliable apply Silas Amsel Box 46 Caro Mill*. But Justine was firm and cool and deliberate. Like her grandfather, she stiffened her pointy chin and set her head at a commanding angle. "It's time we learned to stay in one place," she told Duncan every night when he came home.

"Whatever you say, Justine."

There was something underneath, some considerateness in his voice that made her turn on him. "Don't you think so?" she asked him.

"Whatever you say."

"Not what *I* say. Don't you think so yourself? We've been moving around forever."

"That's very true," he said.

"Why do you keep agreeing with me? Do you feel you have to humor me in some way?"

"No, no."

But he did. She knew he did. It was because of her fetching Caleb. Wasn't it? Duncan seemed to think she had gone crazy, or senile—or who knows?—running off like that to get Caleb. (She had assumed he would understand. She had called the antique shop from Box Hill: I'll be away overnight, I think, Duncan, I don't think I can find a plane out of New Orleans till tomorrow." "New Orleans? Is that where you are? I thought you had left me," he said. "I went home for lunch and you weren't there." She said, "*I* wouldn't leave you"—forgetting altogether that up till that afternoon she had been seriously considering it. She was so excited about meeting Caleb. And it was so good to hear Duncan's voice on the telephone. It had completely slipped her mind how angry she was with him.) When she came back from New Orleans, Duncan gave Caleb a long look and then shook his hand. But the look he gave Justine was longer—a gentle, sad, *pitying* look, which she was going to remember till the end of her days. What could he be pitying her for? He didn't even know that she had done all this illegally, so to speak. Yet during supper that night he had been so soft-voiced and solicitous, as if she were sick. When really there was nothing more natural than having your great-uncle come to stay with you.

Not that Duncan minded having Caleb. He got along with him very well. Better than Justine herself did, in fact. They had long discussions on jazz and blues and Creole food. Duncan would ask about Lafleur Boudrault, and Whisky Alley, and musical funerals and old-time cathouses, about which (Justine was surprised to hear) Caleb seemed to know everything. Caleb played Duncan's harmonica, drawing forth from it such beautiful, disreputable sounds that Justine stood motionless and open-mouthed. *This* was her great-*uncle?*

But he didn't like to be called Great-Uncle, or even Uncle. Perhaps he had been without relatives too long for such titles to sit easy on him. "Just 'Caleb' will do," he said. And there had been so many difficulties in the way of his paying the rest of the family a visit. He was too tired from the trip; he was just getting used to Caro Mill; his arthritis was acting up. Thanksgiving would be better, he said. They could arrive unannounced and take the family by surprise. "Thanksgiving!" said Justine. It was barely November. Was it fair to keep everyone in the dark for so long? She was all for going this Sunday, perhaps, for Sunday dinner at Uncle Two's. But Caleb refused, offering a dozen shiftless excuses. ("I'm scared I wouldn't know anybody's name,'' he said.) Justine sighed. She had to admit there were times when Caleb disappointed her.

No, more than that. Tell the truth. There were times when she almost disliked him.

He had gone so far afield, it seemed. He had journeyed such a distance from his family. Now it appeared that the return trip was not that easy, maybe even impossible. He had a hundred habits and qualities that the Pecks would not have tolerated, skills they neither possessed nor wanted, bits of knowledge they would not know existed. Often he said things that horrified her. "Maybe,'' he said, "we could just *never* let the family know, have you thought of that?''

"Why, Caleb!''

"I mean—Justine, I'm happy here with you and Duncan. Why go anywhere else? It would be like meeting strangers.''

"That's ridiculous! It's ridiculous.''

"I don't have anything in common with them, Justine.''

"How can you say such a thing?''

"Do you think a one of them would recognize me?''

No. Not a one of them. Deep down, she knew it, and he and she would stare at each other in absolute agreement even while she continued to protest.

Sometimes she shut herself in her room and pulled out Caleb's old photo, which she had taken from her grandfather's pocket after he died. She studied it as if it could be read, not merely looked at. The gleam of Caleb's Panama, the set of his shoulders, the perfect crispness of his tie. Nowadays he did not even wear a tie. His old jauntiness had become, somehow, *boldness*; his speech had a sharp, unpleasant tang. There was something spineless and lackadaisical in the way he walked. And she could not help noticing that still, wearing Daniel's clothes and Duncan's aftershave, he had the musty cabbage smell of a public institution.

Well, after all, he had been away so long.

Yes, but he had gone by degrees, traveling only where led, merely proving himself adaptable, endlessly adaptable.

As Justine herself had.

Then a trembling would rise from the soles of her feet, turn her stomach queasy, pass through the hollow of her chest to beat in her throat like a second heart. She stuffed the snapshot beneath a stack of magazines and hurried out to join the others.

In the afternoons, with Duncan asleep on the floor beside his disks, Justine brought Caleb up to date on the family. Even though he seemed not to care, she sat at the table earnestly filling him with history. She was amazed at how little time it took to tell—all those events unfolding over months and years, summed up now in minutes. "Richard did get married but it was annulled, the girl's father had it annulled because she was under age, and since then he's lived downtown in a—"

"Now, which was Richard?"

"Why, Uncle Mark's son," she said.

When she told how her mother died she spoke without inflection, as if hoping he wouldn't catch it, but of course he did. He made no comment. When she talked about fortune telling he only looked interested. What did he really think? She imagined that he was about to define her; that at last, after clearing his throat, he would sum her up, announce where she had been heading all her life. She tensed expectantly whenever she caught him looking around the house, or glancing at her clothes, or staring at some toothless woman in socks and Wedgies who came to have her cards read. Surely he was judging their life, whose skimpiness she had just begun to realize. Any moment now he would give his verdict. But he never did. She kept trying to explain herself, even so. "You see we have always just—Duncan has kept wanting us to move around," she told him.

"Is that right," said Caleb.

"He likes to travel."

"But he hasn't traveled *far*."

"What?" She searched her memory for other family news,

meanwhile absently cracking a coffee bean with her teeth. "Now Aunt Lucy, she always says—"

"Lucy? I didn't remember Daniel had a Lucy."

"Lucy is Two's wife, Caleb. I told you that."

"Ah yes." He nodded. "It must be hard trying to keep all this straight."

"I don't have to *try*. They're family. Now, what was I telling you about Aunt Lucy?"

"You said—who did you say she was?"

So that she grew exasperated. "Don't you have any *memory?*" she asked him. "Don't you feel any connection at all?"

"Memory, yes. Connection, no."

She believed him. At night, tossing in her bed, she told Duncan, "We might as well have picked a stranger off the streets."

"What makes you think so?"

"He's not connected, he says. He *admits* it. That scroungy old man—if he had written a letter when he should have I bet Grandfather would be alive today. He doesn't have a trace of the family left in him and he tells me so as if he's proud of it. He doesn't have a trace."

"He does, though."

"What are you talking about?"

"Oh, use your head, Justine. Who do you know who acts more like a Peck? Consider that he has remained alone his whole life long, never let in anybody who wasn't a blood relative. Never got close to White-Eye, never married that waitress, never was a father to Roy. Can't you read between the lines? Look at what Luray said: it's not as if he were a real relation. You say the Pecks haven't left a trace?"

"You don't know the first thing about it," Justine said. "Of course he didn't get close to White-Eye. He was careful and respectful. He had *tact*." And she would flounce over on her side away from him, preparing for another night of insomnia.

Then the next afternoon, facing Caleb, who wore his

brother's pinstriped shirt, she was full of new hope and energy. "I think you're going to like my cousin Claude," she told him.

"Oh yes?"

"He collects engravings. He's the only one besides you who's interested in the arts."

But, "I believe I'll make coffee out of some of those beans, Justine," he said. Then she would notice how metallic his eyes were, and how there was something raw and uncared-for about his skin, which was stretched too tightly across the bridge of his nose.

He had taken over the kitchen by now, as if he guessed how she felt about cooking. (The first supper she served him was hot dogs scorched in a skillet.) He prepared every meal so seriously and so tenderly that it tasted like a gift. "Eat it all," he told them at suppertime. "If you don't finish it, how can I make more? I want to get started on something new." He would hum as he worked, clattering pots, cursing the scarcity of equipment. "But that's all right, I can make do with anything. Put me in the pokiest diner and I will cook you up a seven-course meal. Why did I ever retire? I let Luray talk me into it. Here I've been thinking I had no means of support, but I do! I'm going to get a job and contribute to the household, I have it all worked out."

But even Duncan looked doubtful when he heard that. "Well, look," he said. "I wouldn't want to discourage you, but *age* might stand in your way, don't you think?"

"Never mind my age," said Caleb. "Oh, for the quality places, yes. But there is always some little café by the tracks or the water where they don't give a hang, and that's where I'll ask."

"Well, at least why don't you wait a little. If we move or anything, you don't want to go through a whole new job application."

"But we're not moving," said Justine.

"Oh, no hurry," Caleb said. "I play it by ear. I wait to see what falls out and who is going in what direction. I always have." He smiled. "It's funny," he said, "I'd forgotten the taste of garlic. Can you beat that? It's peculiar how you associate some foods with people. Or times you used to have, or places . . . Bess always liked garlic-buttered popcorn. The two of us must have eaten bushels of it. Now you could bring me some and I don't know, it would taste so *unfamiliar* somehow. I suppose everybody's like that. Best friend I ever had liked Blue Peter sardines on saltine crackers, but maybe if I were to track him down today I'd find he doesn't even remember them any more."

Duncan listened so hard he forgot to eat. Justine slid a salt shaker back and forth. Why did Caleb have to talk about food all the time? No one else in the family did. All they asked was that their meals be nourishing, and not too unusual in taste. They tended to like white things, foods baked in cream sauce. They would have been horrified by the peppery shrimp casserole that Caleb had served tonight. "Listen!" Justine said suddenly. "How can we be sure you're Caleb Peck?"

Both men stared.

"How do we know you're not some impostor?"

"Justine," said Duncan.

She ignored him. She was watching Caleb. "But who else would bother?" Caleb asked her.

"You're not like them in any way."

Caleb shrugged. (A foreign gesture.) "For that matter," he said, "how do I know *you're* a Peck?"

"We're not even sure that Eli's honest," Justine said. "Maybe he just picked up some stranger and coached him. Maybe the two of you framed this whole story together. After all, there must be money involved. Caleb's share of the will must have been drawing interest for sixty years."

"Caleb didn't *have* any share of the will," Duncan told her. "Justine, I wish you would—"

But Caleb only nodded, sober and proud somehow, as if he were receiving compliments.

* * *

In the night there was a pounding on the door, and shouting and the beam of headlights across the bedroom ceiling. Justine, wide awake as usual, crawled over Duncan and threw a bathrobe around her shoulders. "Just a minute," she called. Duncan stirred and then sat up. From Caleb's room came the rustle of bedclothes. Justine ran through the hallway, breathless and shivering. Someone had died. Something was wrong with Meg. She had never realized how many possibilities there were for disaster, or how calm and joyous her life had been until this moment.

But it was only Tucker Dawcett, whose wife had her fortune told weekly to see if he were faithful and never believed it when the answer was yes. Tucker was just a sweet skinny man with buck teeth. He jogged in a sweatsuit every morning and worked as a, let's see—

Policeman.

Her teeth started chattering again.

Tucker coughed, and then showed her his identification in a plastic envelope. (Why on earth?) For all she knew it was his YMCA card. "Oh. Tucker," she said.

"Could I speak with you a moment, Justine?"

From the hall doorway, Duncan said, "Do you know what time it is?"

"Police business," said Tucker.

Duncan came up behind Justine without a sound.

"Now I have to ask you folks this question," Tucker said. "Are you all related to a Mr. Caleb Peck?"

"You get us up at one a.m. to ask us that?" Duncan said.

"Now I know, I know how trying this must be," Tucker told him. Through the screen his face looked grainy; out of tiredness or embarrassment he kept his eyes down. "Fact is I was sacked out at home myself. Doug Tilghman called from the station asking me to run this little errand. I wanted to wait till morning but he said we would look pretty silly if Louisiana called back in a couple hours and we hadn't done a thing."

"Louisiana?" said Duncan.

"See they got this lady down there claiming a Mr. Caleb Peck has been kidnapped."

Duncan looked at Justine.

"Seems like he was in a home of some sort. This lady, Mrs. Luray Pickett, went to visit him last Sunday and found he'd disappeared. Home hadn't noticed. Seems somebody at the office remembered a Justine Peck come from Caro Mill to visit him, and he was never seen again."

"So?" said Duncan.

"Well, I believe that would be kidnapping, or stealing at least. See, the man was institutionalized. He didn't have no right to be leaving of his own free will. Or would it be aiding and abetting? Well, look. *I* don't care about it. Let an old fellow go where he wants, I always say. But Doug Tilghman said I had to just ask, because some lady somewhere is fit to be tied. Mrs. Luray Pickett. I said, 'Look, Doug, can't this wait till morning? I mean what will the Pecks think of us for this?' I said, and he said, 'Tell them I'm just as sorry as I can be but these policemen in Louisiana have this lady name of Mrs. Luray Pickett who is kicking up a storm, calling them and visiting, asking why they're not doing more. She says she put the man in a Home herself and saw to his every need, never let a month go by without . . . and here he had been removed and not so much as a by-your-leave. She says if anybody thought she wasn't taking proper care they could just come to her in person, there was no need to steal the man, and she will thank the police to get him replaced or she'll know the reason why. And also—' Well, and it's true there's not many Justine Pecks. I mean the *name* is odd. And especially from Caro Mill. Of course you do have that old man staying with you now . . ."

"Tucker," said Duncan, "don't you know that all our family is from Baltimore?"

"That's true, they are."

"And have you ever heard either one of us mention a relative in Louisiana?"

"Well, not directly," said Tucker.

"So," said Duncan.

"Well, I knew there was nothing to it," Tucker told him. "Sorry to have woken you folks up." And for the first time he raised his eyes to meet theirs. "I'll tell the wife I saw you," he said. "Night, now."

"Night," said Duncan.

He turned on the porch light and shut the door. Justine waited, but he didn't say a word. Maybe he was angry. She should have told him from the beginning. Only at the beginning he had been so odd, and after that it was never the proper moment. Now what? Would he make her send Caleb back again? Then it occurred to her that all this time Caleb must have been listening, bolt upright in bed, terrified they would give him away. "That poor old man!" she said, and slid past Duncan to open Caleb's door.

He was gone.

His bed was unmade, and his pajamas lay at the foot. His rubberized raincoat no longer hung from the closet door. Duncan's harmonica was missing from the bureau. And the window was wide open, empty and black, the paper shade lisping in the wind. "Duncan!" Justine called. "Hurry, we have to find him!"

She already had one leg over the windowsill before he stopped her. He took hold of her arm and said, "Let him get a little head start again first, Justine."

ʬ

20

Duncan sat on the floor with a twelve-hundred-piece jig-saw puzzle, "Sunset in the Rockies." He had found all the straight edges and constructed the frame; but now he was simply moving pieces around, picking one up and tapping it against his teeth while he stared into space, setting it down, picking up another, turning several over to expose their gray cardboard backs. He considered turning the whole puzzle over and doing it all in gray.

He considered moving Justine back to Baltimore.

"Is that what you want?" he asked her when she came through wearing her hat.

She looked startled. "What?"

"I asked if you wanted to move to Baltimore."

"Baltimore?"

"Baltimore, *Maryland*, Justine."

She stared at him.

"We'll live in Great-Grandma's house. *Your* house," he told her. "I'll find some kind of busywork with Peck and Sons. You know Dad's always said I could."

"You mean, stay forever?"

"No reason not to."

"Never again move?"

"Not unless you liked."

She thought a while, biting her lip.

"But you might not be happy there," she told him finally.

Which was her way of saying yes. He felt the answer settling on him by degrees, like a large heavy blanket drifting down. He was done for. Yet at the same time he had a sense of relief, almost. What else would you call this sudden giddiness? The other shoe had fallen. He nearly laughed.

Underneath, he must have known all through their marriage that this was where they were headed.

Justine fit books into cardboard boxes. Then machine parts. Duncan let his jigsaw puzzle dissolve and scatter while he took up a new kind of solitaire. Lately he had become talkative and fanciful, almost silly; he was emerging from his silence. But the bourbon and the solitaire remained, because he had lost his job by now and if he didn't look occupied in some way Justine would ask him to help her. That was one thing he could not do. He would feel like a child repacking his pathetic provisions—blanket, alarm clock, teddy bear—after half a night of running away. Or like some sea animal, declawed and deformed by battle, scuttling back to his shell with whatever scraps of himself he could salvage. He remained on the floor, pretending to be deep in his game. Meanwhile his mind had sprung awake again and was playing games of its own. He composed a list of all his favorite words, aloud. "Luncheon. Reality. Silver salver. Ippolitov-Ivanov." Justine sat back and wiped her hair off her forehead.

"Sometimes I wonder why we travel with so much *stuff*," she told him.

One of the puzzling things about Justine was that she always seemed to be shaking lately, and it hadn't stopped when he decided to move her to Baltimore. The streamers of her hat trembled gently, and whenever she drank coffee (which was the only thing she would touch) she spilled it. She reminded him of a fragile tree full of birds. But what could he do that he hadn't already done? He tried diverting her thoughts. "Justine," he said. "You know? In twenty years I firmly believe we will be traveling instantaneously by transposition of matter. You get in this glass box, see, if you want to go to, say, Omaha, and someone in Omaha gets in *another* glass box—"

"I travel fast enough as it is," said Justine, "and way too far."

"You haven't traveled so far," Duncan said. "Then bulletin boards would spring up everywhere: 'Gentleman from Detroit wishes to go to Pittsburgh; does anyone in Pittsburgh wish to go to Detroit?' There would be new hope for the unemployed. Bums could make money being transposed to Cincinnati when someone in Cincinnati wanted to get out. You go to a park bench. 'Look, fellow,' you say—"

"But it would always be me who ended up accepting," said Justine. She rose, and for no apparent reason examined her face in the speckled metal switchplate on the wall. "I can turn into anyone. That's my curse."

Her curse was her ability to see all sides of every question, but that wasn't something Duncan wanted changed and so he didn't mention it. Finally Justine turned away and bent to pack another box.

She was fitting some things of Meg's in now. Each object she handled very gently and lovingly, taking much longer than necessary. She rolled a stray belt meant for a dress Meg might not even be wearing any more, and she tucked it in beside a mildewed high school almanac. She took the lid off a tin of pebbles that Meg had collected on a Virginia beach in the summer of 1965, and she held each pebble up to the light and smoothed it with her fingers before replacing it.

At mealtimes, if he remembered, Duncan made sandwiches and poured two glasses of milk. But Justine seemed to have given up on eating. She didn't even go to the diner; she didn't go anywhere. When he urged her she would take one bite of her sandwich and then set it down. "Come on. Eat," he told her. Though he could see that it wasn't possible. He could tell from the way she chewed; her mouth was too dry, or too small, or something. Never mind, she would eat when she got to Baltimore. Aunts would take her in hand.

He thought of the aunts for the first time with gratitude, imagining how they would relieve him of Justine's dull white face and her limpness. Then he caught himself and looked away from her eyes, which were fixed on him too steadily.

He could always leave her, of course. He could settle her in Baltimore and then go off again on his own. But he knew that he wouldn't. If he didn't have Justine he wouldn't even know how to see things, what to look at; nothing would exist for him if he couldn't tell Justine about it. The first flat-brimmed hat in a department store window would break him. He would be unable to last the night without her rustling, burning wakefulness guarding his sleep. So he put away all thoughts of leaving, and he wrote the letter to Peck & Sons asking for work. But when the answer came, he didn't want to open it. He stuffed it in his pocket, angry already at the phrases he knew it would contain. Finally Justine found it, and opened it for him. "Well? What does it say?" he asked.

"Oh . . . they'll get you something."

"But what does it *say?* Are they glad I'm finally listening to reason? Do they say they always knew we would end up coming home?"

"No, they don't mention it," Justine said.

He snatched the letter away from her—his Uncle Mark's signature beneath a secretary's crisp black typing. Probably, his uncle said, there would be some employment for him although it was hard to say what, on such short notice. And no, the firm had no need of a fix-it man, what kind of a question was that? And of course it was true that Great-Grandma's house was legally Justine's, although really the family had been the ones to see to its maintenance all these years and Esther and the twins were so accustomed to living there . . .

All in all, Duncan thought the letter sounded disconcerted. As if secretly the family had *enjoyed* having the two of them ricocheting around somewhere. He had not expected that. Nor had he expected to feel so offended, once he found it out.

But the wheels were set in motion, anyway, and now they gave notice to the landlord and made arrangements with the movers. ("I'm not hiring a U-Haul," Duncan said. "I don't have Grandfather." But really he was just indulging in his new policy of floating to places. He pictured the Mayflower men hauling out the living room rug by its corners while he remained seated on it, steadily playing forty thieves.) They notified the electric company and the water department, breaking off ties, unplugging all their cords to Caro Mill and reeling them in. They wrote a letter to Meg giving their new address. ("Although," Justine said, "there is no way we can ever let Caleb know . . .") Nowadays when Duncan passed the Blue Bottle he saw an unfamiliar young man established behind the counter, picking his fingernails and gazing idly out the reglazed window with its display of gilded china teacups.

At Thanksgiving they stayed home, since they would be going to Baltimore anyway in another few days. They ate dinner on the living room floor: a combination pizza that Duncan had bought from a takeout place. "Really you shouldn't have," Justine said. She meant because of the cost; their money was nearly gone. They were living on BankAmericard. "But it wasn't expensive," said Duncan, "and I thought you *liked* combination pizzas. I told them to put extra anchovies on. Why aren't you eating?"

She took a bite. She didn't seem to be tasting it.

"Isn't it good?"

"If Caleb were here we'd be taking him to the family today," she said.

"If he were here, yes."

"And they wouldn't have liked him."

He leaned forward and tapped her plate. "Eat," he told her.

The morning after Thanksgiving Dorcas came to have her cards read. She was considering marrying a moviehouse owner named Willis Ralph McGee. "How do you like the name Dorcas McGee?" she asked Duncan.

Behind her, Ann-Campbell said, "It stinks."

"Who asked you?"

Now that it was cold Dorcas wore a car coat heaped with blond fake fur, but her feet were still in spike-heeled sandals. Blood-red toenails glinted beneath nylon, overrun the next moment by the last of Duncan's forty cards. She moved her toes a fraction of an inch away. "You said I would meet somebody soon, Justine, and so I did," she said. "Now I want to know what kind of husband he would make."

"Lousy," said Ann-Campbell.

"Will you hush that?"

"My daddy, Joe Pete Britt, is not ever going to stand for this," said Ann-Campbell. "Here, Justine, I brung in your mail. There's a bill from Howard pharmacy, a Korvette ad—"

"Just *give* it to her, Ann-Campbell."

Justine set down a roll of binder's twine and took the letters. "Well, here is something from Mayflower," she said. "I just hope they're not putting off the moving date."

"I hope they *do!*" said Dorcas. "Just years and years."

"Here's something from—who do we know in Wyoming?"

Justine tore the envelope open. Duncan laid down a nine of clubs, which Dorcas immediately stepped on. "Now I don't want to hurry you or anything," Dorcas said, "but me and Ann-Campbell are going out to Woolworth's for a hot fudge sundae and we were just stopping by *briefly* to get my fortune told."

"You prick a balloon," Ann-Campbell told Duncan, "and see what number is wrote on it. That's the price of your hot fudge sundae. Could be a nickel. Could be a penny."

"Is that so," said Duncan. "Would you move your foot a little, Dorcas?"

"Could be forty-nine cents," said Dorcas. "It always has been."

"Well!" said Justine.

They all looked up at her, but it seemed she was reading a letter. She would read for a moment and then look up, then start reading it all over again. "What is it?" Duncan asked her.

"Well, it's a—"

He waited, but she went back to the letter.

"Reason I'm in a hurry is that tonight we have this special date," Dorcas said. "I have a feeling he's going to propose. Now I don't want to answer without knowing what the cards say, do I?"

"Certainly not," said Duncan.

"Justine? If you don't want to do it all you have to do is tell me."

"Look at this, Duncan," Justine said.

He took the letter, a cream-colored sheet crumpled and gray around the edges.

November 20, 1973

Dear Justine,

I want to apologize for taking so long to write, but circumstances prevented me up until now.

It was very kind of you to invite me to stay with you. The frankfurters you cooked were delicious, and I shall remember my visit with a great deal of pleasure for a long time to come.

Love,
Caleb Peck

Duncan laughed—a single, sharp sound. He handed the letter back.

"It's a thank you note," said Justine.

"That's right."

"A bread-and-butter note."

"That's what they call them."

"I just want to ask you one thing," Dorcas said. "And I want an honest answer. Hear? Now Justine, you have been putting me off all morning and it's not the first time. Other people have noticed too. Nowadays you just *drift* the cards down like your heart's not in it. Anything anybody asks you definite, should they do it or should they not, you don't want to reply. You just shuck it off, like. Well, what I want to know is, do you not really care to read the future any more? Are you trying to phase it out? Because all you got to do is say the word, Justine. Not to keep on going with your mind on something else the way you have been lately.''

''What?'' said Justine.

Dorcas looked over at Duncan.

''Oh, your *fortune*,'' Justine said.

''That's right.''

''Well, let me find my . . .''

She fetched the straw carry-all, unwrapped the cards from their square of silk.

''My great-uncle Caleb wrote a thank you note,'' she told Dorcas.

''Now isn't that nice.''

''Thanking us for his visit.''

''You can always tell good upbringing, is what *I* say,'' said Dorcas, but her eyes were on the cards, which Justine was gently shuffling over and over again. ''Aren't you going to want a table to lay those out on? Or you're just going to go on shuffling evermore.''

''*Oh* yes,'' said Justine. And they went off to the kitchen, leaving Ann-Campbell behind. Ann-Campbell squatted next to Duncan. ''Will Justine let Mama say yes to Mr. McGee?'' she asked him.

''I don't know.''

''Will she tell her to marry daddy again, Joe Pete Britt?''

''Tune in next week and find out,'' said Duncan.

''Huh?''

''Nothing.'' He tipped back his head for a swallow of bourbon.

''Who is this great-uncle Caleb man?''

''That old guy we had around for a while,'' Duncan said.

"Who is either very dumb or very very smart, it's hard to tell which."

"If she marries Mr. McGee I might just come along to Baltimore with you all," said Ann-Campbell, edging closer. "I think that might be what's going to happen. Justine will tell her to go ahead."

"Justine won't tell her *anything*, don't worry," Duncan said. "She hardly opens her mouth any more."

But just then he heard her laugh, a clear light sound that startled him, and he looked up from his cards and met Ann-Campbell's speckled green eyes fixed thoughtfully upon him.

After lunch Justine worked in the yard a while, pulling up yellowed cornstalks. She returned with her face pink. Starchy-smelling air trailed behind her. "Feel," she said, and laid her stinging hands on Duncan's cheek. He drew back. "Doesn't it make you want to get outdoors?" she asked him.

"Not exactly."

"Aren't you tired of sitting here?"

She spun away from him and went off toward the kitchen. A minute later he heard her running water in the sink, clattering dishes, but she must have grown tired of that, because very soon she was back in the living room. She stood at the window a moment, and then took a second pack of cards from the sill and settled down on the floor with them, not far from where Duncan sat playing forty thieves. He could hear her murmuring to herself as she laid them out. ". . . the queen of change, beside the king. The wish card, the journey card . . . why so many journeys? Look how far the loved ones are! This is the card for journeys beyond other journeys, I've never had that one before. The card for, what was it?"

She fell silent. Duncan looked up to find her chewing a thumbnail and staring into space.

Shortly afterward she left, sliding into an old lumber-jacket that used to be Duncan's. She didn't say where she was going. Duncan heard the Ford start up, a burry sound in the frozen air. First he was pleased, but then he wondered if she would keep her mind sufficiently on her driving. He noticed how empty the house felt. There was a strong wind blowing up from the north, whistling through all the cracks. The sky was white, and the room seemed lit by a bleak cold glare that hurt Duncan's eyes. Everywhere he looked there was something dismal to see: packing cases, dry dead plants on the windowsill, a sprawl of tomato-stained pizza wrappings from the day before. He rose and went to the bedroom. He was only planning to rest; he lay on the unmade bed with one arm across his eyes and thought about the turn his life was taking. But then he fell asleep and dreamed about antiques—jewelry that came in clusters and jungles of carved chair legs. Even in his sleep it was impossible to find any space that was pure and simple and clean of line.

When he woke it was dark. Justine was still not back. He got up and felt his way to the kitchen, where he turned on the light and made himself a peanut butter sandwich. The cat watched him from the stovetop. "So this is what it's like to be grown up!" Duncan told her. She blinked and looked away, offended. He took his sandwich into the living room and settled down again beside his unfinished game. It was clear he was not going to win. Still, he shifted cards doggedly and pondered a choice of moves, munching meanwhile on his sandwich. There was nothing else to do.

Then the Ford drove up, and a minute later Justine's quick footsteps crossed the porch. When she opened the door he kept his eyes on the cards; she would never guess how glad he was to see her. "We're out of peanut butter," was all he said.

"Oh, are we?"

He moved a deuce.

"I think I'm losing," he said.

"Never mind." She came to kneel in front of him, a flash of red plaid, and scooped his cards up. Some were left on the rug and some flew out of her hands. "Well, wait a minute," Duncan said.

"Shall I tell your fortune?"

She had never told his fortune in all his life. He stared at her. But Justine only smiled—bright-eyed, out of breath, her hat a little crooked—and began laying cards in a disorderly row that she didn't even glance at. "You are about to alter your entire way of life," she said, smacking down some jack or king. She was watching Duncan's face.

"Yes, well," said Duncan, reaching for his bottle.

"You are going to become a fix-it man for a carnival."

He set the bottle down.

"Your wife will be their fortune teller. You'll have a purple trailer in Parvis, Maryland, and live happily ever after. How do you like me so far?"

"You're crazy," he said, but he was smiling, and he didn't even protest when Justine spilled all the rest of his bourbon while leaning over the cards to give him a kiss.

21

On moving day they got a late start, which was fine because there wasn't that much to move. They were taking only their books and clothes, plus Duncan's spare parts and inventions, packed in a little orange U-Haul van. They were leaving everything else behind. Furniture would be supplied in the trailer. Built in. Justine liked the idea of having everything built in. She enjoyed telling people they were traveling light, and would have thrown away even some things they needed if Duncan hadn't stopped her.

It was a clear, frosty morning in December, with a sky as blue as opals and a pale sun. Some of the neighbors had come to see them off. Dorcas Britt and her husband Joe Pete, and Ann-Campbell with Justine's cat struggling in her arms. Red Emma, Black Emma, old Mrs. Hewitt and her poodle. Maureen Worth from across the street, still in her bathrobe, and Mrs. Tucker Dawcett, who stood a little apart and looked sad and wistful, as if she expected even now to be handed news of her husband's unfaithfulness like a parting gift. Justine went from one to another, setting her face against theirs and giving them little pats and making promises. "Of course we'll be back. You know we will." Duncan was rearranging boxes in the U-Haul, and from time to time he cursed and stopped to rub his hands together. Red Emma threw him a dark, sullen look that he failed to see. "You tell him to bring you on weekends, hear?" she said. "Don't you let him just keep carting you off every which way." She kissed Justine's cheek. Mrs. Hewitt hugged her. "Oh, it just seems like people are always *going*, leaving, moving on . . ."

"But it's not far," said Justine. "And you can all come visit."

"In a trailer? In a cow pasture?" Dorcas said.

"You're going to love it," Justine told her. "*We're* going to love it. Oh, I can feel good luck in my bones, I know when we're doing something right. Besides, next month it will be nineteen seventy-four. Add all the digits and you get twenty-one, add those and you come up with three. Our lucky number. Did you ever see a clearer sign?"

Someone pushed a pot of ivy into her arms. Then a rubber plant. She was carrying so much they had to open the car door for her and help her settle things in. "Just put them anywhere," she said. "The front seat is fine." The front seat was already full of food for the trip—Fritos, Cheez Doodles, salt herring and coffee beans and a box of Luden's. This year she was the only person in the car. Though next year, who could tell? She took the cat from Ann-Campbell, and then once the cat was in she had to get in herself and slam the door, fast, and roll down the window no more than a slit. "Ask Duncan if he's ready to start," she said. The clanging of the tailgate was her answer. "Well, I guess I'll be saying goodbye then." For the first time her voice was sad, and appeared to drift out too slowly on the mist of her breath. "We don't want to hit the rush hour." She stuck a cold silver key in the ignition and kneaded her fingers. Hanging from the gearshift knob was a National Safety Council ad torn out of a magazine: cupids with black straps slanted across their chests, I LOVE YOU, WEAR YOUR SEAT BELT. She turned and looked at the cat, who glared at her from behind a begonia plant. "Well, then," she said, and roared the engine up and left, waving her hand out the slit in the window.

Behind her the U-Haul's engine started too, and the crowd of neighbors moved over to Duncan. "Have a good trip!" "Drive safely, hear?" The truck rolled off. "Oh, aren't you ashamed," Red Emma called suddenly, "taking her away from us like this?'' But Duncan only waved. He must not have heard. Or else he was too intent on catching up with Justine, who by now was only a puff of smoke in the distance.

ANNE TYLER

SAINT MAYBE
It's 1965, and the Bedloe family of Baltimore is living an ideal, apple-pie existence. In the blink of an eye, a single, tragic event occurs that will transform their lives forever—particularly that of seventeen-year-old Ian. Ian is almost crushed under an unbearable guilt until he enters the CHURCH OF THE SECOND CHANCE and discovers that forgiveness must be earned, through a bit of sacrifice and a lot of love.

THE CLOCK WINDER
Elizabeth Abbott seems to have no fixed destination in her life, which is precisely how she lands on the doorstep of the big, neglected house far outside Baltimore and persuades the recently widowed Mrs. Emerson that she needs a handyperson. Soon Elizabeth has not only Mrs. Emerson, but two of the Emerson sons dependent upon her. Elizabeth becomes more and more apprehensive as these entanglements close in on her. Part of her is transfixed as her magic takes hold, until she makes a terrible bungle and irreparably damages another human being.

A SLIPPING-DOWN LIFE
Evie Decker, the second-fattest girl in her Pulqua, N.C., high school, has an unlikely romance with Drumstrings Casey, a small-time rock singer playing in a country roadhouse. The desperate tactics Evie employs to attract Casey's attention, their brief noncourtship, and its surprising results are off-beat, funny, and immensely touching.

ANNE TYLER

THE TIN CAN TREE

The Pike girl has just been buried. Her ten-year-old brother Simon is still unsure what death means and is more immediately disturbed by the withdrawal of his mother's love, numb as she is with grief and guilt. All around him people conspire to restore normalcy: the father, who tries to fill his wife's silence; an older cousin, who has made the Pike children almost her own; the cousin's sometimes beau and his chronically sick, inept brother. But it is Simon himself who inadvertently breaks the stupor of his mother's grief, and they pick up their lives where death interrupted them.

DINNER AT THE HOMESICK RESTAURANT

Pearl Cody is thirty when she marries twenty-four-year-old Beck Tull, a glib and handsome traveling salesman. They have three children and spend their married years moving from one territory to another. Eventually Beck leaves Pearl and the children, though Pearl never admits to them that he isn't just on a selling trip. Beck sends her some money, but it is still a struggle to support the children. Pearl is strict and distant, but she is the center of their lives. Before she dies, she gives her son Ezra her address book and asks him to invite the people in it to her funeral. Beck Tull is the first name Ezra finds.

ANNE TYLER